DEAD

GIRLS

DON'T

SAY

SORRY

DEAD

GIRLS

DON'T

SAY

SORRY

ALEX RITANY

ALFRED A. KNOPF
NEW YORK

Text copyright © 2024 by Alex Ritany
Jacket art copyright © 2024 by Max Reed

All rights reserved. Published in the United States by Alfred A. Knopf, an imprint of Random House Children's Books, a division of Penguin Random House LLC, New York.

Knopf, Borzoi Books, and the colophon are registered trademarks of Penguin Random House LLC.

Visit us on the Web! GetUnderlined.com

Educators and librarians, for a variety of teaching tools, visit us at RHTeachersLibrarians.com

Library of Congress Cataloging-in-Publication Data is available upon request.
ISBN 978-0-593-56926-9 (trade) — ISBN 978-0-593-56927-6 (lib. bdg.) —
ISBN 978-0-593-56928-3 (ebook) — ISBN 978-0-593-81071-2 (intl. pbk.)

The text of this book is set in 12-point Dante MT.
Interior design by Ken Crossland

Printed in the United States of America
10 9 8 7 6 5 4 3 2 1

First Edition

To Kirsteen, for loving this
story out into the world,

To Yasmi, for being Nora's
most stalwart advocate,

And to anybody who has ever
been made to feel small.

PROLOGUE

When Julia was still alive, I think I would have let her get away with anything.

That was just Julia. Impulsive, charismatic, head-turning Julia.

Nobody said no to her, and that wasn't because she was a reasonable person. She wasn't. There was just something about her—or something about the way she asked for things—that meant the only answer was yes.

She was my best friend. She *chose* me. We loved each other just as desperately as we hated each other.

Can't live with her, my mom had mused the fall of tenth grade, *can't live without her.*

We were about as different as it was possible to be, but we still picked each other over and over. It was desperate, hungry friendship, claws sunk deep, no way to escape.

It was a shoulder to cry on, someone to look for in a crowd.

By the summer before grade twelve, it was this: Nora Radford and Julia Hoskins, furious, adoring, blazing, *jubilant;* a two-headed creature hurtling toward the beginning of the end.

ONE

Before

"Nora, are you even paying attention to me?"

I looked up from the wood grain of the table and offered Julia a sheepish grin. "I'm paying attention."

It was halfway true.

She shook her head, exasperated. "How are you supposed to see anything if you don't even *look*?"

"You're the one who wanted to come here," I pointed out.

Our favorite haunt, mostly at Julia's insistence, was a little café within walking distance of both of our houses. It wasn't all that scenic—the view through the dust-coated windows consisted of a persistently shabby parking lot and the back entrance of the even shabbier recreation center—but every Tuesday at ten after one, the back doors of the rec center opened and the members of Centennial High's summer debate team started trickling out, and the view improved.

Spying on people wasn't my style, but it *was* Julia's. So,

with mild reluctance, I agreed to be dragged here once a week all summer. It's what you do for a friend.

"Here he comes." Julia reached across the table and tapped my arm.

"Can you be any more obvious?" I looked around and then glanced out the window. "He's going to think we're creepy."

Nate Gibson, the object of our attention that day, stood outside, deeply involved in conversation with another member of the team.

"Who cares? We *are* being creepy." Julia mimed a pair of binoculars.

I rolled my eyes. "Cut it out."

Julia laughed, tossing her blond hair over her shoulder. "I'm just glad you're finally into someone who isn't *boring*."

I crossed my arms, watching Nate catch a set of car keys with one hand and grin. "The others weren't boring."

"Are you kidding me?" She scoffed. "Please. Collectively, they had the personality of a peanut, and you know it."

"Whatever." I slumped in my seat, knocking my sunglasses down over my eyes. The AC unit next to me ticked to life, raising goose bumps on my calves. Julia always shot down guys I liked, which meant I'd never actually dated any of them. She said she was looking out for me and I should be grateful. We both knew where I'd stood on the social hierarchy when we met, so maybe she had a point.

Nate Gibson was a lot of things, but boring wasn't one of them. He was the sort of person Julia liked to ogle: conventionally attractive, captain of the debate team, decent hockey player, popular. He was smart, too. He'd been an alternate for Team Canada in debate last year, and I knew for a fact that he'd been top of the class in biology. Julia had broken into the school records to change her grade on a social studies project, and she'd shown me a picture of his report card.

Those weren't the reasons I liked him, though.

He had a nice smile, and he wasn't afraid to speak up in class, and once, I'd seen him doodling a field of flowers in the corner of his notebook.

"Nate's not boring," I told her.

"He *certainly* isn't." She raised her eyebrows.

"Hey!" I swatted her arm.

"What? I'd never go for your man. You know that."

"He's not my man." I watched him hoist an amp into the back of the van, then glanced down at the chipped polish on my fingernails.

"Yet." Julia shoved my leg with her foot. "Don't look. He's looking."

"Why are *you* looking?" I slumped even farther in my chair. In the reflection of the half-empty pastry case, I saw the team climb into the van and drive away.

Julia stirred her iced coffee absentmindedly with her straw.

"Can you believe summer is almost over?" I asked.

"Don't remind me." She wrinkled her nose. "I'm enjoying the last of it in blissful ignorance."

I probably wouldn't tell her this, but I was looking forward to going back to school. This year was it. That's how Julia talked about it. She'd clench her fist and say, *This is it.* After this, it was on to the next adventure. An adventure Julia had been planning for years. She had everything sorted, from our destination—McGill University—down to matching sweatshirts, notebooks, and water bottles that we'd bought and bedazzled in bright red sequins.

She was a lot braver about it than me. Daydreaming about

graduating was one thing. Actually doing it, well—that was going to be another.

Julia tapped her straw against her glass. "Hey, you were friends with Dillan Fletcher, right?"

I blinked. I hadn't heard that name in years. "What?"

"Dillan," Julia said impatiently, pointing the straw at me, "Fletcher. You guys were friends."

"Yeah, why?"

Before Julia, it was me and Dillan. His mom ran the preschool we went to, and then we went to the same kindergarten, and then they moved next door when we'd both turned six. I'd never tell Julia, but I was pretty sure that Dillan had been my first-ever best friend.

Dillan and my older brother, Simon, and I spent entire afternoons constructing elaborate forts, having water-gun fights, and digging around in the dirt. Mostly, I remembered a lot of skinned knees and stupid games. We did *everything* together as a Dillan-and-Nora duo, an inseparable unit with inside jokes and a thousand silly games.

He'd moved away right before fourth grade. Julia had arrived in fifth grade like an explosion, raising a dust cloud and filling every gap he'd left behind, and then some.

I hadn't spoken to Dillan much since then, not out of any kind of animosity. It was just harder to see each other when we lived farther apart, and when school had started, we'd drifted.

"You were neighbors," Julia said.

I smiled. "How do you even know that?"

"I know everything."

She did.

"Like, I know he's enrolled at Centennial."

That surprised me. "Who'd you hear that from?"

6

"Through the grapevine." Julia grinned conspiratorially. "Actually, I heard he got kicked out of Forest Lawn."

"*What?*" She had my full attention now.

"Yeah. Expelled. That's what I heard, anyway."

That was just how Julia was. She'd say the most absurd thing in a deliberately offhand way, and then smile like she'd made an excellent joke when I was surprised.

"For what?"

She shrugged and leaned back, pulling her hair into a ponytail. "Dunno. Probably something extreme, though."

I had a hard time reconciling what I remembered of Dillan with this new information. "And he's coming back to Centennial?"

"Yeah." She nodded. "I heard he's got this whole delinquent thing going on now."

"Huh."

Then, like this information was trivial rather than a revelation, she tossed her ponytail and asked, "Are you coming to soccer tryouts?"

I gave my head a shake, still stuck on Dillan. "Uh, yeah? Obviously."

I didn't play soccer. Julia did, though, and she was good. I went to all her games, and I *always* went to her tryouts.

"Good." She took the straw from her glass and tossed it at the trash can. It bounced off the rim and landed on the floor. "I really want to make the team again."

"Of course you'll make the team." Julia didn't need my reassurance. She'd been team captain since sophomore year, but she still liked to hear me say it.

"You're gonna be on the student pub list this year too, right?"

I grinned. "Obviously."

Soccer was Julia's thing. The school newspaper was mine.

"Come on." She stood. "Let's see if we can convince my mom to let us use the projector tonight. I want to watch *Clueless.*"

While Julia jingled her keys and shouldered the front door open, I ducked down and picked up her straw, gingerly dropping it into the bin, and then followed.

TWO

After

Pain is an old story.

People like asking about it until the response starts being the same over and over. Honesty earns discomfort. Dishonesty earns distrust. There isn't a correct answer.

There are no words for this awful, crushing guilt.

My best friend is dead, and nothing will ever be the same.

Eve thinks I'm depressed.

We've never talked about it, but when she thinks I'm not looking, I see her watching me. And sometimes she comes over just to sit on the edge of the bed, and doesn't talk.

Eve was the third member of our trio. Julia, Eve, and me. She's one of my closest friends now. One of my *only* friends. I'm grateful for her for a lot of reasons, but the main one is that Eve has a lot of other people to spend time with, and she never seems to mind that I don't have much to say.

Like today, for instance.

She could be doing other things on the last Saturday before school starts, but she's dragging me to the dog park, like she has nearly every weekend this summer.

I forgot my sunglasses, so I squint at her, the warm September air heavy on my skin.

Next to us, Strider walks along the path, nose in the grass, thrilled to be alive. Since I don't want to be outdone by a dog, I try to take on a similar attitude.

Eve's cut her hair recently. I can't remember if I've already told her I like it, so I don't say anything. It suits her, though: short on the sides, long on the top, the sort of style my mom would probably call funky. She looks like she's spent a lot of time in the sun, too. Eve's always been darker than me, but especially now. Over the summer, she and her family went back to Sri Lanka for a few weeks, and I haven't told her that I didn't follow through on my promise to do something out of the house while she was gone.

I clear my throat. "Are you excited about starting school?"

"I think so." She shrugs. "Feels weird. Like a next step that I'm not quite ready for."

She glances at me, and I pretend not to notice, because we'll both feel better if she thinks I don't pick up on what's underneath that look: *I'm sorry you're not joining us. I'm sorry life derailed your plans.*

"Is Dillan excited?" she asks.

I shrug.

Dillan has refrained from talking about it too much for my sake, but he is, because when he talks about it, he gets this goofy little grin. He's always been excited for new beginnings, and I'm excited for him—that's what friends are for, after all. "I think he's looking forward to getting back into school."

She wrinkles her nose. "Makes one of us."

"I thought you were looking forward to cosmetology."

"I am," she said. "But it's still *school*."

Eve and I are nothing alike. It's been evident in the last year especially—she's only blossomed, grown brighter, while I have the unpleasant feeling that all I've done is shrink further into myself.

My phone buzzes. It's Dillan—I know by the distinctive triple-tap vibration against my leg. Eve chases after Strider, who's seen a squirrel, so I look.

> abducted by aliens???
> how worried should i be

I text him back:

> Sorry
> Meant to text this am, all good

I fell asleep in the middle of our late-night TV show—whenever we're not watching it together in person, we start episodes simultaneously and text about it the whole time. The fact that I forgot to say anything this morning makes me feel an odd twinge of guilt.

He would have texted me.

Eve and Strider come bounding back toward me. She shields her eyes with her hand. "Is that Nate?"

I look up from my phone, about to ask why she thinks I'd be texting Nate Gibson of all people, but she's looking out over the field.

"It is!" She breaks into a smile.

Before I can stop her, she's walking toward him, and I realize that's how Eve makes friends: by ignoring what I consider human instinct and marching right up to people.

I'm still surprised when Eve reaches him and they hug sideways like old friends.

"Eve!" He looks genuinely thrilled to see her.

Strider's cold, wet nose touches my hand, and I jump. The two of us trail after Eve until we catch up.

"Hey, Nora," Nate calls over warmly. "Long time no see—how have you guys been?"

I almost tell him I've been busy, like an excuse, but that would be a lie, and I'm trying to do less of that. I should be okay with not being okay, considering. So I just smile, though the gesture feels foreign on my face, like I can't quite remember how.

"Great!" Eve beams. "I've been working a little, but mostly making mischief. You?"

"Good, good." Nate nods. "I spent most of the summer volunteering up at a camp in BC."

I know this in the peripheral way I know a lot of things: through social media. Over the summer, I watched the rest of my graduating class go on vacations and prepare for their first year of university—which is right around the corner—while I stagnated.

That's the word I heard my mom use.

Stagnating.

She said it to my dad one night, when she thought I was sleeping.

Eleanor is stagnating.

I don't know. I feel justified in it.

Eve and Nate are talking enthusiastically, and I probably

should contribute to their conversation, but I'm unsure of how to interject without sounding awkward.

It comes on all at once. I'm exhausted, and I can't even begin to describe how much I'd rather be at home, or at work, or anywhere else.

I wonder how Eve knows how to do this so well, with such ease. Maybe it's the fact that it's Nate we're talking to, and he used to make me nervous, but my palms are sweating. I've missed the window to say what I've been doing. It's not exactly thrilling, anyway: get up, go to work, come home, wait to sleep.

What's the appropriate etiquette here? Nate and I are sort of acquaintances who were almost . . . something else. Not friends, though.

I miss exactly what Eve says, but it must have been funny, because they both laugh, the sound carrying through the open air.

Dillan would describe them as *zesty*. The thought almost makes me laugh. I want to be able to join in and laugh easily too, but my life's like a TV show somebody's paused, while everyone else has gone on playing.

The sensation is both foreign and familiar. *Wanting,* cousin to jealousy. I really haven't wanted anything since Julia died except for it to not have happened.

I exhale, a long, trembling breath.

"Nice to see you both," Nate says, even though I've hardly said two words.

"You too." Eve's smile is bright. "I'll see you later, then?"

He nods and walks away.

I smile weakly. As soon as he's out of earshot, I turn to Eve. "You didn't tell me you've been hanging out with Nate."

"I haven't. He's been gone. I've been hanging out with his friends."

Eve has lots of friends that aren't me, but I can't picture her with Nate's preppy school pals.

I can imagine Julia laughing about it, and a wave of realization washes over me for the hundredth time: the only person I could talk to about this is gone.

Eve nudges my elbow. "Are you coming to the party?"

I glance at her. "What party?"

She laughs with breathless exasperation. "I texted you about it!"

I'm terrible at answering texts unless they're from Dillan, and that's only because he'll text me twenty times in a row if I don't respond to the first one. And then he'll call. He's the only person I know under the age of twenty-five who *likes* talking on the phone.

I shake my head. "I didn't see."

I think I did, though. The memory feels a little foggy. I haven't told Eve that I have a hard time remembering some things. Only Mom and Dad and the therapist I saw for a few months after Julia died know about that. They all said it was normal, and that it would get better with time. And it has, so I don't make a big deal of it, and as far as I know, nobody's noticed.

I close my eyes for a moment. The text.

Right. My eyes fly open.

"The party," I say, and Eve nods.

There's a back-to-school party. I'd dismissed the idea immediately because for one thing, I'm not going back to school, and for another, I haven't gone to a party in months.

A bird flutters past us, and Strider barks.

Eve is looking at me expectantly, so I shake my head. "I'll probably pass tonight."

When she tilts her head and offers me wide, entreating puppy-dog eyes, I sigh.

"I'm busy," I tell her.

She considers me like she knows I'm lying, but shrugs it off. "All right. Maybe next time, then."

Eve sounds hopeful, but I think we both know that next time, just like this time, and just like the time before that, I'll say no.

THREE

Before

I'd liked Nate Gibson for a lot longer than I'd admit to anyone, especially Julia. When it started, in the middle of eleventh grade, it was a subtle thing.

But by the end of the summer, there was nothing subtle about it. I couldn't stop noticing him. It had turned into a full-blown starry-eyed-sweaty-hands *crush*, and I didn't really know what to do with it.

That wasn't the problem, though.

The problem was that he kept doing things that made me think maybe he noticed me, too. Like when we saw each other at parties, sometimes he'd make eye contact for just a second too long or he'd wave a little *too* cheerily. Sometimes he'd raise his hand for a high five when we passed each other in the hallway.

But maybe that was just Nate. From what I could tell from his series of short relationships, he had a type—outgoing, blond, long legs. I got nervous in front of too many people, my hair couldn't decide whether to be blond or brown, and I didn't have long legs, either.

Julia ticked all those boxes, though. It sort of freaked me out, but she insisted that she wasn't into him. And even though Julia's word didn't tend to mean much, I believed her. It was scarier not to.

The weekend before senior year, there was a party. Of *course* there was a party.

I only wanted to go because Julia wanted to go. That was how it was with Julia. When she was excited, I was excited. When she smiled, so did everyone else around her, either because it was contagious or because they were afraid not to.

Even before we'd arrived, my chest tightened, knowing: *Tonight something will happen.*

I'm still not sure—did something happen that night because it was destined to happen, or because I had decided it would?

As we walked up to the house, a few people were starting a fire in a fire pit in the backyard and music streamed from somewhere inside, not loud yet but nearly there. We stood on the deck, surveying the drink cooler, the warmth of the day fading into dusk.

"You'll DD, right?" Julia asked my reflection in the patio windows, adjusting the clasp of her necklace. The dim evening light made her hair shine.

I leaned against the railing. "You really have to ask?"

It was an old argument.

Julia claimed she enjoyed parties more when she was drinking, and even though I did too, the responsibility often fell to me. Sometimes, even when it was her turn, she'd forget and drink anyway. Then Simon would have to come collect us, which I knew he hated.

"Where's Eve?" I asked.

Julia lifted one shoulder. "Bailed."

I frowned. I'd been looking forward to starting the school year as a unit. "Did she say why?"

She opened her mouth but was interrupted.

"Hey, Hoskins."

Julia turned.

Nate, of all people, walked out onto the deck, carrying several brightly colored cans.

I averted my eyes, but then I couldn't help looking again.

Nate was get-up-on-your-toes tall, with dark hair and a quick smile. Tonight he was in a maroon shirt and dark-wash jeans, grin already bright as he laughed at something somebody was shouting after him.

He nodded to Julia and tossed her a can in a clean arc, then turned to me, eyebrows raised. "Radford? You want in?"

I shook my head and jerked my thumb toward Julia. "Maybe if I weren't babysitting."

"Oh, ha," Julia said. "I thought your job was to be pretty. Leave the jokes to the rest of us."

I flashed her a sharp glance, but she was looking inside the house as she cracked the can with a neat hiss.

Nate laughed, though, and turned to me. "That's your job, hey? Being pretty?"

I sustained eye contact, even though my cheeks were warming. "Apparently."

Nate gave me an appraising look. "You're doing it well, I'd say."

Then, carelessly, he winked, turned, and walked back inside.

Once I'd managed to recover, I whirled on Julia. "What was *that?*"

"Worked in your favor, didn't it?" She handed me a can of decidedly nonalcoholic iced tea. "He was checking you out. Cheers, yeah?"

Reluctantly, I clinked my can against hers.

"Did you know," she said, "we've been friends exactly seven years today?"

I pivoted to face her. "Really?"

She nodded. "Yeah. We moved to Calgary the week before school started. I met you on September seventh. Nine days after that."

"Not that you're counting." I grinned.

She made a face. "First day of school, remember?"

I did. I'd been *so* nervous. Dillan had moved away the year before. Fourth grade without him was miserable and lonely, and I'd convinced myself I would be friendless again. I would have been, without her.

"That was a good day," I told her.

"The best." She looked pleased. "Anyway, it's an omen."

"What, that today is special?"

"This is your night." Julia nodded, then winked. "Big pond, small fish, all that. Or wait"—she frowned—"is it big fish, small pond? Either way, you'll get him. Something something fishing metaphor. Ha."

I rolled my eyes, but she was already downing her can, and I couldn't help smiling. Maybe she was right.

As it turned out, she was.

The next few hours passed in a flush of dark rooms, raucous conversations shouted over the thumping of low bass, reconnecting with school friends not seen since June. At first, I was sober and so was everyone else, but as the party progressed, everyone around me grew louder and sloppier, eventually leaving me wishing desperately that Eve were around. She would have stayed sober with me.

Around eleven-thirty, I realized I hadn't seen Julia in over an hour. I'd been involved in a game of cards with some acquaintances from the yearbook committee, but the game had dissolved, attentions scattered, and I left to wander the halls on my own.

I wasn't sure whose house this was, but it was nice. I had filled a plastic cup with water in the bathroom and started back down the hall, to see if I could spot Julia, when Nate stumbled through an open door and nearly crashed into me.

"Oh," he said, dimples creasing his cheeks. "Hey, Eleanor."

"Just Nora," I corrected, yelling over the music. When I rested my palm against the wall, I could feel the pounding of the bass through it, almost as fast as my heartbeat. Then, "You can call me Eleanor if you want, though."

"Raaaaaadford." He leaned against the wall, beer bottle dangling loosely in his hand. "'S'at what your friends call you? Nora?"

I nodded, taking a sip from my plastic cup.

He jerked his head toward it. "Thought you were baby-sitting."

I tipped the cup so he could see. "Just water."

"Ah." He raised his eyebrows, gesturing at it. "You mind?"

Feeling a little self-conscious, I handed the cup over. As he tilted it back, I tried not to think too hard about how his lips were on the same spot mine had been only a second before.

"Thanks." He set the cup down on the windowsill, the beer bottle next to it. "Where's your ward?"

"Julia?"

"Yeah." He squinted, blinked. "That was pretty weird, when Julia said that, don't you think?"

"Said what?" I frowned, not quite following.

"The thing about jokes."

"Oh." I brushed it off. "That's just Julia."

"Hmm. Well, *I* think you're pretty funny." Then he leaned forward and whispered, "Two separate adjectives."

We were really close. His breath smelled like beer.

"Oh?"

I didn't even have time to be nervous. There was no space for it. I didn't even close my eyes all the way before he kissed me.

It felt like: bass thudding through the floorboards, his mouth warm and wet, hand on my waist.

It felt like: surprise flooding my whole body, alcohol on my tongue, my eyes squeezing shut.

It felt like: the material of his T-shirt under my fingers, intense heat, no time to breathe.

He pulled away for a half second, and then he kissed me again, openmouthed, his hand on the back of my neck.

When he pulled away for real, he grinned, lopsided, then patted my cheek. "Nice."

"Uh, yeah." I blinked, not quite certain I hadn't just imagined that.

My phone rang—Julia.

Somebody hollered Nate's name from farther inside the house.

"Well," he said, glancing over his shoulder. *"Well."*

Heat radiated from my cheeks. I was sure I must be bright red. "Well."

My phone kept ringing in my hand. I held it up so he could see, and he stepped back. I wasn't sure whether to be relieved or disappointed when he picked up the beer bottle and tossed me a loose peace sign.

"Good to, uh . . . *see* you, Nora."

"You too."

Then, just like that, he walked away, and my phone was *still* ringing.

Reeling, I answered.

"Nooooor. Nora." Julia's voice was elastic. "Where are you?"

"Where are *you?*"

"Hmm," she said. "Kitchen. Second kitchen. Basement? I'm going outside."

"Are you ready to go?" I pressed my phone to my ear as I picked up my cup and followed in the direction Nate had gone. "Don't move. I'll come find you. You aren't going to *believe*—"

She hung up.

Finding Julia at a party was easy. All I had to do was ask and follow the pointed fingers.

I found her leaning against the back fence, the heel of her palm pressed to her forehead. She looked up when she saw me, and at first I thought she'd been crying, because her eyeliner was smudged, but then I saw that her shirt was clinging to the outline of her bra.

"What happened to you?"

She gestured flippantly. "Hot tub."

I took her phone and grabbed her by the arm to lead her

into the house, toward the car, weaving through the crowded space.

"Keys?" I held my hand out.

Julia's bright red McGill lanyard jingled as she fished it out of her pocket and slapped it into my open palm. At least she didn't fight me on it.

Someone wolf-whistled as we passed them, eyeing Julia's transparent shirt, and a few of the guys still in the hot tub started clapping.

Julia bowed deep, then flipped them off with both hands.

They clapped louder.

This was a Julia thing to do. She was absurdly confident about her body. I'd never *dream* of getting into a hot tub in my underwear.

A freshman girl cast Julia an admiring glance on her way past us. I knew Julia caught it, because she smirked. Another one to add to the Julia posse at Centennial. I shook my head, grinning.

Julia slung her arm around me. Her mouth was stained blue, and she planted a sloppy kiss on my cheek. I swatted her away. Julia liked to kiss people when she was drunk.

"You ready to go?"

"Nooooo."

"You were the one who called *me*." I jabbed my finger into her shoulder. "And looks like it's good you did."

"Where's my phone?" She turned around. "I don't remember where I put—"

I held it up, and her face relaxed as I closed the front door behind us.

"Oh, good. You're the best." She made a grab for it, but I held it out of reach.

"Nope, not a chance, dude. You're going to break it."

She grimaced. "I am *not*."

"You always do." I sighed and slipped her phone into my back pocket. "I'm keeping it safe, don't worry."

"Hold up." She leaned against the fence. "Just—gimme a second."

I waited while she closed her eyes, hoping she wasn't going to be sick. She didn't look like she was quite there, but I kept my distance anyway as I leaned against the fence next to her.

"What was the thing?" she asked, eyes still closed. "That I'm not going to believe?"

"I thought you hung up on me."

"I heard . . . something. What's so unbelievable?"

I took a deep breath. "Nate kissed me."

"What?" She turned. "Tonight?"

I nodded. "Yeah. Just before you called."

At first, she just stared, but then she laughed, high-pitched and clear. "See? Something something fishing metaphor."

Right then, Julia looked invincible. Like she could do anything if she wanted to.

"Yeah." I smiled sheepishly. "You were right."

"Oh, Nora." Her grin was impish. "I always am."

Then she pivoted abruptly and threw up in a bush.

I held her hair back and afterward let her slump against me. I slung an arm around her shoulders as I navigated us back to her car.

"Come on," I said when her head started drooping. "Let's get you home."

FOUR

After

I don't often see ghosts at work.

The coffee shop where I'm a barista opens every morning at six. I'm there by quarter after five on weekdays, and sometimes on the weekends.

I like the hiss of the machines starting up and I like organizing the pastry cupboard by the glow of a single overhead light. Usually it's just me and one shift supervisor, which means I'm left pretty well alone until the first customers arrive, though the people who come in at six generally aren't inclined toward conversation.

I'm okay with that. It's easy to pour coffee and steam milk. It's not so easy to make polite and cheerful small talk when all I want is to go home and stand in a hot shower until I can't feel my skin.

Nine months later, this pace of life is not as unbearable as it was in the beginning.

Around seven, the flow starts to pick up. Some days the morning rush lasts a couple of hours. Other days, like today, I'm looking for things to do until I can start the midmorning cleaning.

Other days, like today, I turn around and see Julia standing at the register.

My heart stops, strains, and restarts again.

But it's not Julia.

It's her mother.

It isn't *always* Julia's mother. Sometimes it's a stranger with her hair, or an acquaintance who laughs the same way she did.

"Nora," Mrs. Hoskins says warmly. "Good morning."

I haven't been able to figure out how to tell her that I wish she wouldn't come here. So I just smile.

I *think* I smile. It feels plastic.

"Good morning," I say. "What can I get for you?"

The bell for the front door jingles, and even though I know who it is, I look up. It's exactly quarter to nine, and he's always here at quarter to nine on Tuesdays.

Dillan gives me a two-finger salute as Mrs. Hoskins is giving me her order. I'd know it was him even out of the corner of my eye. That's one of the nice things about Dillan—his bright red curly hair makes him hard to lose in a crowd.

After I've put in her order, I whip around, pour a coffee, and slide it across the counter to Dillan. Ordinarily, he and I might talk, but Mrs. Hoskins lingers, making idle conversation.

"How have you been?" she asks while I'm foaming milk.

"Um."

Behind her, I see Dillan pouring an obscene amount of sugar into his coffee. Even though he's mostly turned away, he sees me watching and smiles slyly.

"I'm all right," I say. "You know how it is."

I see Dillan listening intently, even though he's pretending not to.

"Yes," she says, and then heaves a sigh that sounds excruciatingly familiar. When I hand her coffee over, she says, "Keep your chin up, kid."

My throat tightens. I stare at the back of her head, my chest heavy, until she's gone. Then I whisper, "You too."

When I turn back around, Dillan raises his eyebrows at me, but I just shake my head.

It's not until a half hour later, when I clock out for break, that we talk.

"Hey, dude. Scoot." I go to push him over when I reach the couch, but he scrambles sideways before I do, shoving aside his notes and nearly knocking over his to-go cup. "You really have to quit buying those if you're just going to stay."

"I know, I know." Dillan raises his hands in surrender. "I keep forgetting."

"Tell that to the ocean." My tone is a little more biting than I mean it to be. I poke at his papers with my foot. "What are those?"

"Careful with the shoe prints!" he warns, and I pull my foot down.

Even though I'm pretending to be annoyed with him, I'm pretty sure we both know that his presence has dissolved the tension that's been building since I first saw Mrs. Hoskins. Like Dillan is my own personal pressure-release valve.

When I've settled, he glances at me out of the corner of his eye. "You okay?"

I shrug.

The first couple of weeks after Julia died, she was all anyone wanted to talk about. People would crowd around me, asking if I was all right, talking about how much they missed her, and Dillan knew I hated it.

After the funeral, he found me in the side hallway of the church, ashen and shaking. "We don't ever have to talk about her if you don't want to," he said. "Never, unless you want to."

And we don't talk about her. Some wounds are better left untouched.

But now he's watching to make sure I'm fine, and that makes me feel a little less like I'm standing alone in the pouring rain. Like he's holding an umbrella over me without saying a word.

"I've been working on a song," Dillan says, smoothing out the wrinkles on the page. It's sheet music, with notes scrawled across the neat hand-drawn staff lines.

"For work?"

Dillan has a job at Music Center Canada. He was full-time all summer, and now he's down to part-time. I don't really get what he does, but it usually involves sitting with headphones and scribbling notes on a page. When he starts talking about post-tonal harmony, my brain goes staticky. All I know is that he loves it.

He shakes his head.

"For Queen's, then?"

He doesn't look up. "Yeah. Might be good for scholarship applications."

I'd never tell Dillan, but I hate thinking that in a year, he'll be gone.

Not that I'm not excited for him. I'm *really* excited for him. It's just that 2,881 kilometers is a lot of kilometers. I know because I Googled it when he told me he was going. "Isn't it early to apply for scholarships if you aren't transferring until next year?"

His hand goes still, and for a second I worry that I've said something wrong. Then he shrugs. "I just want to get started."

"What's it called?"

"The song?"

"Duh."

"I don't know yet."

I snatch his pencil off the table and lean over the page, then sit back, grinning. "There. Temporary. You can't just call it *I don't know yet.*"

Across the top of the page I've written: *Nora's Song.* My handwriting is sloppy, and I itch to erase it.

He looks slightly stunned, so I reach for the eraser, but he snatches the paper. "Hey! It's written down, it stays."

I slouch back into the couch.

"Has your mom gotten off your back about school yet?"

I shift uncomfortably. His blue eyes are piercing enough that I look away. "Will she ever?"

"Have *you* thought any more about it?"

"No," I say sharply. "And I don't want to. I'll tell you when I do—I mean, *if* I do."

He smirks but doesn't push it further.

I clear my throat. "Do you know who I saw yesterday?"

He humors me, turning and imitating my wide-eyed expression. "Who?"

"Nate Gibson."

Nothing visibly changes in his face, but maybe that's what tips me off—he isn't thrilled.

I cross my arms. "What?"

Dillan turns back to his notes. "Nothing."

It's not nothing, but I don't press him. Instead I watch surreptitiously as he scribbles, morning light filtering through the window and igniting his curls. I've never seen anyone with hair as orange as Dillan's is, except maybe his mom. Julia used to tease him for it. The memory is a thorn in my chest.

Raggedy Ann.

"Nor?"

I blink. "What?"

"I asked, didn't you guys used to have a . . . thing?"

I feel myself flush. I want to ask what Dillan qualifies as a *thing,* and also how he knows. But that would lead to us potentially talking about whether or not *Dillan* and I had a thing, and I'm not exactly eager to bring it up. So I just shrug. "Wouldn't *you* like to know."

He sits back, slowly shaking his head, smile bemused. "What is that supposed to mean?"

I steal his pencil and poke him in the ribs with it. "It means none of your business, that's what."

"All right, yikes," he says pleasantly, then snatches the pencil back. "Sorry I asked."

I don't want to talk to Dillan about Nate. I don't want to talk to *anyone* about Nate. But I don't know whether that's because I care, or because I don't.

All I know for sure is there isn't much to say.

FIVE

Before

The first day of school was especially strange, because it wasn't just a first day. It was the *last* first day.

It went just about how I'd expected it to go, consisting of confusion and clamor and introductions. I couldn't really complain about my schedule, since I had Eve in one class, Julia in another, and both of them in English. I mainly spent the day trying to survive, so I could get home and quit worrying that something was going to go wrong.

I was sort of hoping to see Nate, though. Not that I'd talk to him if I saw him. But I'd been replaying the kiss over and over in my head, and it was hard not to wonder if he'd been doing the same thing.

When I walked into last-period English, Julia was already there. She lifted her backpack out of the seat next to her and smiled in greeting. "How's it been?"

Relief diffused through me at the sight of her.

"Passable." I shrugged, sliding into the seat. The classroom buzzed as I scanned the desks. "Where's Eve?"

Julia shrugged. "She wasn't feeling well, or something."

Then Nate walked in, and my focus shifted.

I wasn't sure if I should look at him or *avoid* looking at him. What were the rules? After a few seconds of indecision, I pulled out my notebook.

Julia leaned over her desk and read my notes from the previous period. "Why did you write 'try not to asphyxiate self' here?"

"I got Fitzner for physics."

"Oh, God. I've heard terrible things."

"Apparently"—I flipped the notebook to a new section—"they're all true."

Then Dillan Fletcher walked through the open door.

Somehow, even though he was older and a lot taller, he still looked the same as he had in elementary school—unassuming, delicate features, analytical eyes.

Honestly, in all the chaos, I'd forgotten he was coming. Or maybe I'd never really believed Julia.

He walked into the room politely, sidestepping a group of girls congregated around one of the front desks. He didn't *look* like a delinquent.

I watched Dillan glance around the room, eyebrows drawn together. Then he saw me.

Nothing in his face changed at all. He saw me, and I *knew* he knew it was me, because his eyes stopped for half a second, and paused again on Julia, and then he continued scanning the rest of the classroom.

My hand was halfway up to a wave before I pulled it back

down. He hoisted his backpack higher on his shoulder and strode to the back of the room.

There were two desks open in the row behind me, and he flung himself into the farther one without looking over.

Julia and I exchanged a glance. I knew by the look on her face that she knew who he was too, which had to mean—

"Oh," she said, voice low, unscrewing the lid to her water bottle. "I forgot to tell you; I already met him. He's in my chemistry class."

I wondered if the way Dillan looked at us had anything to do with Julia getting to him first.

It wasn't that she was unfriendly, exactly. . . . Well, actually, it *was* that she was unfriendly.

"What did you say to him?"

Her eyes widened and she nearly choked on a large gulp of water. "Why do you assume I said anything?"

I tilted my head and looked at her.

"What?" she asked.

"Maybe"—I leaned forward—"you have a tendency to be unfriendly to those not in the inner circle."

"Maybe," she retorted, loudly, "*he's* unfriendly."

I kicked her under the desk, then dared a glance behind me.

Feeling impulsive, I twisted around in my seat. "Hey. Dillan."

Even though he was in the farther of the empty seats, he was still within arm's reach.

I hadn't thought about our handshake in *years*, but when he looked up, wary, it was as though a switch flipped inside me. Instead of sticking my hand out normally, I gave him a set of finger guns with one eyebrow raised.

He wasn't smiling, but there was the suggestion of a smile, and he returned the finger guns, then stretched his hand out.

Julia's eyes followed every motion.

I was more than a little relieved that he remembered it too: finger guns, fist bump, handshake (firm up-down), second fist bump, explosion. We'd spent *hours* arguing about the perfect handshake in third grade. Apparently, some things were muscle memory.

We both hesitated at the end. The last addition we'd made to the handshake had been to end with a pinky swear.

Today, neither of us made a move to do it.

"Ellie," Dillan said. "Hey."

"Nora," I corrected instinctively. "It's Nora now."

"Oh," he said. "Okay. Nora."

I smiled. "Long time no see."

Next to me, Julia frowned.

At the front, Mr. Ambrose cleared his throat, so I turned back around. "All right, folks. I know you've done this quite a lot today, so let's make it snappy. Icebreaker. Name, favorite color, book you enjoyed recently, and something cool you did this summer."

There was a muffled groan from all of us, which he ignored. Picking up the attendance sheet, he pointed to a girl in the front row. "You start, and we'll go around the room."

I *had* done this quite a few times already today, but that didn't make it any easier. Julia wouldn't have a problem with it, but even the thought of standing up and saying my name made my heart pound.

I mostly tuned people out, focusing on calming my breathing and organizing what I was going to say. When Nate stood up, though, I couldn't help but pay attention.

"Nate Gibson." His voice rang clear through the room. "Blue. *The Great Gatsby.* And my debate team killed the provincial championship this summer."

Even the way he sat back down looked confident.

He didn't look at me. Not once.

Before I knew it, Julia was speaking—of *course* she made it sound easy—and then it was my turn.

I closed my eyes for a moment, and when I stood up and spoke, it all came out at once. "Nora Radford, green, *The Scorpio Races,* and—I went camping."

I sat down quickly.

Mr. Ambrose didn't look up from the paper. "All right, nice. Thanks, Nora. Okay, last one."

Behind me, I heard Dillan stand up, and while I only turned my head to look, heart rate still higher than usual, Julia twisted right around in her chair.

He cleared his throat. "Um, I'm Dillan. Fletcher. I like, uh"—he did a complicated half shrug—"yellow? I liked *Indian Horse* by Richard Wagamese. And I went backpacking in the Rockies this summer."

Julia mouthed the word *expelled.*

I barely resisted rolling my eyes.

"Thanks, Dillan." Mr. Ambrose still didn't look up.

Dillan's chair scraped along the floor as he sat back down.

"Got a sort of Raggedy Ann look going on, don't you think?" Julia twisted back around in her chair, clearly making no effort to lower her voice, then gestured to her head, making a flopping motion with her hands. "Think that worked on the Forest Lawn girls? Couldn't be me."

Several people around us snickered.

My heart sank. There was no way he hadn't heard. And

sure enough, after I'd glared her into silence and glanced back, his head was ducked low as he intently scribbled something on a piece of paper. The tips of his ears were pink.

"Julia," I hissed. "*What* is your problem?"

"Okay." Mr. Ambrose shunted the stack of papers onto his desk. "Let's get started, folks. I have a bet with Mx. Anderson in the other English class to see who can be most hated by students in the shortest amount of time, and I intend to win."

There was a brief pause. Nobody laughed at his joke, except for one girl in the front row, and that was mostly a nervous giggle.

He cleared his throat. "So, your first assignment is going to be a group project. A partner project, actually."

Nate raised his hand.

Mr. Ambrose let out a weary sigh. "Yes?"

"Is this that egg project? Or bag of flour, or whatever?"

Mr. Ambrose pinched the bridge of his nose. "Do I look like a life skills teacher to you? Or whatever?"

Nate smirked and leaned back in his chair.

He *still* didn't look at me.

"No." Mr. Ambrose leaned against the desk. "This is not that egg project *nor* is it whatever. It's simple, it's easy, it's a chance to work with a friend, or not a friend, I don't care. It's a book report on *Of Mice and Men*. That's all."

To the general groaning, he raised both hands. "I know, I know. We have to do a group project at some point, and we may as well get it out of the way early in the semester so you can all go back to—*no texting in my classroom, Mr. Allen, thank you.*"

One of the boys in the back scowled and pocketed his phone.

"Here's the silver lining, if you will." He cleared his throat. "You get to choose your partners."

Julia nudged my foot with hers. I nodded.

"I'm going to leave a sign-up sheet here, and you can take the next ten minutes to find yourself a partner. If you'd rather I assign you a partner, I'm leaving a list for that, too, so don't freak out if your 'BFF' isn't in this class." He traced quotation marks in the air. "Okay. Ten minutes. Then we'll reconvene."

To my surprise, Dillan was among the first to sign up, standing quickly and striding to the front of the room.

I watched him covertly as he hunched over the list. There was no way this quiet guy had been *expelled*. He looked like the worst thing he'd ever done was accidentally cut someone off in traffic.

Julia turned to me as Dillan sat back down.

"Go." She jerked her head. "Sign us up."

"Me?"

"Who else?"

Sighing, I went up to the front. When I looked back, she was staring into space, absently biting at the corner of her thumbnail. Behind her, Dillan's head was ducked low so that his face was hidden, but the tips of his ears were still pink.

I pulled my pencil from behind my ear and wrote my name in small, neat letters. Without even really knowing why I was doing it, underneath my name, I started a new set.

Julia Hoskins and *Evelyn De Zilwa*.

Then, beside my own name, I wrote: *Dillan Fletcher*, and crossed his name out from the list of singles.

As I walked back across the classroom, Julia raised an eyebrow. "All good?"

I nodded. "Yup."

I couldn't help but wonder exactly how this would come back to bite me in the ass.

Honestly, I wasn't even sure why I'd done it. Logically, I knew Dillan would probably be fine on his own. I wouldn't need to face Julia if I'd just put her name down.

But at the thought of the way his ears had turned pink when Julia had made fun of him, shame burned in my gut.

That's what it had been.

Shame.

SIX

After

The days are mostly the same.

One of the mercies of consistent shift work is that the minutes and hours blend together, and the resulting days tend to slide by.

Not today.

My friends went back to school, and I didn't. I don't know precisely what emotions this brings up, but there are a lot of them, and none are good.

I come out of my room when I hear Mom in the kitchen. She's still in her work clothes, but she's pulled her hair out of her usual tight bun and is leaning against the counter, rubbing her temples.

"Hey, you." She looks up at me with a weary smile, which lasts until her phone lights up. Then a frown creases her forehead, and she puts the phone in the cupboard and closes the cabinet door.

I ask her about work, and she makes a series of grumbling apathetic noises. She asks me about work, and I echo her sentiment.

"I haven't thought about dinner yet." She peers into the fridge, and I pour both of us a glass of water.

This is good, because even if the rest of today was not routine, at least this part is. Mom never thinks about dinner until the threat is imminent. We'll probably make a quiche or pasta, because it's fast.

While her back is turned, I take her phone out of the cupboard and put in on the charger, because otherwise she'll forget.

It's a Thursday, which means Simon's at work and Dad has a meeting, so it's just us. Mom pulls out a carton of eggs. I put on some music, and we cook and eat in companionable silence.

After both of our plates are clean, she drops her semi-usual, "Have you thought at all about school?"

We both know it's a stupid question. Obviously, I've thought about school. I run my fingers along the edge of the place mat. "I don't really want to talk about it."

She leans back in her chair, closes her eyes, and takes in a quick breath. "We have to at some point, you know."

I keep my tone even. "Is it urgent?"

"Of course it's urgent, Eleanor."

"Why?"

"Don't you *want* to go to school?"

"I don't know."

"You always have. You had dreams, Eleanor. Wouldn't Julia have wanted you to keep writing? Wouldn't she have wanted you to be happy?"

I feel like I'm going to shatter. We both know that was a

step too far, but she can't know the real answer to that question: *I'm not sure.*

"What's the point? You know what happened," I say bitterly, spitting the words out like they're poisonous. "TMU *rejected* me."

And I don't write anymore. I dropped the school paper after Julia died. Even though I miss it so badly it hurts, I can't. Now, whenever I get in front of a blank page, all I can do is stare at it until the blinking cursor goes blurry.

Mom just looks at me. I wish she *would* say something, because I have venom swimming through my bloodstream right now and I would give anything to direct it somewhere.

I push away from the table, but she stands up.

"Honey. Eleanor. I know what happened was hard, but you can't let it derail your future. A no from one school doesn't mean it's a no across the board. You got accepted—"

"Don't." I stare at her.

"I know things were hard last year, and I think it was wise to defer, but you have to move forward. That's the only way. You can't just keep on . . ."

"Keep on what?"

She doesn't say anything. We both already know.

I cross my arms. "I'm just . . . happy with what I'm doing right now."

This is a lie. It feels like *everything* is a lie. I told Mom I deferred my university acceptance, but I didn't. I let it lapse, because it had felt impossible to even consider going without Julia, and now the idea of reapplying is humiliating.

"I'm happy," I repeat. "For the time being."

She watches me sadly, and I look back at her, defiant, both of us knowing I will stick to this story even if it kills me.

"Good night," I say wearily.

"It's not even seven-thirty."

"I have to be up early. I'm tired."

Even though she knows this is a lie too, she doesn't argue. She just lets me go.

I go through the motions of getting ready for bed. When I text Dillan to ask him about his first day at university, he doesn't respond.

I don't really know why he's still here. He was accepted to Queen's four months after the accident, in the spring, which means he could have gone this fall, but he chose to do a year at the university here and then transfer. We haven't talked about why, but I'm pretty sure it has something to do with Julia.

Whatever his reasons, I'm grateful. Dillan was the only one who really understood, after she died.

People must think it's weird that we hang out so much. I'm pretty sure Mom thinks we're secretly dating, but it's not like that. Not anymore, at least.

Sitting on the edge of my bed, I try not to think about anything, especially not Dillan at school because that means thinking about school in general, and that's basically the same thing as thinking about Julia.

I don't like doing that, even though it happens a lot.

I look at myself in the mirror and run my hand through my hair. It's the longest it's ever been, down to my waist. I'm thinking about cutting it, but I can't quite bring myself to do it. I lie down on the bed, but I don't get under the covers.

Julia called Eve and me her birds, sometimes. Eve was her raven, and I was her sparrow, because Eve's hair was dark and mine was in the middle. At least that's what Julia said.

We were her birds, but I never asked her what she was.

She was just Julia, except for the fall of ninth grade, when she made us call her Lee. That didn't last, though, because by then she was already Julia, and if you're already something, she eventually decided that ninth grade was too late to change it.

Sometimes she was Jules, but I was the only one who called her that. She wasn't a bird. She was too much to be a bird—she was so *herself.*

Sometimes I wonder if I would have been like that if it weren't for her.

SEVEN

Before

"Oh, this bitch is going *down*." Julia grinned at her phone.

I scooted up onto my elbows, craning my neck to look at her screen. "Who's going down?"

We were on Julia's bed, all lights turned off except for her fairy lights overhead. Julia's laptop lay ignored, playing an old episode of *Gilmore Girls*. I'd been dozing, I was pretty sure, like I always did when Julia played with my hair. I always loved it when she did that. Right from our first-ever sleepover, I'd felt like Julia was weaving promises into the plaits. *You don't have to be alone ever again. You've got me now. I'll always understand you best.* She was good at making promises like that.

She was even better at keeping them.

Julia turned her screen to show me a text from somebody named Mayu. I didn't recognize that name, so it was probably one of the first-year students Julia was indoctrinating into her group of friends, like she did every year.

Julia's face lit up when my eyes widened.

"Thanh's the one who was gunning for the captaincy, right?"

Julia preened. "And she's not going to get it now."

I bit my lip. Thanh hadn't exactly been a saint, but even I could tell that she was a brilliant player, and she'd already been bullied all through junior high for her accent, so I'd been hoping Julia would just leave her alone. "What are you going to do?"

"Nothing she didn't have coming." Julia sat up abruptly. "Let's go."

"Go? Where? It's after midnight!"

Julia was already putting on a pair of sweatpants.

"I was almost asleep," I said, somewhat grumpily, but I sat up anyway, swinging my legs off the bed. Another Julia adventure was at hand, and as her aide-de-camp, I was duty bound to join in.

"This won't take long."

"Where?" I asked again.

"They're at a party."

I glanced down at my fuzzy pajama bottoms covered in polka dots.

Julia laughed. "No, don't worry, it's a kid party, basically. They're ninth graders. We're just going to pick something up."

"You're not going to do something really stupid, are you?"

She just grinned.

My stomach twisted.

"Come on." With the glow of the fairy lights behind her, Julia looked like some kind of angel, but her expression—cunning and pleased—sent a shiver up my spine.

"Come *where?*" I asked.

"Out," Julia said, sliding her window open.

My jaw dropped.

"Julia, it's after midnight," I reminded her again.

Even though we both knew Julia's mom wouldn't care, we also knew there were cameras in their entryway, and Julia had a strict curfew. There hadn't been consequences for breaking it in years, but Julia swore that was more due to not being caught than it was due to her parents letting her off the hook.

I wasn't sure I agreed with that, but if Julia wanted to think it, that was fine by me, because I hated it when Mrs. Hoskins got mad.

"And duty calls," Julia said, giving me a salute, and before I could object, she jumped out the window. Duty *indeed*.

I rushed to the edge. It was only a four-foot drop, but I always freaked out when Julia did it. I hissed at her, "You're going to give me a heart attack."

"I'm *fine*," Julia said, then held her hand out. "Are you coming? I need my partner in crime."

I jumped out the window after her, shivering as my socked feet hit damp grass. "We could have at least gotten shoes."

"It's not that far," Julia said, looping her arm through mine and pulling me closer.

You've got me now.

She was right.

This party was only two blocks over. She spent the walk there talking about Thanh—how she had talked shit about Julia for weeks, how she hadn't listened when Julia told her to knock it off, how she'd even flirted with the coach.

And now she was going after Julia's place for captain.

"There are consequences for these things," Julia said, flipping her hair under the streetlight.

"What are you going to do?"

She just smiled.

The pit in my stomach twisted. Sometimes Julia took things too far. She was a whiz with computers, which she said made it *too* easy. The year before, she'd gotten somebody suspended for accusing her of plagiarism. She took her honor very seriously.

"The rumor mill never forgives," she'd told me, more than once. "You have to stay on top of it, or it'll come back to bite you."

Then, as we were walking, I thought about asking her if she would consider just leaving Thanh alone.

But I kept my mouth shut. Sometimes that was easier.

There was somebody waiting for us outside the house where the party was happening.

I didn't recognize her, but she looked young standing there. Did Julia notice that she looked nervous?

"Excellent," Julia said, taking the bag the girl handed her and peeking inside. "Aila, right?"

The girl nodded, eyes enormous in the dark.

"Tell Mayu I owe her one." She smiled widely down at Aila, who mostly just looked how I felt. A little uncertain. "Have a good night."

I watched Aila walk away, feeling uneasy.

Julia hoisted the bag onto her shoulder. I wasn't sure if she wanted me to ask.

I didn't break until we got back to her house, standing beneath her window, and then I couldn't take it anymore.

"Okay. What's in the bag?"

Julia grinned. She produced a small digital camera.

"A picture," she said, like it was a priceless secret, walking the edge between joking and cruel, "is worth a thousand words."

When Julia talked like that, it could be chilling. One time at dinner, my mom jokingly referred to her as "the kingpin," which made us both laugh so hard lemonade actually came out of my nose. Mom had a point, though. Julia was at the center of a web, and I was just glad I was in it with her, and not on the outside. Like Thanh.

"What's on it?" I asked finally, turning the camera around.

Julia smiled at me, devilish. "Does it matter?"

My stomach dropped. "I don't know. Is it something really bad?"

She rolled her eyes. "I didn't know you cared about Thanh so much."

"I *don't*." I sighed, frustrated. "I'm just curious."

But Julia wasn't about to answer me.

"Come on," she said, grabbing hold of the windowsill, grinning at me over her shoulder. "Boost me back up."

EIGHT

After

I t's been weeks since I've been to Julia's grave.

September sunlight beats down on my head as I notice that the last bouquet I left her is wilted and mostly gone. Except for a single rose with a touch more life that sits atop the gravestone, there's nothing else.

There used to be lots of flowers. Right after she died, it seemed like half of the school was here on a weekly basis, but people have stopped coming in the last few months, which makes me angry.

Especially because I'm one of them.

I stand with my head bowed. I want to feel like coming here connects me to her, but I don't feel like she's here. I barely feel like *I'm* here.

It's eerily quiet, but my head is loud. I wonder if grief feels like this to everyone else, too, slippery and echoing. As though sometimes memories dart just out of reach and leave only a hollow ache behind, and other times one moment sticks like a song on repeat, as crystalline and sharp as a shard of glass.

I sit on the grass, and I have one of those moments.

The first summer Eve hung out with us, after she'd forgiven Julia, we spent a lot of time sitting on my front lawn, grass prickly on our bare legs. One of those afternoons, Julia put her hand out and said, "Jen forever!"

Both Eve and I were confused because neither of us knew a Jen, and we thought that was what she meant. But then Julia explained "J.E.N.," like our three first initials together.

I reminded her that it should be "J.E.E." because we were Julia, Eve, and Ellie, but she looked at me all funny and said, "Who wants to have a group name like 'Jee'?"

That was when I stopped being Ellie and started being Nora.

I loved being Nora, because Nora was special. Julia was good at making me feel that way—especially back then. Maybe back then, she meant it.

My breath shakes. I miss how *certain* she always was.

Does anybody else do this? Does anyone else come here anymore? Julia was so well known. People flocked to her. Hell, she had a whole posse at one point.

But she chose me. Over and over, Julia chose me.

And look where that got her.

I stare at the gravestone until it blurs, and I wish I could cry, but I can't.

I wonder if I'll ever feel anything other than this hollowing guilt.

NINE

Before

Even though I hadn't missed one of Julia's soccer tryouts since eighth grade, I didn't particularly enjoy them.

For starters, they were boring. Also, I didn't really like soccer, so mostly I just sat there, feigning interest. It's what you do for friends.

Thanh was nowhere to be seen.

Julia waved from across the field. As I shot back a double thumbs-up, I caught sight of a flash of red hair by the school doors.

I hadn't seen Dillan since earlier today, when Mr. Ambrose had handed out blank booklets with our names printed across the top. When Dillan had gotten his, he'd looked up at me like he was certain there'd been a mistake, which kind of made me wish I hadn't done it, especially because Julia's face wore the exact same expression dialed up to one thousand.

Wincing, I wished I could forget the conversation—interrogation, really—Julia and I had after class. She'd been incredulous that I wouldn't want to work with her and had needled me about changing it until I'd slung an exasperated arm around her and told her what was done was done. It was just one project, after all. Once it registered that I wasn't changing my mind, Julia had sulked for ten minutes, done quite a lot of dramatic sighing, then given it up.

Now Dillan walked across the parking lot with a few kids I knew were in band. He said something and all of them laughed; one of them even lightly punched his shoulder. He grinned, a hand on his backpack strap.

This guy was supposed to be a delinquent?

Then, as Dillan turned, he saw me sitting there watching. My instinct was to be embarrassed, but he just smiled and lifted a hand in my direction.

I waved back.

There was a general uproar from the field—a goal. I turned back just in time to see Julia do a victory dance. She looked my way, then beyond me to Dillan. For a moment, I thought she was annoyed, probably because I'd missed her goal, but then she shot me a thumbs-up before she ran toward the coach.

When I turned back to the parking lot, Dillan was gone.

My phone vibrated in my hand. I looked down, expecting a text, but it was an email from—

I clapped a hand to my mouth. *Toronto Metropolitan University.*

Congratulations, Eleanor Radford! We are pleased to offer you a conditional acceptance to the Toronto Metropolitan School of Journalism.

I skimmed the email, trying to figure out if this was some kind of joke. Julia had my email passwords, so she could have easily sent this as one of her pranks, like when she'd snuck onto the school computers and changed the grades of the boys' soccer team. But no, there was the university logo, and the email address was from the registrar, and it was—it was—

Real.

I scrolled down.

*Please note that your offer of admission is **conditional on submitting your transcripts and a personal essay,** which are required to complete your offer.*

My heartbeat hammered in my throat. An essay. Just an essay. I could do that. I read through the instructions, stomach inching higher and higher up my throat with every second. They'd sent a list of questions to choose from—I had *options.*

There was one essay between me and a spot in the TMU journalism program.

I'd mostly applied on a lark. Their program would be a dream come true, so of course when they had sent notice that they were interested in young journalists applying, I'd filled out everything I needed to. But I hadn't thought I really had a chance! For one thing, Julia and I had made plans to go to McGill ages ago. For another, TMU's journalism program was intensely competitive.

Despite the uproar on the field, I couldn't look up. I was frozen in place, heart beating like I'd just been running for my life.

TMU had never been anything but a daydream.

But now . . .

Early acceptance, depending on an essay. As I read the rest of the instructions and conditions, I realized that if I wasn't accepted now, that would be it unless I wanted to reapply next year. This was my one shot.

But it was still a shot.

I read and reread the email for the rest of the tryouts.

This was real.

After, Julia jogged over to me. She was beaming like she'd already gotten on the team, like it was a sure thing that she would get what she wanted.

Guilt blossomed in my gut. *McGill.* Julia would hate this.

"So?" she asked, out of breath. "Thoughts?"

I blinked up at her. Could she *possibly* already know just based on my face? But then—

"I think I did okay," she said.

"You've got it in the bag." I gave her a tight smile and picked up my backpack. "Obviously."

She grinned. "I hope so."

"I *know* so."

On the way to the car, Julia talked about soccer teams at McGill—the knife of guilt twisted in the pit of my stomach again—and how she wanted to try rugby, and how fun it would be when I got to watch her play on a real team. By the time we were heading home, I wanted to tear my hair out.

When we got back to my house, she looked a little annoyed, probably because I hadn't been enthusiastic about the way she'd apparently *totally showed* Kelly Offenheimer. I stared at the Polaroids hanging from Julia's rearview mirror. Us in McGill sweaters. She'd stuck scarlet rhinestones all around the edges.

I should just tell her right away. But Julia didn't like when plans changed, especially not big ones like this, and she was so thrilled about the tryouts, I didn't want to burst her bubble.

I wasn't even sure I'd get in, and I knew from experience that when Julia didn't get her way, things didn't go well. Like when we'd first gotten to high school, we'd been in different homerooms and Julia had bothered the administration until they gave up and let us be together. Or when I'd wanted to go on that trip with Eve . . .

"How were tryouts?" Mom asked us as soon as the front door closed behind us.

"The usual." I shrugged, walking into the kitchen and leaning against the fridge. "She's a shoo-in, for sure."

"Like there was ever a doubt," Mom said.

"Right?" I turned back around, arms spread wide, then shot a pointed look at Julia. "Please tell her to stop freaking out."

"I'm not freaking out," Julia grumbled, but looked begrudgingly pleased when Mom squeezed her shoulder; then Julia pulled her phone out and started furiously typing.

A moment later my phone buzzed.

> when is the snack coming home

I glanced up at her and raised one eyebrow.

She looked pointedly at my phone, so, shaking my head, I typed out a response.

> Stop pretending you have a crush on my brother it's weird

> i'm not pretending. i'm in love w him

> He has a date

> WHAT

> Aren't you going to ask who

> no i'm busy trying to drown myself

Julia caught my eye and tipped back the glass of water in one go. I couldn't help laughing, and then she did too, nearly choking.

Simon chose that moment to walk into the kitchen. He dropped his bag on the floor and announced, "I think I got it this time!"

"Good interview?" Mom asked.

Simon nodded.

Julia glared at me and wiped her mouth, cheeks flushed. "You're a liar and a terrible friend."

I was busy erupting in a second fit of giggles. Simon blinked when he noticed her. "Oh, hey, Julia."

"You were at a job interview?" she asked him, hopping onto the counter and crossing her legs.

"Yeah," he said, presenting his cheek for a kiss as Mom walked past him. "I think it went pretty well."

"So if you get the job, does this mean you'll finally get a decent car and sell me yours?" Julia asked him.

Simon flipped her off and grabbed a water bottle from the fridge. Pointing at her with the end of it on his way out, he said, "I would drive it off a cliff before giving it to you."

Her mouth dropped open. "Hey! I drive just fine!"

Simon and I snorted.

For a moment, Julia looked furious and indignant, eyes bright, but then she burst out laughing too. The sound shot through me like a balloon deflating, the anxieties of the day easing all in one go.

"Come on," I said, walking over and bumping my hip against Julia's leg. "We have homework."

"You spoil all my fun," Julia said, but there was no heat behind the words. She hopped off the counter and slung an arm around me. "Fine. Let's go."

TEN

After

"There *isn't* a freezer section at Shoppers. I'd bet my life on it."

"Prepare for a short life, dude," I say as we walk through the sliding doors. "I don't know why you're arguing with me about this. I've literally bought chicken nuggets here."

Dillan shakes his head. "There's no way."

I'd been sort of nervous that he wouldn't have time for stupid nonsense like this now that his semester has started, but he showed up today just like he always has.

Two minutes later, after I've proved him wrong and he's finished sulking about it, we aimlessly wander the store. The employees probably hate us for it, since we never buy anything, but it's fun. Afternoons like this—out of the house, with somebody who isn't afraid of upsetting me—have sustained me for the last few months.

I stop in front of a bin of sale items, pick up a floridly colored stuffed bird, and hold it in front of my face.

Dillan snatches the bird and looks down at it in disbelief. "This thing is *ugly* ugly."

"*You're* ugly ugly." I hold my hand out for it.

He grins good-naturedly but shakes his head, holding the bird high out of reach. "I'm keeping this, thanks."

I'm about to respond when I spot a familiar figure farther down the aisle. Dillan must see my surprise, because he turns, and his eyes widen ever so slightly. I don't think Dillan would be able to hide an emotion if he tried. This particular expression says a lot of things all at once, like: *My day was going so well* and *I definitely still don't like this guy.*

Nate Gibson is standing in front of the sunscreen. I don't think he's seen us, but I still turn away.

"What do I do?" I whisper.

Dillan looks utterly bewildered. "About what?"

I jerk my head toward Nate.

"Do you want to talk to him?"

"I don't know!"

"What's that supposed to mean? I thought you didn't like him."

"I never said that."

Dillan glances over his shoulder, incredulous.

Nate looks up and I can see the exact moment he realizes who we are, because he tilts his head.

I'm glad I wasn't looking *right* at him, only peripherally. But then, as if this isn't already awkward enough, he saunters over, a bottle of sunscreen in each hand.

"Hey, Nora. What do you think?" he asks, as though

we're great friends. "I don't know which is better. It's for my mom."

I want to disappear into the vinyl flooring.

Dillan places the stuffed bird back in the bin.

I can feel my forehead getting warm, but I try to play it cool by crossing my arms and raising my eyebrows. "You should ask Dillan, he's the sunscreen guy."

Nate looks at Dillan like he's only now noticing him. He gives Dillan a cursory nod in that strange way that guys do.

Dillan acknowledges him coolly. "Gibson."

"Fletcher." Nate holds the two bottles up. "What do you think?"

Dillan knocks his knuckles lightly against the yellow bottle. He doesn't smile. "I'd go with this one, if I were you."

Seeing the two of them interacting is strange. Nate smiles at me.

For a second, the three of us just stand there. Then Dillan seems to read something in the situation that I don't, because he ducks his head. "I'm, uh . . . I'll be over here."

He shoves his hands into his pockets as he strides down the aisle, only stopping once he gets to the magazines and picks one up.

I watch him go, feeling a little helpless. I know he's only pretending to read by the exaggerated furrow of his brow, and also by the way he's holding the magazine upside down.

Nate clears his throat. "So, you and Fletcher?"

I have to stare at him for a second before I understand what he means. "What? Oh, no. We're just friends."

Nate glances over at Dillan, who has now turned the magazine right side up. "Huh."

"He knew Julia really well too." I don't know why I'm saying this, since Nate knows. I don't know why I'm mentioning Julia at all. Thinking about Julia in a Dillan context makes me feel ill.

"I remember." Nate flips the sunscreen once. "Hey, I don't want to be, like, insensitive or anything."

I watch him toss it again. It flips a 360.

"I know it's probably a touchy issue for you. I just know you and Julia were really close, so . . . how's it been?"

It's the weirdest way anyone has ever asked me about her. I don't really know how to answer. "Uh . . . physically, I'm fine. I only broke my arm, so . . ."

The same night that stole a life left me with only a cast.

"Everything else . . . I don't really think it gets easier. That's what lots of people say, anyway."

There's no way Nate would understand the full truth. Because it's not just losing her. It's everything else that happened before, too, all the things I've tried not to think about since.

He nods once, then again. "She was really cool."

There's a lump at the base of my throat. "Yeah."

It's a half-lie.

I rock on my heels.

"Hey, is your number still the same?" he asks, running his hands through the hair at the back of his neck.

"Yes?"

"Cool." He tilts his head. "Good thing I ran into you."

"Yeah." I laugh nervously. "Good thing."

"Thanks for the advice." He raises the yellow bottle of sunscreen. "I'll see you . . . sometime."

I stop myself from pointing out that it was Dillan who gave him the advice, and instead I just wave as he backs away, disappearing around the corner.

A *wave*? Really?

Once I'm sure he's gone, I cover my face with my hands. When I look up, Dillan is back, looking bemused.

"Where did you go?" I swat his shoulder. "You left me alone!"

He sounds a little weary. "What kind of friend would I be if I weren't at least a good wingman? What was all that about, then?"

I swallow. Then, after a moment, I tell him, "I have no idea."

ELEVEN

Before

The first time the four of us studied together, it was *almost* a disaster.

For starters, I was in a terrible mood. Two weeks into school, I'd resigned myself to the fact that Nate and I—whatever we'd been—were over. As far as I could tell, Nate didn't even know I existed. I couldn't decide between being angry and hurt, or surly and sullen. On top of that, I couldn't think of a good essay topic for my TMU application, *and* I hadn't told Julia yet. Every time I thought about telling her, I just froze up.

It was a small mercy that we were picking up Julia last, because that meant for a little while, it was just Eve, Dillan, and me in Eve's car. On the bright side, Eve and Dillan seemed to be getting along like they'd known each other for ages. On the less bright side, neither of them seemed to notice my gloominess.

"So." Eve twisted around so fast that her long dark braid

nearly whipped me in the passenger seat. "Did you really get kicked out?"

I shot her a look. "Eve!"

Dillan blinked. "From where?"

"School, duh." Eve stopped at a stop sign and stared at him through the rearview mirror.

He looked utterly nonplussed. "What are you talking about?"

"Word on the street is that you got kicked out of Forest Lawn, and that's why you're back."

Dillan let out a small helpless laugh. "No, I didn't get kicked out. Where did you hear that? My family moved again."

It didn't *really* surprise me, because I had been starting to suspect that the rumor was only a rumor, but I still felt relief sharp in my chest. "Where'd you move?"

"Back to Sundance."

"Huh." I wondered why he hadn't said anything until now. We'd been living in the same neighborhood again and I hadn't even known.

Eve snorted, then, triumphantly, said, "Julia owes me ten bucks."

"No way she actually still believes that," I said, then felt a little guilty, because I'd thought it was possible too.

We turned the corner onto Julia's street. Her neighborhood was full of homes with large, sweeping driveways, fountains, and perfectly manicured lawns. She was already waiting on the sidewalk, which wasn't a surprise. Julia hated spending time at her house. She always said it was either too empty or too full of her mom.

Eve stopped.

"What's up, losers?" Julia slid into the backseat, then frowned. "Dillan."

He regarded her coolly. "Julia."

"I thought it was just us girls today." Julia's voice was neutral, but there was danger in her eyes.

I scoffed. "What am I supposed to do at the library without my partner?"

"Whatever." She slumped back, arms folded, looking like she was trying to pretend Dillan wasn't there.

The first few minutes of the drive were tense. Then Eve spoke up.

"I heard about Thanh."

Even though her tone was nonchalant, I saw Julia's shoulders tighten. "What did you hear?"

"Isn't it . . . ?"

Julia scoffed. "Spit it out, De Zilwa."

"Aren't you worried that targeting her is a little racist?"

"Racist?" Julia spluttered, gesturing to Eve. "I'm friends with *you*. How could I be racist?"

Dillan caught my eye in the mirror and winced, lips pressed together.

I resisted the urge to cover my face in my hands and slide down in my seat. Sometimes it felt like Julia didn't know where the line was, or if she did, she just didn't care. I turned toward her. "You don't want to get canceled, do you?"

"I'm not getting canceled." She sniffed, looking down at her nails. "I don't see color."

Eve rolled her eyes, and I shot her an apologetic look.

"Oh, the horrors," Dillan said, deadpan. "I think people should get canceled more often."

The look Julia gave him was positively withering. "I'm *not* racist."

But Eve grinned at Dillan through the mirror. I could tell that regardless of what Julia thought, she liked him just fine.

"I'm not racist," Julia insisted. Then she leaned forward, as though she was trying to let all of us in on a secret. "I'm just not wrong about Thanh."

"We know," I said, smiling back at her, teasing. "You're never wrong."

"Speaking of never being wrong," Eve said slyly. "Like I told you, Dillan wasn't expelled."

Julia's mouth dropped open. She and I made wide-eyed eye contact through the rearview mirror. "You just *asked* him?"

"You're the one that said it! You owe me ten."

"I can't believe you sometimes." Julia rolled her eyes. Then she turned to Dillan. "Sorry. Some *people* in this car have no tact. What's the story, then?"

Dillan just shrugged. "It's fine. I moved, that's all. Where'd you hear I got expelled?"

Julia muttered something, but Eve laid on the horn and her words were obscured.

"Just 'cause you're a fossil doesn't mean you should drive like one!" Eve rolled down her window and made a rude gesture, then slammed her sunglasses back onto her face.

Dillan burst out laughing, and to my relief, Julia laughed too.

At the library, we set up at two separate smaller tables, laptops open. As Dillan unloaded his backpack, I was surprised that the bookmark in our assigned novel was already close to the end. When I pointed it out, he laughed.

"What, you didn't think I'd do the reading? Is it because I'm a guy?"

"No! Actually"—I risked a glance backward at Julia and Eve, who were looking at Eve's screen, whispering together, and lowered my voice—"it's that I'm usually partners with Julia for stuff like this, and she *never* does the assigned reading."

"Really?"

"She's more of a SparkNotes gal. It works for her, but it's sort of a pain for group stuff."

He shifted back in his seat and grinned. "Huh. If I'd known I could have gotten away with freeloading . . ."

I bent over my backpack to hide my smile.

Dillan cleared his throat. "So, I looked at your notes on the Google Doc. You use a lot of big words."

"I *like* big words." I riffled through the booklet Mr. Ambrose had provided.

"I heard that he'll dock points if you use too many."

"As if. I work with him on the school newspaper. He knows I have a propensity toward them."

Dillan grinned and mouthed *propensity*.

"I read the article you wrote," he said, after a moment.

I blinked up at him. "What?"

"The one from the June edition," Dillan said, twirling his pen between his fingers. "It was really good."

My cheeks warmed. "Oh. Thank you."

I had liked that piece. It had been on the front page right before school let out. Julia had it framed on her wall. I'd written it about the school's carbon footprint, with interviews and everything.

"I liked it. It was funny. And clever," he said, with an easy smile. "You're going to do just fine."

I grimaced. "Thank you, but this is different. It's a

presentation. I hate them. I'm going to have to hide behind some big words."

"He's going to think I'm a lot more literate than I am." Dillan wrinkled his nose as he scanned the document. "Who unironically says 'incorrigible'?"

"Insufferable know-it-alls." I flashed him my brightest smile and started typing.

"You said it, not me."

"Hey!" Eve snapped her fingers at us. "Stop flirting for a second and help us."

My cheeks burned. The chair scraped against the floor as I pushed it back. When I glanced at Dillan, his head was bent low over the paper, but the tips of his ears were flushed pink just like they had been the day I'd chosen him as a partner.

I glared at Julia and Eve when I reached them, and hissed, "I wasn't!"

Julia tossed her ponytail over her shoulder. "Come on. Why *else* would you have picked him?"

"We're friends! Or—we were." I didn't need Eve's knowing smirk to tell that my cheeks were still flushed.

She and Julia exchanged a glance. Sometimes it was hard to remember that Julia had *hated* Eve at first. I'd been the bridge between them. And after that, time had worked magic. And a similar sense of humor.

"Look," I told them. "Neither of you knew him. We were best friends when we were kids. Don't make it weird."

Julia put her hands up in surrender.

"Did you actually need my help, or did you only call me over here to harass me about my *friendships*?"

They erupted into a fit of giggles.

"No, we did actually have a question," Julia said. "But mostly it was for harassment purposes."

To my relief, Eve pointed to a question on the pamphlet.

I answered to the best of my ability, then turned to leave, but as I did so, Eve whispered, "Have fun with your *friendship*."

I threw my hands into the air and stalked back to my chair, scraping it along the floor with such deliberate force that the librarian shot me a warning look.

"What was that about?" Dillan asked, his pencil hovering over his notebook.

"Nothing." I covered my cheeks with my hands. "They think they're so funny."

He smirked. "You could say . . . incorrigible?"

I couldn't help the begrudging smile. "You could."

TWELVE

After

"Nora?"

Oh, God.

My first thought is to hide, but I can't. I'm on an open train platform, and there's nowhere to go, and no way to pretend like I haven't heard her. For a moment, I hardly recognize the girl walking toward me, but then she snaps into context and I let out a startled huff of laughter. *"Kayla?"*

"Hey, it's good to see you." Kayla Pham smiles at me. "It *is* Nora, right?"

I have to do some quick recon to think of everything I know about her: that she's just clever enough to have annoyed Julia, that she used to take photos for the school newspaper, and that we were classmates all through high school without ever really being friends.

Besides that, I'm drawing embarrassing blanks. What sort of person sees an acquaintance from school and doesn't just give them a little awkward nod and move on? *Other* than Eve?

"Yeah," I say, at last. "That's right."

She's wearing a black leather jacket, and she looks different than she did when we were in school. Like she's standing up straighter, maybe.

"It's good to see you, too," I rush to tell her. That's the right response, isn't it? Then I clear my throat. "How's school been?"

"A good distraction. Feels a little unreal to be at university, actually." I can *see* that she's wondering whether I'm going back to school or not.

I give her my most encouraging smile but don't offer any information. "Are you studying at U of C?"

"Yeah, I am!" She practically lights up. "My classes are really good so far."

I nod, and then there's a beat of silence that's a little bit awkward.

"How are you?" she asks. "I mean, really. I know it must have been really tough, after . . ."

The temptation to laugh out loud is nearly overwhelming. Why do people always ask me that? They only ever want me to say *fine*.

I just shrug. "I'm all right."

She gives me a swift look that makes my spine tingle, like she's got me all figured out. I remember that look. Usually, she hid it behind a camera. She took photos of the soccer team. I still have one of Julia above my desk. For a second, I think she's going to push it, but she doesn't. "Where are you off to?"

"Work," I tell her. "You?"

"School," she says, with a wide smile. "I've got a study group."

The train pulls into the station. While the announcer is telling us to stand back from the yellow line, I clear my throat. "This one's mine."

I'm a little relieved that Kayla has to catch a different train. She waves, which I return a second too late, and then I get on the train and very determinedly don't look back.

What happened to the version of me that used to find this so *easy*? Meeting new people used to feel so natural. Julia would do most of the talking, and I would know when and where I was supposed to come in. Without her, I feel the same way I did the year before we met. Alone. Small. Like I don't know any of the rules. Like I'm sitting by myself at lunch again.

Like the source of my magic is gone.

I'm so off that when I brew the coffee at work, I forget to toggle the switch that seals the machine, and half-brewed coffee flows through the spigot and drenches the floor. My manager, who knows all about Julia, doesn't say anything. She just starts to mop and sends me to the back to take inventory. I lose count halfway through and have to start over.

The shift is long and frustrating, and when I come home, all I want to do is soak my feet in the bath and take a nap. Instead, when I open the door, the landline starts ringing, like whoever is on the other end knows I'm there now.

I don't normally pick up, but cautiously, I check the caller ID.

It's a punch to the gut.

HOSKINS.

I answer the phone.

"Hi," I whisper. "Nora speaking."

"Nora," Mrs. Hoskins says. "You're actually just who I was hoping to get. I wanted to talk to you about something."

"Oh?" I ask.

"We're going through some of Julia's things," she says, and her voice hitches. "I wanted to extend the opportunity for you to come and take a look."

She's always talked like she's still at the office. Even to Julia. I stand there in silence for a lot longer than is probably normal.

Then again, if anyone is going to understand the impossibility of *normal*, it would be Mrs. Hoskins.

"Nora?" she asks, so softly it feels like she's touching my cheek with two fingers, gently, like she did at the funeral, because she didn't know she was supposed to hate me.

"When?"

"We're going to hang on to it for a little while," she says. "Some of it we'll keep, and the rest we'll donate."

"Can I think about it?" I ask, because the idea makes me feel numb and awful.

"Of course," she says. "Call me when you're ready. It's not a one-time offer."

"Thank you," I whisper, and my throat feels dry and cracked and ruinous. I can barely stomach the idea of going back to Julia's house again. Standing in her bedroom, looking at the mirror where we used to take selfies. Sitting on her bed with the light pink duvet, where the fairy lights cast a warm glow. Surrounded by photos and her soccer trophies.

Julia and I binge-watched TV shows in that room. Painted each other's toenails in that room. Braided each other's hair. Dreamed of university. Made fun of cringey Instagram posts. Filmed *horrendous* attempts at TikTok dances, then erased them. (Well, not *all* of them.)

There were fashion queries over video chat, and homework marathons, and shit-talking. There were conversations whispered under the blankets even though nobody was listening, secrets shared we promised to take to the grave. There were laughter and joy in that room, and tears and fighting and insults, and sometimes it was *hell*, but—

This is the hardest, worst, most terrible part of it all, now that I know what I know.

Sometimes it was hell, but sometimes it was heaven, too.

We sat on her carpet in that room and talked until the birds started chirping. We talked about the future. To be back there again . . .

I stand with the phone pressed to my ear long after Julia's mother hangs up.

THIRTEEN

Before

"Matching duvets," Julia said from her perch on my bed, looking down at me on the floor.

She did that sometimes: skipped straight to the point of a conversation without seeming to remember that she hadn't brought me with her.

I looked up from my homework, one eyebrow raised. Julia wasn't even pretending like she was doing hers—it was a Friday, and she always said doing homework on Friday nights was criminal, even though I liked to get it out of the way at the beginning of the weekend. She was lying flat on her stomach, looking at me instead.

"I was thinking," Julia said, then paused.

"Congratulations."

"Asshole." Julia grabbed my pillow and whomped me with it.

I yelped as papers scattered everywhere, leaping to my feet to snatch the pillow and missing it as she yanked it back and scrambled off the bed. Julia brought it down twice more before I managed to win it from her and wallop her. She went down like a sack of potatoes, collapsing back onto the bed, laughing.

I smacked her with the pillow again, for good measure.

Julia held her arms over her head, protesting through her laughter. When I tossed the pillow back onto the bed, Julia blew her hair out of her face and grinned.

"So I was *thinking.*"

I sat back down on the floor by my homework. "Make sure you don't strain something."

She laughed. "You are such a dick."

When I looked up and saw her grinning at me, I winked. "What were you thinking about?"

Julia hesitated. "We should start looking at the stuff we want to get for our room."

I blinked, confused for several seconds before my brain caught up. "You mean our room at—"

"McGill."

"We haven't even applied yet." I laughed, tapping my pencil rapidly against the page.

"Come on," Julia said. "We're both going to get in. I've got good enough grades. You're *brilliant*—"

"Oh, stop."

"I'm serious!" Julia poked my shoulder. "You're the smartest person I know."

I looked up and caught her eye. Her smile was loose and amiable. "Thank you. And you could hack into their system if they don't let you in."

Julia preened. "Obviously. I'm just saying, we're going to get in."

"I know." I didn't look at her. I knew that my real thought—*I don't know if I want that anymore*—would not go over well, but I couldn't help that it was true. Besides, nothing with TMU was anywhere *close* to confirmed, so why bother saying anything at all?

"I was on their website, and they have a virtual tour of the dorms," Julia said. "I thought we could look at it together."

"Maybe later," I said, glancing back down at my homework.

When she didn't respond, I rushed to say, "I don't want to jinx anything. You know, just in case."

Julia nodded, but she still looked unhappy.

I cleared my throat. "You want to get matching duvets?"

She shrugged.

After she stayed quiet for several seconds, I tried focusing on the page in front of me, but it blurred. It was hard to concentrate when Julia was upset.

We used to have blowup fights when we were younger, so bad that our parents had to get involved. We'd have horribly formal sit-downs in my living room or at Julia's house and try to negotiate how we were feeling. For the last several years, I'd been trying to avoid those conversations, because I always left them feeling inside out and upside down, like I hadn't gotten to say what I wanted to say at all. That was usually because of Julia's mom. Or maybe Julia.

Probably both.

Steamrolled, Mom had muttered to my dad once in the car when she thought I had earbuds in. *That's what they do. Good to know she's learning it somewhere.*

Her voice had been biting and sarcastic, and I hadn't understood what she meant by it at the time.

I did now.

In any case, I hated fighting with Julia. The last fight we'd had, we'd almost stopped being friends entirely, but that was in eighth grade, so we were on a hot streak. Maybe that was because I just avoided disagreeing with her.

I gave my head a little shake. We weren't fighting. We *weren't*.

At any rate, dreams weren't certainties. That was just life. My phone buzzed. Relieved by the distraction, I saw a text from Dillan, responding to an earlier question.

> what about me makes you think i'd be good at calculus

I glanced surreptitiously at Julia, who wasn't looking, then responded.

> I was hoping you were because I'm not

> i can count to like . . . 11
> i do have notes from monday if you want though
> i don't know if you guys are doing the same thing in your class

"Who are you texting?"

"Nobody." I glanced at Julia. She was chewing on her pencil's eraser, staring at the wall. I texted Dillan back.

> I owe you a life debt

i didn't think it would be that easy
i had all of these elaborate plans and all it took was calc notes?
what am i supposed to do with all of these hired assassins
so are we bound together by fate now or

> I take it back

you can't take back a life debt

> I Take It Back

that's illegal

"Seriously." Julia peered over my shoulder. "Who is that?"

I jolted, startled. I knew that if I said *nobody* again, she would get suspicious, so I told the truth. "Dillan."

In one fluid motion, Julia snatched my phone, ignoring my squawk of objection, and climbed back onto my bed. There was no point in fighting—so I just sat back, resigned, as she squinted at the screen, scrolling up. Her eyes widened. "You guys talk a lot."

"We're project partners."

"None of this is about the project, though." She started reading aloud. "Christ, he's not afraid to double-text. 'What's your favorite class so far?' 'How was the Forest Lawn experience?' 'What are you doing this weekend?'"

She looked up from the screen. "You're talking about journalism."

I flushed. "So?"

Telling Dillan about it had felt like reliving the whole journey. Really, I hadn't charged into writing with any huge dreams. Julia had been the one to get me into it. She'd prodded me for weeks about joining the school newspaper until I gave in and said I'd try. It had been a slow-growing love, born of tiny triumphs and patience and lots of *really* crappy practice writing.

Later, Julia said she always knew I'd be a genius at it.

"Journalism is a big deal to you," Julia said, then gestured like I was missing something obvious. "Nora, do you *like* him?"

"Dillan?"

"Obviously."

"No, I don't like him!" I scrambled for my phone. "We're just—catching up. That's all."

She sat up and held the phone above her head, still reading, her eyebrows arching. "He said he was so glad to have a class with you, because he knew it was a big school and he was hoping you'd be friends again?"

I snatched the phone from her and shoved it into my pocket. "Don't make it into a thing, okay? It's not a thing. We're just friends."

She bit her lip.

"What?"

"I don't know. Isn't he sort of weird?"

I laughed, placing a protective hand over my pocket. "Since when is weird a bad thing?"

"I don't know. His family just seems kind of . . . out there."

My mouth dropped open. "Julia, come on! You can't say that."

Her brow furrowed. "Well, they do."

"Having two moms isn't out there."

"That's not what I meant." Julia rolled her eyes, but didn't offer another explanation. She just sighed. "Anyway, what are you going to do if he likes you?"

My breath caught. I wanted to ask why she cared, but her frown stopped me.

"Oh, come on." I scoffed, even as the idea took root and unfurled inside me. A balloon of hope expanded against my rib cage before I could stop it. "He doesn't."

She just raised an eyebrow. "But if he *did*?"

I shrugged, flustered. "I don't know. I'll deal with it, all right?"

For a moment, it looked like she was going to fight me on it, but then she just shrugged and actually opened up her homework.

I didn't turn back to mine, though. Instead, when I picked up my homework to sit at my desk, I caught my reflection in the mirror. My hair was getting longer than I knew what to do with anymore—and I itched for change.

I didn't really think before I spoke. I just blurted it out. "I sort of want to cut my hair."

"What—off?"

I turned to her, trapping my hair between my fingers just below my collarbone. "To right here."

She just stared.

"Should I do it? I've been thinking about it for a while."

Julia got off the bed and stood behind me. She looped a

strand of my hair around her finger. For a second I just looked at her as she wound it around and around, her face bathed in the soft purple glow of my bedroom. She said, "Don't do it. You'll regret it."

"Why?"

She turned my chair around so I faced her. "If you cut your hair, how am I supposed to braid it?" Then she grinned, exposing her canines.

I smiled back. When Julia smiled like this, she was like a warm bath of relief and she became all I could see. I was forgiven.

She said, "Trust me."

And I did.

FOURTEEN

After

I love being at Dillan's house.

There's not one specific reason. There's artwork by kids plastered everywhere, and there's almost always music playing, and it smells nice, like cinnamon.

Dillan's mom Sara runs a preschool out of their house. His other mom, Maria, is a lawyer, which means she's often not home, but when she's there, she talks to me like she's really interested in my opinion. She's always been like that, even when we were kids. Maybe that's why Dillan is the same way.

Some people have an issue with Dillan having two moms. He got teased for it at school. I know Julia thought it was weird at first, even though she'd never admit it. I don't know. I think theirs is a lot more of a family than some others with both a mom and a dad.

When I walk in, Dillan's little sister, Angie, barrels toward me and throws her arms around me so hard that I have to take a step back.

She buries her face in my stomach, and I laugh, squirming away. "Hey! Watch it."

Angie offers me a macaroni bracelet, and I hold my arm out without hesitation. She shows me the identical one she's wearing, bright against her dark skin, and tells me, "I made them at school."

"It's very cool." I smile fondly.

Dillan peers around the corner. "Oh, good, you're here. We're in the kitchen."

I hear an outburst of laughter—Sara's—and don't even bother trying to suppress a grin.

Angie grabs my arm and I barely manage to slip out of my shoes as she tugs me along. I can't help but stare at her hand around my wrist. She's grown so much since I met her last year.

Instead of her leading me all the way, I grab her by the waist. She's almost too big for me to pick up, but not quite, and she squeals as I heft her over one shoulder.

I turn the corner. "Incoming!"

I pass Angie off to Dillan, who holds her upside down.

Even though they're not related by blood, Dillan and Angie have exactly the same curls, only his are bright orange and hers are jet black.

She squirms in Dillan's arms, yelling at him. "Put me down!"

"Should I just . . . drop you? What do you think, Nor? Should I just drop her?"

I grin wickedly. "Make sure she lands right on her head."

Angie lets out an ungodly screech, dissolving into laughter.

Maria winces as she opens her arms to me.

Dillan wrinkles his nose and carries Angie into the living room, where he drops her onto the couch.

She's up in an instant with a joyous shriek. "Do it again!"

I hug Maria first, then Sara. They're both dressed up. "You guys going somewhere?"

"Out on the town." Sara checks her reflection in the glass of the microwave, then points to the living room. "Oh, Dillan, honey, I meant to tell you."

He pokes his head back into the kitchen. "What?"

"There's an exhibit for kids coming to Studio Bell in a few weeks. I thought it might be fun if you guys took Angie."

"Like, me and Nora?" Dillan's eyes dart to me and away again quickly, like he doesn't want me to notice.

Immediately I know why.

The last time we went to Studio Bell was his birthday last year. That was the night I kissed him. My cheeks burn.

"No, like you and the cat." Sara rolls her eyes. "Yes, you and Nora."

Dillan won't look at me. "Do you know when it opens?"

Sara waves a hand. "Use the Google or something."

Angie ducks around Dillan, narrowly missing his elbow, and thrusts a yellow plastic disk into my hands. "Look!"

I turn it over. It's a clock, with movable hands. I give one of them an experimental spin. "You're learning to tell time?"

She hooks her fingers around one of the loops on my waistband and tugs me with her into the living room. "I'm so good at it!"

As I let her drag me past Dillan, I shoot the rest of them a thumbs-up. "Studio Bell sounds good to me."

Angie yanks the clock out of my hand and catapults herself

onto the couch. She shows me every hour while Sara and Maria are getting ready to leave, and after she's dutifully accepted their goodbye kisses and the door is closed behind them, she shows me every half-hour increment too.

She's about to start on the fifteens when Dillan comes in from the kitchen to sit on her other side.

The night I kissed him we were right here, actually, on this couch. I wonder if he's remembering too, and then I feel weird, because I sort of hope he isn't.

"Hey." Dillan shakes his wrist. "Matching."

I look over, and he grins widely. He's also sporting a macaroni bracelet, except it looks much less ridiculous on him, like it's something he might actually wear of his own volition. When I tell him so, his mouth drops open and he places a hand over his heart in mock offense.

"Hey!" Angie pokes my cheek. "This is six-forty-five."

I glance down, then back up at Dillan. "It sure is."

He shakes his head, but he's still smiling.

"What time is it now? In real life." She looks up at me entreatingly.

I'm about to check my watch when Dillan lurches forward and yanks her into his lap. When she squeals in protest, he stands up and hauls her over his shoulder with some effort. "Bedtime!"

"That's not a real time!"

"It is!"

"Is not!"

I can hear them arguing all the way up the stairs.

"How old are you?"

"Seven!"

"And your bedtime is?"

"Seven!"

"See? Told you. Bedtime is a real time!"

I wait on the couch until Angie comes back down in her pajamas to say good night. She climbs on top of me and squeezes my neck, and for some reason, tonight this makes me want to cry. I mumble into her shoulder, "Stop getting bigger."

"I can't," she reminds me. "Dillan says I'm pho-to-synfasizing too much."

"He *what?*"

She's clinging to my neck so tightly my laugh gets cut short. I pat her shoulder. "Okay. Okay. Time for bed."

"Three squeezes first."

I oblige with three of my tightest squeezes. This makes me weepy too, and I look away as she scrambles off me and thunders back up the stairs. Angie and I made them up together. I'm the only one allowed to do three squeezes.

The pitiful part of me wonders if I'll still be invited over after Dillan leaves. Then I squash down the idea, because I don't want to think about Dillan leaving, even though it's a whole year away.

I lean onto the armrest and press my face into a couch cushion, which means I don't hear him come back down the stairs, and I'm startled when I feel him sit down on the other end of the couch.

"Did you pass out?" he asks, amused.

In response, I groan into the cushion.

Dillan pokes my foot with one of his. "That sounds . . . not great."

I emerge from the pillow and shake my head. "No. I'm good, really. Just . . . a long week. Did you tell Angie she photosynthesizes?"

"She said she wanted to be a sunflower when she grows up."

I shake my head, laughing. "You're absurd. What are we watching?"

Dillan grins, reaching for the remote. "I've definitely beaten you this time."

"That's impossible."

"This one has aliens."

"I don't think aliens were on the list."

"Terrible CGI aliens qualify. *And* it was a blockbuster. Somehow."

Dillan and I have an ongoing competition for who can find the worst movie. An evolving list of qualifications decides the winner, and even though there's no real prize, only gloating, I love it. It's something to do with our Saturday nights, and it's fun to mock them together, plus I'm the reigning champion.

He flicks through Netflix until he finds it, and presses play. I don't recognize the title, but somehow, I *do* recognize the music. I yank a blanket out of a basket beside the couch and cocoon myself in it as the introduction rolls. As promised, the CGI *is* terrible.

I think he's beaten me.

We throw out sarcastic commentary like it's popcorn, and the hour and a half passes quickly. When the end credits roll, I let out a cheer that's more of a groan.

Dillan gives me a cheeky grin. "So?"

I roll my eyes. "Fine. You win."

"The third one comes out in three weeks."

"Ugh. The *third* one? You mean there's a second? Spare me. I don't think I can handle any more."

Dillan whacks me gently with a cushion. "What else did

you think we were going to do tonight? And you have to come see the third one."

I let out a belabored sigh. "No more aliens. Please. God."

"Oh, come on. You're telling me you *don't* want to see more aliens? Not even *in theaters*? It's supposed to be worse on the big screen somehow."

I groan.

He presses onward. "We'll go to the old-people showing, even."

"What do you mean?"

"The one that's at a stupid time, like four-thirty in the afternoon. So you don't have to be out late."

I'm running out of excuses to not see this idiotic movie. I roll my eyes, but I'm laughing. "Maybe I have plans."

"Last time I checked, you don't have plans on Monday afternoons."

"Shut *up*. Maybe I'll have made plans by then. On purpose. To avoid this."

"Call it a birthday present to me."

I raise my eyebrows. "That's what you want for your birthday? For me to go with you to this stupid movie?"

"Yes." His smile is mischievous. "That's what I want."

I sigh heavily. "Fine."

He grins. "I'll get tickets, then."

"I'll e-transfer you."

"Don't be stupid. You singlehandedly save my bank account by comping me coffee all the time."

"That's just a thank-you."

Even though I'm looking at the carpet, I can see his eyes on me. "For what?"

I wonder if Dillan knows he's my best friend. I wonder if I'll ever be able to say it out loud. It feels almost sacrilegious to refer to someone other than Julia as my best anything.

I give a halfhearted shrug. "I don't know. Just being there, I guess."

There is something quiet and careful about the way he says, "Of course."

My phone vibrates.

I glance down at the screen, and my heartbeat goes weird. It's Nate. One word:

> Hey

I stare at it. So does Dillan.

"I didn't know you guys were talking," Dillan says.

"We aren't," I tell him, and I'm glad it's the truth. I'd convinced myself Nate wasn't ever going to text me, so now that I see his name on my screen, I don't know how to feel.

"Will you?" Dillan asks.

"I don't know, that's like, one word. *Hey* doesn't mean anything."

He looks away. "Would you want it to? Mean something?"

I stare at his profile. What kind of question is that? "I . . ."

Dillan shakes his head. "You should respond."

I keep staring at him, but his face reveals nothing. "Should I?"

He shrugs. "If you want to."

I don't know if I want to. I don't know if I *should* want to. And now Dillan looks almost annoyed, and I don't know what that's supposed to mean.

So I text Nate back.

A typing bubble appears, and I watch it for a full twenty seconds. What could Nate be trying to figure out how to say? Is he trying to say something about last year? Is he apologizing? The bubble disappears. A few seconds later it reappears, and then I get:

What's up

I laugh a little, out loud. *That's* what took him so long to say?

Dillan snorts.

I glance up at him. His face is as neutral as a glass pool. For a second, I think I see a flash of annoyance, but if it was ever there, it's gone.

Dillan picks up the remote. "We don't have to watch the second one."

"Don't be stupid. Put it on."

The main reason I want to watch it is that I want to stay here. I don't want to go home yet. The house will be empty, and I'll have to be alone with my thoughts about Nate.

Sometimes when I'm at Dillan's, my thoughts turn off. At home they exhaust me, playing on loop. The quiet in my head here is sweet relief.

I barely pay attention to the movie. It's somehow, impossibly, even worse than the first one. Considering how bad it is, I thought Dillan would be more into making fun of it, but he's uncharacteristically quiet.

For a while, I'm afraid to look over and see if he's annoyed with me, but when I finally do, his eyes have drifted shut and his chin is on his chest.

I poke him, and he opens his eyes blearily just in time for a huge explosion on-screen, and then his lids drift down again.

That's when I notice exactly how tired he looks. I knew that the first week of school would take it out of him. He never does anything halfway. I told him five classes plus work was ambitious, but he was set on it.

I place my palm on his shoulder, which startles him enough that he's partially awake, but then I push him over so that he slumps against the pillows.

He mumbles a protest, but he's not coherent enough to fight me, because he doesn't sit back up.

The rest of the movie plays, but I'm not paying attention. I'll look up the plot on Wikipedia before we see the third one. I like sitting there in the dark with the noise and the lights as a distraction, even though Dillan is fully asleep, which means I'm alone.

Mostly alone.

My own voice in my head is there, but sometimes, on nights when I'm tired, or overwhelmed, or just desperately lonely, I hear Julia's, too. The worst part is that I know exactly what she would think.

She approved of Nate. I met him through Julia, but we'd barely had a real conversation before he kissed me at that dumb end-of-summer party last year. I wonder if Nate ever thinks about it.

It seems funny that I've only been kissed twice in my life, because Julia made a habit of kissing people, like a night out was disappointing if it didn't end that way. But as far as I know Eve hasn't kissed anyone at all, so it's not like I'm alone. It just feels weird because the two kisses of my life were as different as they could be.

As the credits roll, I wonder if *Dillan's* ever kissed anyone else. We don't talk about that sort of thing.

It occurs to me that I've never seen him sleeping before. It feels oddly private, like I'm witnessing something I shouldn't. I consider waking him, but he looks like he's *really* asleep, so instead I just extricate myself from the blanket and drape it over him.

When I leave, I close the front door quietly behind me.

FIFTEEN

Before

It was strange to see Dillan in my house again after all these years.

The sight lived on the needle edge of uncomfortable, like all the memories I had of him didn't quite join up with this older version of him. It had been *kid* Dillan and Ellie who had played countless stupid games and built forts in the living room and had Nerf wars that went on for days.

We were both different people now.

Dillan didn't look uncomfortable, though. He stood for a moment in the entryway, surveying, and then he smiled. "This is so weird. It's just like I remember."

"Yeah, well. Not much changes around here." I led him through the living room, hoping to sneak past my parents.

No such luck.

Mom and Dad had been waiting, apparently, and Mom beckoned us into the kitchen.

I offered Dillan an apologetic smile.

"If it isn't Mr. Fletcher." Dad laughed as he slapped Dillan's shoulder. "When did you get so tall?"

"And handsome!" Mom patted the side of his cheek, smiling fondly.

Dillan flushed, rubbing the back of his neck. "Good to see you both."

When I was sure he wasn't looking, I stole a glance over at him. It hadn't really occurred to me that Dillan might be handsome, but Mom was right—he had nice cheekbones and long eyelashes.

He was actually sort of pretty, if I thought about it, but thinking about it felt weird, so I just shook my head and grabbed an apple from the fruit bowl.

"I hear you're at Centennial." Mom stepped back to survey him. "That's exciting!"

Dillan squeezed my shoulder. "Nice to be back with friends."

I leaned against the counter and bit into the apple. "Can we use the office?"

Mom raised one eyebrow.

"We have a project. I told you."

"Oh, right."

When she nodded, I picked up another apple, tossed it at Dillan, and yanked my backpack over one shoulder. "Cool, thanks. You'll know where to find us, then."

I led Dillan down the hall and into the office, but before we left the kitchen, he offered a salute, which my dad returned.

I closed the door behind us.

"Your parents are just as nice as I remember."

I was sort of surprised. "Yeah?"

He shrugged, setting the apple down on the desk. "Yeah. I—it's good."

"How are you enjoying being back?"

"In general?" He shrugged. "I don't know. It doesn't really feel different here than it did at my last school. Eve's cool, though."

When he mentioned Eve, he glanced at me, almost like he was double-checking something, but I couldn't figure out what. I knew they were getting along, because I saw them together in the hallways all the time, but that didn't feel particularly significant. Whatever he saw on my face didn't appear to clarify anything, and he looked away.

"Good," I said. "I'm glad it's not been a total nightmare."

Dillan grinned. "Not a nightmare at all."

"You must miss Forest Lawn, though."

"Some. I had friends there, I guess, but I was a drifter, so there was nobody I was devastated to leave behind. Not like it'd be for you with Julia and Eve."

I tilted my head, debating whether to ask. But I *was* curious. "Nobody special there, then?"

"Oh." Dillan smiled. "No, nothing like that. I didn't date, really."

"Got skeletons in your closet or something?"

He laughed. "No! I just wasn't interested in anyone there."

"Fair enough."

I looked at him as he started unzipping his backpack. Afternoon sunlight spilled through the blinds, casting a striped pattern across his shoulders and hair. I felt as though I were living in two moments at once: this moment, and another, ten years ago, when we had sat in this office and pretended to be foreign spies. When everyone called me Ellie and things were simpler. Before Julia turned up in a whirlwind and gave me a new name, and a new best friend. A new life.

My phone buzzed in my back pocket with a text from my mom.

Door open.

!! Don't even

;)

I didn't open the door.

"What?"

I hadn't realized Dillan was watching me. I shook my head. "Just my mom."

At first, we worked in silence. We'd gotten our presentation date—beginning of November—so there was no urgency to finish the project, but I'd been relieved when Dillan had agreed that it was better to get a head start than to be left scrambling when midterm papers were all due.

Even though there was almost a month between now and then, I was already nervous. When I'd told Dillan, he'd said he was surprised because I'd been such a loud kid. I'd assured him that I was still loud, just not in front of large groups.

When I looked at him, he looked at me, then glanced away, the slightest frown on his face.

"What?"

He trapped the end of his pencil between his teeth, then sighed and set it down on the desk. "Why'd you pick me?"

It was clear that it had taken him quite a lot of courage to ask, because as soon as he said it, he looked away, and didn't look back.

"What, for the project?" I hooked my foot around the desk leg and pulled the chair closer to the computer.

He nodded.

"We used to be friends. Is it so wild that I'd choose you?"

"I don't know. I thought you'd pick Julia." He pulled a book out of his backpack and thumbed it open.

I inclined my head. "Why?"

"Well, you guys are so close."

"Hey, I'm my own person." I crossed my arms tight.

"That's not what I meant."

"I know." I paused, trying to decide how much to say. "I thought it would be pretty shitty of me to leave you out in the cold, especially after Julia was being an asshole. Don't take that personally, by the way. She's just like that."

"So it was because you felt sorry for me?"

I looked up from the screen just as he looked up from the page, and when our eyes met, some of my indignation must have been visible on my face, because he looked slightly abashed.

"No," I said, as pointedly as I could. "It's because we used to be *friends*."

His ears flushed bright red. Then he looked back down at his notebook and started writing.

I watched him for a moment longer, even after he probably knew I was looking.

The way he tilted his head made me think about what Julia had asked me, and right then, I decided that maybe if Dillan *did* like me, I'd be flattered.

SIXTEEN

After

"I'm not saying you *have* to," Eve says, running a hand through her short dark hair. "I just think maybe she's right."

I groan. "Don't tell me you're actually backing up my *mom.*"

Dillan laughs.

We're sitting in the back of Eve's truck at Peters' Drive-In. Dillan's got one leg dangling off the tailgate, mostly preoccupied with Strider, who's spent the last twenty minutes with his head in Dillan's lap trying to mooch one of his French fries. Evening air trails fingertips across my exposed arms.

The last time I was here, I was with Julia. Julia loved Peters'. Once, she'd joined a flash mob here just for fun, without knowing the choreography or anything. She'd dragged me with her, and we made such fools of ourselves that my stomach hurt from laughing.

When I close my eyes, I can see her sitting cross-legged

on the top of her car, drinking a milkshake while she made up stories about passersby, and for a moment it feels like she's still here. I can see her thousand-watt smile. Hear her laughter. Remember how it fe—

"Maybe your mom has a point," Eve says, yanking me out of my reverie. "She's—"

"Don't," Dillan warns, and Eve grins widely.

"You can't always agree with my mom because you think she's hot," I say.

Eve throws a fry at me. I dodge it and Strider jumps up and grabs it before it even hits the ground.

I shake my head, exasperated. "TMU rejected me, re-member?"

Immediately, I wish I hadn't said it out loud. I rub my throat. The memories about TMU live there, choking, threatening to rise up at any moment.

Dillan and Eve exchange a glance.

I ignore it and take a deep breath. "So really, that's that."

"Just, considering the circumstances . . ." Eve taps her fingernails on the truck bed. They're long and the loudest yellow I've ever seen, which would look awful on anybody but Eve. "Maybe it would be worth reapplying."

I cross my arms tight, like making a shield out of them will show her that I don't want to talk about this. "You sound like my mom."

It works on Dillan, who stays quiet.

"I'm just saying." Eve reaches out like she's going to touch my arm, but doesn't. I guess my shield is working on her, too. "You could explain that you—"

"I don't *want* to."

Toward the end, it had felt like TMU or bust. There are other schools, but I just—

An unexpected bubble of laughter escapes, and Eve and Dillan look at me like I've finally—possibly reasonably—lost it. "What am I supposed to do, go to McGill?"

The unspoken *without Julia* hangs between us.

Eve looks to Dillan, but he just shrugs. I have a flash of appreciation for him.

Eve thinks I should apply to a local school. She and Dillan are both local. She's at cosmetology school, and he's at U of C. Well, just for the year. Next September, when Dillan goes off to Queen's, we'll be separated.

"You could tell them what Julia did," Eve says.

Dillan looks over at me with a sharp intake of breath.

"It wasn't her fault," I whisper.

I can practically feel the psychic energy bouncing between Dillan and Eve.

"It wasn't," I insist. "It was mine. I could have clarified, and I didn't."

I don't know if I believe that, but it's easier.

Across the parking lot, a group of guys are hooting at each other and laughing. Eve shoots them a dirty look.

Dillan looks across the lot and grimaces. The face he makes when he's annoyed always makes me grin, so I'm smiling when Eve catches my eye and raises an eyebrow.

My cheeks warm. I *hate* when she catches me looking at Dillan, especially because it doesn't mean anything. It's not like that with us anymore, and really, it never was, so there's no reason for her to look like she knows some secret.

If I were still hung up on Dillan, I would be the first to know.

Sometimes I regret telling Eve about what happened with us, because I know things now that I wish I didn't. Like how Dillan refuses to talk about it, which feels a little bit like missing a step going downstairs whenever I remember.

If I were in his shoes, I wouldn't be keen to talk about it either.

Anyway, I'm never going to tell Eve the whole story. I don't even want to think about the truth. I told her half of it, and if that earns me sidelong glances, so be it.

Dillan whistles low. "Earth to Nora?"

I blink. "Sorry."

Eve and Dillan exchange a glance. Sometimes it feels like they decided to be the unofficial committee in charge of making sure I don't implode.

The guys across the lot are still making a lot of noise. Eve's watching them when her eyes widen and she smacks my knee.

"Ow," I say. "What—"

"Nora!" She jerks her head across the parking lot.

At first, I don't see him. It just looks like some guys messing around, like they always did at school, but then I get why she's reacting like this.

One of the guys is Nate.

"Oh my God," she says. "Look."

"I'm looking," I say.

I recognize some of the other guys too.

"Go!" Eve urges, making a shooing motion with her hands. "Come on. Maybe school is a step too far. But you could at least, you know . . ."

I stare at her while she wiggles her eyebrows, my cheeks heating up. "Seriously. Are you in cahoots with my mom, or something?"

"It's *Nate!*" Eve says, loud enough that he might be able to hear, but when I glance wildly over, he has his head down. "It could make you feel better. Go!"

"Go?" My hands are sweating. "Talk to him? In *person*? No way."

"Yes!" She smacks my shoulder. "It'll be good for you!"

I look to Dillan, but he's absorbed in his phone and smiling at something.

"Go!" Eve urges again.

She's staring at me so meaningfully that I'm almost convinced.

"I was going to get a refill anyway," Eve says sweetly, like she can sense the fact that I'm actually considering this. "You could go for me."

I sigh.

I don't start regretting my life choices until I'm on the way back from the counter and I'm facing Nate's direction. And he sees me.

"Radford!" Nate says, and for a second, it feels like we could be at school again. He smiles the same way he did that night he kissed me, which makes me feel super weird. "It was cool talking to you the other night."

It was. Not that we talked about much. It was mostly catching up on the basics, which means now I scramble for something to talk about.

In my peripherals, Eve makes a triumphant gesture.

"Yeah, I enjoyed that," I say, trying not to wince. *Enjoyed that?* What am I, fifty? Must recover quickly. "It was lit."

It was *lit*? I want to lie down on the pavement and disappear.

But Nate just laughs, gesturing at me with his phone.

"You're funny. Hey, I was thinking, we should hang out some-time."

I'm pretty sure I go bright red. "Um."

Nate grins.

"Yeah," I manage, a second too late. "Yeah, definitely."

If Julia were here, she would laugh. Or scoff. It's hard to know whether she would be happy for me. It's even harder to tell if that matters. If I allow myself to be honest, I know it does.

I clear my throat. "What were—what were you thinking, exactly?"

I'm doing this. I'm actually doing this. I'm doing *something*.

"I'm pretty into spontaneity." He tosses his phone from one hand to another, which makes me nervous, because come on, it's only one slip of the fingers away from death by con-crete. "I like to play it by ear."

"Oh, yeah. Totally. Me too. I love being spontaneous."

I absolutely do not.

"Cool," he says. "I'll text you?"

"Yeah," I say.

"Good to see you," he says.

"You too," I squeak, and turn around.

When I get back to the truck, Eve is waiting with raised eyebrows.

I frown, looking around. "Where's Dillan?"

Eve chews on the end of her straw. "Had to go home."

"Oh," I say, faintly disappointed.

As I'm sitting down, she gestures at me with the straw. "So . . . Nate?"

I give her a look.

"Oh, come *on*," Eve says. "He was obviously flirting with you—what's up?"

I shrug, looking around the parking lot. Dillan is nowhere in sight. I sort of hate that he left without saying goodbye.

"I wish I knew what Julia would think of this," I confess.

She wrinkles her nose. "Seriously? Why?"

I know it was easier for Eve to let go of what Julia thought, because of everything that happened in the week before Julia died. But I secretly wish she would understand why I can't.

"You know Julia never gave a shit about whether you were happy, right?" Eve prods.

I give her a reproachful look. "That's not true."

Eve sighs.

"It's not," I reiterate. "She was trying her best."

"Well, her best wasn't good enough," she says.

That makes me want to curl up in the tiniest ball and block out the whole world. I know full well that anyone doing their best can still cause destruction. Julia doing her best might have hurt feelings.

Me doing my best got her killed.

"So . . ." Eve drags the word out, like she can sense that a topic change is needed, and then blows air at me through her chewed-up straw to get my attention. "Are you going to give it a shot with Nate?"

I look at her. And I think about how she looked at me when she caught me looking at Dillan. And I think about how I don't want to feel like I'm lost in a black hole anymore. Something needs to shift. "I think I might."

SEVENTEEN

Before

I was supposed to be good at writing essays.

I slammed the lid of my laptop shut and pressed the heels of my palms against my eyes.

The sounds of the café filtered through my headphones—the hiss of the steamer, a low murmur of conversation—until it was all I could hear.

I wrenched my headphones off. I'd thought a change of scenery would inspire me, but so far . . .

I'd narrowed down my options for the TMU essay to one topic, which would show how high school politics reflected governmental politics, but I couldn't focus. Thoughts drifted just out of reach as soon as I tried to snatch at them, my head full of static.

I couldn't stop thinking about Julia. Finding out about this would kill her. I knew she'd take it as a betrayal.

But then, it wasn't like I'd already gotten into TMU.

So why did I feel so guilty?

The war in my head got louder and louder. I sank down in my chair and squeezed my hands over my ears, as if I could silence it. Like I could erase the premonition of her face falling when I told her—*if* I ever told her—the truth. *If* I ever had a reason to.

Was I even capable of keeping a secret like this from Julia without it eating me from the inside?

I *had* to tell her.

Didn't I?

The thought of my essay gaining me a final acceptance offer loomed. Did I even want this? Was this something I wanted for myself?

If I wanted it, that meant saying goodbye to Julia.

I pulled my phone out of my bag, my stomach twisting at the dozen or so notifications.

All Julia.

> Hey
>
> Call me?
>
> Wyd????
>
> Wtf where are u
>
> Did u die

I sighed, suddenly weary, and started packing up. On my way out of the café, I called her.

"Julia," I said as soon as she picked up. "Hey."

Julia sighed, relieved. "Where *were* you tonight? I know you don't have plans on Thursdays."

"Sorry," I said as I zipped my bag shut. "This was kind of last-minute."

"You never make last-minute plans."

I ignored her comment, rifling through my backpack for my mittens, walking toward the front.

"Anyway," Julia said, once my silence had grown pronounced. "I know it's still a few weeks away, but—"

I nearly bumped into somebody on my way out, ducking out of the way at the last second, then whirling around as I recognized the familiar hair.

Dillan blinked at me and half turned around too, still walking in the opposite direction. He gave me a quizzical look that I was probably reflecting right back at him.

". . . *you* could probably get us invited," Julia was saying.

I gave Dillan a distracted wave. He returned it, then promptly tripped over the upturned edge of the carpet and pinwheeled for a moment, nearly falling over.

"Hello?" Julia asked. "Earth to Nora."

"I'm still here," I told her through my fingers, where I had covered my mouth in an attempt not to laugh. "Sorry."

Dillan glanced back, saw that I had been watching, and flushed bright pink.

"Where even are you?"

I gave Dillan a second, smaller wave and a grin before I stepped out into the cold. Then I told Julia, "On my way home. What were you saying?"

Julia didn't take the bait. "On your way home from *where?*"

"Second Cup," I told her, with resignation, because I knew she'd find out some way or another.

"*Without* me?"

"It was a spur-of-the-moment thing." I crossed my fingers, hoping that she couldn't tell I was lying. Ironically, Julia was brutally perceptive about dishonesty. I'd never been on the receiving end of her wrath about it, but that was mostly because I never gave her a reason to think I wasn't telling the truth. I'd seen what she was capable of. Once, two years ago, when a girl on her soccer team lied to her, Julia had gone through her social media and pulled an old tweet vastly out of context until the whole school had canceled her.

It had been so horrible, I'd even voiced an objection, but Julia had stared at me like I would be next.

"She should have told the truth," Julia had said, like it was simple.

Now she sounded sullen. "You could have invited me."

"Sorry," I said, even though I didn't feel particularly sorry, then let out a slow breath of relief. "I was working on something."

"On what?"

My stomach twisted. "Homework. Tell me your idea."

At last she let up. "I was thinking we should go to the Halloween party."

I didn't have to ask which one. Every year the guys' hockey and soccer teams got together to host a Halloween party. It was always the place to be the weekend of Halloween, and whether I'd wanted to or not, so far Julia and I had gone every year of high school.

I sighed. "I don't really want to, though. Remember last year?"

Julia scoffed.

"You threw up in my bathtub," I reminded her. "And you promised we wouldn't have to go this year."

"Come on. It'll be *fun*. You could interrogate Nate. With your face, maybe."

I rolled my eyes, trying to ignore the way my heartbeat went weird at the sound of his name.

"Come *on*. I keep telling you he likes you. You could totally get invited," Julia said suggestively.

"*You* could get invited. You're on the soccer team."

"I'm *trying* to be a good wingwoman," she said, and I could hear her grin. "You should talk to Nate. I think you should put your mouth on his mouth again."

"You're horrible," I said, without any heat, trying to ignore the pang in my gut. Did she really think that was a good idea after he'd ignored me for so long?

"You love me," she said.

"Yeah."

"Get invited," Julia said, then hung up.

EIGHTEEN

After

When I bump into Kayla for the second time in just a few weeks, it feels a little fated.

I'm at U of C, waiting for Dillan, when Kayla and I turn and clock each other at the same time.

"Nora!" Kayla says, nearly dropping her phone. "Hey!"

"Hi," I say, almost breathless. "I didn't recognize you!"

"What are you doing here?" she asks. "I thought you weren't . . . ?"

"I'm just waiting for a friend." I glance at my watch. "Class just got out, so . . ."

She squints at me for a moment, and then laughs. "Wait. It's not Dillan Fletcher, is it?"

"Yeah, it is."

"I'm in the same class, so I see him around. We study together." She smiles. "Nice to have a familiar face."

Dillan hasn't mentioned anything about studying with

Kayla, but then, when I try to figure out a reason for why that sort of bothers me—like a grain of sand working its way under my skin—I can't think of one.

She pulls a few strands of hair out of her ponytail to frame her face. "He talks about you a lot. Dillan, I mean."

I can't stop myself from smiling. "Really?"

"Yeah." Kayla eyes me sideways. "I mean, I knew you guys were close because of everything that happened last year. . . ."

"Yeah."

Thinking about Dillan makes my chest constrict. The past few days we've been a little stilted, and I'm not exactly sure why.

"He's been really great with everything since the accident," I tell her, breathing low, trying to steady my heart. "You know, he's just really constant. He knew Julia too."

Something behind her eyes shifts. We're not in light-hearted territory anymore. Her voice is quiet. "How—how has that been? How are you? I meant to ask the other day, but then . . ."

I just shrug, before she has to figure out how that sentence is supposed to end. "I'm all right. It sounds like a terrible thing to say, but it feels almost like . . . I'm getting used to it."

"That's not terrible." Kayla looks confused.

I stay silent.

"It's good you have Dillan, at least," she says simply. "He seems like a great guy. And no one should have to go through that alone."

The way she says that last part makes me shiver. I wonder what it's like to live in her head. She says it like being alone is harder than having company.

Friendship, at least for me, has never been anything but complicated. I'm always waiting for something terrible. As I think that, I realize I'm waiting with her, too, for something to go wrong, for her to say something that makes me wilt on the inside. I'm always waiting.

Even with Dillan. I'm waiting for him to leave. He's been my anchor. The person who held me together, who set aside all his own baggage about Julia to make sure I was all right, who's somehow still trying to show me there's a way to live in death's echo . . . he'll be gone too.

At least I'll have time to build armor before he goes, so that it'll hurt less.

I am so, so tired of feeling like this. I want . . . I want . . .

"Are you okay?"

Her voice jerks me back to reality. At first I nod, and then I shake my head. "I don't know."

When I'm by myself, feelings about Julia choke me, and I have to put headphones on to make it stop. But now that I'm talking about it, I've run out of words. I have to stop before I say too much. Friendships are always complicated, but mine and Julia's was messy in a way I don't even know how to articulate.

Julia was messy.

When I meet Kayla's eyes, I smile. "It's not easy."

"I'll bet."

What comes out of my mouth next surprises even me. "Sometimes, though, I think it's easier."

I can see the questions forming—*Easier how? What do you mean?*—and I press on in a rush. "Anyway. What's the class you guys are in?"

Kayla's smile is apprehensive. "English comp."

That's when Dillan turns up beside me, bumping my elbow with his and startling me so badly I jolt. Both he and Kayla laugh.

The full force of my admission doesn't catch up with me until much later.

I don't think about it while the three of us are trying to figure out what to talk about, or when Dillan and I eventually say goodbye to Kayla. I don't think about it while I'm with Dillan that afternoon, or when we're confirming our plans to see that stupid movie next Monday, or even when I'm on the train home. I don't think about it until later that night when I'm safe in my room.

• • •

There's something funny about the way I process. I can think I'm fine for an embarrassing amount of time, until suddenly it hits me that I never was all along.

I have that exact sensation the moment I turn the lights out to go to sleep. I'd meant to flip the switch and get under the covers, but instead I flip the switch and just stand there in the dark, thinking about Kayla and trying *not* to think about Julia, but the barrier between not thinking and thinking is paper-thin.

My fingers are still on the light switch. I should turn it back on. But I don't. I let the darkness pry my heart out with creeping fingers.

Easier? Sometimes I think it's easier?

I don't know what to do. How is it that nights still catch up with me like this? I slide from my bed to the floor, pushing myself across the carpet until my back is pressed against the wall. I can't breathe.

I shouldn't be here. I shouldn't be allowed any of this. Not when it's my fault she's dead. I should turn the lights on. I should get up. I should do *something*.

I am frozen. My lungs are simultaneously blazing and icy cold. My fingers fumble with my phone.

I call Dillan.

He answers, a little bleary. "Hi."

"Hey."

There's a muffled sound on the other end. "You okay?"

I suck in a breath that feels like static. "Did I wake you?"

"No." It's a lie. He sounds like he's still half submerged in sleep; the word comes out sticky and slow. He asks again, "Are you okay?"

I don't know what to say. I don't know how to say any of it. *I never am. I need it to stop. I need to feel something else. I want to stop running but I don't know how.*

"Hey." His voice goes awfully quiet as I gasp for breath. "Hey. What happened?"

"Nothing." My voice cracks.

"Just a bad night?" Dillan lets me lie. He's been letting me lie for months.

"Yeah. Just . . ."

"Talk?"

Tears burn, but they won't come out. They never do when I need them. I'm just relieved that with Dillan, I don't have to say what I need. "Please."

He talks. He tells me about school, and his family, what Angie's been up to, the details about a song he's working on, music software he's looking into trying.

I listen to the cadence of his voice, the familiarity of the way Dillan shapes sentences. I listen until I feel like I can move again. Then I slide under my duvet and pull it over my head, and I keep listening inside the cocoon.

He doesn't ask me any questions. He doesn't have to; I think we both know it would be a repeat of the same conversation we've already had a hundred times. *I miss her.* I know. *I'm angry.* I know. *It's my fault.* It isn't.

This is what I've never said: *I'm relieved.*

This is what I've never said: *I'm terrified of what it means to be relieved.*

This is what I've never said: *I wish it had been me.*

The idea spreads like rot; I feel it in my bones and my blood. She was so much more, she was so full of life, I wish it had been—

"Hey." Dillan's tone shifts. "What?"

I'm breathing hard. I wish I could cry so badly that pain blooms under my ribs. "I wish it had been me."

It's the dark of the room, it's the dark in my head, it's not real, it's not true, but maybe it is.

"Nora," he says. Then again, "Nora."

I'm silent—I'm afraid of saying anything more, and of not saying enough—and shivering even though I'm not cold.

He says, "I wish . . ."

I grab a pillow and hug it to my chest.

"Just, please—don't." His voice breaks to a whisper. "Don't say that."

She should have lived. She should have lived. She should have lived. My voice is steadier. "It should have been me. That would have been the fair thing."

"No, it wouldn't have."

Time is supposed to heal wounds. That's what they promised.

It isn't healing this one. I'd thought that weeks and months would lessen the ache, but nothing has gone dull; it's just as sharp and fresh as that very first day afterward.

"Are you still there?" I whisper.

His voice is barely audible. "Always. You know that."

NINETEEN

Before

I was never quite sure why happiness felt like a surprise. Happiness—real happiness, the kind that started slow and took on speed—snuck up on me and sank hooks in.

It felt like it had taken a lot longer than usual, but finally, halfway through October, life was starting to form a routine.

I liked the rhythm of sameness.

I liked that I had lunch with Julia and Eve every day. I liked that I was getting consistently good marks. I liked that Julia's soccer team met three times a week after school, and that I got to stay and sit in the library until it was over. I liked that decisions about school were still a long way off. I liked that in English class, Dillan was sort of part of our group.

It had happened slowly. I wasn't sure when it stopped being Eve and Julia and me having conversations that Dillan listened to, but soon all four of us were talking all the time, which Mr.

Ambrose sort of hated, but I couldn't help it. Dillan was really funny, and it was hard not to laugh at the comments he'd mutter just loud enough for us to hear. I'd always thought of Julia as sparkly inside, something I was drawn to even if I wasn't sure what I would find. But Dillan . . .

Dillan was different. He made me feel like *I* was the sparkly one.

I didn't think about it too much until one day after school, I realized that I wasn't the only one noticing that Dillan was in our group too.

Eve, Julia, Dillan, and I were standing outside, and Dillan was in the middle of asking me a question about our project when I noticed that Nate was watching from across the courtyard.

I tried not to be aware of it, but I could feel the *way* he was looking.

Did the sight of me standing so close to Dillan make him jealous? I wondered if I even cared.

"I mean . . ." I swallowed, trying to stay focused. "I don't know if it's worth using presentation time to talk about the book being banned, since we already have so much—"

"Shh!" Dillan grinned widely, winking at Eve and then turning back to me. "You're going to give away our secrets!"

Nate was still watching.

"Oh, come on. It's not like it's *classified*." I laughed louder than I might normally. Then I touched Dillan's shoulder, lightly, like I was making a joke, then let my hand fall.

Julia wasn't looking, but I knew Eve was, because her face went through a series of strange expressions one after the other in rapid succession.

The way Dillan smiled sort of made me forget that I'd only done it because Nate was watching. Part of me wanted to do it again.

"Anyway." I shook my head. "I keep going back and forth about it, and—and I . . ."

Julia looked at me, at Dillan, over my shoulder at Nate, and then pointedly back to me, eyebrows raised.

I couldn't help it. I glanced over my shoulder, and when I did, he was *still watching*. My cheeks turned hot as I fumbled to complete the thought. "Um. And I just think that it would mean we'd have to get into cultural history, which isn't really the point of what we're talking about, right?"

Julia and Eve made deliberate eye contact while Dillan was nodding.

I didn't look when Nate and his friends left, but I could hear them going. The muscles in my back didn't loosen until they were gone.

Julia shoved my shoulder, her eyes flashing. A warning.

I blinked at her, confused.

Dillan raised an eyebrow. "What?"

"Nothing." Julia tugged her hair out of her ponytail and shook it loose, then looked at me again. She wasn't smiling.

I could tell that Dillan knew it wasn't *nothing*, but he didn't push it.

A younger student I didn't recognize approached Julia and passed her something without saying anything.

"Thanks, Mayu," Julia called after her, which earned her a wave.

Dillan tilted his head quizzically.

"Julia has a posse," I told him, leaning closer. Frankly, I was surprised it had taken this long for him to see evidence of it.

Julia had a knack for figuring out who was the social leader of the grades below us and befriending that person. She'd be able to do anything she wanted after she graduated, but I thought she'd have a real future in espionage if she gave it a go.

She said she liked to be connected. I said she had bad FOMO. Once, last year, Eve made a comment about how Julia reminded her of a spider in the middle of a web, and Julia didn't speak to her for a week.

"I do not have a posse," Julia said, flipping me off without looking as she opened her hand and unfolded a piece of paper.

I guessed *posse* wasn't the right word. Maybe *circle of admirers* was a better description.

"You totally have a posse," Eve said. "And what happened to Cade, anyway?"

Last year, Cade had been the person who brought messages to Julia. Evidently, Mayu had replaced him.

Julia waved a hand, not looking up. "Cade is out. We hate Cade."

I swatted her arm, remembering his coming out the previous year. "You can't say that, Julia."

"Oh my God!" She looked up at me, rolling her eyes. "I don't hate him because he's gay. Minorities aren't automatically saints. I hate him because he's *annoying*."

Eve bit her lip when I caught her eye. I could tell she didn't believe it.

"Anything good?" I asked Julia, gesturing at the page, feeling suddenly uneasy.

Julia looked back down at the paper, visibly amused. "Somebody in ninth grade peed the bed at a sleepover."

"Oh, *goody*," I said, shooting a bemused grin at Dillan. "Do you know who?"

"Of course," Julia said, looking pleased with herself.

"You're not going to—"

"I'm not going to *tell* anyone, Nora." Julia crumpled the piece of paper into a tiny ball.

Julia rarely acted on the information she collected. I think she just liked to know. And to tell. Julia told you other people's secrets in a way that made you feel special. I always did, anyway.

Even though there were teachers nearby, she yanked a lighter out of her pocket and set the paper on fire.

God, the *dramatics*.

She let it fall to the ground and watched it shrivel and smolder before she ground it into the concrete with her foot. "I'm not a monster."

"People just . . . tell you this stuff?" Dillan asked.

Julia gave him a cool look, but then she smiled. There was something nearly wicked about it. "Fletcher, people tell me *everything*."

◆ ◆ ◆

After school, I sat on the bleachers with Eve, waiting for Julia's soccer practice to be finished. I hunched over my journal, propped on one knee, while Eve lay back and read.

Well. It looked like she was reading.

I didn't notice she was watching me for quite a while, until she spoke.

"You and that journal."

Her eyes were trained on the journal, and she didn't sound like she was teasing, so I just smiled. "I like it. Helps me think."

"I know," she said. "It's cool."

"Thanks." I closed it, and when Eve turned her face back into the sun, I watched her.

Light caught in her dark eyelashes and turned them ochre. She'd always been lovely, I thought. She had the best side profile out of the three of us, with her long straight nose and pointed chin. I'd always wondered if Julia was jealous of her for it.

Sometimes with Eve, you could tell when she was going to say something, like she'd already started talking but somehow without words.

This felt like one of those moments.

So I waited, and for a long time, Eve stared across the field, eyes tracking Julia's movements as she jogged.

Then she said, carefully, "I wonder about her sometimes."

I followed her gaze. "Julia?"

Eve nodded. "She says things. . . ."

I didn't have to ask. "That's just Julia."

"Why do you defend her?" Eve asked, propping herself up on her elbows. "Even after the trip, you defended her, and you still defend her."

"That was *years* ago." I folded my arms. "We've all grown up since then. She's not so . . ."

I didn't know how to finish the sentence.

Eve pressed her lips together. "Maybe."

"Julia's a good person, she just says stupid things sometimes. We all do."

She bit her lip.

"Nobody's perfect," I told her.

Eve paused, then nodded and let a long breath out between her teeth. "Do you think Julia's actually homophobic?"

I blinked, once.

A cool wind pushed Eve's bangs off her forehead as she frowned.

"I don't know," I said carefully. "I don't think so. Why?"

"She says things, sometimes." Eve sounded uncertain. "Like earlier, about Cade. And she'll make these jokes that make me wonder. Like, homophobia *lite*, if you know what I mean. The 'there's nothing wrong with it as long as I don't have to interact with it' kind."

I wrinkled my nose, shielding my eyes from the sun. "That does kind of sound like her."

"Yeah."

I'd been sort of waiting for Eve to bring this up for a long time. "Well, I'm sure if she, you know, had a friend who was gay, she wouldn't say those things."

Eve let out a huff, like she was frustrated. Then she said, "She *does* have one."

"Yeah?"

She caught my eye and held my gaze, and whatever she read on my face must have been comforting, because she relaxed and let out a shaky laugh. "Yeah. I just . . . I don't know. But I wanted to tell *someone*."

"Cool," I said, smiling. "Really, it is. I'm proud of you."

Eve smiled.

"How long have you known?"

She shrugged. "I don't know. A long time? I thought it might go away if I ignored it."

"But it isn't going away?"

Eve nodded.

"You know there's nothing . . . wrong with liking girls, right?"

She laughed. "No. I know that. Obviously. It's just . . . complicated. I don't know how Julia would react."

I wished I could reassure her, but Julia was unpredictable about sensitive issues, and that was putting it mildly.

"Dillan knows," Eve said.

I blinked. "Okay."

"I just—I thought he'd understand. And he did."

"Makes sense." I nodded. "Thank you for telling me."

Eve's voice was quiet when she said, "Don't tell her."

I was even quieter when I responded, "Of course."

TWENTY

After

The next few weeks slide by with unsettling ease.

The beginning of October blends into the middle with no more bad nights, and before I know it, the month is almost over. Dillan's birthday is right around the corner, which is a little awkward. Fortunately, we have an unspoken agreement not to make a big deal out of it. Neither of us is eager to reminisce about last year, so it's just the alien movie and nothing else. I brought up having a mini-celebration, and he mumbled his way out of it, which is fair. I don't want to think about it either.

It's almost been a year.

And that feels impossible.

"So," Eve says. "Nate."

I lean both elbows against the bar and groan.

This is the second time I've been to a bar with Eve. She didn't turn eighteen until after Julia died. The first time I went out with her, trying to celebrate, I got so nervous and sad that

I had a panic attack in the bathroom and had to call Simon to come and get me.

Anyway, this time it's going better. Mostly.

I pick up my glass of Coke and swirl it so the ice cubes clink. "You are obsessed with the idea of something happening with me and Nate."

"Aren't you?" she asks.

For a second, I have the strangest sense of déjà vu, as though I've had this conversation before, as though I'm having it with someone else. Maybe my memory is playing tricks on me again.

I glance at the empty chair next to us. What would this moment have looked like if Julia had been here? What would she have thought?

I shake my head. "I don't know. I guess it would be nice."

Truthfully, I don't know if I want Nate, or if I just want to feel something. Admitting that makes me want to curl into myself. I can picture the way Julia's nose would wrinkle if she knew how confused I was.

Eve hums noncommittally, chin tilted up.

The question comes unbidden, like somebody else is yanking it out of me. "Do you ever think Julia was unfair?"

Eve startles. "What?"

"Do you think . . . ," I begin, and I don't know how to continue. I'm not even sure what I'm trying to ask. "I've been thinking about Julia."

She looks a little wary. "And?"

I tap my fingers lightly against my kneecap. A thousand words swirl near the surface. "I don't know. I guess I'm just . . . starting to think of myself differently."

"How so?"

"You know how Julia used to kind of . . . assign us roles?"

She shifts uneasily. "Not really."

"You remember, though. I was the creative one, she was the funny one, you were—"

"The gay one?"

My mouth drops open. "Hey! I wasn't going to say that."

Eve laughs humorlessly. "You remember how she used to be."

I bite my lip.

She sighs. "In answer to your question, I guess . . . yeah. I do think she was unfair. *Obviously.*"

I watch her closely.

"It was over between her and me even before—" She cuts herself off and looks away, then sighs. "You guys were always a unit. But I knew it wasn't all wonderful between the two of you. It couldn't be, could it?"

I don't say anything, but I press my lips together and nod.

"You guys seemed so unbreakable. I felt left out sometimes. But I don't know if it bothered me that much, you know? The differences between Julia and me were sort of irreconcilable."

That's true. Sometimes it feels like that night at the Christmas market is imprinted into my brain. I might never understand the entirety of what happened between Eve and Julia, and thinking about it makes my stomach bottom out.

"Things weren't the same with me and Julia. Not like how it was with the two of you." Eve doesn't look at me. "I mean . . . you were always her favorite."

"We were a trio."

She shakes her head. "No. We were a duo plus me, until I left. But you already knew that."

I swallow hard. "I guess that sort of answers my question, then."

"What question?" Eve looks almost expectant, though I'm not sure what she wants from me.

I think back to the most recent text from Julia's mom. *Just wondering if you'd given it any more thought.* "The Hoskinses asked me if I wanted to go look through some of Julia's stuff."

Eve's eyes widen. "Oh."

"I was going to ask you if you wanted to join me. But you don't have to."

For a moment, I think Eve is properly upset with me. Like I've disappointed her somehow. But then she just sighs. "For you, I would. But not for her. I'll think about it."

Even though I wasn't planning to stay out late, we stick around for another hour.

It's not until two drinks later that I realize Eve is the best person I know. Like, she's incredible. All I can think about is how she forgave Julia back in eighth grade, even when she didn't have to. And she stayed friends with me. She invited me to her house for fish curry and sleepovers, showed me the best comedy specials, taught me a few words in Sinhala, and hung out with Julia even though she didn't like her, at first. And since Julia died . . .

I grip her arm. "How do you do it?"

"Do what?"

"You did so good after she died. How'd you do that?"

"I did *not* do good. Oh my God. I cut all my hair off."

"Yeah, but it looks great."

"It's a coping mechanism." She waves a hand lazily. "I wanted to be someone else so bad."

"I thought it made you look more like you."

She looks like she might cry, but she leans against the bar and buries her forehead in the crook of her elbow.

I lean back, let my ponytail dangle behind me, trying to tease the tension out of my neck. It's so *heavy*. Then I blurt out, "I should cut my hair."

"Oh, *fuck* yeah. You should definitely."

"Julia always said I'd regret it."

Eve snorts. "You won't."

"I want to cut it off," I say, and suddenly I'm resolute. "I want it off."

Eve stands. "Let's do it, then."

"Now?" I twist in my chair.

She runs her fingers through my ponytail. "Literally you are out with a cosmetology student. The scenario could not be more perfect."

"You've been drinking."

"I cut better when I'm tipsy."

"This is a terrible idea."

"I'll sober up on the way, then."

I stare at her, and she stares at me. Then I grin. "You know what? Fuck it."

TWENTY-ONE

Before

At some point, I stopped hanging out at the library on the days Eve didn't stay for Julia's soccer practices.

Instead, after English class, I'd hang out with Dillan in the hallways before his band rehearsals while the rest of the school emptied out.

On one such afternoon, I was struck by a sudden realization.

"It's your birthday soon, right?"

He side-eyed me, closing his locker with a snap. "You remember?"

"Dillan." I rolled my eyes. "We used to share birthday parties. I remember yours every year."

Our birthdays were exactly one month apart.

He smiled. The smile looked almost like some kind of secret I wasn't sure I was supposed to see.

"I remember yours, too," he said. "I thought it was just me."

"So, what are you doing this year?"

"For my birthday?"

I punched his shoulder. *"Obviously."*

"Rule of thumb." He rubbed his shoulder, but he was still grinning when he shrugged on his backpack and started walking down the hallway. "I don't have birthday parties."

"Why?"

"First off, I'm not five." He held one finger up, then another. "Secondly, whatever I choose to do always gets overshadowed by Halloween. Everyone is having parties. I have more reasons. I can keep going."

"We can't just do nothing." I wrinkled my nose. "You're going to be eighteen!"

He shook his head. "It's not that big a deal."

"It *is*!" I insisted. "You only turn eighteen once."

He looked exasperated. "You only turn *sixteen* once, and same with seventeen, and I didn't celebrate either of those. No trauma from that."

"Come *on*. Let me think of something fun."

Dillan scratched his head. "Uh, I guess? If you feel that strongly about it."

I *did* feel strongly about it, and that was strange to acknowledge, so I tried to shrug the thought away. I crossed my arms. "I'm going to think of something."

He paused, then smiled and shook his head. "All right. If you want to."

As we turned a corner, I nearly walked straight into somebody.

"Nora!" Mr. Ambrose said. "Hello!"

I nodded. "Mr. Ambrose."

"Fantastic work on that editorial you sent," he said. "You

laid out the issues around student mental health really well. I've sent it out to some of my colleagues."

I grinned. I'd written that one over the summer, but had only sent it in recently. "Thank you."

"I got your email about TMU, too." Mr. Ambrose offered me a wide smile. "Congratulations, by the way!"

My face warmed. "Oh," I said, folding my arms tightly. "Thanks."

Dillan gave me a funny look, and I realized with a strange, swooping sensation that I hadn't told him anything about TMU.

On a whim, I'd emailed Mr. Ambrose about the essay over the weekend, desperate to talk to *somebody*. Which means I'd let exactly *one* person in on my secret. It was about to be two.

"I'd absolutely be willing to give you a hand with your concept," he said. "I don't think I'm allowed to assist overtly, but if you need somebody to run ideas past, I'm happy to be an ear."

"Thank you so much." Relief swelled through me. "I'd appreciate that."

"I'll email you and we can set up a time to chat. When's the submission due?"

"November fifth," I told him. "So I've really got to get going on it."

"You're going to do great," he said, with a nod at me and then at Dillan. "So, you two, then?"

I blinked at him for a moment, not sure what he meant, but when I saw the slightly stunned look on *Dillan's* face, I got it.

"No!" I shook my head, laughing nervously. "No, we're— we're just friends."

Mr. Ambrose nodded without missing a beat. "Friends also make great listening ears."

Then he winked at me.

My cheeks burned, a match to Dillan's ears. "Right," I said, suddenly desperate for a way out of the conversation.

Fortunately, Mr. Ambrose took our embarrassment as a cue to take his leave.

Dillan cleared his throat, and as soon as Mr. Ambrose was out of earshot, he asked, "What's this about TMU?"

Just as I was opening my mouth, I caught a flash of blond hair coming down the hallway. Julia's soccer practice must be over. I grabbed Dillan's sleeve and yanked him down the side hallway.

He looked amused.

"You can't tell Julia," I said, whirling around to a stop.

He raised both eyebrows.

"You can't. Pinky swear."

His eyebrows arched even higher.

"I mean it," I said. "It's important. Look, I'm dead serious, feel my heart."

I grabbed Dillan's hand and put it to my chest, where he could feel my heart pounding double-time.

His whole face flushed.

Suddenly all too aware of what was going on, I let go and cleared my throat. "That's just from *thinking* about her finding out."

Dillan looked first at me, then at the floor, then down the hallway, and back to me, like he wasn't quite sure what he was supposed to do.

I caught a breath and held my pinky out, gathering myself. "Seriously, Dillan."

Dillan shook his head, but then he extended his pinky too.

"Good," I said as we shook.

"You're the only person that still makes pinky swears, you know that?" Dillan asked when we unhooked, grinning.

"Are you calling me juvenile?"

"Extremely." Dillan folded his arms. "So. TMU?"

"Right." I took a deep breath. "TMU."

Make that *two*.

TWENTY-TWO

After

I can't get used to not having long hair.

I'm constantly reaching to pull it into a ponytail, and it's a shock every time my palms brush against short ends. My hair rests just above my collarbone, but Eve said if I curl it, it'll be almost chin length.

Just like Julia told me not to.

I like it, I tell myself firmly. I like it a *lot*. I always laughed when Eve said new hair felt like a new beginning, but I'm starting to think she's right. I still feel like me, but a newer, confident version.

Eve cut off a full ten inches. When I woke up on Sunday morning, I felt like I weighed about twenty pounds less. My mom hasn't been able to stop smiling about it.

Now it's Monday evening, and my closing shift is about to end. All the regulars have commented on my look, and both of my supervisors had to do a double take. I think it makes me look both older and younger at the same time.

At any rate, it makes me look *new*.

When I push through the double doors after my shift, I almost bump into someone and then freeze.

It's *Nate.*

He blinks, and instead of *hello,* he says, "You cut your hair."

Instead of *hello,* I say, "I did."

"It suits you," he says, but it sounds like something he thinks he's supposed to say.

My smile fades, and I adjust my purse. "What are you doing here?"

"I asked around, and I heard this is where you work."

I'm so flustered that I blurt out, "I thought you were going to text me."

He shrugs. "I guess this was just easier. Are you free?"

"What, right now?"

"Yeah."

I take a second to think. It feels a little like I'm forgetting something, but I can't remember what it is, so I just shrug. "I guess so." Seeing Nate made my brain blip even before the accident. I guess it makes sense it would choose now to freeze up. "I was just leaving anyway."

Honestly, it's probably good that this is the way he's asking, because otherwise I'd have time to freak out and try to get out of it.

Nate grins and turns around. I follow him to the parking lot, and he pauses with his fingers on the door handle of his truck and raises an eyebrow. "Hey, do you wanna drive?"

I blink. "It's your car."

He grins and tosses me the keys.

What am I getting myself into?

I get in. The truck is very tall, and I have to adjust the mirrors. It smells like hot leather and dust.

When he slides into the passenger seat and closes the door, I turn to him. "Where am I driving?"

Nate gives me a half smirk that makes my heart skip a beat. I don't know whether I love or hate that he can make me feel like this. For God's sake, my hands are sweating on the steering wheel. He says, "I'll direct you."

I turn the key. "All right."

"I wish girls would drive my truck more often. It's kind of"—Nate surveys me as I turn to back out of the parking spot—"hot."

I blush furiously. "Thanks?"

It feels wildly unnecessary, since the sun is setting, but I pull my sunglasses down to hide my eyes.

We don't talk much while I'm driving, and I can't tell whether it's the good kind of silence or the kind I'm supposed to fill. Either way, I act like driving is taking most of my attention until he's directed me to the highway and we've started descending into the valley.

"Fish Creek?" I ask.

"You go much?"

I nod. "I used to."

Julia liked Fish Creek. She liked to roller-skate on the paved pathways in the summer. She liked to wear those little bralettes and skin-tight shorts and spin like she was in some eighties montage.

I've never been to the parking lot Nate directs us to. There's nobody else here, and for a second, I can hear Julia's voice saying *This is how you get murdered* until I block it out.

As I'm getting out, I reach up to toss my hair over my shoulder and I'm taken aback yet again to find that there's nothing there.

At first, I think we're going to walk, but then Nate gets into the truck bed.

I don't know how I feel about that. Remembering Nate, he isn't exactly the type to take things slow. But then I remember Eve telling me I should go for it, and what else am I supposed to do? Say I don't want to?

It's not particularly comfortable in the back, but I try to settle as best I can.

My phone vibrates against my leg—Dillan's distinctive triple tap—but I don't look, because I don't want to be distracted.

"You good?" Nate asks.

"Yeah," I say. "It's nice out here."

"It is," he agrees. "Quiet."

"Do you come here a lot?" I ask.

"Sometimes," he says, and then he doesn't say anything else, which is annoying, because I don't know what to say.

My phone buzzes against my thigh again, but I don't pick it up.

Nate asks, "Do you still write?"

I blink up at him. "Sorry?"

"You used to write," he says.

"How do you know that?"

"I used to read your stuff in the school newspaper all the time."

My phone buzzes again, and again, and I realize somebody

is calling me. I flip the phone over, and Dillan's name lights up the screen.

Nate glances. "Are you going to get that?"

I turn the screen back over. "Not important."

Nine times out of ten, it isn't. This is just how Dillan is.

Still, his name triggers a second strange sensation that I'm forgetting something. I just can't think of what it is.

"Sorry." I turn back to Nate. "You read my pieces?"

"Yeah," Nate says, sounding faintly surprised. "They were great. Weren't you, like, their top writer or something?"

Just like that, I feel like I'm back in school again. Like I'm crushing *hard*, and all he had to do was remember one thing about me.

My cheeks warm. "I guess so. Sort of, I mean. Mr. Ambrose was really great about giving me opportunities."

Maybe being here with Nate is taking back something I lost—even though I don't quite know what that was or how I lost it.

He doesn't ask again whether I've kept up with it, and I'm glad.

Nate looks like he's thinking hard. My phone begs for my attention, and for a second, I'm tempted to turn it over and see what Dillan needs. But instead, I power it off, and I train my eyes on the horizon. Dillan doesn't usually stop at ten calls, let alone one.

"Okay," Nate says. "Question. Why'd you never join debate? If I remember, I think I told you to consider it."

I shrug. "I didn't think I'd be any good. Being quick was always . . . Julia's thing. She was the clever, funny one."

If he hears the hesitation in my voice, he doesn't let on. He just shakes his head. "Ha. That's weird."

I glance up at him. "What?"

"I always thought *you* were the clever, funny one."

"Yeah, right."

He grins. "I'm serious. You look surprised."

"I *am* surprised."

"Why?"

"I don't know. I guess I didn't think that was my brand."

Now he looks surprised. Then he reaches up and tugs lightly at my hair. "Hmm. I thought you were funny, if it makes a difference. I thought you were a lot of things."

It *does* make a difference. "Things like what?"

"Funny, nice, pretty. I thought you had it all." He hasn't let go of my hair, and he pulls gently so that I lean toward him. "I was busy being stupid, though, so I didn't pay the right kind of attention, I guess."

I blink. "You think I'm pretty?"

As soon as I've asked, he laughs, as though it should have been obvious. "I've said that once before, right?"

I remember, so I nod.

Then he leans forward and presses his lips to mine.

I've replayed kissing Nate in my head a hundred times in the last year, but here's the funny thing about thinking through the same moment over and over: what you end up with is nothing like the original. I thought I remembered what it was like, but it's only once it's happening again that I remember for real.

I think, *Oh.*

I thought I'd feel something *more.*

He pulls away.

I look at him, and then I keep looking at him. There's a small part of me that wonders if maybe I'm broken, but then he whispers, "You're *really* pretty," and something behind my ribs does a funny little flutter and I feel better.

This time I lean in first. It's nicer to kiss Nate when I'm sure he wants to, not just because he's been drinking. It's easier to enjoy kissing when the kiss itself feels like the promise of another.

He lets go of my hair to cup my face and pull me closer. For a little while, I'm not sure what to do with my hands, but then I reach over and slide them around his neck, which seems right. I like it when he snakes an arm around my waist, and I like the way his hair feels under my fingers.

The first time he kissed me it was nothing like this. When I kissed Dillan, it wasn't like this either. With Dillan it felt like a story, like I was saying something and he was saying something too. This doesn't feel like communication at all.

I don't want to think about what Julia would say, but the idea floods in anyway. As soon as she's in my head, I can't get her out. Julia treated relationships like they disgusted her. Like it was beneath her to want that kind of connection with someone, and in a way, I was beneath her for wanting it at all.

I'm being kissed by the guy I spent high school infatuated with, and all I can think about is how she'd probably make fun of me for it. Her left eyebrow would arch, as if to comment, *What do you want me to say? Congratulations?*

Nate's fingers slide up my spine.

I wonder if Julia ever did this. She never had boyfriends. Not because she wasn't interested in anybody at *all*, exactly, but she never described feeling the way I did about people. Sometimes I think she saw feelings as stupid, which didn't make sense. It was easy for me; I fell in love with people and places all the time. I loved like I hadn't learned to be afraid yet, like it didn't matter if I kept breaking my heart over and over again.

I only understood what that fear was like after she died. After that, life only happened in fragments. What would it be like to feel whole and happy again? Not like this, I think.

Nate pulls back. "What?"

I shake my head. "Nothing. I'm fine."

Keep trying, Nora.

I hadn't even realized how far into my head I was until he pointed it out. I try to stay present when he kisses me again and again, on my mouth and my jaw and down to my neck, except now I'm thinking about—

I can't keep up.

One of the many things Julia used to say about me and guys. I can still taste the disdain in her voice, even though it was almost a year ago.

Nate sits back with a huff. "Seriously. What's up?"

My chest has gone so tight that I can hardly feel it, let alone figure out how to get words out. "I'm fine."

"We're chill, right?" he asks.

I nod, breathless. "Totally. I'm just—"

He leans in and kisses me again, but this time it feels like I can't get enough air. My heart is beating hard in my throat and my ears and my fingertips but it's not nice or pleasant, it feels like static and dismay and I have to pull back.

"I'm sorry," I whisper, and I can't breathe. "I'm sorry, I'm sorry, it's not you, I don't know what's wrong with me, I—"

"It's fine," Nate says, but it doesn't really seem fine. He pulls back and wipes at his mouth and for some reason that's the thing that makes me feel like I'm disintegrating into a million pieces.

I know this is over before he gets up.

It's dead silent in the truck on the way home.

He drives.

He doesn't turn the engine off when he gets to my house, or pull into the driveway. He just stops and waits.

For a second I think he's going to say he'll text me, but he doesn't. He just gives me a nod as I climb out, and when I nod back, he looks through the windshield and drives away.

TWENTY-THREE

Before

The Saturday before Halloween, Julia and I sat on the curb outside 7-Eleven with Slurpees, just like we used to after school when we were in junior high.

I'd been trying to convince myself it was still warm out, even though it was miserable and cloudy and one stray snowflake floated lazily to the ground in front of me.

I couldn't stop thinking about Dillan's ever-growing smile when I'd told him the details about TMU. He'd been happy for me.

I hadn't even realized how anxious I'd been about it until the tension left me like a balloon deflating.

A relief. It had felt like a relief.

And I'd found out that he was applying to Queen's, which is in Kingston. TMU was in Toronto, so we'd be practically neighbors. It had been surprisingly steadying to realize that I would be only a two-hour bus ride away from a familiar face.

If I got in. *If.*

I looked over at Julia.

She was already looking at me, smiling just a little around her straw. "So. Matching duvets."

I laughed, but it felt hollow. "Right."

She seemed to be watching me closely, so I looked down at a crumpled receipt rolling past us on the pavement, propelled by a crisp wind.

Julia sighed.

I was pretty sure if I didn't change the subject, she was going to start talking about school. So, as I stared into my Slurpee, feeling a little sick, I told her, "Nate invited me to the Halloween party."

She blinked. "Oh! That's— When did this happen?"

I shrugged. "The other day."

"And you didn't tell me?" Julia smacked me. "Dude."

"It's not a big deal."

"What is with you?" Julia asked. "I thought you'd be stoked. We *are* going to go, right?"

It occurred to me that I didn't really want to go to the party with her. If I was going to go, I'd probably want to go alone, or maybe with—

"I—" I shook my head, trying to clear my thoughts, then looked down at my fingernails, trying to think of an excuse. "I actually might already have plans that night."

A lie. Julia was a bloodhound for my lies.

She squinted at me. "*Don't* tell me you're hanging out with Fletcher."

"It's school stuff," I mumbled, even though that wasn't true either. I didn't have plans at all. I could feel my cheeks warming, though I didn't know whether that was because of the lies or because of Dillan or because of the way Julia was looking at me like an X-ray.

"So," she said, slowly and pointedly, as though she didn't believe me but had decided not to press it. "You and Fletcher. Is he a rebound?"

"For who? *Nate?*"

She nodded.

I shook my head rapidly, hating the way she said that. It made it sound like Dillan was an object, or something, when he wasn't. Besides, I had a feeling Julia still didn't like him, based on the looks she gave me when we were all together. I'd already been thinking it, but this just confirmed that there was no way I could talk with her about him. Besides that, I wasn't sure there was even anything to say.

Even if there *was* something to admit about Dillan, I couldn't, not now. Not after I'd emphatically denied it mere weeks ago. I felt sort of like if I told her what I was feeling, she'd somehow take it as an admission of guilt.

It did give me a strange little thrill that Julia was the second person in the last several days to wonder, though.

"No," I told her. "Dillan's not a rebound."

She gave me a look, and then stirred her straw through the ice slush at the bottom of her cup, looking annoyed. "Right."

"He's not just some random guy. I *know* Dillan. We're—"

Julia snorted.

"What?"

"No, tell me how it is between you," Julia said, but it didn't sound like she wanted to know.

"I was *going* to say we're friends."

She hummed low in her throat and didn't say anything more.

I hated how this felt. Usually, talking to Julia was easy. She pulled the truth out of me like a magnet. She was safe. Julia was my best friend. She was my number one cheerleader, as she'd told me hundreds of times.

So why did I feel like I couldn't be honest with her?

TWENTY-FOUR

After

My alarm doesn't go off.

When I wake with a start at quarter to five, bleary-eyed and confused, I scramble out of bed. It's not until after I've brushed my teeth and combed my fingers through my hair that I realize I never turned my phone back on after I turned it off with Nate. I spent the rest of the evening in a disoriented haze, trapped in my head.

I power it on.

I have several texts and a voicemail from Dillan, and a text from Eve, but I can't look at any of them, I'm so late.

I speed most of the way to work. My shift supervisor looks annoyed when I roll in ten minutes past when I'm supposed to start, but promises not to report me when I explain.

I scramble through opening duties. It feels like my heart doesn't stop pounding even when everything is ready on time—there's a tiny part of my brain that says *See, you aren't even good enough for this*—and all morning it trips in my chest to remind me that I'm here and awake, whether I like it or not. It doesn't slow for what feels like hours, until after the morning rush has died down.

When I drag the mop out from the back, the bucket gets stuck in the deep grooves between the tiles. I pull so hard that it topples, sending a wave of warm soapy water over my feet and pooling all across the floor.

I'm in the middle of thinking my morning can't possibly get any worse when Dillan walks in.

I smile at first, because Dillan always came in on Tuesday mornings, but then I see the look on his face, and I realize it's *Tuesday*, and yesterday was *Monday*, and my stomach drops down to my feet.

I know what the voicemails were about.

The mop sags in my hand.

The movie. I forgot about the stupid alien movie. That was supposed to be yesterday.

He's got both hands shoved in his pockets and he ambles over, eyes trained on the display of coffee.

I don't really remember how to breathe.

The first thing he says is "Nice hair."

I feel like I'm going to choke, but I manage to gasp, "Thanks."

He's still looking at the floor. He blinks once. "You didn't even call."

"Dillan, I'm so sorry." I feel my stomach clench when I think about him waiting at the theater for me. I never showed up. "I totally forgot."

I'm the *worst*. I'm the worst friend.

Cavernous silence.

He knocks his knuckles against the bar, and finally looks at me. His expression is completely flat, and that's how I know I've really blown it. "You didn't miss much."

I swallow. "I'm *so* sorry."

He glances down at the floor, at my wet shoes, and he doesn't laugh at the sight. I can see that he is choosing his words with care.

I hate seeing Dillan like this. Like regular Dillan but with the volume turned down. "Dillan. I'm so sorry. I had my phone powered off."

"What were you even doing?" he asks.

I can only swallow and look at him helplessly.

"Were you with Nate?"

He looks at my face and he knows.

"I'm happy for you." He kicks aimlessly at the tile. "I'm happy you're happy. It's just—I thought we were friends."

"We *are* friends." I don't even think, I can't put a filter on my thoughts. "You're my *best* friend."

His eyes snap up to mine. Neither of us has ever said that out loud.

"You know that, right?" I feel like there's something heavy trapped in my chest. "I mean it."

"I thought . . . ," he says, then squints like the words burn him. "I thought best friends come first. Before . . . boyfriends. Or whatever."

"He's not my boyfriend." The assertion tumbles out before I can think about why I want to clarify. "Definitely not."

"That is"—he flexes his fingers—"not the point. It's just . . . I feel like— God. I hate that I feel like . . . like I'm being re-placed."

I shake my head. "Dillan. Nobody could replace you."

He winces. "That's—those are just *words*, Nora. They're nice, I'll give you that, but . . ."

Annoyance bristles. At first, I think my aggression is directed at him because it wasn't *that* terrible of me to forget, but then I realize that I'm furious with myself, and it *is* terrible of me. How could I have forgotten? He hadn't confirmed our plans, but I hadn't bothered to either.

He lets out a long breath and says, "I've got to go to class."

"Dillan, please." I feel like I've been trampled. "I'm *sorry*."

He shakes his head. "Whatever."

The back of my throat burns as I watch him turn around. I want to say something to make it better, but what is there to say that won't make it worse?

I want to run after him, grab his arm, make him listen. Instead I stand there in wet shoes and watch the door close behind him.

He doesn't look back.

It's only after he's gone that I remember words I hurled at Julia once—*Why are you trying to make me feel replaceable?*—and my heart sinks.

I'm just like Julia. I'm acting *just* like her. I remember so vividly how she made me feel stupid and unimportant and like I didn't matter, even though I *knew* that wasn't what she really thought. The idea sticks and won't let go, clinging, ugly, choking.

Between blinks I see Julia's face, the tension in her jaw, accusations flung my way. The way her chest heaved when we spat poisonous words back and forth. How those were some of the last words we ever said to each other. Heat rushing from all sides.

It's not until an hour later, when I'm running through the inventory, that I see today's date: October twenty-ninth.

I sit down right there in the middle of the back room and bite my palm to stop myself from crying.

It's October twenty-ninth.

It's Dillan's birthday, and I didn't say anything, because I forgot that, too.

TWENTY-FIVE

Before

It was Dillan's birthday.

He and I skipped last-period English to get to Studio Bell before it closed, which was what he'd finally admitted he wanted to do after I'd needled him about it for ages. Originally, Eve and Julia were supposed to come too, but they both bailed at the last minute.

I wasn't that upset, though, since that meant it was just the two of us. We were supposed to give our presentation in a week, and I was starting to worry about what was going to happen after. Would he find other people to hang out with? I knew I wasn't his only friend, because he was always bumping knuckles with people in the hallway, and it was a weird day if I didn't hear "'S up, Fletcher" at least once during lunch.

We took the train downtown. It was an unseasonably nice day, and maybe because of that, or maybe because it was a weekday afternoon, the Studio was almost empty. I'd never been, but Dillan had, so he showed me around, seemingly pleased when I was impressed by the vaulted ceilings and expansive displays of Canadian music and its history.

It was a strange little glimpse into the person Dillan had become over the years. I knew he was in band at school, and I knew he liked music, but watching him ardently admire the collection of guitars made me realize how much I'd missed.

I sidled up to him. "Do you want to be a musician?"

He laughed. "You mean, like, a performer?"

When I nodded, he shoved his hands in his pockets. "Nah. I wouldn't be good enough for that."

"But you love it."

"Yeah." He looked at me sideways. "I've thought about— actually, I *do* write music. Sometimes. Just stupid stuff, though."

"I bet it isn't."

He just shrugged, ambling through the arched doorway into the next room, where a series of pianos lined the walls.

"What *do* you want to do, then?"

His lips quirked into a smile. "Sound engineering. Don't laugh."

"I wasn't going to."

"It's what interests me most about music. Like, figuring out how it all works. Plus, it's a blend of passion and practicality. It's a surprisingly lucrative field."

I wasn't really that surprised that Dillan knew what he wanted to do. He seemed like a decisive sort of person.

He stopped, and for a moment it seemed like he might look my way, but instead he kept his eyes fixed on one of the pianos. "You want to be a journalist, right?"

I nodded.

"Have you heard anything from TMU?"

"I haven't even submitted the essay."

"You're going to do well."

"I'd better." I swallowed. "If they don't like it and I get rejected, I can't reapply until next year, and by then I'd probably be at a different school, so it's sort of my only shot."

"Well, you're halfway there. Your stuff in the school paper is great. *I* believe in you."

"Thanks." I flushed, then gestured toward one of the pianos. "Do you play?"

"Oh," he said, and when he looked at me, he grinned. "Nah. I can't play piano for shit."

Right then it felt like there was something different between us, though I couldn't quite put my finger on it.

Maybe it was because it was his birthday. Eve always claimed there was such a thing as "birthday glow." That might have been it. Or maybe it wasn't.

For a second, I let myself think that this was a date.

Then Dillan cleared his throat and looked away.

We took the train back to his house.

If it had felt weird to have Dillan at my house, it was even weirder to be at his new one. Even though I'd never been inside, there were enough pieces of furniture that I recognized that it felt like I *should* have been there before. Even the entrance rug was the same.

"I don't want to overstay my welcome." I leaned gingerly against the kitchen counter. "It *is* your birthday, after all. Don't want to disturb your plans."

"Oh, yes." Dillan nodded. "My thrilling plans. Options included ordering a pizza and locking myself in my room or ordering a pizza and hanging out by myself in the living room."

"That *does* sound thrilling." I crossed my arms. "Where's your family?"

"Mum's got some conference thing, so they're out for the evening," he said. "Shitty timing, but it is what it is."

"Oh." I frowned.

"We celebrated last night, you don't have to look like I've been kicked."

I laughed.

"My sister—did you ever meet her? No? She's a little twerp—is at a friend's house for a sleepover."

"And they just left you here, on your own?"

He nodded.

"That sucks."

Dillan shrugged. "Not really. I don't mind. Like I said, we had a birthday dinner last night, and I'm going out with some buddies over the weekend. Mom looked like she was going to cry when she realized the conference was tonight, but Mum *had* to go, so it is what it is. Can't really complain."

"Still. It's your actual birthday, and you're stuck here with me."

He looked at me like he'd meant to look away just as quickly, but then didn't. "I could think of worse things."

The air in the room felt charged, like I'd create static just by moving. I broke eye contact first.

Dillan knocked once on the counter, a sharp rap. "How do you feel about breaking the law?"

"Where are we on the scale of one to murder?"

He tilted his head. "Considering that *your* birthday is in less than a month, I'd go with a solid one-point-five."

Then he opened the fridge and pulled out a cider.

"Oh." I shook my head rapidly. "Oh, sorry. I don't believe in underage drinking."

He blanched for a half second but recovered quickly, eyebrows high. "Wait—really?"

"No." I rolled my eyes. "Obviously not. Give 'er."

He grinned as he handed it over, shaking his head slowly. "You sure are something else."

He said it like it really meant: *You make me laugh.*

Then, after he'd cracked his cider and briefly touched his can to mine, he stepped into the hallway to order pizza.

I let my gaze wander around the kitchen. Even though it was a different house, it still reminded me of where Dillan lived when we were kids. It was something about the way it smelled. I recognized the elaborate picture frame his mom had hung on the wall, but almost all the photos were different. I recognized the old black-and-white photo of two young men in air force uniforms, because I had run past it nearly every day when I was younger. There was Dillan with braces, Dillan with his mom, a younger Dillan (the way I remembered him) with his arms around two older men, him hugging a much younger girl, her skin as dark as his was light.

"What are your thoughts about mustard on pizza?"

I jumped. When I turned around, I just stared at him. "What are my thoughts on— Excuse me?"

He shrugged. "Mustard on pizza."

I blinked, once. "I have literally never devoted brain space to considering it."

"Okay." He winced. "Not, like, baked *on* the pizza. As a dipping sauce."

"*Mustard,* as a— I don't know if that makes it worse or not." I wrinkled my nose.

"Don't knock it till you try it!"

Exasperated, I shook my head. "You are so strange."

I said it like it really meant: *I don't think I mind it at all.*

Before the eye contact could start to feel like anything, I turned back to the photos. "So this is your sister?"

He nodded.

"Cute."

"She's really great. Super-smart kid. And really nice." Dillan grinned slyly. "It's genetic."

I elbowed him.

When the pizza came, we sat on the couch to eat—the mustard wasn't good—and he put on music and taught me the rules to a convoluted card game. I proceeded to forget the rules so badly that we had to give up, and then we found a TV show we both liked, and we drank ciders and laughed over nothing.

It felt a little bit like hanging out with Julia, in a way. It wasn't weird, or awkward, or any of the things I had worried it might be. But it wasn't like hanging out with Julia, actually, because I was nervous. Not *anxious,* just nervous. Jittery. My hands were more nervous than my heart was.

When Simon texted me that he was on his way home and could swing by to pick me up, I almost wanted to tell him not to. It was only a ten-minute walk, and I didn't want to leave yet.

But it was also a school night, and the ciders were starting to make me feel a little bit fuzzy, so I texted Simon the address. When he said he'd be there in five minutes, I tried to convince myself I wasn't disappointed.

Dillan closed his eyes and leaned his head back against the couch, less than a foot away. "Who's that?"

"Simon." I put my phone down on my lap. "He's going to come get me."

"Oh, man. Simon." He opened his eyes and ran his hands through his hair. "We were such imps when we were little, weren't we? *God,* we were annoying."

I laughed. "I'm sure he still thinks I'm annoying."

"Do you remember," he said, a lazy smile spreading across his face, "that time we tried to convince him that it was a school day but it was really Saturday?"

I laughed, covering my face with my hands. "Oh, God. And he was just like, 'Why is Dillan at our house on a weekday, then?' and we thought it was *so funny.*"

"What was it, April Fools' or something?"

"Something like that." I laughed and looked over at him, but when I found his face, I couldn't look away. A lamp lit up his hair from behind, which made him look like he was glowing. I had the sudden, strange urge to kiss him.

"What are you thinking right now?"

The question sort of startled me, and I found my face flushing warm, even though there was no way he could know what I'd been thinking. There must have been some of it visible on my face, though, because he was looking at me with a quiet sort of wariness.

I wanted to kiss him.

Like, *really* wanted to kiss him.

He looked a little like he wanted me to.

"I'm thinking . . . ," I whispered, and then I leaned forward. We bumped noses, and both of us laughed, even though it wasn't that funny.

Then I kissed him.

He tasted like cider. For a brief moment, he was so perfectly still that I was afraid I'd imagined it and he didn't want to after all, but then he kissed me back.

He was a good kisser. I don't know why that surprised me, but it did. I didn't have a whole lot of experience, but this didn't feel like kissing Nate had. This felt like my heart was hammering in my mouth, like if we were still enough, he'd be able to feel how nervous I was.

I meant to pull away, but then I didn't. I'd thought about what it would be like to kiss Dillan before, but only sort of, and never in detail.

My phone buzzed against my thigh, but I shoved it aside.

Real life was nicer than what I had imagined. His lips were soft against mine, and each kiss felt like a question, gentle and uncertain, warm.

He reached up and touched the side of my face, fingers feather-light.

We both jumped when a car honked outside, and we sprang apart. My phone rang.

Dillan looked a little wild-eyed.

Simon's picture lit up my phone screen. Blushing furiously, I swallowed hard and answered. My ear burned against the cool glass. "Hi?"

His voice was gruff on the other end of the phone. "I'm outside, dipshit. What are you doing in there?"

I glanced over at Dillan. He was smiling, and the tips of his ears were pink, the same way they'd been in class all those weeks ago. As soon as we made eye contact, his eyes dropped to the floor. I said to Simon, "Give me two minutes."

I stood and swayed on the spot, holding a hand to my head. "Jesus."

I felt a hand on my elbow, and I nearly tipped over when I spun around. Dillan's grip tightened, and when I looked up, his face was right there.

Being this close to him made my stomach do a series of funny flips, and even though I'd just kissed him, I wanted to do it again.

But instead I just looked at him, because I didn't know how to look away. He had lovely eyes. Pretty, sort of. People were probably thinking about eyes like his when they wrote songs about blue-eyed boys.

"Dillan," I said.

"What?"

Then I laughed, because it was so terribly funny. I wanted him to kiss me. I wanted him to start it this time, so that I'd know I wasn't making it up. "I don't know."

He grinned, and then let go of my elbow.

My skin felt cold where he wasn't holding it anymore, but then when he reached up to brush his fingers lightly across my cheek, I forgot about that.

He said, "I don't know either."

He kissed me.

• • •

When I finally closed the front door behind me and scrambled down the steps, my heart was beating double-time. I felt strangely unsteady as I opened the passenger door, though I was fairly certain it didn't have much to do with the ciders.

"That wasn't two minutes." Simon looked annoyed, like I'd personally meant to inconvenience him. "What, were you making out in there?"

My face gave me away, and I turned when his eyebrows arched.

"Wait—*were* you?"

"No!" The objection squeaked out. "Maybe."

"You guys were *making out?*" He shook his head, but there was a ghost of a smile on his face. "You and Dillan? The fuck."

He didn't ask any questions, and I didn't expect him to. Even though it was cold, I rolled down the window and shoved my face out, letting the air cool my cheeks and neck. It bit at my skin, but it didn't feel as intense as it'd felt when Dillan touched my cheek.

When we got home, I went straight to my room, where I collapsed on the bed and called Julia.

"What is *up,* Nora-nora?" Julia sounded chipper. "How was the birthday whatever thing?"

I couldn't keep it in even for a second. "Guess what?"

"Are you actually going to make me guess?"

"Julia. *Julia.*"

Now she sounded a little annoyed. "What?"

I just laughed.

"*What?*"

"I kissed him."

She was quiet for so long that I wasn't sure I'd said it out loud.

I closed my eyes and lay down on the bed.

My phone buzzed against my ear. I put her on speakerphone, then checked my notifications—it was a single text from Dillan.

:)

I was typing out a response when Julia finally spoke. "Wow."

I took her off speaker before I'd sent it and pressed the phone to my ear. "Wow? That's it?"

"Just . . . I thought you didn't like him."

"I didn't know."

That wasn't quite true, but it was safe.

"Wow," she repeated. "How did it happen?"

I was starting to feel my heart sink. "Are you happy for me?"

"Should I be? Are you happy?"

"*Yes.*" I took a deep breath in, but it was like inhaling dark clouds—Julia-shaped. When I closed my eyes, Dillan's face swam right up close. I touched my fingers lightly to my lips. "Yeah. I'm really happy."

I heard running water on the other end of the line, then Julia sighed. "Then yes. Yeah. I'm happy for you."

She wasn't. *Why?* Why couldn't she let me have this?

Maybe this was just Julia being Julia. Maybe she needed time to adjust.

She sighed. "Did he seem into it?"

"Uh." I laughed. "I'd say."

I felt my cheeks warm when I remembered his hands on my waist, fingers pressed against my back. I couldn't *stop* thinking about it.

"Yeah." I sighed. "He seemed happy."

And despite her lukewarm attitude, so was I.

"Well," Julia said, and more than anything she seemed bewildered. "I'm happy if you're happy."

But it didn't sound true.

TWENTY-SIX

After

Forgetting Dillan's birthday feels like stepping off a ladder into nothingness.

Every time I remember it, my stomach lurches. So far, I've been good at being patient with myself when I forget things, but this feels like a crime, and I'm so angry with myself that hot tears burn behind my eyes the whole rest of the day.

How could I?

When I get home from work, I don't even think about whether this is a good idea. I don't have room in my head for thinking, only a high-pitched and insistent buzzing that won't leave me alone.

I walk to Dillan's house.

Standing at his front door, though, I'm not sure. Normally I'd just walk right in, but it doesn't feel appropriate now.

I stand on the porch with my hands in my pockets, trying to figure out what to say.

When I finally knock, it's weak and uncertain.

I think I have my speech all sorted, but when I hear foot-steps coming to the door and the lock turning, I forget what I was going to say.

He opens the door, and all I manage is "Dillan."

This is the first time since last year that he doesn't look pleased to see me. His eyebrows draw together, and for half a second I get the impression that the sight of me on his door-step has caused him physical pain, but then the expression is gone and the idea vanishes with it.

"Nora. What?"

"I—I . . . ," I stammer. "I'm really sorry."

He sucks in a fast breath and lets it out slowly. He doesn't invite me in.

I try again. "It was a really stupid and shitty thing for me to do. I feel terrible. And . . . happy birthday."

The last part comes out horribly stilted. I meant to imply that I hadn't forgotten, that I'd never forget his birthday, but instead it sounds all wrong, like an afterthought.

"It's just—it's the principle, isn't it?" He speaks in a quiet rush, like he hasn't thought about the words and now they're suspended between us. Slower, more carefully, he says, "I don't want to be your second option. It's—it was like this before, wasn't it?"

Is he talking about Julia?

"I don't know how to make it better," he says. "Maybe I just need to get used to it."

"To *Nate*?" I shake my head. "No. It's not like that."

"Nora," he says firmly. "I just—don't want to talk about it right now. Okay?"

If this were any other day, if I weren't standing on his porch,

I'd want to talk about what happened with Nate. I'd want to tell him how I still feel like I'm bleeding on the inside without Julia to help me figure this out. "But . . . it's your birthday. I don't want us to be fighting on your birthday."

From inside the house, I hear the familiar sound of a stool scraping backward. "It's your birthday?"

I blink, trying to place the voice, but I can't. I'm so surprised when I see Kayla that I can't even formulate a greeting.

When she sees me, her face brightens, and she waves. "Hey, Nora!"

My wave is halfhearted.

Dillan explains before I ask. "We're working through an assignment together."

She comes to the door and shoves Dillan's shoulder, repeating, "It's your birthday?"

When he nods reluctantly, her mouth drops open. "And *this* is what you're doing? Why didn't you say something?"

He shrugs. "I have plans later."

I know him well enough to know that this is intentional, that he wants me to know he's made plans without me, and it's so uncharacteristically cruel of him that I just stare.

He doesn't meet my eyes.

Don't cry, don't cry.

I clear my throat and blink rapidly, eyes burning. "Well, I didn't mean to interrupt."

The idea of Dillan and Kayla hanging out together makes me feel weird, an unpleasant sort of weird, but maybe that's just because right now everything is tinted with the ugliness that's settled between my lungs.

I kick at the wood under my feet. "I'll just go, then."

He doesn't stop me.

TWENTY-SEVEN

Before

Dillan wasn't in school the next day.

I realized the next morning that I hadn't ever responded to his text, so when I woke up, I sent a quick "thanks for yesterday:)," but he didn't respond to that or to the three other messages I sent asking where he was.

In English, I asked Julia, "Do you know what's up with Dillan?"

Her eyes darted toward me, then to his empty seat. "What about him?"

"Where is he? He's not answering my messages."

Julia didn't look at me. "I'm not sure. I haven't heard from him either."

I didn't see Dillan until Thursday. Halloween. When I spotted him in the hallway, I rushed after him, sidestepping a girl with a skull painted on her face. "Dillan!"

He glanced over and I *knew* he saw me, but then his eyes darted away.

"Hey. Dillan!" I jogged after him as he spun the combination on his lock, feeling dismay sinking through me. "About the other night—"

He shook his head sharply and started shoving books into his locker. "We don't have to talk about it. We were drinking, it's whatever."

My stomach fell. Like, full-on plummeted.

I wasn't sure what I had wanted him to say, but that wasn't it.

I stopped in my tracks, blinking.

He stared into his locker. "You cool with that?"

I stared at him. "Oh. Okay."

He nodded a bit grimly, and then closed his locker door, hard. "I've got to get to class."

Dillan didn't look back as he walked away, and then he didn't come to English, either.

The class passed by in a blur. I hardly noticed when the bell rang. This felt like how it had with Nate at the beginning of the school year, except *worse*, because I hadn't had a friendship with Nate to lose overnight.

What was it about me that made people disappear without warning?

Julia waved a hand in front of my face. "Hello? Earth to Nora."

"Hmm?"

"You look like shit."

I barely refrained from rolling my eyes. "Yeah, *thanks*."

"No, that's not what I meant. You look like you need a pick-me-up." She slid her notebooks into her backpack. "We're still going to the Halloween party tomorrow night, right?"

The way she was looking told me that if I said no, it would be an argument. So, even though it was the last thing I felt like doing, I agreed.

But by ten o'clock on Friday night, the only place I wanted to be was at home, in bed, which was unfortunate, because I was surrounded by drunk classmates.

What was there to say? It was a Halloween party. Some of us were dressed up, some of us weren't. Some of us—namely, me—were utterly miserable.

I felt possessed. By what, I didn't know, but—

But I had been *so sure.*

I'd been sure Dillan had liked it, wanted it, even. His hand on the back of my neck was a phantom, one I was positive I couldn't have gotten rid of even if I wanted to.

A horrible voice in my head whispered, *Nate seemed to like you too.*

Where was Julia? Why was I here? I didn't want to be at this party. I didn't even want to be awake. I knew I was being melodramatic, that really, there was no reason to feel *this* miserable, but the living room was loud, and I was tired, and sadness ate away at my sternum like it was ravenous.

Then I saw Dillan. Just for a second.

I felt like all the air was being sucked out of my body.

He was standing in the doorway, scanning the room.

I hadn't thought he'd be here. I'd thought this would be the last place Dillan would want to be. I was staring, but I only had a second to be self-conscious, because then we locked eyes, and he was staring back.

I looked at him, and he looked at me, and I *kept* looking at him, and then he looked away. He must have seen somebody else, because he frowned. I wanted to go over, but more than that I wanted him to come explain what was going on.

His frown deepened and he walked away. I followed his gaze a second too late. All I saw was a flash of blond hair disappearing around a corner.

A hand on my arm stopped me from following.

"Hey, you made it!"

Nate.

He was wearing a costume—sort of. He'd just put on his hockey jersey, which effectively blended with the garish colors around us.

"Yeah." I glanced over my shoulder. Dillan was gone. I offered Nate a weak smile. "I'm here."

"I'm glad." He squeezed my arm. "You good?"

"Yeah. I'm fine."

I felt sick.

"There's a hot tub out back. You want in?"

For a second it occurred to me that Nate might be trying to rekindle whatever we'd had at the last party. I wondered if I'd have been excited about it before Dillan.

All I felt right then was worn out, like a bit of paper that had been crumpled and flattened so many times it was soft to the touch.

I swallowed. "Uh, no, thanks. Have you seen Julia around?"

He blinked, like he hadn't expected me to say no. "Oh. Okay. No, I haven't."

I glanced over my shoulder again.

He sounded far away when he said, "You know where to find me if you change your mind."

When I looked back, he was gone.

I turned to follow Dillan, but the house was large and laby-rinthine.

After about twenty minutes of fruitless searching, I found Julia.

She was leaning against the fridge, talking to a boy I vaguely recognized from our calculus class. From her posse, probably.

I grabbed her arm. "I need to talk to you."

She looked annoyed. "Now?"

When I nodded vehemently, she pushed off the fridge and shot the boy an apologetic look.

I dragged her into the hallway. "Did you see Dillan?"

She nodded.

"Where is he?"

Julia shrugged and tossed her hair over her shoulder. "Not sure. I think he left."

"Left? I thought he just got here. Did you talk to him?"

"A little," she admitted.

"What did you say to him?" I hissed.

For a second, she looked genuinely surprised. Then she slung an arm loosely around my shoulders. "I was giving him a piece of my mind."

I tried to shrug her off, but she gripped me tighter. "What did you say?"

"Does it matter?"

"Julia." I managed to wrench myself free. "What did you say?"

"It's not a big deal." She rolled her eyes.

"It *is* a—"

She grabbed my arm. "Nora? It's not a big deal."

I blinked at her.

172

"You can't trust Dillan," Julia said, with frightening intensity.

I stepped back, shrugging her off. "What?"

"You can't trust him," she said.

"What are you *talking* about?"

Julia sighed. "Okay, you know what, I didn't want to say any of this, but it seems like you need it laid out for you, so here it is: first he led you on, then ghosted you, now he was just flirting with *me*."

"He was what?" I felt my chest sink.

"I didn't *let* him," Julia said. "I told him off for being an asshole to you."

A bubble of nausea rose slowly. "What did you say, specifically?"

She crossed her arms. "You know what? You need to—you need to cut it out, for a second. Just for a second, Nora."

Even though Julia was quite a lot taller than I was, I wasn't often aware of it.

I was aware of it then. I set my jaw, looking up at her. "What's that supposed to mean?"

"You're always letting yourself get so influenced by what a guy thinks of you. First you like Nate, then you don't. You don't like Dillan, now you *do*. It's exhausting to keep up with you."

"Keep *up* with me! What are you talking about?"

"You're *so* fucking emotional. All the time! And I'm just trying to, like, be supportive, but I *can't keep up*. You're welcome for having your back, by the way."

I stared at her, biting back a thousand equally cutting words. "You know what? Find another DD. I'm out of here."

She rolled her eyes. "Like you'd just leave without me."

"Watch me."

For a second, I thought I saw a flash of panic in her eyes. But then her expression settled to stone. "Fine."

We both knew it wasn't.

I threw her keys at her, turned, and walked away.

I didn't leave, though. I don't know why I didn't. Maybe it was because I knew Julia would call, and because we both knew that nothing could ever stop me from helping her when she needed it.

She did call, well after midnight. I was sitting on the porch, letting the cold air leach through the concrete into the backs of my thighs. I stayed on the phone with her until I found her in the bathroom, leaning against the shower. I hoisted her arm around my shoulders and guided her out to her car.

This is what friends do, I told myself, resolute. *Even when they fight.*

"Sorry," Julia slurred while I was wrestling the car door open. "I didn't mean to say those things."

"You're fine," I said.

"I have your back," Julia told me, snaking an arm around my neck. "I would do anything for you. I would destroy anybody if they were mean to you."

"You," I told her, depositing her in the passenger seat, "are wasted. Please don't destroy anybody."

Julia said, "Nnghh."

She fell asleep on the way home with her cheek against the glass. I watched her while I was sitting at a red light. When she was asleep, Julia looked younger. She always had. She reminded me of the girl she'd been when we first met, when she dragged me out of myself and into the world.

She had my back, and I had hers.

I thought nothing would ever change that.

TWENTY-EIGHT

After

I hate parties.

I always have, on some level, but they're especially terrible now. I haven't been to many since Julia died, and every one has left me drained dry. But this is a Halloween party, and since Eve asked me, I'm here, even though the memory of last year's party still stings.

I'm leaning against the wall in someone's dining room. I'm not sure whose house this is.

Eve gives me a nod from across the table. "You good?"

I swallow. "Yeah."

I wish I could be as certain as Eve. Even the way she dresses—tonight in a dark green blazer, with a tucked-in button-up shirt—seems to say that she knows who she is and she's not afraid of it.

In the next room, I hear a vaguely familiar burst of laughter, and a second later, Kayla walks in.

She brightens when she sees me. "Hey, Nora."

Beside me, Eve's eyebrows arch, and she suddenly averts her eyes out the window, raising her glass to her lips.

"Kayla!" I'm relieved to see another familiar face. "What are you doing here?"

"I'm *mostly* here because I thought it would piss Rafael off." She flips her hair over her shoulder.

I have no idea who he is, but I nod anyway.

"Not that I really care what he thinks, but I also sort of want to make him mad, and I knew he'd be here."

Across the table, Eve snorts into her drink, gaze dropping away from Kayla to the floor.

"You and Rafael were a thing?" I ask, mostly to be polite.

"Emphasis on *were*," Kayla says.

Eve is still watching us with curiosity.

Well, me. She's watching me, but her eyes dart over to Kayla every so often. I should probably introduce them, but Kayla is still going.

"And then Dillan asked if I wanted to go, and I said sure, but then he bailed last second."

The muscles in my back tense. "Dillan was going to come?"

One of Eve's friends, a girl with a red ponytail, skids into the room and yanks on Eve's arm. Eve smiles apologetically as she's dragged away.

"Yeah. Hey, is everything good with you guys? You don't have to tell me, but he seemed a little tense after you left the other day."

The large gulp of iced tea lodges in my throat as if it's solid, and I have to force it down. "Uh, yeah. It's fine," I cough. "It's my fault. Something stupid. I'll talk to him about it."

I don't tell her that I've *already* been trying to talk to him about it, but he isn't answering my calls. That's so far out of the ordinary that I'm not sure what to do. I miss his incessant texting. What's the protocol after you've been a cataclysmically horrendous friend?

My feelings about it are raw and stinging, and I can't stop thinking about how he must have felt standing there, waiting for me. I also can't stop thinking about what he said about birthday plans. Who was he with?

Kayla's expression is calculated and knowing, and right then, I wonder if he might have told her. Would he have done that?

"Ah, well." She shrugs. "He's an easygoing guy. It'll probably blow over."

She looks across the room as anxiety brews in my gut. I try to think of something—anything—to keep the conversation going.

The door Kayla came through opens again, and two girls I vaguely recognize come in, whispering to each other. They're both dressed up as cats. They're maybe fifteen or sixteen, too young to be at this sort of party, and it makes me a little sad.

Then, abruptly, as one of them turns and I catch a glimpse of her face, I realize how I know them.

Stepping forward, I ask, "You're Mayu, right?"

She raises an eyebrow. "Yeah?"

The other one doesn't say anything.

"You were friends with Julia."

Mayu and the other girl exchange a look.

"No." Mayu scoffs. "No, it wasn't ever like that. We just did things for her sometimes."

I blink, taken aback. "Why?"

She shrugs.

The way Julia talked about them, I thought they were friends. Or that at least they liked each other. The way Mayu responded makes me think they were barely acquaintances.

I'd thought they admired her. But Julia's family had money, and Julia had influence, and maybe they were friendly with *that*.

"Like, I don't know," Mayu says. "It was more like I did her little favors."

I have a sinking, dreadful feeling. "What do you mean? What sort of things did she have you do?"

She just laughs. "I thought you'd know all about her *business*."

I shake off what I'm pretty sure was meant to be a barb. But I remember these two girls, and it's with a horrible feeling that I ask, "Did she ever have you take a picture for her?"

Mayu doesn't say anything, but by the way she's looking at me, I know she knows what I mean.

I've been doing my best not to think about that picture for *months,* but it's still branded behind my eyelids whenever I close them. Dillan's hair in the dark. The way the moonlight bounced off it. The moment frozen in time. How it felt like the world was ending when I first saw it. My chest squeezes.

"That was real?" I ask. I feel light-headed. "It wasn't . . . Photoshopped, or something?"

Mayu looks at me sadly. "No—I was there. I took it for her."

I swallow hard.

"Aila was there too," she says, turning to the other girl. "Right?"

Aila's hazel eyes are luminous in the low lighting of the room when she nods. She looks apologetic.

"Right," I say, trying to act as if I don't feel like the floor is tilting up toward me. "Right, yeah. That's all I wanted to know. Thanks."

Mayu gives me a weird look as she passes by. For a second, it looks like the other girl—Aila—is going to just leave with her, but at the last moment, she turns around.

"I'm sorry," Aila whispers. "About Julia."

I don't have time to react before she's gone.

They didn't even like her. They weren't her friends, they didn't admire her. Why had I thought otherwise? Julia made it seem like she had friends everywhere. She deserved a fucking Oscar for her performances. Can I trust *anything* I thought I remembered?

Next to me, Kayla has the attention of four or five other people, students by the looks of them, and I'm trying to tune in to what they're talking about when the speakers beside my elbow fade out. When the next song starts playing, my chest turns to ice.

Julia's favorite song.

I try to fight my way through it, offer weak smiles at their jokes, but I'm not hearing them anymore. There's only a terrible roaring in my ears. My fingers wrapped around the plastic cup feel fake.

My breathing quickens.

The guitar riff of the pre-chorus thrums through my bones. *No, no, no. Not now.* It feels like every sound is being sucked out of the room.

It's like Julia won't let me go even now.

Or maybe I'm the one who can't let go of her.

Someone is asking me something. But the part of my brain that is responsible for answering is frozen.

I don't feel myself let go of the cup. I only feel it once it lands on my feet. Cold liquid sloshes through my shoes and onto the floor.

"Nora!" I feel Kayla's hand on my arm. "Are you okay?"

My heart beats unusually hard in my chest and I blink at her. Then her face comes into focus and all the sound rushes back into the room.

"Are you okay?" she repeats.

"I'm sorry," I say, and squat down to the floor, scrabbling for the empty cup. "Sorry."

A girl thrusts paper towels into my hands.

Kayla is crouching next to me. She watches while I sop up the mess, then gently pries the paper towels from my hand. I hear her saying something to somebody else, and what feels like a half second later, she's been handed a wet rag.

She wipes down the floor.

I'm still crouching. My hands don't feel real. I murmur, "Sorry."

The word is stiff like cotton in my mouth, I've said it so many times.

"It's okay." She puts a hand on my knee. "Hey. You're okay."

I nod blindly and let her guide me up again.

She pulls me by the elbow out into the hallway. "What's going on? Are you okay?"

My socks are wet, I think. I mumble, "'M fine."

"What?"

"I'm fine," I repeat, a little clearer.

Her face is etched full of pity. I hate it. I *hate* it.

I pull my elbow out of her grasp. "I'll be fine."

Kayla doesn't believe me.

"Thanks for—you know."

"Anytime," she says. "If you ever want to talk, I'm—"

"Thanks," I repeat. "I'm okay."

She sighs.

"I'm gonna go find Eve," I whisper, and I turn and walk away.

I don't go find Eve, though. I go outside and stand on the front porch, letting the cold numb me.

All I can think about is that damn picture.

TWENTY-NINE

Before

"So." Julia propped herself up on one elbow. She was back to normal, though she'd spent most of the weekend hungover and groaning about it. Now, on Monday night, she was painting my toenails.

I raised an eyebrow in my best attempt to feign innocence. "So?"

"Ugh." She flopped backward on my bed. "Dillan? Heard from him at all?"

I turned a bottle of nail polish over and over between my fingers. When I spoke, I tried to be as nonchalant as possible, even as annoyance bubbled under my skin like an itch. "I thought you didn't want to hear about that."

Dillan had been MIA all weekend, and then today he'd skipped English again. I was starting to move past disappointment into anger. Had the kiss really repulsed him so badly that he didn't want to be in the same room with me? And had he really been flirting with Julia? Was she right that I couldn't trust him?

I'd *thought* I could trust him.

Julia's words were still ringing in my ears. *I can't keep up.* Not that we'd talked about that. For now, at least, we were both acting like it had never happened.

Julia tapped my ankle with her index finger. "Nora. C'mon. I'm just looking out for you."

I shook my head, trying not to doubt her. "I haven't heard a word. You haven't heard anything, have you? Like, from your little posse?"

Julia rolled her eyes. "Stop calling them my posse. They're my *friends.*"

I stared down at the polish bottle. "But they haven't heard anything about Dillan?"

"No," Julia said, sounding bored. "I haven't heard anything. But I don't really need to. He turned out just like I expected."

Heat flared in the pit of my stomach. "Oh? And what were you expecting?"

She looked up at me and said, coolly, "That he'd play nice and then treat you like shit."

"You didn't even *know* him," I said. "How could you think that?"

"I was right, wasn't I?" Julia asked. "He hadn't been nice to *me* until we were at the party the other night, so maybe that's just his game."

"I am *tired* of games," I said.

Had it just been a game? *Could* it have just been a game?

Maybe Julia was right.

"Games," she said, sounding disdainful, "are *fun.* That's why people play them, Nora."

I ground the heels of my palms against my eyes. "I just don't think that's what's happening here."

She shrugged and looked down at her handiwork. My toes were vivid purple. "He's an idiot."

"What?"

"His loss," she said. "You're a catch. He's an idiot for not seeing it."

The way she said it sounded so *final*.

"I'm serious," Julia said. "Any guy would be lucky to have you. You're brilliant, and you're kind, and you're a better friend than anyone I've ever met."

A stab of guilt shot through me like an electric shock.

"Thank you," I said, leaning forward and resting my cheek against the cool wood of my desk. Then I reached for my journal and ran my fingers lightly down the spine.

"You write about him in there?"

I jolted, startled both by the question and the hard edge to her tone.

Julia let out a hiss. "Watch the toes."

I kept still. "Uh. Not really. A little?"

She laughed, but not like she thought it was funny.

"What?"

"Nothing."

"*What?*"

"Well, you're a little obsessed with him."

I crossed my arms. "What do you mean? *You're* the one who has been asking about him!"

"All I mean is that you're not acting like yourself," Julia said. She was looking down, but there was something dangerously casual about her tone.

I hummed, low in my throat.

"If I didn't know better," she said slowly, "I'd think you were keeping secrets."

Then she looked up at me.

She knew.

I was certain of it. She knew about TMU. She wasn't saying it out loud, which meant . . . What did it mean? Was this a free pass? I felt like I'd swallowed ice. "I'm not keeping secrets."

I should tell her. I *should*. The thought yanked in the pit of my stomach.

Nothing was certain, though. I wouldn't hurt her over nothing.

"I'm just feeling off recently, that's all," I said.

She made a derisive sound.

"What? It's the truth."

"If you focused on your real life instead of some guy, maybe you'd feel more *on*."

I stared at her. Were we still fighting about Dillan, or was she talking about something else? "What is your problem?"

"I don't have a problem."

"Julia, come on. The things you said at the party . . ."

She didn't say anything.

"He's not just *some guy*." I crossed my arms. "Dillan is my friend. It's not just a stupid crush. We were friends, and I really liked him, and now he's pretending like I don't exist. And I'm worried that I've permanently ruined our friendship or something. I just—I don't see how *my* feelings are hard for *you*."

"I didn't mean for you to take it like that," Julia muttered.

I swallowed hard. And then, even though I didn't want to, I whispered, "It's okay."

It didn't feel okay.

Even after Julia had moved on, screwing the cap back onto the nail polish, I still felt every word echoing.

Vague and unpleasant helplessness pulled me under. Was this it? Would this be the next four years of my life? If TMU didn't pan out, or if Julia talked me out of it and we ended up at the same school, would this same pattern continue forever?

I wasn't sure I could bear it.

I squirmed. Julia's hooks went deep, maybe deeper than I ever realized. When I let myself think about TMU—and somehow separating myself from Julia—it made me feel like maybe I didn't recognize myself. Did I know what I wanted?

And did I know what I'd be willing to do to get there?

THIRTY

After

I'm not used to being angry.

Or, at least, I'm not used to this kind of anger. I'd gotten used to the low simmer of desperate outrage at the universe, but this new fury is stabbing and reckless and entirely directed back at myself.

When Dillan doesn't show up for his usual morning coffee, I'm not sure if I'm disappointed or relieved.

Every time my thoughts wander to our argument, something tightens in the pit of my stomach. It's completely my fault, which makes it bad, and he has every right to be upset and want space, which makes it worse.

But now his absence drips unease down my spine. He might have midterms, but I feel weird that I don't know when they are, or what his classes are like. That's the sort of thing we used to tell each other.

I almost consider calling him on my break, but what would I say? I'm a terrible friend.

Without him here, I have nothing to distract myself from the slideshow of memories that have been flooding in since the party. Julia, face contorted in anger and hurt. Julia, laughing with people who weren't actually her friends at all. Julia, gone.

Gone. A shout into the darkness met with silence.

I suck in a breath.

I'd always thought my knee-jerk negative reaction toward parties was because of the night Julia died. It's only been occurring to me in slow increments that it might stem from nights before that. The Halloween party last year was a mess. That was the beginning of Julia and Dillan, and it only got worse from there.

I'm holding on to a tangle of truths and lies.

I believed so many stories.

I let her play me like a chess piece in her games.

I ask my shift supervisor if I can run through the task list instead of standing at the register. I must look awful, because she agrees without hesitation.

My hands are sweating. I swipe them reflexively on my jeans.

I can't block Julia's voice out. I can't stop hearing the things she used to say. I feel increasingly ill, the knowledge looming, and I can't stop it, and I'm thinking it even though I don't want to: Julia was wrong.

The way she treated me was wrong.

There's a part of me that whispers, *Liar, liar. She was a liar.*

I was a fucking marionette, and Julia is still pulling the strings, dictating what I think, what I do, and how I feel.

When I think about what she did, it makes me feel sick.

When I think about how it felt to look her in the eyes and know that she would never take ownership of any of it, I have to stop what I'm doing and count my breaths.

It makes that new anger leap to the surface. I've been furious for months, *years,* even. Rage sneaks up and wraps a slender tendril around everything, tying it down. It only speaks the language of permanence, and this awful, guilty, hot, burning fury won't give up without a fight.

I've been so stuck in the mire that I hadn't even noticed how sick I am of being angry. I'm sick of hurting, of wishing things had been different. I'm sick of the worst feeling of all: relief.

Sometimes, when I think that I'll never again have to find a way to untangle her words and reweave them so that they don't hurt me, I'm so relieved I could cry.

Then I remember why I'll never have to, what *I* did, and that's when I wish it had been me instead, because I know now what I didn't know then: I'm the same. I'm stitched together with the same thread, stuffed with the same carelessness, the same compulsion toward destruction. She didn't listen to the heart of what people said—

I don't listen. I think about Eve, and how she'd confessed that Julia had excluded her, and instead of even bothering to ask if she was okay, I made it about me.

Julia hurt people. I hurt people. Julia hurt me. I . . .

Julia hurt me. She's dead.

During my break, I check my phone. Nothing back from Dillan. That sours my mood even further, which I didn't think was possible.

I'm scrolling mindlessly through Instagram when I decide to do it.

The idea hits me all at once and out of nowhere in two separate instances, first in the vague but urgent: *Get out of here.* It's only a half second later that it formulates into something more substantial: *It's time to try again.*

Instinct tells me that I can't—shouldn't—and then it doubles back and tells me that I have to. The *shouldn't* is an echo of Julia's voice, and it's time that voice shut the fuck up.

It's as though my subconscious has been holding back all of these urgent desires, and now that I'm aware of them they come like a flood. I've been resistant to consider reapplying for months, but there's a folder on my computer that has everything ready to send. I compiled everything in a burst of motivation months ago: explanations about what happened, the essay I'd written . . .

I could do it tonight.

Applying doesn't mean I'm going.

My first instinct is to tell Dillan, which feels like a rock dropped into my gut. I miss him like I might miss a vital organ.

I call him again. This is probably my eleventh voicemail in the last several days, so after I listen to him cheerily instruct me to leave a message after the beep, all I say is "Dillan . . . please."

I decide right then, after I hang up. I'm going to do it tonight.

THIRTY-ONE

Before

The night before the presentation, I wound myself into an anxious frenzy.

Dillan's disappearing act was impressive. As much as I wanted to be angry with him—as much as Julia thought he deserved it—I couldn't find room for anything other than hurt.

I wanted to call him, ask if he was nervous too, but the idea of talking to him made me feel a little sick. The email he'd sent with his notes had been polite and professional, like we were business colleagues.

I hardly slept, though it was hard to tell whether that was from nerves or the fact that I couldn't stop worrying about Dillan.

He regretted the kiss, that much was clear, but how much longer was he going to avoid me? At first, I'd been surprised by how much I missed having him to joke around with. Now every text message that wasn't from him was a reminder that Dillan didn't feel the same way I did.

But was this it? Had I ruined everything?

Did I really *want* to be friends with him, if it was so easy to forget me and go after Julia? I'd seen him in the hall walking with her, his head turned in close. Julia had been nothing but honest about everything he was doing and saying—how he was hanging around her when I wasn't there, pestering her with questions, *flirting* with her—so it wasn't her I was worried about. Betrayal from *Dillan* was a knife that dug into bone. If he could do this, would he tell her my secret about TMU?

Julia had always told me I was too trusting. I just wanted to believe the best in people, even if it made me blind to the truth.

Because truth hurt.

The next day every period was a countdown to our presentation. All I could think about was how much fun we'd had preparing, and how spectacularly we'd crashed and burned at the end.

I'd forced my brother to sit through my half of the presentation, and he'd told me I didn't sound like a total asshole, so I knew it was okay.

When I sat down at my desk, my hands were shaking, and Dillan wasn't there. Julia and Eve were whispering, working through a pile of flash cards covered in Eve's messy handwriting.

For a second, I thought he wasn't going to show up, that he was going to abandon me to do the presentation on my own, but then he walked through the door and relief diffused through me. He didn't look my way, though.

Eve and Julia exchanged a tense look, and I stared down at the desk, letting my hair fall around me like a curtain.

I tried to even out the pulse tapping wildly in my neck. Class started in two minutes. My eyes burned. If I didn't get ahold of myself, I would cry right there. Breathe in. Breathe out. Count, one, two, three, four . . . I pinched the web of skin between my thumb and pointer finger.

I could do this.

Mr. Ambrose walked into the classroom, carrying his briefcase under one arm. He greeted us with a slight wave. "Afternoon, folks! Presentation day. Hope you're ready!"

I wasn't.

When I glanced over at Dillan, he gave me a tight smile and returned his attention to the front of the classroom.

Watching the other presentations was awful. At least I wasn't the only one nervous. Eve looked like she was about to pass out when she was in front of the class, and Julia carried the whole thing, even though I was sure she'd only done about five percent of the work.

Nate's presentation was the most fluid by far, but I could barely pay attention. Every part of me was counting down until it was my turn.

And then it was.

I hated every step up to the front of the classroom. It didn't help that Dillan didn't make eye contact with me until right before we started, and that made me lose my train of thought. I wondered if it made other people suspect something was wrong too, which only added to the tangle of nerves making a mess of my insides.

He introduced us, but I barely heard him.

Somehow I didn't miss my cue to start, and I only stammered once while reading through my first card.

Dillan was good in front of people. Not like Nate was, but it also didn't feel quite as staged. In the first two minutes, he made the entire class laugh.

My chest eased and then tightened again.

The whole presentation was a blur. I know it happened, because at the end Julia gave a thumbs-up, but I felt strangely detached.

As soon as it was over, Dillan stopped looking at me.

After listening to Mr. Ambrose's feedback, Dillan turned stiffly and walked to his seat, where he started doodling on the corner of his notebook. He didn't look over for the rest of the class, and as soon as the bell rang, he was the first out of the room.

Was I really *that* repulsive?

I swept my note cards into my backpack.

"Radford," Nate said. "Hey."

I blinked. "What?"

"I said, nice presentation."

I scrambled to zip my backpack. "Oh, uh, thanks. You too."

He offered me a perplexed smile as he turned and left.

"What was that about?" Julia asked me under her breath. "Nate is, like, all over you today."

"Yeah. I don't know." I wasn't sure that qualified as *all over*, but I didn't have the energy to argue.

She'd implied I was boy-crazy. About *Nate*? I'd prove to her I wasn't.

I sighed. "I'll meet you after your practice, okay? I have to do something."

If Julia was going to object, I didn't see, because I was out of my seat and after Dillan like a shot.

I caught up to him in the hallway. "Dillan—wait. Hold on—*please.*"

At that, he stilled.

I said, "I hate this. I hate it."

"What?"

"Come on." I crossed my arms, feeling immensely self-conscious. "You know what I mean."

He sighed. "I don't know what I'm supposed to say."

"Look, if you don't want to talk about it, that's—okay. That's fine. Just . . ." I trailed off.

He turned around, at last, and looked me in the eye.

I felt something in my stomach drop.

His eyes were very blue.

I couldn't look at him for long, so I lowered my gaze to the floor.

He said, "Just what?"

I could feel my confidence withering away. "I don't know. We were friends."

He crossed his arms. "Yeah. We *are* friends."

"Then—can you *not* ignore me? We don't have to talk about it. I just don't want to feel like it ruined everything."

"It didn't," he said simply, and started to walk away.

I caught hold of his arm. "Dillan."

He stopped, like my touch burned him.

When he turned around, his jaw was set. "Nora. It's okay. We can still be friends. You don't have to look at me like that. We don't have to talk about it."

What if I wanted to?

I swallowed, and said, "Okay."

Then he said, "Nice job, by the way. On the presentation. You didn't look nervous."

"I didn't?"

He nodded, and then smiled. It wasn't a real Dillan smile, but it was still a *smile*. "Yeah. You did really well."

"Oh. Well, thanks. So did you."

He let out a long breath. "So . . . do you want to walk with me to band?"

It was an olive branch, and we both knew it.

"Sure." Relief surged between every heartbeat as I matched my pace to his.

Maybe it would take a while, and maybe it wasn't what I wanted, but if we could get back to where we'd been before everything had gone horribly wrong, I could be happy with that.

I just hoped he could too.

THIRTY-TWO

After

When Dillan finally calls me back, I answer immediately. Dishwater drips down to my elbow. "Hello?"

"Hey." He sounds weary. "I, uh. I got your messages."

"Sorry." I wipe my hands on my jeans. "I got carried away."

"Are you free right now? Or—"

"Yes. Yeah, I'm free."

"Okay, good." He lets out a relieved huff. "I'm outside."

Something slots back into place between my lungs. *That's* Dillan. That's a Dillan sort of thing to do.

I let out a breathless laugh as I switch the phone to my other ear. "Okay. I'm coming out."

I don't even let him get out of the car, opening the passenger door and hurling myself into the seat, letting the door slam shut. "Where are we going?"

Dillan gives me a *look*. I'm not entirely sure what it means, but it feels significant. "Froyo?"

I lean my head back when I nod. "Okay."

There's a moment of silence before he starts the car in which neither of us looks at the other, and then we both start talking at once.

The words are stumbling and halted, and when we stop, it's clear neither of us has heard anything the other said.

Dillan lets out a shaky laugh and takes a deep breath. "I'm sorry for being a dick when you came over."

"No, *I'm* sorry. For everything. You were right about—all of it, really."

He starts the car and backs out of the driveway. "I didn't actually make plans without you. I couldn't stop thinking about that. It was a lie. I feel really bad for saying it."

I close my eyes, I'm that relieved. "Oh."

"It was just me and Angie and my parents," he says. "And they were asking why I hadn't invited you, and I told them I wanted it to be just family, but that felt stupid, because even if it were true, I'd still have wanted you there."

I might cry.

"Anyway." Dillan heaves a sigh. "Yeah. I overreacted, and I'm sorry."

"Dude." I open my eyes and punch his shoulder. "I was the asshole here, remember?"

"Well, yeah, sort of." He grins, and it's right then that it all feels okay again.

I shake my head. "I feel terrible for standing you up like that. I really don't know what came over me, but I hated thinking that I hurt you. I'm so sorry."

He tilts his head for a second. "Forgiven. Just . . . warn me if you're going to do that again."

"Never." I shake my head vehemently. "I'm *never* doing that again."

As we pull into the parking lot for the frozen yogurt place, he admits a little meekly, "I hated ignoring you."

"Me too."

"I don't want to do it again." He puffs out his cheeks as he lets out an exhale. "Ever."

Right then I sort of wish that Dillan and I were the kind of friends that hug. But we never have been. There's something in me that says *Careful,* and so I just smile at him. "I'm glad. I thought I was going to lose it."

I climb out of the car and follow Dillan inside.

As always, I make his froyo, and he makes mine. He's done a lot faster because I only like pistachio and Dillan likes a combination of every single flavor, and pulling all the levers takes forever.

Eventually, I slide his paper bowl across the table. "Have your . . . abomination."

"Hey." He shoots me an annoyed glance. "It's *good*. It's like, every spoonful is something new. If I *mix* it, then it's everything at once."

"It's *disgusting,* Dillan."

"Oh, fuck you," he says, but with affection. His face twists into a smile. "I was never going to mix it."

I roll my eyes and look at my bowl. Dillan made the froyo into a perfect spiral, and I flick off the tip with the tiny plastic spoon.

I consider telling him about my applications. It still feels a little surreal, but it's done. I hit submit, and they're in, and I have no idea what to expect, because my grades from my final semester after Julia died were terrible. But that's a problem for future Nora. For now . . .

When I look back up, his smile is gone, and his knee is bouncing. I eye him warily. "What's bugging you?"

He shakes his head. "Nothing."

I roll my eyes. "Come on."

At this, his mouth pulls into a wry smile, but it quickly fades. Then he's silent for a full minute.

Dillan is entirely incapable of concealing emotions. Usually, I can read him like a book, but right now I can't tell whether he's upset. He just looks like he's thinking.

At last, he asks, "Are you happy?"

His eyes are fixed on a poster on the wall.

I pause. "I haven't thought about it much. Why?"

He sighs. "Nora. I have to tell you something."

"What?"

"I'm going to Queen's."

I nod, frowning. "I know."

He lets out a slow breath. "In January."

At first, I think I've misheard him, but then I realize I've understood him perfectly and my chest goes concave. "You're . . . January?"

He nods. "I didn't want to tell you until I was sure you were, you know . . . okay."

I sit up straighter and cross my arms. "How long have you known?"

He shrugs. "A couple of months."

My jaw drops. *"Months?"*

"I'm going to visit in three weeks. Just to see what it's like. I found a bunch of people who are also starting in January, so we're meeting up to see the campus and get to know the city a little bit." He says this all in a rush, as though he's terrified to tell me. The same way I was terrified to tell Julia about TMU. "Term starts on January sixth."

My head is whirling. "So . . . you're leaving?"

He bites his lip and slouches down into the chair. Then he nods.

"Why are you only telling me this now?" I'm angry, though I don't realize it until I've already asked. "Did you think I'm so fragile that I couldn't handle it?"

"No!" Dillan exclaims, but he won't meet my eyes. "I just—"

"You just what?" I feel a lump forming in the back of my throat.

"I just wanted to make sure you were okay. I knew I could always push it back to September if you weren't."

"You're not supposed to be making major decisions like this around me!" My chest tightens. "Why would you do that?"

He sucks in a sharp breath. He's still not looking at me. When he speaks, his voice is quiet and miserable and full of pent-up frustration. "Nora."

It's one word.

It's just my name.

But the way he says it sounds like it physically hurts him, and some part of me understands.

The implication registers like a stone dropped into my stomach. I shake my head vigorously. "No."

He doesn't react. He still won't look at me. I see that his eyes are moving, reading and rereading the words on the poster across the room.

I'd be lying if I said this idea had never crossed my mind—of course it has, over and over, but I haven't been able to give it any weight. The idea that Dillan stuck around so faithfully because he's *interested* in me creates a rush of a thousand complicated emotions.

I clench my jaw. "This whole time?"

"I don't . . . want to talk about it." He picks at a tiny hole in his jeans. "I just wanted to make sure you were happy before I told you."

I look down. "What about Julia?"

"What *about* her?" Dillan asks, sounding frustrated. "She's gone."

My heart sinks. Right. Of course. That's why. This is *because* she's gone. It's not me, it's not anything that makes me special. But . . .

"Nora." He sounds wrecked.

My shoulders tense.

"You're my best friend first. Always. None of this is because of . . ." He pauses. "I'd never."

Misery wells up in me. It doesn't matter what he says right now, because all I can think about is the countless days and afternoons we've spent together. I was learning to be happy again. Was *he* happy?

None of this is fair.

"I'm not asking for anything," he says. "Obviously."

He's leaving. It's a hundred times worse now. It's a *thousand* times worse. I can think of a million questions all at once, but the only thing that comes out of my mouth is "Dillan."

He shakes his head. "I didn't mean to—I wasn't going to—that's not what I was going to say tonight. I was just going to tell you I was leaving early, and then that was going to be it."

"*Dillan.*"

"You don't . . . have to say anything."

I'm relieved. What is there to say?

At last, he looks at me, but as soon as he does, he shakes his head and his eyebrows draw together in a way that makes me think he'd rather be anywhere else.

I want to ask him about the kiss last year. I want to ask him what changed. He brushed me aside afterward like he never wanted to talk about it again, and then—and then *Julia*. It feels different now, but my questions are stuck inside and I don't even know where to start.

Right now, all I feel is horribly confused.

THIRTY-THREE

Before

There were a lot of nights in the last few weeks where I'd felt pretty awful, but none of them had been as bad as this one.

The worst part was that there was no real *reason*.

It was 10 p.m. I pressed the heels of my palms against my eye sockets. I wasn't going to sleep. Not like this.

I pulled out my phone and opened my last messages to Julia. Then I swiped back and opened a new message, my fingers hovering over the keyboard.

I texted Dillan, because I could. Because he'd offered me an olive branch. Because I wanted to.

> I kinda want to go get juice
> Do you want juice?

I had to wait less than a minute before his response buzzed in.

is that an invitation?

Maybe. You're the one with a car.

i want it on record that i know you're using me
for my sweet ride
for hydration purposes of all things

You drive a '91 Honda Civic & you named her
Gertie
You're calling that a sweet ride?

i am Deeply offended
you've hurt her feelings

...

gimme 10 minutes

I didn't need Dillan's message to know he was here. I heard the low rumble of an engine and slipped quietly out the front door without telling anybody I was going.

I expected it to be awkward. It was. Dillan didn't meet my eyes when I slid into the passenger seat, and when I muttered hi and thanks, he just made a noncommittal noise in the back of his throat.

My head fell back against the headrest as I let the day out between my teeth in a long breath, wondering if this had been a bad idea.

I was intensely aware of the fact that this was the first time we'd been alone together since I'd kissed him. The memory of it burned on my lips and behind my eyes every time I closed them.

Don't think about it. Don't think about the maybe. Don't think about the what-if.

I wondered if he was thinking about it too. What about the kiss did he regret?

I turned to look at him. "Hey."

He was already turning to back out of the driveway, but he stopped when we made eye contact. "Hi."

For a second, we just looked at each other, suspended in the moment. The kiss was playing on repeat in my head, and in a different moment, in an alternate version of me, maybe I would have just done it again. But the look on his face when he'd seen me in the hallway was fresher and hurt worse, so I didn't.

He backed out of the driveway.

"Safeway has the best juice."

"Shawnessy?"

"Yeah." I reached up to fiddle with the radio until I found a good song and turned it up.

"Where's Julia tonight?"

"Out of commission." I chanced a look at him, but he was looking at the road. "Why?"

"I'd have thought she'd be your first choice for a late-night juice run."

"I've never brought Julia on a juice run," I said.

His voice was a little quieter. "Consider me flattered."

We drove the rest of the way in thick silence.

I didn't break it until he'd pulled into a parking spot and taken the keys out of the ignition. "You still want to be friends, right?"

He looked a little annoyed, and I thought I saw his hand

tighten on the wheel. Then the annoyance was gone. "I'm here, aren't I?"

"I wasn't sure." I just opened the car door and got out, shutting it firmly behind me as I wrapped myself in my coat.

I let him walk in front of me as we crunched across the icy parking lot. My breath came in clouds of frost-mist, and when we walked inside, I couldn't stop shivering, even with warm air blasting from above.

"So, juice?"

I nodded, and he followed me to the juice aisle, a few steps behind. "It's only a good juice run if we get whatever is on sale. It's the rule."

"You make it sound like you go out specifically for juice often."

I twisted around, pretending to look surprised. "You don't?"

He rolled his eyes, but he was smiling as he peered down at the sale tag. Then he wrinkled his nose. "It's strawberry-kiwi."

"Gross."

"Right?"

"There's a reason it's on sale." I put my hand on the handle of the fridge. "It's because nobody is buying it, because anything strawberry-kiwi should be illegal."

"Or strawberry-banana."

I tilted my head, considering. "I concur."

"Well? Are you going to get it?"

"It's *strawberry-kiwi*." I looked at him in mock horror. "Also, I can't believe I'm agreeing with you on something food-related, you mustard-dipping heathen."

He grinned. "You'd break your own rule? Just like that?"

"Rules are only created in order to be broken." I stared at the juice, daring it to call me a liar.

"Damn. Would've thought you'd have stronger morals."

I pressed a hand to my chest. "Excuse *you*. I'm going to buy it just to prove you wrong."

I bought the juice, thinking vaguely hostile thoughts toward it. I knew I probably wouldn't drink it all, but it had sort of stopped being about the juice.

We stood by the doors for a second, looking out into the dark.

He asked, "Now what?"

"We drink the juice."

"The terrible juice that you bought to spite me."

"Yes."

"D'you want to just . . . sit in the car? Or drive around?"

I shrugged. "Up to you."

We climbed back into the car. He backed out of the parking spot and I didn't ask where we were going. I just cracked open the juice and tilted it back like I was dying of thirst.

It felt strange. Here I was, in the passenger seat beside a boy who'd rejected me, drinking juice I didn't like.

I asked the question before I could think about it for too long. "Why'd you leave the party so soon?"

Would he admit he'd been trying to hook up with Julia? Would telling me clear the air?

He didn't say anything for a long time. The glow from the streetlight spilled across his face, disappeared, and reignited in a hypnotic rhythm. If he knew I was watching him so carefully, he didn't let on.

Then he just said, "I was tired."

I wasn't sure what I had wanted him to say. Not that.

He held his hand out for the bottle, and I passed it to him, careful that our hands didn't touch, trying not to think how it was a kiss by extension. He tipped it back, swallowed, and shuddered a little. "Gross. Why'd you really want to get juice?"

I didn't have to stop and think about whether or not I was going to tell him the truth: I already knew I was. "I don't feel right."

He didn't say anything as he handed the bottle back.

I clasped it to my stomach. "Things are weird with me and Julia."

He nodded.

"It feels like things have been weird for a long time."

"She really supports you, you know," he said. "She's . . . something else."

"Was she that bad at the party?"

"At the . . . ? Oh." He nodded. "I mean . . . yeah."

"I'm sorry," I said, and I pulled my jacket higher up around my neck. "I didn't ask her to do that."

I didn't tell him I knew about the flirting. I just couldn't picture it. Dillan hadn't even flirted with *me*. He'd just sort of existed until being around him made me feel like I was going to explode.

He shrugged. "I figured. Plus, she was sort of right. It was a dick move for me to ignore you like that."

"That's what she told you?"

"Among other things."

My stomach bottomed out. I pressed my index finger against the window until it was so cold that I couldn't feel it anymore. Then I lightly rested it against my temple where my pulse was throbbing. "I'm sorry she did that. I don't need her to fight my battles."

"Your battles?"

"That was a weird way to put it." I shifted in my seat. It

didn't matter how I sat, I couldn't get comfortable, like there was something wrong in my bones. "Not . . . my battles. I don't know. She gets involved even when I don't ask her to."

"She's got an interesting grasp on boundaries, that's for sure." Dillan shifted toward me. "Actually, I was talking to Eve the other day. . . ."

I kept looking at the road. "Oh?"

"We were both—I guess we're sort of worried."

The idea that Dillan and Eve were discussing me felt strange. What did she know about what happened? I cleared my throat. "About?"

His eyes were serious. "She told me she and Julia didn't get along, at first."

Understatement of the century.

"She didn't give me any details, and you don't have to either, but she said—she said Julia lied to you about her."

"She was looking out for me," I said, resolute, even though the memory made my stomach tighten. "Julia knows me better than anyone else. She thought she was protecting me. She's had my back, always."

"I thought you just said things were weird."

"They are," I said. "But not *that* weird. Why are you worried?"

"I don't know," Dillan said, but it didn't sound true.

It occurred to me right then that I didn't really know him at all.

I sighed. "Maybe it's stupid. It's just a gut feeling that something is off. That happens sometimes. It usually goes away."

Dillan asked, "Are your gut feelings usually right?"

I couldn't look at him. *He'd* been a gut feeling. "I'm not so sure anymore."

THIRTY-FOUR

After

"Oof," Eve says, letting out a low breath. "You didn't say it was going to be a shrine."

"I didn't know," I tell her, stepping into the room.

I called Eve to ask if she would come. She was silent for so long, I almost thought she'd hung up on me.

"I wasn't sure you were serious," she said.

"Please," I whispered, feeling sick and guilty even as I asked. "I can't go alone."

Julia's room is the same as the last time I was in here, except now there are boxes *everywhere*. It's like anything that could conceivably remind the Hoskinses about Julia has been squirreled away. I remember the first time I came over here a few months after, and every photo of her had been taken down. I hated it.

Eve steps past me, toeing aside a box of school supplies. "Holy shit. This is a lot."

"I know."

I walk into the center of the room and turn in a slow circle. In any other version of this moment, Julia could be here. She could be *right* here, or at her desk, or standing under the strip of LED lights she'd fastened to her ceiling.

I sit on the bed, tugging listlessly at a shoebox full of knick-knacks. Every single one of them is a stab of memory: Julia and me making friendship bracelets at the summer camp my brother worked at; the first tiny plastic soccer trophy she ever won and how she jumped up and down; a set of CDs we burned together the first year we were friends with Eve.

And a photo.

My stomach plummets. When I reach for it, my fingers shake, and for a second I think I'm wrong, that it's not what I think it is, but then I recognize Dillan's hair.

I'd thought I would never see this again. I had no idea she'd made a physical copy of it. I turn it over. On the back it says:

For Julia
—M

It was true.

"What are you looking for?" Eve asks me from across the room.

I shove the photo back in the box. I don't want her to see. Maybe if nobody but me sees, it will make it less real. My heart pounds. "I don't know."

She walks over and sits next to me. "You holding up okay?"

I'd thought this would help, but I didn't know what exactly

I thought I needed help with. Whatever it was, being here isn't bringing any lightning bolts of clarity.

Haltingly, I shake my head.

We don't stay long after that.

There's nothing I want to keep. Especially not that photo. Remembering any of this makes me feel like I'm about to puke. The idea of forgetting is worse. In the end I don't take anything at all.

"Come on," Eve says when we get outside and I just stand there. "Let's go."

It starts to snow while she's driving, and I pick at my cuticles and look anywhere but at the road.

Eve drives us to her house.

I close my eyes and absorb Eve's home: warm, brightly lit, smelling like coriander and turmeric. Ordinarily, it's louder, but today we're the only ones here.

Eve grabs a jar from the kitchen and leads me down the hall to her bedroom, where she sits on the bed and gestures for me to join her.

When I do, she doesn't ask questions, just offers me a piece of Sri Lankan milk toffee from the jar, and waits.

Sweetness bursts on my tongue, and I'm relieved for the moment it allows me to compose myself. I'm trying to figure out what to say when I get two texts from Dillan. The second one makes my chest squeeze.

> i'm still taking angie to studio bell tomorrow
> you don't have to come

I tap out a reply.

I look up from my phone. At long last, I formulate words. "When did Julia start to care about Dillan?"

There's a brief silence after I ask.

Eve frowns. "Care?"

"She cared," I say. I'm not quite ready to tell Eve everything I know. If I talk about it out loud I might actually throw up. "She hated the idea of us together."

"She was jealous, wasn't she? You started choosing him."

But I know this already. Julia's expression in the moments right before she died is etched into my brain.

My eyes catch on the little wooden elephant statue on Eve's desk, and I stare at it. "Friendships aren't about *choosing*. It was never her or him. I was friends with them both."

Even as I'm saying it, doubt creeps in.

Eve tucks her feet underneath her. "Yeah, but she wasn't like that. Julia didn't like to share."

There's a stone in my chest. It's always been there, but now I'm precisely aware of the size and shape and weight of it. It's true. Julia wasn't like that. I might have been able to forge close friendships with multiple people, but Julia had a singular focus.

The elephant statue blurs.

Eve laughs, and I'm startled by how bitter she sounds. "You know she only ever talked to me when she couldn't talk to you?"

I stare at her.

"Yeah. Did you notice that she never wanted to come over here? We were always either at her house, or yours. She and I never did anything together unless you were busy, or you guys were fighting or something. I was always lesser. Always."

The gravity of her confession sucks me downward. "I didn't know."

"I know." Her voice goes soft. "That was never your fault. I just wanted her to need me the way she needed you. I guess she was sort of electric that way, you know?"

I do know. Julia had a way of making you feel more than alive. Like you were everything.

"But I knew she never would." Eve swallows. "She *was* a little racist. I'd never be on the same level as the two of you, and some part of me knew she was the sort of person who would out me."

I don't deny it. Just the thought is a sick ache.

"You know she told me you guys had decided not to go to that party?"

When I stare at her blankly, she rubs her temple.

"The one at the beginning of the year. I saw her Instagram story where she was in some guy's hot tub, when just earlier that day she'd told me you both had decided to cool it before school started." She makes circles on the comforter with her thumb. "And it *hurt*, obviously, but I didn't say anything about it, because I *never* said anything."

"I had no idea," I whisper. "She told me you bailed."

She laughs. It's a tight, bitter sound. "Of course she did."

I bite down on my lip.

"Whatever." Eve sighs. "Look, it was horrible, and I'm sorry it all happened the way it did."

"I'm sorry," I tell her.

She just looks at me.

"I am," I say. "I never meant to exclude you."

"I know," she says. There's a moment of silence before she adds, "Forgiven."

I let out a breath. My eyes burn. "No."

She blinks.

"No," I repeat. "I'm sorry for more than just not seeing it. I wish I'd stood up for you more. I wish I'd disagreed with Julia more. Out loud, I mean."

She nods.

"And then when you tried to tell me about how hurt you'd been, I just steamrolled over you and asked you to come help me with Julia's stuff when I knew it would hurt. . . . I'm so sorry."

Eve relaxes. For a moment, all she says is "Aw, Nora."

I wait.

"I forgive you," she says, and her eyes are a little glassy. "Of course I forgive you. I know what she was like, and you've been through a lot."

"That doesn't excuse—"

"I know," she says, wiping at her eye. "But I know you mean it. So, yeah. I forgive you."

I deflate.

"Ugh, emotions." Eve gives her head a little shake. "Gross. Anyway, I'm changing the subject now."

I let out a wobbly laugh. "Okay."

"Did anything ever happen with Nate?"

I surprise myself as much as I surprise Eve when I burst into tears.

"Oh, shit." She sits up straight. "Nora, I'm sorry, I didn't think—"

"I'm fine," I say, scrubbing at my eyes. "I am, really, I just . . ."

"What happened?"

"He's an asshole. We drove to this park, and—and he kissed

me, and it was nice, but then I couldn't stop thinking about Julia and what she would say, and I totally freaked out."

Eve has never seen me when I get really bad about Julia. Only Dillan has. But she reaches for a tissue and waits for me to keep talking. Eve is a good friend. A *true* one.

"I don't even know what was wrong with me," I tell her, after I blow my nose. "Is she going to run my life forever?"

Eve touches my hand. "No. No, she isn't."

I suck in a deep, shuddering breath. "He didn't even say goodbye."

That's not what I'm upset about, and we both know it.

Eve shakes her head.

"It's fine," I say. "I didn't even like him."

"I'm sorry he turned out to be a dick."

"Boys," I say, wiping my eyes, and she laughs.

I'm desperate to talk about anything else, so I let out the deep breath I'd been holding and lie back on her bed.

"What about you?" I ask. "What's happening in your love life? Got your eye on anybody?"

If I didn't know her so well, I'd probably miss the deliberate way her gaze shifts to her phone before she shrugs. "Not really."

I reach up and shove her shoulder. "Who is she?"

Eve raises her eyebrows as a dark flush creeps across her neck. "Uh, no one?"

I wait.

"It wasn't anything serious. Just a one-night thing." Her eyes dart toward me and then away again.

"*Who?*"

She shakes her head. "It doesn't matter. It wasn't anything."

"Do I know her?"

She just flushes even darker. "I will not be taking further questions at this time."

"Oh my God. Eve. Do I know her?"

She shakes her head. "Talk about something else."

I'm grateful for Eve. I don't think many other people would stick around the way she has. When I tell her that, she ducks her head.

"Aw, man. That makes me sound better than I am." She reaches over and tugs lightly on a piece of my hair. "You're easy to stick around for."

"Thanks for coming today," I whisper.

She just nods.

THIRTY-FIVE

Before

The next day at lunch, when I stopped by my locker, I was surprised to find Eve waiting for me, hunched over like she was in pain.

"Hey." I slid my backpack off my shoulder. "Are you okay?"

She was worrying her bottom lip. "You guys teamed up against me?"

"What?" I stared at her, eyes wide. "Who? Me and Julia? We haven't—"

"Not you and Julia," Eve spat. "You and *Dillan*."

I blinked, then repeated, *"What?"*

"Tell me," Eve said, eyes shining, "why somebody in art asked if it was true that I'm gay."

My mouth dropped open.

"She said she heard from somebody else, who heard from somebody else who heard it from Dillan. So basically, he told, and now it's going around the school."

"Dillan wouldn't do that." I shook my head. "He wouldn't. I mean, his parents—"

"That's what I thought!" Eve scrubbed away a tear. "I trusted him, and I trusted you!"

"Why do you think *I* had anything to do with this?"

"You two are as thick as thieves, aren't you? You're the only two people I told."

It felt suddenly as though we were standing on opposite sides of a glass wall. I hadn't told Eve about the kiss, or anything that had happened after it. "I *just* saw him the other night, he wouldn't—"

"See? That's what I'm talking about. Julia told me that you and Dillan are—or were, whatever—some kind of item, so you had to have known he was going to—"

"I *didn't!*"

"For all I know," Eve said, then swallowed hard and had to start again. "For all I know, you could've been telling people too."

I stepped back. "Do you really think I would do that?"

"Your name got dropped with Dillan's," Eve said. "I don't know what to think anymore."

Then, abruptly, she turned and walked away.

I called after her, "Wait—Eve! I *didn't.*"

She just kept walking.

• • •

After school, I was sitting with Julia in her car, waiting for the parking lot to empty out.

I shifted in my seat to face her. "Did you hear the rumors?"

Julia looked out the windshield. "What rumors?"

"About Eve."

"Oh, that she's a dyke?"

"Julia!"

"What?"

"That's offensive! It's a slur."

She scoffed. "It's not a slur."

"Yes, it *is*. At least, *you* can't say it."

"Fine, then she's . . . into girls. She's gay. A lesbian. Whatever," she said loftily.

I let air out between my teeth and sank into my seat. She almost sounded *angry*.

"Do you think it's true?"

I looked out the window. "I don't know."

"You'd tell me if she'd talked to you about it, right?"

I sighed. "It wouldn't be my secret to share."

"She hasn't even said *anything* to me," Julia said, and there it was again, that bite of anger. "Eve's my friend too."

Eve's face swam in front of me every time I closed my eyes. Hurt. Betrayed. She'd accused *me* of outing her. She'd accused Dillan. None of that made sense.

Words my mom had spoken years ago echoed in my head.

She's angry. It doesn't matter if it makes sense to you. Just give her time.

Mom had been talking about Julia then, but it felt like it applied now, too.

That fight had also been about Eve, actually. It was our last big one. We'd argued since then, but not like that. I'd almost walked away from Julia entirely, but Mom had talked me out of it, saying everyone deserved a second chance.

You're a liar, I'd shouted at Julia. *How could you?*

Julia had just stared at me.

Now Julia flipped down the sun visor and examined her reflection. "But what if she *is* gay? Wouldn't that be sort of weird?"

"What? No! Why would it be weird?"

"We've had sleepovers together!"

"Just because she might like girls doesn't automatically mean she likes either of us." I rolled my eyes. "Julia. Don't make it a big deal."

"I'm not making it a big deal. It *isn't* a big deal. I can't believe she was so upset."

I stared. "You talked to her?"

"Not yet. I heard from somebody else that she was freaking out in the bathroom, but I couldn't find her."

"She got outed," I reminded her gently. "That part is a big deal. This is a really hard thing for anyone to go through."

"I'm a minority, too," Julia pointed out. "I know what it's like."

I closed my eyes. "Women make up half the population, Julia."

"I guess." She started the car. "I just can't believe she would keep it from us. If it is true."

"She doesn't owe us anything." I sighed and opened my eyes, shaking my head, as Julia started to back out of the spot.

Someone smacked the trunk as she nearly backed into them.

"Watch it," I hissed, gripping the seat.

"I *know*," she growled. "I have eyes."

Then use them.

I bit down my retort and simmered, wondering about Eve. It just didn't make sense. Why would Dillan out Eve? He *wouldn't*.

But if he hadn't started the rumor, who had?

THIRTY-SIX

After

The day I go with Dillan to Studio Bell for the second time, it's sunny.

For a split second, when Angie sees me walking onto the train platform and waves, grinning widely, I think everything might be okay.

But Dillan's smile doesn't quite meet his eyes, and my hope dissolves.

As I buy my ticket, I think about the way he said my name. My fingers feel robotic. *Nora.* All misery.

Since the other night I've been doing my best not to think about it. Of course, that's not working particularly well, because all I can think about is Julia, and the damn photo, and the way Dillan looked at me that day in the hallway.

I'm not thinking it, but I know what I'm feeling.

Who do I go to first with news? Who do I call at night when I need someone? It's not even a question. It's never been a question. It's always been Dillan. Even before Julia died.

My heart clamors. Uncertain, certain.

When I reach them, I shove my hands into my pockets to ward off the sharp, cold air. "We cool?"

He just nods. "Yeah. We're cool."

It doesn't feel true yet.

The overhead speaker blares for us to stand behind the yellow line as the train snakes slowly into the station.

When we get on, Angie sits with me, and Dillan sits alone on the other side of the aisle. Normally I wouldn't even notice, but it feels deliberate that he's left space between us.

The moment I *finally* let myself think it, everything feels ugly in just the same way it's lovely. The sunlight filters through Dillan's eyelashes, caught, bright, as he looks down at the floor, his knee bouncing.

I'm instantly aware of everything: the rumble of the tracks as the train hurtles forward, the tinny music from the headphones of the girl in front of us, his hands, his *hands*.

He's got freckles spattered across his knuckles, fingers long and slender, drumming a rhythm on his knee. Something sharp sticks behind my ribs. I find his hands bewilderingly interesting, like I could consider them for hours, like maybe the existence of Dillan's knuckles in the sunlight is somehow connected to the way my heart feels trapped higher in my chest than it should be.

It's the truth all at once, and I keep it hidden, and I don't look at it, and then I do, and I think it and it's stark and unrepentant and true:

I'm in love with Dillan.

Maybe I've always been. I've been loving him for so long I

forgot what it meant, stuck in the space between not-allowed and not-wanted and not-certain. I'd told myself to stop loving him so often that I believed I had.

But loving someone isn't about the butterflies and the sweaty hands and the lurching agony of wondering.

Loving someone is about calling them first. It's hearing a joke and thinking they'd laugh. It's listening to a song and knowing, without even having to ask, that they'd love it. It's wanting to be around them more than wanting to be alone.

I can't keep looking at him. I look away, at the buildings racing by. My heartbeat matches the rhythm of the tracks beneath.

I hear Angie chattering, and I hear Dillan responding, but I don't hear the words. One question whirls through my head. *What now?*

When we get off the train, Dillan gives me an odd look. He catches my shoulder, but then lets go like I've burned him. "You okay?"

I keep looking ahead. "Sure."

It's funny that we're back at Studio Bell. It's funny that this realization is happening here. Except it isn't funny at all, and I have to consciously remind myself how to breathe. I wonder if he's thinking about the last time we were here too. Every moment of it is playing on repeat.

I don't let myself look at him as we walk through the front doors or as we buy our tickets, voices echoing under the arched ceiling. I don't let myself look at him as he guides Angie toward the conference room where they've set up an exhibit of brightly colored interactive booths.

I don't look at him as he pushes her toward the middle, where a group of kids has already gathered around a woman using a puppet to talk about music, and I definitely don't look at him as he settles next to me, leaning against the wall, hands in his pockets.

And then I steal a glance, and it's a mistake, because once my eyes have landed on his face, a dozen memories fly by like a film: Dillan signing my cast with careful deliberation the week after the funeral, me writing *Nora's Song* at the top of his paper, the countless late-night drives as I got used to being back inside a car, watching him laugh, the look on his face after I stood him up at the theater, the way his hand ghosted across my cheek when I kissed him, his hair in the photo Julia showed me. It's too much, and I excuse myself to go to the bathroom, but once I'm there I just look at myself in the mirror like maybe I'll finally see something about myself that I'd forgotten.

It seems so obvious now. Dillan isn't my best friend but nothing else, he's my best friend and *everything* else.

I don't know how long I stay in there. It might be ten minutes; it might be thirty.

When I finally make my way back to the conference room, the woman isn't speaking anymore, and Dillan and Angie aren't there.

I check my phone. A one-word text from Dillan.

upstairs

I find them in the stairwell. Neither of them sees me yet.

Dillan watches Angie with immense fondness as she reads from a large poster, dragging her index finger along and stopping to sound out the big words.

When she reaches the end, she whoops and leaps toward

him with a force that nearly knocks him over. After he sputters his indignation, he catches her by the waist and hoists her over his shoulder, though it seems to take significant effort.

Angie laughs like being upside down is the funniest thing on the planet.

"You're a menace," he tells her, but he doesn't look annoyed, only amused. She kicks her legs and shrieks with glee.

Dillan laughs and sets her back down when she lets out a second ear-splitting screech, glancing over his shoulder. His face lights up when he sees me, and a moment later something shifts and his smile dampens ever so slightly. He turns back to Angie. "Hey. Inside voice, remember?"

She claps a hand over her mouth.

Dillan filtering parts of himself around me makes me physically ill.

It feels like nothing else matters. Nothing Julia said matters, nothing about the past matters. There's just now.

I have the urge to reach out and grab his hand, or even to walk over and wrap my arms around him, but I resist. I want to do it right. Besides, Angie is here.

He quirks an eyebrow. "Where'd you go?"

"Bathroom," I tell him. "Stomachache."

When I reach them, I ruffle Angie's curls, and she giggles.

I think, *Everything is different.* But that's not true. It's not different. The way Angie looks up at me and grins is the same. The way Dillan tells a joke and we laugh is the same.

I think, *Everything is the same,* but that's not true either. The way my stomach flips when he looks at me is not the same.

I don't get it right until the third try.

Everything is more.

THIRTY-SEVEN

Before

By the end of the week, thinking about TMU made me feel sick. Technically my essay was finished, and I'd had an encouraging meeting about it with Mr. Ambrose, but what if I didn't get in? What if I *did* get in? What if I told Julia and she decided not to forgive me? It wasn't like she'd kill herself over it.

Right?

I stared down at my journal, where my notes from the meeting were staring back up at me. Just a few tweaks and I'd be done, which was good, because it was due tomorrow.

"What are you working on?" Julia asked, shifting in her perch on top of my kitchen counter. "Application stuff?"

I snapped my journal shut. "Um. No."

Julia squinted at me. "You've started, though, right?"

For a moment, it was tempting to just lie. But historically, lying to Julia didn't have a promising success rate. So I rubbed my nose with the end of my pencil, praying she hadn't seen what I was looking at. Not that I was really worried. Even Julia—who knew all my passcodes to everything and proofread my texts before I sent them—knew my journal was off-limits. "Not yet."

Julia frowned. "Why not?"

"I don't know. I'm just still thinking."

"What is there to think about?" she asked, eyes trained on me, laser-focused.

"Nothing."

She obviously didn't believe me, but I was spared the agony of being interrogated by her phone buzzing on the counter.

Dillan.

I blinked at it.

Julia had her message previews turned off, so I couldn't see what the message said, but his name was right there.

I hadn't spoken to him since Eve had talked to me the other day, and he hadn't tried to reach out. What did that mean?

Could it be true? Could he really have outed Eve?

I cleared my throat. "Why is Dillan texting you?"

Julia let out a tight laugh and picked up her phone. "Do you care?"

"Should I?"

"I thought you guys weren't friends anymore."

"I never said that."

She wrinkled her nose. "I thought he rejected you."

"Wow. Nice, Jules. Thanks a lot."

"Nora. I didn't mean it like that. I just didn't know you guys were still hanging out."

"I didn't say that, either."

"Jeez, cryptic much?"

"He's my friend. Or he *was*."

"Didn't he out Eve?"

I thought I might cry. Sometimes talking to Julia made me feel like I was going insane. It didn't help that all our conversations lately seemed to devolve into something unpleasant.

Julia swung her legs over the edge of the counter so she faced me and stared at me for what felt like a moment too long.

Then she said, "I'm sorry."

"For what?"

She shrugged. "I didn't know you liked him that much."

I looked down at the tile and curled my foot. "I didn't either. It snuck up on me."

Julia sighed. Then she slid off the counter and held her arms out.

I hesitated to see if she was kidding. But she wasn't, so I opened my arms and rested my head on her shoulder. She smelled like a sleepover, which made my eyes burn.

"It'll be okay," she said gently.

I didn't realize I was crying until I was making her shirt wet. I pulled away, embarrassed, but she just repeated, "It'll be okay."

I hoped she was right.

THIRTY-EIGHT

After

I'm sitting on the couch in the dark, blanket wrapped around me. Lately it's too confining in my room, and if I can't sleep and I know I'll have to get up in a few hours anyway, I'll just sit in the living room until I either doze off or I've thought myself into a stupor.

Tonight feels more like the latter. I'm thinking about Dillan, which means that in a roundabout way I'm thinking about Julia and trying not to think about the two of them together.

I know what I want with Dillan. I want to kiss him again like I mean it. I want to ask him a hundred questions. I want to keep having movie nights forever, but now I want to lean against him and rest my head on his shoulder.

The idea that he's leaving in two months is a punch to the gut.

I wonder when it changed for him. After I kissed him last year, he acted like I'd mortally offended him, like it was too much to even *look* at me. And then there was the secret about Julia. Now he's pushed back going away to school for an entire semester, just to be here.

For me.

We never talked about university in the months after the accident. We didn't really talk about anything at all. He would come over, and we would watch movies until I fell asleep. He let me be silent and sad because that's what I needed. It's probable that he had applied and gotten into Queen's, and then pushed it back without ever saying anything. I can only speculate, though, so I'll have to ask him when I talk to him.

When I talk to him.

The idea sends a thrill up my spine. What am I going to say?

Hey, remember when you sort of said you liked me, and I didn't say anything at all? Let's revisit that conversation.

I close my eyes. I can see him looking at me, wary and uncertain. I'll look at him, and maybe reach over and touch his shoulder. I'll fight with my subconscious because it's screaming *Not allowed not allowed not allowed.* And I'll remind myself that it is.

When I check my phone, I'm surprised to see missed texts from Mrs. Hoskins.

> Took some of Julia's stuff to a storage unit.
> Thought of you. Hope you're well.

I'm not going to respond. My mom would tell me I should, but my mom does a lot of things because she *should.*

My mom and Julia's mom weren't exactly friends, even when Julia was alive. They were friends because we were, in the sort of way that meant they got along, but only because they had to. My mom used to make this face sometimes when Mrs. Hoskins would say things. I realized later that it was her *Well, I guess she gets it somewhere* face.

She wore it when she heard Mrs. Hoskins talking about a diet she and Julia were trying, and when Mrs. Hoskins barely acknowledged Julia in front of people and then wouldn't notice as Julia's eyebrows spiked inward and down. Julia's mom was always so worn out and busy she hardly had anything left over to give to Julia. When Mrs. Hoskins got a new job our freshman year, she practically vanished. By then, we weren't little kids anymore. I saw who she really was—somebody so focused on chasing success that she forgot her job was also to be there for Julia.

And maybe I made it my job to do it when her mom didn't. I remember hating her a little. Before, it was because she sometimes acted like Julia didn't exist. After, it was because she sometimes acted like she *never* had. It wasn't easy to hate her, either, because she wasn't always like that. Sometimes she was warm, and soft, and sometimes Julia loved her desperately and sometimes she didn't.

In any case, I don't think I have any hate left in me.

My phone buzzes again, and my stomach clenches, but when I look, it's not from Mrs. Hoskins.

It's from Kayla.

dillan asked me out

I stare at the text for several seconds.
I squeeze my eyes shut. My phone buzzes again.

cool with you?

The remaining air in my lungs vanishes. A million thoughts are hurtling against my skull, and it *hurts*.

It's the kiss all over again.

I thought—I *thought*—

I've been an idiot *again*.

What am I supposed to say? No?

I can barely move my fingers, but I text back:

> Go for it

The moment I send the text, all I feel is a *waterfall* of regret. How else could I have responded? It's not like I have a claim on him. I can't fault him for this. I want him to be happy.

I thumb back over and stare at the message from Mrs. Hoskins until I don't feel anything anymore, until all that's left is the same thing that's been there for the last year.

I am very tired.

THIRTY-NINE

Before

Submitting the essay wasn't nearly as dramatic as I'd thought it would be. One click at the end of hours of work.

At least because I'd submitted everything else already, I wouldn't have to wait long to hear back.

Early acceptance. The thought was enough to send a shiver through me.

"So. Have you made any more progress on the application?"

My stomach tensed. "What?"

Julia and I were walking to my house the morning after I'd submitted. Her car was out of commission for the week because she'd backed it into a pole. I curled my fingers inside my mittens and shoved them into my pockets. It had snowed properly the night before, and we were skidding on the icy sidewalk.

"McGill," Julia said, sounding cross.

Oh. I let out a breath. "Yeah, a little."

"When are you sending it in?"

"Soon," I said.

Eventually, I thought, we'd have to have this conversation. I just didn't want it to be now.

Beside me, Julia pressed her mouth into a tight line.

We walked up the driveway to the side door, and I wrestled with my lanyard in my pocket.

"How soon is soon?" Julia asked.

Frustrated, I ripped my mitten off and ignored the stinging cold as I shoved the key into the lock. "I don't know. Soon. I promise. It's not like I'm not going to."

A lie, maybe. At this point, I didn't know.

When I finally got the door open, we nearly tripped over each other trying to get in. I slammed it behind us.

After several minutes of stamping feet, Julia said, "Sometimes"—she blew on her hands—"it feels like you don't even want to go to McGill."

There it was. My perfect opening.

I swallowed.

And I couldn't do it.

"I want to," I said. "I've just got lots on my mind."

Julia followed me into the kitchen. "Like what?"

I shrugged. "You know. Homework. Eve, the Dillan thing . . . lots of things."

When I started making tea, Julia backed off. I knew she'd bring it up again later, but we were always quiet for this part. It was a ritual, and I liked it. Scroll through Instagram while waiting for the water to boil, prepare the mugs, pour the water. Black for me, milk for Julia. The simplicity of it soothed my nerves.

When I handed a mug to her, though, she looked troubled. And not like she had when we were talking about McGill. As though there was something else bothering her.

"What? Too much milk?"

She shook her head. "No. It's . . ."

I leaned against the cabinet. "What's up?"

She bit her lip, and when she spoke, she turned away from me, knocking her ankle bone lightly against the wall. "Since we're being honest, I need to tell you something."

"What?"

"I just—I'm worried that if I don't tell you, no one else is going to."

"Julia." I turned to her, alarmed. "What's going on?"

"It's not a big deal." Julia didn't look at me. "It was just something I heard Dillan saying."

I felt like somebody had poured a bucket of ice water over my head. "What did he say?"

She looked down at the ground. "Well— He was just . . . I'm sure it was nothing."

"*What?*"

"He was talking about you, so I stopped to listen in. Maybe I shouldn't have."

I felt a little like throwing up. "*What did he say?*"

Julia crossed her arms and looked out the window. "He was sort of . . . making fun of you."

My heart stopped. "He was what?"

"Do you want to know?"

I couldn't speak.

She told me before I could answer. "It wasn't about you guys kissing, or anything. It was just more like . . . general."

I could feel my heart again. It was beating in my eyelid.

"He was joking around with some kids in band. They were asking if you guys were an item, and he was like, *no,* not really. And when they asked him why he said it's because you were sort of . . . dumb."

I blinked.

"And that you were fun to hang around with, but that it was mostly a joke, and—"

"Julia, *stop.*"

She stopped, staring at me. "What?"

"Why are you telling me this?"

"I thought it was my job. Shouldn't you know if someone isn't really your friend?"

I put my mug on the counter and took a deep breath. If I told Julia every bad thing I heard people say about *her,* she'd be apoplectic.

"I just want you to know." Julia paused. "I'll always be there. When other people disappoint you, I'll always be loyal."

"Thanks," I said, uncertain.

"Just remember, I was there when no one else was."

I knew she meant it to be reassuring, but it sort of sounded like a threat.

She pulled her phone out of her pocket and swiped at a notification, typing with one thumb while her other hand curled around the mug.

I watched her for a long time. Would Dillan have said that? If he could do something like that, could he also have outed Eve?

I gave my head a shake. What was going on? Julia had lied to me before, but she *knew* how important this was to me, and besides, she'd changed since eighth grade. She wouldn't lie now, not after it had almost cost us our friendship once before.

Julia let out a soft snort.

"What?"

When she turned her phone screen around, she was showing me a list of somebody's Instagram followers.

I looked at her blankly.

"Eve unfollowed Dillan," she said.

A pang of dismay tore through me. Thinking about Eve getting outed made my chest hurt. I would never do that to a friend. I'd never do that to *anyone*.

Would Dillan? *Why?*

My gut told me something wasn't right here. *Something was wrong.*

I hadn't outed Eve.

I couldn't imagine Dillan had either.

That didn't make *any* sense.

Julia had been so nonchalant about it. Even the way she'd asked—*Didn't he out Eve?*—had felt like it almost didn't matter.

Several puzzle pieces slotted into place.

Julia tilted her head at me. "You okay?"

"Fine," I said, even though my heart was beating in my throat.

Julia had said Eve hadn't talked to her about being queer. *Didn't he out Eve?*

Eve had thought Dillan was behind the rumors, and I only knew that because she had told me.

But I hadn't told Julia. So how did she know? A real journalist would find out.

"Why were you looking at Dillan's followers?" I asked, as casually as I could.

She shrugged. "I was curious. Cyberstalking."

"How did you know he was the one behind the rumors?"

Julia blinked. "What?"

"I didn't tell you that," I pointed out.

"People tell me things," Julia said smoothly, then crossed her arms, leaning against the counter. "You know that."

"Who told you?"

"Why are you interrogating me about this?" Julia asked. "I don't remember who told me. People tell me all kinds of secrets."

I took a deep breath. Now or never. "Was it you?"

Julia stared at me. "Was what me?"

"Did you start the rumor about Eve?"

I'd seen Julia surprised before, but never like this.

"Who do you think I am?" she asked. "You really think I'd do something like that?"

Yes.

I shook my head. "No—of course not. I'm just paranoid. On her behalf."

"What the hell is your problem?" Julia asked. "Come on. Seriously."

"I just wondered how you knew, because *I* didn't tell you."

"You're not the center of the universe," Julia snapped. "I have friends that aren't you, Nora."

"I'm not saying you don't!" I objected, helpless. How had this turned around so quickly? "I'm just asking!"

"Don't you trust me?"

I stared at Julia and she stared back at me. "Yeah," I said, at last. "I trust you."

"I look out for my friends. Didn't I look out for you?"

I was about to reply, but she was already continuing.

"I'm not the one who was alone when we met," Julia said, voice deceptively light.

My mouth dropped open.

"Don't forget that."

My shoulders curled inward. "Why are you trying to make me feel replaceable?"

"I'm *not*. I'm always going to want what's best for you," Julia said. "And I'm always going to watch out for you. And you're accusing me of—"

"I'm not accusing you of anything!" I gestured aimlessly. "I am just asking questions."

"Why? You think I'm going behind your back?" Julia asked, tone scathing. "Oh, that's rich. Were you ever even going to tell me about TMU?"

It felt like all the air left the room.

I blinked at her.

"Yeah," Julia said, after a moment. "That's what I thought."

"How did you—"

"*That's* what you're concerned about?" Julia asked me. "What happened to being roommates?"

"That wasn't ever confirmed," I said. "It was a nice idea, but it wasn't—it was a maybe."

"Nothing's a *maybe* if you really want it," Julia said. "What's TMU got that McGill doesn't?"

"I never thought they would be interested in me!" I burst out. "I didn't think they would be, but they are, and you know how important journalism is to me, right? You know it's my dream. I just—if I've got a shot at something that would make me happy, don't you want me to take it?"

Julia just stared at me.

I was breathing hard without even realizing how worked up I'd gotten. I took several deep breaths, trying to steady myself.

Julia sighed, and her shoulders slumped. "Why didn't you tell me?"

I took another deep breath. "I didn't want to upset you when it might not even happen, and then I didn't know how, and then I was scared, and I thought you'd be mad at me."

"Well, I'm not." Julia's tone was level. "Mad at you."

I wasn't sure how to react to that.

"Maybe TMU will pan out," Julia said. "Maybe it won't. I just wish you'd told me."

"I'm sorry." Shame flooded through me. Had I really turned Julia into such a monster in my head that I thought she would be furious with me? Had I thought the truth would turn her mean?

"You're still going to apply to McGill, right?" Julia asked, and there was a teasing edge to her tone.

I let out a shaky breath. At first I thought what I was feeling was relief, but then as it faded, the knife-sharp edge of dread settled between my ribs. "Yeah," I said, ducking my head and running my hands through my hair. "I'm going to."

"Good," Julia said.

She quietly sipped her tea. Why was she so relaxed about this? And how had she known? It felt like Julia knew everything she wasn't supposed to know. Had Dillan told her after all?

I tracked Julia's gaze out the window, where she was watching a bare branch wave back and forth in the wind. I'd expected a *terrible* reaction, but she looked eerily serene.

"I just want you to be happy," Julia said, and then she smiled.

It didn't meet her eyes.

FORTY

After

'm starting to wonder if I should follow in the Hoskinses' footsteps and take down my pictures.

I sit on my bed, staring at them. Julia's in almost all the photos on my wall. Every so often I think about taking them down, but it feels sacrilegious.

Looking at the pictures, no one would know there was a time when we weren't friends. There's only one photo from before then, of me and Simon and Dillan on Halloween.

I don't like thinking about the year before I met Julia. When Dillan moved away, it felt like the end of the world, and not just because I missed him. We'd been best friends long enough that everybody had already made other friends. I'd been a shy kid even before he left, and then without him, I didn't fit anywhere.

Julia called it my lonely year. It was mostly a joke to her, but it wasn't to me. I was the kid who sat alone at lunch, who didn't get invited to sleepovers, who was never paired up for partner projects. I wasn't bullied, but being invisible was its own kind of torture.

On Julia's very first day of school, she marched up to me at lunch.

"Why are you sitting by yourself?" she asked, holding on to her tray.

I looked up at her. What kind of question was that? Did she think I was alone on purpose? She didn't look like a mean girl, exactly, more like she *could* be. She had the colorful elastics in her hair that I always asked my mom for but never got. I remember worrying that she was going to find something about me to pick on, or that this was a prank.

But after a moment of silence, she just shook her head and set her tray down across from me, sliding into the seat.

"I'm Julia," she told me. "I'm the new kid, but you already know that, obviously. Want a gummy worm?"

Julia had chosen me. I owed her.

She came into my life like an explosion. One moment I'd been alone, and then she was everywhere all at once, sitting with me every day at lunch, asking me first to be on her team in PE, coming to my house after school, talking me into dance classes and staying up way too late on the weekends. There was no adjustment period for Julia Hoskins. I'd never been loved like that before.

That was the sweetest version of Julia I ever knew. She bought me my very first journal. She got a credit card when she turned thirteen, mostly for emergencies, but we knew her mom threw money at problems. Julia said she didn't mind. I never really believed her. In any case, she went along with it, saying that being bored on a Thursday afternoon counted as an emergency. Or when we were supposed to go out for dinner with her mom and she bailed last second. Or when there was a sale at Zara.

The memories sting.

It was just us for two years. Then I met Eve in eighth grade, when Julia and I were in totally opposite classes all year. And I remember all too well how that went.

My box of journals still lives under my bed. There are five inside. All black leather. All not quite full, but almost. The last one is only halfway full.

My journals have always been a checkpoint for the truth.

There is no truth, Julia always told me. *Only stories. It's about who you believe most.*

Back then, my truth revolved around the facts. That always made it easier when Julia was being confusing or when I felt like I couldn't trust my own thoughts. Stories were built from the facts. That's what always made writing essays feel so easy.

I pick up the journal on the top of the pile. My last entry is from December second of last year.

It's odd looking at the blank page. I run my finger along the paper as my eyes look everywhere but at that underlined last sentence. I know what it says.

I know why it's the last one.

I close the journal and pull out another. This time it falls open to another page I've revisited over and over. March of eighth grade. I've spent more hours trying to make sense of this in the last year than I did all through high school, and I still don't get it. But then again, I don't really understand Julia anymore, do I? Sometimes I don't think I ever will. And maybe I have to be okay with that.

I can still hear the hurt in her voice. *You were going to—*

I slam the journal shut. Sometimes it feels like Julia's right here with me still, knowing what I'm thinking. I take several deep breaths before I can open it again, and another before I can start reading.

> *Today Eve invited me and Julia to go to Vancouver with her for the weekend over spring break with some of her other friends. I don't think Julia wants to, but she said we should go anyway. Julia's been to Vancouver loads of times, but I've never been. I'm excited to get to know Eve better, too. Sometimes it feels like she's just as much my friend as Julia is.*

Then, four days later:

> *I think I'm uninvited from the trip. I'm not in the group chat for it anymore and I didn't leave it myself, so I don't know what happened.*
>
> *I'm at Julia's for a sleepover. She said it would be a good idea to stay distracted, and said she's staying home in solidarity. We've put our phones in a drawer so that we won't be tempted to look tonight or tomorrow and see them having fun without us.*
>
> *I asked Julia what she thought about why I was uninvited, and she told me that Eve said she never wanted me to come at all, which doesn't make sense. I mean, she invited me, right?*

◆ ◆ ◆

Eve and her friends went on the trip. The pictures look fun. Eve is ignoring me now.

• • •

Julia lied.

I talked to Eve and she said I was an asshole for ghosting her last second. When I told her I had no idea what she was talking about, she said I left the group chat and wouldn't answer her calls the night they were all leaving.

I told her I wouldn't do that, but I don't think she believed me. Then I told her what Julia had said about her not wanting me on the trip, and she said that wasn't true. She said she never told Julia anything like that.

When I got home, I checked the call log and all the missed calls were there, but I don't remember her calling. I would have seen them in the morning, wouldn't I?

• • •

Julia deleted the calls from my phone in the morning so I wouldn't see them. Texts, too.

She said it was because she thought going on the trip was a bad idea, and that she wasn't sure I should be spending so much time with Eve. She said I was irrational for being so upset. I just don't get why she lied.

Did she think I wouldn't find out?

• • •

Julia and I fought for *days*. I called her a liar and a sneak, and she said she was only trying to look out for me, and didn't I care that she was protecting me?

That was the time my mom told me I should stay, work things out. After all, Julia was my best friend.

Best friends don't lie, I told Julia.

No more lies, Julia said.

I thought it was a promise.

FORTY-ONE

Before

*S*ort of . . . *dumb.*

The worst part was I could hear him saying it. I'd thought about it so often that it had stopped being Julia's voice in my head. It became Dillan's, over and over.

Dumb. He thought I was *dumb*? Maybe he *had* outed Eve after all. Maybe I didn't know him like I thought I did.

When Dillan walked into class the next day, I pretended to be deeply involved with my journal, even though I was just writing the date over and over.

I didn't look up, and I didn't say anything even when he and Julia struck up a conversation.

How strange that they were the ones talking now. I'd been glad they were on the way to being friends, considering how hostile she'd been to him, but now it made me feel a little sick. How could she talk to him with such an easy smile, knowing what he'd said? Was everything Julia did so calculated?

I couldn't stop thinking about how calm she'd been about TMU. *Too* calm. Was I just being paranoid? Over the last twenty-four hours, the question of how she'd figured it out whirled so fast it made me dizzy. Only two people besides me had known, and I hadn't told her. Had Mr. Ambrose been the one to let something slip? Or . . .

I didn't acknowledge Dillan's presence as class started, and I didn't turn around once the whole time, not even when he was answering a question. I was intending to leave without speaking to him, but he had other ideas.

"Hey, Nora."

I turned around.

Dillan's brow furrowed. "You walking home?"

I nodded.

"I'm walking too." He swallowed. "Want to go together?"

Julia was packing up my backpack. She handed it to me with a tight smile, side-eying Dillan. Her eyebrows arched for a fraction of a second, in a way that was clearly saying, *You good?* She had to stay after school for a meeting with the soccer coach, which meant I'd be on my own.

"Don't have a car today?" I asked him.

"Mum needed it. Figured it wouldn't kill me to actually use my legs for once." Dillan watched me carefully, like he was nervous I would say no.

"Fine," I said.

Still, the first few minutes of the walk were tense. It wasn't as cold as it had been recently, so I tried to focus on that instead of Dillan walking beside me, my hands shoved in my pockets.

"So," he said.

I looked over at him. "So?"

"Are you okay?" He didn't look back at me. "Something feels off today."

I shook my head. "It's nothing. I'm just thinking."

How was I supposed to tell him what was bothering me? I didn't have proof of anything, just suspicions. If Dillan could have told Julia about TMU, what else was he capable of? Eve's face swam in front of me. Eve said Dillan had outed her, and she said my name was being thrown around, but I hadn't told *anyone.* I would never. I'd only written about it in my journal, and that was private.

My stomach lurched. Journal. My journal. I hadn't checked to see if I'd brought it with me.

"Hold on." I stopped in my tracks. "I've just got to check for something."

I dropped my backpack onto the sidewalk, even though it was snowing. Crouching beside it, I rifled through every pocket.

Dillan just stood there. "What are you looking for?"

"My journal." I huffed. "Stupid—ugh, it's not here. I must have left it at school. I'm *such* an idiot."

"Hey." Dillan looked at me sideways. "No, you aren't."

I had to stop myself from rolling my eyes as I muttered, "Of course you'd say that to my face."

"What was that?" He sounded confused.

Both relieved and annoyed that he hadn't heard me, I heaved my backpack onto my shoulder. "Nothing. It's not *here.*"

"Should we go back?"

"No—I'll just go in early tomorrow."

"It's not, like . . . personal, is it?"

"It's a journal, Dillan. Of course it's personal."

He looked a little annoyed. "Okay, whatever. I was just asking."

"It's just, I had some stuff in there." My cheeks warmed as I remembered what I'd written about him.

"Seems important."

"It *is*."

"The office is open until four," he said. "We can still go back."

Julia's story still stung. *Dumb*. Losing my journal was a dumb thing to do. Freaking out about it was even dumber.

"Nah. I'll get it tomorrow."

"Are you sure?"

I swallowed, then nodded, resolute, even though on the inside I felt like I'd been turned upside down. "Yeah. Yeah, I'm sure."

FORTY-TWO

After

When Dillan doesn't show up at the coffee shop at his usual time, my heart sinks.

I mentally run through every conversation we've had in the last week. Did I do something wrong again? Dillan is never late.

He texted me just last night, and nothing *seemed* off, beyond the general awkwardness that comes with the "I asked out someone else" territory.

I gave them my blessing. Was that the right thing to do?

I hate it, and at the same time, what else could I have said?

If Dillan asked her out, that must mean something. Dillan doesn't just *do* things. If he asked Kayla to go out with him, it's because he wanted her to say yes. If he wanted her to say yes, it follows that it's because *he* was interested.

Second-guessing is my least-favorite game, but I'm playing it so much I even see it when I close my eyes. Maybe I overestimated what Dillan felt. Maybe I let myself get trapped in my head, riding waves of euphoria. Maybe I shouldn't be surprised. This is exactly what he did last time.

Still, even if he's already moved on—even if that means he never felt the way I thought he did—my relief when his car pulls into the parking lot is palpable.

When he walks into the café, his grin is bright enough to light the world. "Hey. Sorry I'm late."

I let out a slow breath between my teeth as I turn to pour him a coffee and slide it across the counter. "I thought you were mad at me or something."

"Oh." He looks at me carefully. "No, sorry. I just had to drop Angie off at school for Mom."

Dillan backs away from the counter when another customer comes in, and he stays back until I've finished ringing her through and making the drink.

I watch him out of the corner of my eye until I feel like it's too much.

He watches the customer settle into a chair on the other side of the coffee shop before he walks back over. "How's the morning?"

I shrug. "Slow. Someone's kid knocked over a drink, which was sort of funny."

I can't look at him when he laughs, so I duck down behind the counter to grab the rag from the sanitizer bucket and begin attacking the side of the espresso machine as though it's done me a personal offense.

"Hey, are you going to the Christmas market this year?" I try to keep my voice light. "I'm trying to decide."

"I don't know." He scratches the side of his head. "I was thinking of asking Kayla."

I meticulously rinse a pitcher as my stomach bottoms out. "Oh?"

When I look up, he has one eyebrow raised. "What?"

I try to be nonchalant, even though I can feel my heart beating in my temple. "Nothing. I just didn't know it was that serious."

I can hear him scuffing his foot.

"Who says it's serious?" He's drumming his fingers on the countertop, his eyes fixed on his shoes.

I shrug, uncomfortable. "I don't know. I was just thinking that's what you meant when you said you were taking her."

"I didn't say I *was* taking her." There's a defensive undertone to his voice. "I said I was *thinking* about it."

I take the rest of the pitchers and rinse them, too, even though they don't really need it.

"Besides, taking her doesn't mean it's serious." He's mumbling now. "We used to go together all the time when we were kids. And we went last year, right?"

I put the pitcher down hard. "Yep."

I don't mean to, but I pop the *p*.

I want desperately for him to ask me what I think, but instead he rocks back on his heels, raps the top of the counter once, and shoves his hands into his pockets.

"Okay," he says. "Cool."

He's staring out the window. I feel like someone is squeezing my heart, he's so beautiful. I want to touch his curls. It's an urge so new that it catches my breath.

"I'm still not sure I'm going to," Dillan says. He looks at me, and for a moment, we just stand there staring. "There's plenty of time, besides."

"Yeah." I hope my voice doesn't sound too flat. I'm

surprised by how unpleasant the idea is, the two of them. I have no right to feel this way, but I do. "There's time."

The bell rings, and the last person I want to see walks in.

"Hey," Dillan says, raising a hand as Kayla swishes into the café.

No, really. She *swishes*. Kayla takes up space like she does it on purpose. The only other person I know like that is Eve, and she wasn't that way in school. Not until after. I wonder if Kayla learned how to be this way too, or if it's just natural.

Kayla hugs Dillan.

I look away.

"Nora!" Kayla says. "I didn't know you worked here."

I nod. "Where are you guys headed off to?"

They exchange a glance.

"We were just going to stick around here," Kayla says.

"Great," I say, hoping my cheery tone doesn't sound too false. "What can I get for you?"

Kayla orders a green tea, and the two of them go sit at the table in the nook by the window, which makes me want to punch something. I don't know how many times I've joked with Dillan about that being the *date* table.

They sit and talk, and the table is far away enough that I can't hear what they're saying.

But they both look radiant in the sunlight. Dillan smiles at her like he means it. They're laughing about something almost every time I look over, which is a *normal* amount of times.

So basically, it's horrible.

This feels deliberate. Pointed. Or maybe I'm just being horribly self-centered.

Either way, I hate it.

FORTY-THREE

Before

The journal wasn't at school.

I'd checked that morning. Nothing. So either I'd *really* misplaced it, or somebody else had it. The idea made me feel vaguely ill.

When I walked into Julia's kitchen the next night and found Eve sitting at the counter, for a moment I thought I was hallucinating.

She looked up at me. At first I thought she was still mad, but then she sighed. "Hey, Nora."

"Hey." I set my backpack down. "What—"

"I'm sorry," she said, all in a rush. "I shouldn't have accused you of outing me. I know you wouldn't do that."

"What changed your mind?" I asked.

"Julia," Eve said. She opened her mouth as though she was going to say more, but she didn't get the chance.

"Party time!" Julia announced as she walked in, as though we'd summoned her. "Everyone ready?"

"We're not going to a party, are we?" I asked, suddenly uneasy.

Julia laughed. "No, *we're* the party. It's been way too long since we did something just the three of us."

I thought I saw Eve's smile go slightly strained for a moment, but then she turned and started digging through the pockets in her jacket. When she reemerged a moment later, she looked fine.

Almost *too* fine. Eve never looked this chill.

"What were you thinking of doing?" I asked Julia, dragging my attention away from Eve.

"We need to plan your birthday," Julia said.

Eve's phone rang. She looked at the caller ID and frowned, then, without looking at either of us, said, "I'll be right back."

I turned to Julia the second Eve walked out of earshot.

"You convinced Eve I wasn't behind the rumor?" I asked.

Julia shrugged. "Well, it wasn't you. And it seemed like you needed some convincing that I'm not a terrible person."

I was pretty sure she was joking, but part of me wondered if she really thought that. "I don't think you're a terrible person."

She smiled. "Good."

Eve walked back in, looking unhappy.

"That was quick," Julia said.

"Dillan." Eve leaned against the wall and folded her arms. "He keeps calling me."

My stomach went tight. "You really think it was him who . . . you know?"

"Please." Julia scoffed. "Who else would it be?"

Eve said nothing.

Julia smacked the counter. "We need drinks."

I watched her grab a bottle and glasses from the cabinet and pour an equal amount of red wine into each. "What's the occasion?"

"We need a toast!" Julia exclaimed, handing out the glasses.

"To what?" Eve raised an eyebrow.

Julia smiled at me. "The birthday girl."

I had to laugh. "Seriously? I thought we were just planning. My birthday isn't until next week."

Julia knocked her glass against mine. "Cheers anyway."

I knew it wasn't about the birthday. Julia just liked to drink.

Eve and I clinked glasses, and after she and Julia had made contact, I tipped my glass back. I didn't much care for wine, but this wasn't bad, sort of sweet.

I swirled it around in my glass and pretended to consider it. "Hmm. Initial notes of . . . wine. With an aftertaste reminiscent of . . . wine."

Julia laughed, then asked me, "What do you want to do for your actual birthday?"

I shrugged. "Same as always."

Every year, Spruce Meadows, the huge sports and entertainment complex in Calgary, hosted their first weekly Christmas market in late November, and every year the three of us went.

"You don't want to . . . I don't know. Go out somewhere?" Julia leaned back on her elbows. "You'll be eighteen! You'll be legal. Alberta, baby!"

She moved to high-five me, eyes twinkling with the inside joke. Not that it was *really* an inside joke. Kids in the States have to wait until they're twenty-one to drink, which Julia and I had always found especially amusing.

Eve and I made slightly tense eye contact.

I cleared my throat. "Why don't we do that for Eve's birthday in the spring? Then all three of us can go."

"Yeah." Eve snorted. "Like any of us would actually *enjoy* clubbing."

"I'd enjoy it," Julia insisted.

"Anything with all three of us is great," I said. "But I'd be really sad if we missed the Christmas market."

"Up to you." Julia shrugged. "We'll follow in your footsteps."

I sighed. "I'll think about it."

There was a moment of silence.

Then Julia turned to Eve. "Did Nora tell you about TMU?"

Eve gave me a blank look.

"I've got an opportunity for early acceptance for journalism," I told her. "I submitted an essay, so now I'm waiting to hear back."

"Really?" Eve tilted her head. "That's so cool, Nora. You're going to be great at that."

Julia rolled her eyes. "Of *course* she will. Our Nora's going to be the greatest journalist of all time. Follow her dreams."

I was pretty sure that was a jab.

That was sometimes how Julia gave compliments. Technically, all the words added up to something nice, but it still felt a little bit like missing a step on the way down the stairs.

"TMU, though?" Eve asked, glancing between me and Julia. "I thought—"

"It's not official or anything," I interrupted hastily.

"I'm starting to think I'm going to have to chain her to a chair to apply to McGill." Julia laughed brightly. The sound rang through the air and hung for a moment in the following silence.

"I'm still applying," I told her.

"I hope so." She picked up the bottle and topped off her glass, but she didn't look at me. Then she straightened her shoulders. "Movie?"

Eve and I exchanged a knowing look.

Once the movie started and I'd situated myself on the floor in the basement in front of Julia so that she could braid my hair, it almost felt like old times. The tug of my hair, the feathery touch of her fingertips against my neck, the rhythmic drag and pull of the braid once she got going.

Eve sat on the edge of the couch, a few feet away. Every so often she'd glance over at Julia, but not for long. They were the sort of glances that didn't want to be caught. I wondered what she was thinking. I wondered if she was okay.

Halfway through the movie, I let out an enormous yawn.

Julia laughed.

"Sorry." I gave my head a little shake, then whispered, "I was at school extra early this morning."

"Why?"

I sighed. "I lost my journal."

She frowned. "Seriously?"

"Yeah," I said. "I can't find it, and I'm worried someone else might. I looked at the front office, but no luck."

"I'm sorry," Julia said, squeezing my arm sympathetically. "At least you put your phone number at the front so people can call you and return it if they find it, right?"

"Right," I said, not sure why the statement made me feel so strange.

I didn't figure out what was wrong until later, when I'd already gotten home.

My mom was in the kitchen, looking a little harried. She barely looked up when I walked into the room. The single dome light illuminated the top of her head, highlighting her graying roots.

"Hey, Mom," I said.

"Hey." She was bending over some papers, a pen trapped between her teeth. Then she straightened up and took it out of her mouth. "Are you planning on having Julia stay over for your birthday?"

I just shrugged.

"I had an odd conversation with her when she came by," she remarked, shuffling papers into neat stacks. "It's been a while since I've seen her without you."

I put my keys onto the hook, then straightened them. "When was that?"

She looked up at the ceiling, thinking. "This afternoon. Didn't she tell you?"

I frowned and shook my head, leaning against the doorjamb. "Did she say why?"

"I'm not sure. I think she had something for you."

At least you put your phone number at the front.

I'd never shown Julia the inside of my journal.

The more I thought about it, the more certain I was. Maybe she'd seen it in passing? But I was careful. I didn't *want* her to see it.

There was no explanation for why she'd know about the phone number I'd scribbled in the front.

Except one.

I held a finger up and went to my room.

On my desk, underneath a few textbooks, was my journal.

I hadn't put it there. When my fingers closed around the leather spine, I turned right back around and marched into the kitchen.

"Was it this?" I held it up for my mom to see.

She looked at it and sighed. "I don't know. I didn't see it."

That wasn't what I wanted to hear, but I didn't need her confirmation. I felt something like a gasp starting in my chest, but it wasn't a gasp, because I didn't make any noise at all. It just felt like one second I had oxygen, and the next moment I didn't.

Did she *want* me to know? To put the pieces together? To understand that she was in control? It didn't feel like a Julia thing to try to scare me.

My mom must have seen something in my face, because her expression softened. "What's the matter?"

I just shook my head. "Nothing."

Everything was the matter. I turned on my heel and called out "Good night" to my mom as I went back to my room.

Closing the door behind me, I flung the journal at the wall. It hit with a sharp crack and fell to the floor, pages open.

Julia had taken my journal. She must have taken it that day in English, right before it went missing. I let out a long exhale in a thin hiss.

There had to be a good reason why she'd taken it. We told each other everything important, didn't we?

But why?

Eve.

I dashed over to the journal and frantically flipped through the pages. There it was, in my neat handwriting.

Today Eve told me she likes girls.

Those were incriminating words. I'd thought it wasn't possible that Julia had found out from me. But the truth was unavoidable.

She must have been reading my journal for *weeks* when I wasn't paying attention. *Why?*

Julia *was* lying to me. How deep in denial had I been that I hadn't noticed? Was *anything* true?

If I started crying, I might not be able to stop. I was choking on thoughts, drowning in them.

I. Am. Alone.

The three words stuck, one per heartbeat. I gasped and hugged my pillow to my chest so tightly it almost hurt, and I *wanted* it to hurt. I wanted it to fill in the hollow space beneath my rib cage.

Tears ran down my neck. Julia was lying to me. Not a lie by omission or trying to protect me. She was *actively* lying to me. Even if Dillan wasn't a traitor, he thought I was dumb and shallow—

Didn't he? Or was that a lie too?

For a moment, the thought was so startling I sat there blinking at the wall. Then the crushing loneliness settled again. How could I ask him something like that? What if it *was* the truth? Between everything going on, I didn't really know Dillan at all.

And Eve was . . . I had no idea what she thought.

I. Am. Alone.

It felt like the truest thing I had known in a long, long time. I fumbled with my headphones, shoving them over my ears, desperate for *anything* to distract me, but that turned out to be a mistake, because all of the songs reminded me of Julia.

I was crying for real now, ugly, shuddering sobs, trying to

be quiet, trying to remember why it mattered. Half of me wanted my mom to hear, and rush in, and fix it. But I knew she would be at her desk with her music on, and I was in here alone in the dark. The idea of anyone knowing—*judging*—was so repellent that I just tugged my arms around myself more tightly. I wanted to hit something, to let it out, but it felt like a scream that was trapped inside me.

I fell sideways on the mattress, letting the tears run down the sides of my cheeks. I hadn't known it was possible to feel this tired. I just lay there and listened to music and cried until I couldn't anymore. Then I lay there and listened to music and tried to feel nothing at all.

Just remember, I was there when no one else was.

Bullshit.

Bull*shit.*

I am alone. I am always alone. I tried to tell myself everything was fine. It was fine, even if it wasn't. It had to be okay. But that wasn't true, not at all.

I wanted people to want me around so badly it physically hurt. I wanted them to be honest. Was I surrounded by people who were just pretending? There was a secret underneath all of this, and I knew it, and I hated it: if I wanted to know what was going on, I had to be ready to break my own heart.

FORTY-FOUR

After

Kayla lives downtown in an apartment with her brother. She is doing her best to not make me feel left out of whatever she and Dillan have, but it's mostly serving to remind me about it every ten seconds.

I'm doing my best not to be bitter.

She's invited me over for a movie. According to Dillan, they watch movies sometimes after the study group Kayla hosts.

Apparently they've been doing this for weeks.

Today, the study group is off, so I'm their third wheel.

Well, I would be, except Dillan isn't here yet.

I stand awkwardly with my arms crossed in the middle of the kitchen.

It's the only place in Kayla's apartment that looks lived-in, because the fridge is covered in brightly colored magnets inexplicably arranged to read *chicken nuget,* with one *g* missing.

There's a single pot next to the sink. A whiteboard on the

wall listing the days of the week is covered in tally marks, and at the top, someone has scrawled *HAS FAT BASTARD BEEN FED?*

I raise both eyebrows, but Kayla doesn't have to answer because a half second later I hear a piteous meow from the hall.

She sighs. "Fat Bastard."

Kayla disappears down the hallway.

I can't stop my mouth from dropping into an O when she walks back in, carrying the most enormous tabby cat I've ever seen.

Fat Bastard has wide, round eyes, and when they zero in on me, he begins to squirm in Kayla's arms. When she sets him down, he trots right back out of the room.

"Doesn't like strangers." Kayla sighs again. "He used to be just Bastard, but then he started conning us into double dinners."

I laugh despite myself.

Kayla pulls her phone out of her pocket. "Dillan's on his way."

He hasn't texted me.

"How's it been going?" I ask, after I've recovered from the sound of his name in her mouth. "You know, with you guys."

She just shrugs. "We've only gone out a few times. It's still super casual. He seems like a good guy, though."

I'm surprised that I'm furious to hear this, though it takes me a second to figure out that it's not just maddening jealousy.

The idea that Kayla could be going out with Dillan and not think the world of him makes me *angry*. I have to remind myself that technically she hasn't done anything wrong, but resentment still burns.

"Think there's any future there?" I regret asking immediately.

Kayla watches me carefully. "I guess I'll have to see."

I twist the fabric of my T-shirt between my fingers.

"He thinks you're avoiding him."

"He said that?"

Kayla shrugs. "Well, not in those words exactly, but that was the implication."

"Oh." It's true, sort of. I've been distancing myself, because it's a little bit painful to see him and know he's picking somebody else. "I'm not avoiding him."

"Hmm." Kayla looks like she doesn't believe me.

There's a long pause where I decide whether that bothers me. When I open my mouth, though, what comes out is a surprise.

"Last year, I applied to TMU."

"Yeah, Dillan told me," Kayla says casually.

I feel like she's slapped me. "What?"

She looks slightly wary.

"What did he tell you?"

"Just that you applied, and it didn't pan out," she says, raising both hands.

My shoulders relax. "Oh. Well, that's true."

She leans her hip against the counter.

I watch her for a second, and then I decide to take a risk. I tell her, "I've reapplied."

She brightens. "Really?"

"Yeah. And to a couple of other schools out east."

Kayla looks a little concerned.

I fold my arms. "What?"

"Wouldn't it be easier to stay?"

I look at her blankly. She knows what happened. How could I stay?

"I mean, it'd be a lot less adjusting," Kayla says. "You could still live at home, and you wouldn't have to worry about moving away from—"

"From who?" I ask, sharply, because I think she means Dillan, who is *leaving*, but her eyebrows arch.

"Eve."

"I didn't know you even knew her."

"We're friends," Kayla says, bristling. "She didn't tell you?"

"No?" Is everyone in my life suddenly buddy-buddy with Kayla?

"We met at that Halloween party a few weeks ago, remember? Well—" Kayla looks slightly frustrated. "Anyway, if you stayed here, you'd have familiar faces."

"I can't stay," I burst out.

Kayla blinks.

"I can't," I say, and I can feel my breathing getting shallower.

"You can't?"

"No." My throat tightens. Why does she even care? "No, I can't. But that's just—"

"Why?"

Shouldn't she know this? Do I really have to say it aloud? It comes out strangled. "Julia."

Realization dawns on her face, a second too late. "Oh. *Oh.*"

"Everything here reminds me of her," I gasp. "Everything."

"Nora, I'm sorry." She reaches for my arm, but I back away.

"Sometimes I feel so crowded by all the things that remind me she isn't here anymore." My chest is heaving, but I'm not sure when I started breathing like this, like it hurts. "I wouldn't be happy here."

"Nora." Kayla's voice is quiet. "Sorry. I didn't—think."

My heartbeat is thunderous.

There's a terribly awkward silence in which I watch the second hand on the clock tick around the dial and she looks out the window.

Quietly, Kayla asks, "Does Eve know? About the application?"

I want to ask her why it even matters, but she's already shaking her head.

"Never mind. I won't get in the way."

"I haven't told her yet. I don't know what she'll say."

"I'm sure she'll support you," Kayla says.

I nod.

There's a moment of silence. Then—

"Eve didn't like her," I blurt out. "She never did. Before Julia died . . ."

"I know," Kayla says, quietly.

"I really didn't know you and Eve were that close."

Something about that makes Kayla balk. "It's new."

"It's cool," I say, even though I haven't decided how I feel about it.

"I know bits and pieces of what Julia did," Kayla says. "It sounds like a really complicated situation."

I wonder if she's heard more about it from Eve or from Dillan. I wonder if she knows it was my fault. I wonder what *they* know. I want to tell her that Dillan is the only person in the world who really understands, but I don't say anything, because I don't want to step on her toes. Dillan is the only one I can talk to about Julia, and even then, he doesn't know *everything*. Julia spoiled that between us.

I take a deep breath. "She ruined—"

Kayla watches me carefully.

"She messed up a lot of things," I burst out. "She broke things I can't fix."

I'd thought saying it out loud would make me feel better. Instead, I feel uglier. Messier.

I hate that it feels like home.

"I'm really sorry." Kayla sighs. "Are you okay?"

I don't have an answer. I feel trapped. And Dillan's coming, and I don't—

For the first time that I can remember in a year, I don't really want to see Dillan. I don't want to talk to him about this.

"I have to go," I tell her.

She looks dismayed.

"I'm sorry," I say. "Really."

"You don't have to go," Kayla says. "I don't mind any—"

"Have fun with Dillan," I say, shoving my feet into my shoes. "Tell him I say hi."

FORTY-FIVE

Before

I was walking down the hall the next day in a daze when somebody grabbed me by the arm and dragged me into the nearest bathroom. "What—"

"Shh!" Eve shook her head, pulling me farther in, glancing toward the mirror.

There were two girls whispering by the sink. It took me a moment to recognize them as some of the ninth graders in Julia's posse.

Eve stared at them until the shorter one noticed.

"Mayu, come *on*," the girl said, and she and her friend scurried out of the room.

"What was that about?" I asked Eve once the door had swung shut.

Eve shook her head. "If I ask you a question, will you answer honestly?"

I let out a nervous laugh. "What? I mean, yeah."

"It wasn't Dillan," Eve said. "The person who outed me. It wasn't him."

"That's not a question." I looked wildly over my shoulder, but the rest of the bathroom was empty.

"It was Julia, wasn't it?" Eve asked. "Why didn't you tell me you told her?"

"I didn't," I said. "She's been reading my journal. Maybe."

Her eyebrows shot up. *"What?"*

I rubbed at my forehead. "I think she stole my journal."

"That *bitch*."

I flinched.

"Oh, come on." Eve snorted. "It's true."

I didn't want it to be true. I wanted to go back to before everything got so messy.

"I asked around, and yeah, Dillan's name came up, but nobody could confirm who started the rumor. Until I asked that one girl—what's her name, the one who was just in here, Aila?—and she caved and said it was *Julia*." Eve smacked the counter. "I knew it. I kept thinking, there's no way he would do something like that, and he's known for ages, so why now, right? Anyway, Aila said Julia told her and her friend that she'd heard it from Dillan."

Even though I knew it was probably true, I didn't want to believe Julia would go so far. I rubbed my forehead. "But why lie about it?"

"Why does Julia ever lie?" Eve asked. "I don't know. Maybe she was trying to split us up. Maybe she just enjoys it. Hell, maybe even she doesn't know why! Or maybe, she just hates Dillan's guts."

"Why would she have wanted to split us up?"

At that, Eve's shoulders slumped. "I don't know. It's just a theory."

I closed my eyes. "How long have you known about this?"

"A few days."

"So the other night, at Julia's house—"

"I was trying to figure out if you were in on it."

My eyes flew open. I took a step backward and my back hit the door of the stall. "What?"

"Sorry," she said. "I just—I feel like I've been going insane. I don't know what's real."

That I understood. "Look, if this is all true, I just . . . know that I never would have told her."

"I know. I'm sorry for being so closed off about it. I just feel like . . ."

"Like you don't know who to trust?"

She laughed, a little bitterly. "Exactly."

"What are you going to do? Are you going to confront her about it?"

Eve let out a long, low breath. "I don't know."

"Maybe I should do it," I said. I was mostly joking, but Eve's face lit up.

"You should! I mean, she's reading *your* journal, right?"

"Supposedly," I said.

Eve looked at me as the warning bell rang.

I sighed. "I'll think about it."

She started to leave the bathroom, but I grabbed her arm.

"Hey." I swallowed. "I'm really sorry this happened. And I'm sorry I ever made you think I would do something like that."

Eve smiled. "I don't think I ever really thought it was you."

I exhaled long and loud, relieved, and then followed her out of the bathroom.

My peace was short-lived.

On the other side of the bathroom door, Julia was walking past. She saw the two of us and stopped for a moment. A junior kid walked straight into her from behind and her expression hardened as she walked away.

"Oh, for God's sake!" Eve yelled. "We're just *talking*."

I shot an apologetic look to her over my shoulder as I rushed after Julia. "Hey!"

"Hey yourself," Julia said coolly when I caught up.

I followed her down the hallway until we got to her locker. "What are you mad about?"

"Mad?" Julia asked, fingers working furiously at the combination. "Why would I be mad?"

"Julia?"

"What?"

"Can I ask you a question?" I did my best to keep my voice even.

"Yes." She frowned. "What?"

I took a deep breath. "Did you take my journal?"

My knees were shaking.

She blinked, and then she didn't say anything. She just looked at me. "What?"

"Did you take it?"

Something in her expression shifted, and her gaze turned stony. "Why do you always do this?"

"Do *what*?"

"Everything you do—it's . . ." Julia smacked her locker shut. "It's *what*?"

"Why are you always looking for new ways to drag

attention back to yourself?" She crossed her arms. "What is *up* with you?"

"Julia!" I hissed. "You stole my journal."

"I did *not* steal your journal!"

"That was what you were returning yesterday, right? My mom *saw* you."

"You'd just—what—take your mom's word over mine?"

I gaped at her. "Yes, obviously! Why would she lie about that?"

"Why would *I* lie to you about this?" She was *still* trying to squirm out of it. "Don't you trust me?"

"I want to trust you—"

"Oh, great, you *want* to trust me." Julia snorted. "You know what? I've had enough of this."

She turned and started walking away.

"Aren't you *tired*?" I shouted after her.

She didn't turn around, but she did stop walking.

"Of making stuff up and pretending?" My anger was white-hot, racing up and down my spine. "I thought we were supposed to tell each other the truth!"

Finally, she turned, slowly. "I *am* telling the truth."

I let out a low exhale, deflating. There wasn't going to be any truth today. Maybe not ever. Maybe that was how it had always been with Julia. Half-truths mixed with real truths felt more authentic than a lie.

"Nora," she said, and her voice was eerily calm. "I don't want to talk about this right now."

She walked away.

And I let her go.

FORTY-SIX

After

The Fletcher house has never looked as intimidating as it does now. I'm standing on the front porch, staring at the door.

I don't knock. I don't really know why until I'm sinking down onto the front step. It's way too cold for this—I'm pretty sure the temperature has dipped below zero—but I'm already feeling shaky and numb enough that I don't care.

I have to talk about Julia, even if I don't want to. Even if I *really* don't want to. My outburst at Kayla's the other day made me realize that I have to get it out, or it's just going to keep on festering. I summon my last spark of courage, and then call Dillan.

He doesn't pick up.

The line rings and rings, and I sit there feeling stupid when I get sent to voicemail. I hang up, realizing that I'll have to make a new plan.

But then Dillan calls me back, and relief diffuses through me.

"Hey, sorry, I was— What's up? You okay?" Dillan asks, and it's him, and normal, and my heart hurts.

"Are you free right now?" I whisper.

"Yeah," he says, "I'm just about home."

I blink down at the stone steps. "Oh. Where are you?"

Dillan snorts. "Just about home."

"Asshole." The knot in my chest is starting to loosen. "You know what I meant. Where are you coming from?"

"Where are *you*?" Dillan asks, ignoring my question.

"I'm outside your house," I tell him, before I can chicken out.

Dillan pauses. "So am I."

"You're outside my house?" I ask.

"No, I'm outside *my* house. Why are you sitting on my front porch?"

I look up, and see Dillan coming down the sidewalk, hair furiously bright under the streetlamp one moment, all dark the next.

He waves, and I wave back.

"Are you on a walk?" I ask him, into the phone, as he's turning onto the path up to the house. "Dork."

"Hush, now."

I hang up once he's within earshot.

"Sorry I missed you at first," Dillan says, lowering his phone. "I was fighting with my mittens."

"No worries," I say, standing up, and I can't help how my shoulders are hunching.

"Hi," Dillan says, smile flickering as he surveys me. "Are you okay?"

"Fine," I say, even though that's not quite true.

"No offense, but you turning up at my house out of the blue doesn't bode super well, generally speaking."

"I need . . . ," I say, worried about how my brain is going to end that sentence, so I shut it down before it can.

Dillan must sense my uncertainty, because he just kicks his shoes on the welcome mat to knock snow off and opens the front door. "You know it's cold as ass out here, right?"

"I don't think ass is particularly cold," I say, before I catch on to what he's doing and realize that it's working, I'm distracted.

"Speak for yourself," Dillan says, ushering me inside. "My ass is plenty cold."

"That's on you for going for a walk at eight o'clock at night."

Dillan just shrugs as he closes the door. "Well, the walking part was slightly unexpected."

I give him a sidelong glance, relishing the warmth of the house as it washes over me. "What were you doing?"

"Hey, kiddo," Maria calls from her office, heels clicking toward us. "How was— Oh! Hi, Nora."

I wave.

She seems slightly more surprised than I would expect, but I don't have time to figure out why before Dillan nudges my elbow. "C'mon. Downstairs?"

Sara smiles at me from the kitchen as we pass, raising a mug in greeting. I follow Dillan down the narrow staircase into the basement.

He flips on the light switch, revealing the colorful playroom, which currently looks like a Toys "R" Us threw up.

"Oof," he says, toeing brightly colored action figures aside on his way to the couch in the corner. "Sorry."

"I don't mind," I tell him. It's true. I've never minded Fletcher clutter.

Dillan snags a remote off the shelf and turns on the fireplace, then flops onto the couch, letting out a low groan.

I sit on the other end of the couch, two feet away, and as I remember what I'm here to talk to Dillan about, I start to feel vaguely nauseous.

I can't count the number of times we've sat here. This is where we go to talk, but usually not about anything particularly serious.

"Where were you tonight?" I ask. "Before you came home."

"Nowhere," Dillan says, which is so not like him it's almost alarming.

"Seriously, you can tell me."

"It wasn't important."

"I'm just curious, that's all, you don't have to—"

"I was with Kayla, okay?" he bursts out, like admitting it is annoying.

"Oh." I draw my knees to my chest. "That's . . ."

Dillan doesn't look at me, just stares at the fireplace.

"You don't have to be . . ." I search for the right words. "I don't mind, you know."

That is probably the biggest lie I've ever told, but I don't need him to know that. Julia was a damn good teacher in that department.

"Dillan, it's fine to talk about her. I want you to be happy."

He laughs bitterly, like I've told half of an inside joke I'm not privy to.

"Whatever. What's going on?" Dillan asks. He looks exhausted, the crook of one arm slung over his forehead. "You need to talk about something?"

I take a deep breath. "Yeah, actually. I want to talk to you," I say, careful and even. "About Julia. I just want to ask you a couple of things."

I see the exact moment his whole expression shutters. It's distressing.

"You promised," I whisper. "But I don't . . ."

Dillan shakes his head, inching away. "Look, that promise wasn't just for you."

I knew it was coming, but it's still a nasty confirmation. "It's been almost—"

"I don't want to talk about her either," he says, sounding scraped raw and hoarse. "I just—I don't, and especially not to-night."

"What's tonight?" I ask.

Dillan just curls forward and presses the heels of his palms against his eyes. "It hasn't been a super-awesome day, okay?"

"Oh," I say. "I'm sorry. I didn't mean—"

"I know you didn't," he says, and he doesn't sound annoyed with me, just tired, and a little miserable, and I don't realize how I didn't see it before now.

Am I always this selfish?

Am I just like her?

"I think I should go," I whisper, moving to stand.

"No," Dillan says, and he doesn't look up, but his hand shoots out to grab my wrist. "Stay."

I look down to where he's holding on to me, where the two points of us connect, and then because I could never say no, I sink back down. "Okay."

And I stay.

FORTY-SEVEN

Before

That night, I felt like my blood was on fire.

It had been a week of waiting. Waiting for news about TMU, waiting for the frostiness between me and Julia to dissolve, waiting to decide what to do.

Restlessness ate at me. I couldn't sit still.

My mind was on repeat. My life was on repeat. Was this how it was going to be, again and again?

I called Dillan.

He answered on the second ring.

"Drive me somewhere?"

When he arrived, ten minutes later, I slipped out of the house, quiet as the darkness.

I felt immense, then. There was something about climbing into the passenger seat when it had been dark for hours that felt illicit, and I felt brave, brave, *brave*.

My fingers burned, and I didn't look at him, because if I

did, I'd overflow with myself, with the beingness of the now, bleed myself dry.

It wasn't him. I was pretty sure I'd always known that, but relief ate away at my complicated mess of feelings. He hadn't outed Eve.

Neither of us spoke as he drove, and I watched his knuckles on the steering wheel. Who was this version of me? I was unraveling the tangled surface, and underneath it was just me, or the me I was becoming.

I looked at Dillan, watched the movement of his fingers as he flicked the turn signal. Right then, it didn't quite seem possible that he'd said any of the things Julia had overheard. Who was he? If I was a stranger to myself, he was someone I hardly recognized.

Under the streetlight his hair turned translucent and faded to rust as he made a left turn, and in that moment, I recognized him. Being friends with Dillan felt like relearning a language I had known once. When he glanced over at me, eyebrows quirked in an unspoken question, I recognized him then, too. We locked eyes and I felt invincible; I contained a cosmos on fire, igniting and flickering to a low smolder on endless repeat; I was ablaze with want and fury and hunger and a hundred other emotions I couldn't name.

Finally, he asked, "What happened?"

I didn't want to talk about it. I wanted him to turn to me and say that he hadn't meant any of it at all, that he *wanted* to talk about his birthday. I wanted to ask him to pull over and to climb over the gearshift and kiss him until I forgot who I was. I *wanted*. I just shook my head. "Julia. Being Julia. You know."

There was something behind his eyes when he turned to look at me, indescribable. Maybe it was fear. Maybe it was pity.

"I just—" I rubbed my eyes until patterns bloomed, luminous, out of the darkness.

He waited.

"I feel like I'm losing it, Dillan."

He was so silent that for a second, I wasn't even sure I'd spoken out loud. Then he just asked, "Why?"

I let my hands fall. "It sounds so stupid. I shouldn't even—"

I exhaled a long breath through pursed lips. My hands skittered to my phone, and I checked it to see if she'd sent me anything. She hadn't.

"I think Julia's been reading my journal." My voice cracked a little as I corrected myself. "I *thought*."

"The one that was missing?"

I swallowed and nodded. "I found it."

"Well, that's good, isn't it?"

I shook my head rapidly. "I found it at home. I *know* I brought it to school that day. And then my mom said Julia had been over to return something, but Julia never mentioned anything to me, and she knows stuff I don't remember telling her— See? I sound paranoid."

He considered this for several long moments, and with every second that passed, panic blossomed under my ribs, until I realized with a terrible jolt that it had been an absurd idea to tell him anything. If he really thought I was some dumb and shallow idiot, wasn't I just reinforcing that?

"Sorry," I blurted out. "It's stupid. I shouldn't have said anything. *I'm* stupid."

He looked over at me, one eyebrow raised, and shook his head. "You're not stupid. And it's not stupid either. I'm just thinking."

Think faster. I wrapped my arms around myself as he

merged onto the highway, cursing myself for every stupid decision that had led to this moment.

Then he asked, "If she did read it, what would that mean?"

Leave it to Dillan to ask the right question wrapped up in the wrong one. Right, because it was what needed to be asked, wrong because I didn't want to answer it.

Something squeezed hard in my chest, and I closed my eyes. "It'd mean she's been lying to me."

"Are you going to ask her about it?"

A sob threatened to leap out. "I tried. She made me feel like I was an idiot asshole friend for even asking."

He made a low sound of acknowledgment as he took the next exit, but he didn't say anything. He didn't say anything for nearly three full minutes, until I thought I was going to explode.

I cleared my throat. "You look like you're having a lot of thoughts."

"I am." He didn't take his eyes off the road, but he smiled still. "Unusual, I know."

"I wasn't going to say that."

Dillan laughed, and it was a quiet laugh that wasn't quite all the way there.

"What are your thoughts about?"

His eyes locked with mine for barely a fraction of a second. "About what it would mean if she was reading it."

A hard lump formed in my throat. "I don't want to think about that."

"I don't think I do either."

I didn't realize we were going back home until he pulled back onto my street.

"Why would she do it?"

"Read my journal?"

"Yeah."

It had started to snow, lightly, and I watched the flakes flash through the beam of the headlights. "I don't know. I mean, we're friends! I'd tell her anything if she asked me. But now I feel . . ."

"Like you can't trust her."

"Like I don't know if I should."

He pressed his lips together and was quiet until he pulled into my driveway. "What are you going to do about it?"

I held my fingers against my eyes again, waited for the patterned lights, then let my hands drop. "I don't know."

I looked over at Dillan. Could he really have meant any of the things Julia said he had? Had he even *said* them? If she was lying about the journal, could she be lying about that, too?

"I have to ask you something."

His hands tightened on the steering wheel. I probably wouldn't have noticed if I hadn't already been admiring them. I remembered the brush of his knuckles against my cheek and had to look away.

Friends. Friends. Friends.

"What?"

"Please don't lie." I risked a glance over at him, but he avoided my eyes, looking instead across the lawn, at the soft sprinkle of snowflakes falling through the light cast by the motion detector.

He said, "I won't lie."

"You had nothing to do with it, did you?" I whispered. "Eve?"

Dillan paused, and then he shook his head.

"Why didn't you say anything?"

"I did," he said. "I told her."

"And to me?"

He swallowed. "I didn't know you thought it was me until just now."

"I didn't," I told him. "Not really."

Something in his face unraveled, and he closed his eyes. "Good."

"I have another question."

"Okay."

"Do you think I'm dumb?" I tightened my arms, making fists with my hands, as I turned my head away. I didn't want to see his face, so I peered through the neighbor's hedge.

"What?" I heard him turn in his seat. "Nora. I don't think you're dumb."

Something was knotting and unknotting itself in my stomach. I had to select my words carefully. "If you did, you wouldn't talk about it with other people, would you?"

"I *don't*. And no! What gave you that idea?"

I made myself turn my head, slowly, so that I was looking at my house through the windshield. There was no truth, right now. Only stories. I just had to choose which I believed. "I heard . . ."

Dillan was absolutely silent.

"I heard from someone that you'd said that." I knew it was stupid to disguise where I'd heard it. He'd figure it out, or maybe he already knew.

"That I said you're *dumb*?" He sounded incredulous.

"Among other things."

"No." He made a soft sound of disgust. "Nora. Obviously not."

Relief loosened the muscles in my body just in time for anxiety to draw them taut again.

His voice sounded like truth. But so had hers.

It would always come down to a choice.

Dillan was watching the snow falling through the headlight beams.

He tilted his head, thinking hard. "Who said that I said you were dumb?"

I'd never been more certain that a question was just for show. He knew, and so did I, and that meant that we both understood that the truth was sometimes worse than a lie.

My exhale came out shakier than I thought it would, and I didn't answer him. I didn't want to know what the answer would mean.

I wanted to ask him about his birthday. The question was *right there.* I felt like maybe if I asked it, everything would change. I wanted to know what he thought almost as much as I didn't want to know, but the memory of the way he'd looked at me like I was an afterthought made something turn solid in my chest, so I just drew my jacket around me. "I should go in."

He sighed and nodded. Then as I made to get out, he said, "I'm sorry."

My hand was on the door handle, but I stopped before I opened it. "For what?"

"That you'd think I said that. That I didn't make it obvious I wouldn't. You're not dumb."

I swallowed.

His face looked terribly earnest.

"Thanks for the drive," I whispered, and opened the door before I could do something really stupid. Then, after I'd climbed out into the cold, I told him, "I'm just sorry I believed it."

FORTY-EIGHT

After

In a lot of ways, it feels like my whole life is ending.

Not ending like it's *over*, but like doors are slamming shut. My nineteenth birthday passed quietly. I celebrated with my parents and Simon, and the next night Dillan and Eve came over to watch a movie. None of us acknowledged the one-year anniversary of that awful night. I wonder if I'll ever stop feeling like my birthday is stained by it.

So just like every day, I stand at the register and I take coffee orders, but this time I'm not just on autopilot with my head as empty as I can get it.

My thoughts whirl.

I love my job, but there are a lot of hurt-shaped memories here. The itch for something new burns in my veins.

I can't think about Julia, because it makes me hate myself.

I can't think about Dillan, because everything here reminds me of him and what could have been.

He's leaving tomorrow, for that trip to Queen's. He'll be gone a week, and I probably won't see him before he leaves.

I hear the jangle of the door, and when I look up from the register, Kayla is standing in front of the counter. "Hey."

"Hey, Nora." Kayla looks fantastic. Radiant, even.

I bite my lip. "I'm sorry about the other day. I didn't mean to freak out."

"All good," Kayla says, and it sounds true. "Happy belated birthday, by the way!"

"Thanks! How are you?"

"Great, actually." Kayla smiles. I hate that it makes me anxious.

I take her order, then duck down to the fridge to retrieve the almond milk.

"How are *you* doing?" She leans against the counter. "Any updates in the life of Nora Radford?"

"Not *really*." I steam the milk and lower my head so she can't see my face.

It's not really lying.

I ask, "How's it going with Dillan?"

All casual.

Kayla raises an eyebrow. "He didn't tell you?"

I shake my head, bracing myself. They've probably made it official, or maybe they slept together. The idea makes my throat tighten.

She shrugs. "We broke up."

I almost knock over the pitcher. "What?"

"If you can call it breaking up. We weren't really ever together."

"You broke up? *Why?*"

She shrugs again.

I pour her drink and set it on the counter.

"He wasn't my type. I guess I didn't really think it would work out."

My mind is whirling.

"And—" she starts, then breaks off, shaking her head.

"What?"

"Nothing. It's not my business."

My mouth has gone dry. *"What?"*

She raises her hands, shaking her head again. "It's nothing."

It's not nothing.

I look at her, trying to keep it together. "Was he upset?"

"Dillan?" She turns and looks out the window. "Oh, not really. I think he was sort of relieved."

I rinse my hands. "Why?"

She sighs, and looks at me then, steadily. "You know why, Nora."

I feel my heart stop.

I don't know.

I think I do.

I *hope* I do.

I want it so badly it can't be real.

My heart starts again, a fast staccato up in my throat and in my ears. "What did he tell you?"

"He didn't have to tell me anything." She rolls her eyes. "Come on. And if I weren't already pretty sure you were interested in him, the way you're looking at me right now would have confirmed it."

"He—you." I raise one hand to my ear. "I thought he asked you out?"

"Yeah, but that didn't *mean* anything. It was *so* obvious that he was just trying to get over you. It honestly felt like we were just friends hanging out. We held hands, a bit, but that was it. Honestly, it was pretty weird.

"Also . . ." Her eyes dart toward the door. "I was sort of maybe seeing somebody else. Which might have factored into the decision."

I raise one eyebrow. "Who? Do I know him?"

Kayla pauses for a second, then swallows. "Um. Her. And yes."

"Who?"

"Uh. Don't be mad at me for dating your friends. I promise I'm not trying to. It's just—like I said, we met at that Halloween party, and then it sort of spiraled from there. But it might turn into something, and . . . yeah."

I blink once, then again. *"Eve?"*

She doesn't look at me, but she nods.

"Dude. You have *serious* game."

She laughs. "So, you aren't upset?"

"No!" I laugh too. "Just surprised. I didn't know you were . . ."

"What, bi? Yeah. I am." She shakes her head. "Anyway. Please tell me you're going to call him."

"Should I?"

"God." She raises a hand to her face. "Nora. Please. *Enough* waiting, already. Just *talk* to him."

"That wouldn't be weird for you?"

She scoffs. "Nora. Come on. He was always yours."

Always mine.

Is that possible?

"Okay." She smacks the counter. "Tell me how it goes. I've gotta run, but, uh, good luck."

As I watch her retreat, it feels like my brain is working extra hard to wrap itself around all this new information.

The rest of my shift is agony.

I clock out the second it's over. My boss looks at me, eyebrows raised, and laughs. I doubt she's ever seen me this eager to leave. I toss my name tag into the bin and practically rip my apron off.

I've pressed the button to call Dillan before I'm even out of the back room. *Please pick up. Please pick up.* I know he has a midterm today, but it's still forty-five minutes away. I might be able to catch him.

I shove open the heavy door that separates the café from the back. The phone rings and rings. I burst through the doors back into the café and wave to my boss. My heart thuds as I practically fly across the room.

Dillan answers just as I'm wrenching the front door open.

"Hello?" He sounds a little out of breath. "Are you still at work? Don't—"

I careen into somebody and let out a little screech of surprise.

"—leave yet," Dillan says in front of me at the same time he says it into my ear.

I look up at him.

He's flushed and panting, as though he's been running.

"What are you doing here?" I let the door close behind us as I press end on the phone call. It's bitterly cold out, but I don't care. I can't stop looking at him.

He leans over, hands on his knees, breathless. "Jesus Christ."

I grab his arm, but I let go just as quickly. "Did you run here from the station?"

He's looking everywhere but at me. His eyes are a little wild. "Sort of, maybe. Kayla—she texted me—"

For one horrible second, I think I'm wrong. I think Kayla is wrong. I think I've been reading into things because I want it so badly.

Then he finally looks at me, and I see *hope.* "She said—"

I throw my hands up in the air. "Stop!"

He blinks, but goes quiet.

"Sorry." A bubble of laughter rises up in me. My heart is beating so hard I can feel it in my ears. "I want to be the one to say it. I don't want it to be because of something Kayla told you."

He's looking at me with the quiet intensity I'm starting to recognize. "Nora."

I take a deep breath and open my mouth, but I can't form any words.

I can't *look* at him. "I thought you were happy with Kayla."

His fingers are on my wrists and he pulls my hands away from my face.

"Dillan, I—if you still feel—" I just want to get past this part, but I know I can't let him say it for me. "Do you remember your birthday? Last year."

He lets go of my wrists, gently, and he laughs somewhat incredulously. "Of course I remember."

I shake my head. "I wasn't sure."

"I wondered if *you'd* forgotten."

I swallow. "I didn't. I meant it. I meant for it to mean something."

He stares at me for a second. Then he raises both hands and tugs them through his curls, looking across the parking lot.

I wait for him to say something, but he's just thinking. And since he's not looking right at me, I blurt it out. "I like you, Dillan. I liked you then, and I like you now."

His eyes snap back to me, and he's just *looking*.

I'm almost uncomfortable with how intense his gaze is.

Dillan asks, "You're not just saying that?"

"Why would I?" I'm starting to feel a little helpless. I thought he'd be a little happier, but he just looks pensive.

"Because of what I said. About school, and starting late, and—"

"No. No. It wasn't because of that."

"I've been feeling like shit for telling you," he says. "I crossed a line and . . . I didn't want to influence you or anything."

Something is tightening in my chest, and not in a good way.

"You really meant it, back then? The kiss?"

I nod. There's no going back now. "I thought maybe you did too, but then everything was so complicated after, and you said we didn't have to talk about it, and I was so confused."

He sucks in a long breath. "Nora. Nora."

I look at the ground, because I can't look at him anymore, and then I close my eyes because it isn't enough to just look away.

"I meant it too," he whispers, and my eyes fly open. "I meant it so bad. I wanted it to be . . . You really wanted . . . ?"

Hope and relief bloom in my chest at once, and my laughter comes out sounding exasperated. "Yes."

I look at his shoes because I can't look at his face.

"Me too," he says. "Of you. I—wow. Words."

I laugh, and that's when I notice my hands are shaking.

He groans. "I sort of thought I'd be a little more eloquent if this ever happened."

I finally look back up at him, and I'm glad I do, because I

catch the tail end of a really good Dillan smile. It's the kind of smile I reflexively mirror, and for a second, we just stand there, grinning at each other. I want to memorize the way his face looks right now.

Then, because I have no idea what to do, I flounder until my brain latches onto the least important thing I can think of and won't let go. I grip his arm. "Your midterm. You said you have a midterm, right?"

He looks a little startled, but he flips his wrist to look at his watch, and exhales. "I can skip it."

I punch his arm. "Dillan!"

"Ow—I was kidding!" He looks a little offended. "I'll still make it if you'll walk with me back to the station."

"I'll do you one better." I jerk my head toward the parking lot. "You parked here, right? I'll drive and drop you off."

For once, he doesn't argue. I sort of hope it's because he doesn't want to say goodbye, because I certainly don't.

I might be the most pathetic person on the planet. I'm only on the other side of the car without eyes on him for about three seconds, but it's enough that when I slide into the seat and I see him again, something releases in my chest.

He closes his eyes and leans his head back against the head-rest.

I start the car, but I don't—can't—tear my gaze away from him. When he turns his head and opens his eyes to look at me, his whole face is smiling.

I've been in a car with Dillan a hundred times before, but everything is different now.

The leather of the steering wheel looks different. My hands on top of the leather look different. The way my heart beats feels different.

"God," he says. "Did I just die? I sort of feel like I died."

I laugh, and it feels like my chest is about to burst. "I hope you didn't."

I don't know what to do with myself—my hands, my fingers—and I don't know what's allowed. The rules changed in an instant and now I don't know them anymore, but it's not distressing, just strange.

I navigate out of the lot and Dillan puts on the radio station he likes. When I start laughing, he looks over at me, one eyebrow raised. "What?"

"I can't believe you ran from the train station."

He ducks his head low, and his ears turn pink. "What? I was worried that you were going to leave after your shift. I wanted to catch you."

"You could have called or something." I'm really glad no one else is in the car with us, because I know that the way I'm looking at him is probably embarrassing, but I can't stop smiling.

"You don't exactly have an awesome track record for picking up."

My mouth drops open. "Hey!"

His grin is devilish. "What was I supposed to do? You should have seen what Kayla texted me. Of course I ran."

Of course he ran. My chest squeezes so hard it almost hurts. "What did she say?"

He leans back in the seat. "Well, to back up, I had just gotten to school—I was planning to study for an hour or two before the exam—"

"Sorry."

"It doesn't matter. Anyway, I'm standing on the platform, and Kayla texts me 'go get your girl.' " At that, Dillan stops and flushes bright red.

I slow to a stop at a red light and cover my face with my hands. "What a meddler."

He shakes his head, ears scarlet. "I didn't really know what she meant, but then she said she just saw you at work, I figured she might have said something. So when the train going back home came, I just got on. I spent the whole ride thinking about what I might say when I saw you."

It's a good thing I'm driving, and we're in the middle of a busy highway, because I feel like my self-control is dangling by a thread. The adrenaline is starting to wear off, and my fingers are jittery and starving for the way his skin feels under them. I clench the steering wheel and glance at the clock.

Dillan sees me looking. "We'll make it."

"I just . . ." I shake my head, trying to wrap my mind around everything that's changed in the last twenty-four hours. "I don't really believe it."

"What part?"

"All of it. I really thought I missed my chance. I thought you'd moved on. That you liked Kayla."

"Yeah, well, you didn't miss anything," he says; then he stops, as though he's thinking through what he's trying to say. "It's always been you."

I let out a shuddering breath.

"Don't get me wrong, she's nice, but it wasn't fair to her. It's a good thing she's smart."

I take the exit for the university. "I guess so."

I can see in my peripherals that he's looking at me, and the way it makes me feel means that I have to determinedly look at the road. I can't really believe this is happening, but it's starting to sink in. It's real. Kayla's words ring in my ears: *Always yours.*

"You *like* me." I can't stop myself from grinning. "Ha. Sucker."

"Oh, yeah, whatever."

I can *hear* the smile in his words.

"*You* like *me*," he points out. "So that makes us even."

"Yeah." I keep my voice light. "I like you."

When I look over at Dillan, he's already looking back, and the way he's looking feels enormous.

"Would you have ever told me?" I ask. "If Kayla hadn't started it?"

"I don't know." Out of the corner of my eye I see him fiddle with his watch strap. "That's not how it happened, so. Hard to say."

I tap my fingers on the wheel.

"Maybe I would have. Only if I thought you felt the same way."

"Did you ever think I did?"

"Sometimes."

He's not going to elaborate, and it's with a tiny sigh that I turn off the road and onto campus. I glance at the clock again. "You would definitely not have made it if you'd taken the train."

He grins. "Definitely not."

"You can't just *skip* a midterm. Dude."

"Would have been worth it."

"Dillan!" I object, but I can't stop the warmth that kindles in my chest and spreads out through the rest of me.

"My professor likes me. I'd have figured it out. Do you think that matters more than this?"

I don't even know how to answer that. The way he asks tells me I don't have to.

I maneuver into a parking spot, and my heart leaps a little. What happens now?

Dillan turns to me suddenly as he undoes his seat belt. "Come with me to the Christmas market tonight."

"Okay." I'd probably go anywhere if he asked me right now. "I'll drive your car back to the station? Leave your key at the café?"

He nods. "Thank you. I'll pick you up tonight. Six-thirty?"

He reaches toward me—I lean toward him instinctively—and when his fingers graze my jaw I shiver.

"Okay."

For a single heart-stopping moment I think this is it, but instead he just lets his hand fall back down.

He whispers, "Nora."

I whisper back, "Dillan."

"I really, *really* want to kiss you right now. But if I start, I guarantee you I won't be able to stop, and I have a midterm in"—he flips his wrist to glance down at his watch—"three minutes, so."

I can't stop looking at his mouth. "So."

I don't think I could ever get tired of the way he smiles at me right now. "I gotta go. I'll see you later, yeah?"

I'm embarrassed by how breathless I sound. "Yeah. Good luck—for your midterm."

He tilts his head, as though he knows some kind of secret. "Thanks."

Then he's getting out of the car and I'm watching him leave and it all feels impossible, like there's a little impenetrable bubble of ebullience floating in my chest. He looks back twice, and just before he ducks into the building he grins and pauses, raising a hand to his lips. At first, I think he's going to blow me a kiss, but he just lets his fingers rest there, and then he smiles, shoulders the door open, and disappears.

I sit there for a full five minutes before I drive back to the train station, convincing myself that it's real.

It's real. It's *real*.

FORTY-NINE

Before

In a lot of ways, that night was the spark that started the blaze.

In other ways, it was just continuing the disintegration—it had always been happening, and it was happening now. Burning. We were taking turns stripping each other down to nothing, carving away at the truth and coming up with handfuls of smoldering ash.

I'd been more than a little reluctant to follow through with our plans for my birthday. The whole day had felt wrong. Every year for the last seven years, when it was my birthday Julia had decorated my locker. It was tradition that I wouldn't hear from her until I got to my locker and found it covered in glittery stickers and spiraling streamers, so it wasn't weird that I didn't have a text from her. But it felt like a punch to walk through the hallway and see only the bare gray-blue metal. She still wished me a happy birthday when we met up at lunch, but it was distant and almost cold.

I was in trouble, I knew, both for accusing her of stealing from me and then for not bending over backward trying to apologize. But I just couldn't bring myself to do it. I hadn't been able to all week.

It seemed wrong and inside out that we were still going to the Christmas market when everything else was falling apart and all of us were fighting. But it was happening anyway.

I had thought it would feel worse to stay at home by myself when I'd know every minute what we *would* have been doing. Right then, though, sitting in the passenger seat of Eve's car, it just felt terrible.

"I can't believe you invited *Dillan*." Julia slouched in the backseat.

"Hey." I whirled around. "It's *my* birthday, all right? I get to choose who's coming."

Julia blinked.

I didn't think I'd ever talked to her like that before.

But she must have known that she wasn't in a position to argue, because she just closed her mouth and looked out the window.

It was true. I'd invited Dillan, and though I wouldn't tell him this, it was mostly because I couldn't stomach the thought of a whole night with Eve and Julia without a buffer.

They'd mostly been acting like nothing was wrong, and Julia and I were acting like we hadn't fought, and it all felt like a farce. Like we were actors and none of us had scripts.

We were in front of Dillan's house. He walked out the front door and tossed me a bright smile.

"I can't believe you're still friends with him," Julia growled.

I shot what I hoped was a venomous glare toward the backseat.

"Hey." Dillan opened the door and slid into the car next to Julia. "Happy birthday, Nora. Again."

He'd been the only one at school to wish me a happy birthday and sound like he meant it. Even Eve hadn't been really enthusiastic, though I understood why.

I mumbled a "Thank you" as Julia glowered at him.

He frowned, and they exchanged a complex look that was strangely charged. "Wow. Tough crowd."

I was glad it wasn't a long drive, because the four of us were awkwardly quiet. For a second, I wished Julia weren't there, because Eve and Dillan and I would get along just fine.

When we got there, I was relieved to see that it looked just the same as it did every year—glittering fairy lights lined the entrance, and once Eve had parked and the four of us wandered in, there was the usual collection of stalls displaying ornaments, knickknacks, homemade knitted goods, soaps, and various trinkets.

Julia had been to Europe, and normally every year she couldn't resist informing us that it looked *just like* the German Christmas markets. This year, though, she stayed silent and sullen.

Christmas music drifted down from above, bright and cheerful, which felt strange, because I was not feeling bright or cheerful at all.

"I'd forgotten about all this," Dillan said appreciatively, looking up at the ceiling, where more Christmas lights had been draped.

Right up until I'd invited him, I'd forgotten that years ago, Dillan's family used to come with mine to the Christmas market. It had probably been eight or nine years since then, though, and while I'd still been going every year, watching him was sort of like seeing it with fresh eyes.

We started wandering around, and the whole time I was praying that things would get less awkward, or this was about to be a really short night.

"Now that you're an adult, what are you going to do differently?"

Thank God for Eve.

"I'll get a job," I told her. "I could do with some extra cash. Plus, I'm going to try and save up for my own car."

"What, you're going to *drive* all the way out east?" Julia scoffed. "Isn't buying a car a waste of money?"

"So—this job," Eve said, ignoring Julia, who looked positively mutinous. "Where would you want to work?" She leaned against a giant nutcracker display, which wobbled, and she stepped aside nervously.

"I'm actually looking into interviewing at Second Cup." I picked up an ornament and held it against the light. "Do you think my mom would like this?"

Julia stopped walking. "Wait, like the coffee shop?"

"Yeah."

"You'd hate that, wouldn't you?"

I shrugged. "I don't know. It might not be so bad. Being a barista could be fun."

"You hate coffee."

"I hate *drip* coffee," I pointed out.

"I think you'd be good at it," Dillan offered.

Julia rolled her eyes, but I pretended I didn't see it.

"Thank you," I said, placing the ornament back on the shelf, "for not being a huge party pooper."

Julia scoffed as I turned away.

I tried to make my face a neutral mask, the way I saw Dillan do sometimes. Tonight was supposed to be fun, yet everything about it made me want to throw myself into oncoming traffic.

It took less than three minutes for Eve and Julia to get involved in a heated argument over something stupid on one of the display shelves, and so, feeling anxiety build in my chest, I started walking away.

The same helplessness I'd felt the other night was squeezing my lungs. I felt a hand on my shoulder.

"You okay?" Dillan's voice was quiet.

A few steps away, I heard Eve object loudly to something.

"I'm fine."

He just sighed. Then he asked, "Has Julia ever lied to you? Besides the journal?"

I thought about Eve. I thought about countless other examples over the history of our friendship. I just whispered, "Yeah."

He frowned. "How far do you think she'd go?"

"What do you mean?"

"Has she ever lied to you about anything important?" He looked over to where Julia and Eve were still bickering, and when his eyes landed on Julia, he looked almost pained. "Like, sensitive stuff?"

My stomach dropped. I recalled what Julia told me about Dillan flirting with her. Had she hurt him somehow? Had he—did Dillan have feelings for Julia?

I was about to respond when my phone buzzed in my pocket. Two buzzes for an email. My heart jumped up into my throat. Distracted, I asked, "What kind of stuff?"

Dillan was still looking at Julia. There was something very

complicated in his expression, so I pulled out my phone, just to avoid it.

My breath caught.

TMU.

"What?" Dillan asked.

"TMU emailed," I said, breathless.

"Seriously?" he asked, eyes wide. "And?"

"I can't look." I unlocked my phone, handed it to Dillan, and covered my eyes. "I can't look, you read it."

There was a moment of silence while he read, but then he stayed quiet.

"What does it say?" I whispered, heart sinking.

Dillan didn't say anything.

I let my hands fall. "Dillan?"

He was looking down at the screen, expression crestfallen, and he said, "I'm sorry."

My fingers trembled as I took back the phone. Maybe this was a joke. Maybe he was just messing with me.

But there it was. *We regret to inform you—*

I squeezed my eyes shut. "It's fine."

Looked like Julia was getting her way regardless. I'd finally finished my application, and the school counselor had told me I was pretty much guaranteed to get into McGill.

Matching duvets it was.

Dillan let out a low breath. "I'm really sorry, Nora."

"It's fine," I said, keeping my eyes squeezed tight so I wouldn't cry. "It's okay."

Damn, and on my birthday.

"Nor, I—"

He broke off. Whatever he was going to say, it was interrupted by the sound of somebody shouting.

Even though I'd vaguely started to register the sounds behind us, it wasn't until I saw Dillan's face that I whirled around.

I'd thought we'd all be able to get through this evening in one piece.

I was wrong.

Eve and Julia stood practically nose to nose.

"You want to know?" Eve yelled. "You want to know the truth? Fine. *Here's* your truth. It's all true!"

"What's all true?" Julia took a step back.

"You want me to say it out loud?" Eve stepped forward. "That's what you want?"

Julia didn't say anything.

"I *know* it was you." Eve's voice was vicious. "I'm not *stupid*. Who else would do something like that to me?"

"I—it wasn't me," Julia stammered.

I'd never seen Julia look like that before: a little wild, *very* afraid. I'd never seen Eve stand up to Julia—or anyone—like that, either. I wished we hadn't come. I wished—

I backed up into Dillan. His hand grazed my shoulder.

"It's *true*, Julia, I'm gay." Eve threw her arms out wide. "But you already knew that, didn't you?"

Julia stared at her, openmouthed. "That doesn't mean I spread the rumor!"

"But you did, didn't you?" Eve asked. "Didn't you!"

Julia goggled at her. Then she seemed to realize that Dillan and I were watching, and she crossed her arms tightly.

Eve balled her hands into fists. "You read Nora's journal, and that's how you found out?"

Julia didn't say anything, but apparently the lack of denial was enough for Eve.

"That's it." Eve shook her head and sucked her lower lip in. "That's it. I can't."

"What do you mean, can't?" Julia took a step toward her, and Eve stumbled back.

"This is *it,* Julia. That's what I mean. I'm done with this. I'm done with you. You're *such* an asshole, all the time, you know that?" Eve was trembling. One tear spilled down her cheek, and she swiped it away furiously. "I'm sick of it! I'm sick of rolling over and not being myself because I'm afraid of how you'll react!"

Julia opened her mouth, but Eve shook her head violently, a finger in her face.

"No. I'm done. And I'm not afraid of you anymore."

She was crying hard when she turned to me, her shoulders shaking. "I'm so sorry, Nora. I'm sorry I ruined your birthday."

I shook my head. "No, no. You didn't."

That's when I noticed Julia staring at me, indignation written all over her face.

"What?" I stared right back. "Did you seriously expect me to take your side here?"

The reproach in her expression said it all.

I shook my head, and my voice quivered. "No."

Her jaw hardened.

When I spoke again, my voice didn't shake. "No, Julia. I'm done taking your side."

FIFTY

After

When Dillan's car pulls into the driveway, I practically fly out the door.

"How was your midterm?" I blurt out, before I'm even properly in the car.

He grins, which makes me feel a bit dizzy. "I think it went okay. I was a little distracted."

I feel my cheeks burning. "Sorry." Then I add, "Me too."

For a second, we just sit there, looking at each other, then he reaches over and twirls a strand of my hair around his index finger. "I forgot to tell you I like this. Did Eve do it?"

I was already smiling, but I find space to smile even wider. "Yeah. Thank you."

He takes in a breath. "This is real, right? I didn't imagine it?"

"It's real," I whisper.

I can't stop looking at him. I want to kiss him. I want to reach over and pull him toward me, but he's already taken his hand away to turn the key in the ignition. "I still can't really believe it."

"Me neither." I'm drinking in the sight of him.

"You know," he says as he backs out of the driveway, "when I first saw you with the haircut, after . . . Well, you remember. I almost forgot I was upset with you."

I cover my face with my hands. "Oh my God."

"It was like my brain totally stopped working for a second. I had come in with this whole speech planned out and then all I could think was *Holy shit holy shit that is a* very *good look.*" He smacks the wheel and repeats, *"Holy shit."*

I'm certain I'm blushing to my roots. "I'm glad you don't hate it."

"I *definitely* don't hate it." He grins.

Then he turns and gives me a look that would have been a kiss if we weren't merging onto the highway, and it makes something curl in the pit of my stomach.

On the way there, we talk about nothing. It's the sort of frivolous conversation that occurs between two people who are tired of talking but don't know how to stop, and so I hear about his midterm, and I tell him about my shift, and when we pull into the parking lot, we haven't really talked about anything at all.

The market is alive and awake. I feel strangely like I'm living two lives at once—there's Nora, a year ago, walking through the market with Dillan beside me but not allowed, and Nora now, walking through the market again, and Dillan is still beside me, and now it's allowed.

He ambles past a vibrant display of Christmas ornaments, hands shoved deep into his pockets. When he sees me looking, the corners of his mouth pull up.

I'm thinking about kissing him. Again. It makes me think about the last time. I keep my voice casual. "I have a question."

"Go for it."

"Why did you tell me we didn't have to talk about it? The kiss last year, I mean. If you meant it too."

I'm surprised by the look on his face. He picks up a bauble and turns it between his fingers, expression bleak. "I'm not sure I should say."

I feel my stomach turn over. "What? Why?"

He presses his lips together. "It was because of Julia."

It seems improbable that this should surprise me, all things considered, but I still struggle to wrap my head around it. "What did she do?"

"We don't have to talk about it if you'd rather not. I don't want to break my promise."

I grip his arm. "Dillan. What did she do?"

He sighs, and the bauble stills in his hand. He places it back on the shelf, offers the saleslady a grim smile, then shoves both hands in his pockets and starts walking again. I let go of his arm. "She called me that night."

I struggle to contextualize this. "What?"

"She said you'd told her what happened, which I initially thought was a good thing." He doesn't look at me. "But then she said you were freaking out about it, and that you didn't know what you'd done. She said I was an asshole for taking advantage of you when we'd both been drinking, and that you'd said it had been a mistake."

The axis of my world shifts. Again. Again.

How could I have not known?

"I never said any of that."

"I sort of figured that out later, when I realized more about what was going on with you two, and with the whole thing about your journal. If she was lying about that, then maybe she was lying about other stuff too. But then there was the accident, and I wanted to give you space, and . . . timing. You know."

I stop walking. My thoughts whirl too quickly to make sense of anything. "Julia told you that I'd said it was a mistake?"

"Yeah. I mean, I wasn't about to ask you. What if it was true?" He shakes his head. "I confronted her about it, actually. It was the same day of . . . It was earlier that afternoon. Right when you were talking with Mr. Ambrose. I asked her about it, and she wouldn't admit to it, but the way she was talking around it made me realize that she lied."

Why would she have done that? I think back to a conversation with Eve. *Julia didn't like to share.* But would she really have gone that far?

"That's why you were going to come over that night?" It's not cold in the market, but I'm shivering, and I can't stop. "To talk about it?"

He nods. "I thought about it a lot that week, but it didn't seem fair to dump it on you after everything that had happened at the market with Eve and Julia. And then after . . . well. It didn't seem right."

I look at the ground. "Was she the reason you weren't at school the day after your birthday, then?"

"Ha. No. I really was sick." Dillan gives me a wry smile. "Although Mum says she thinks I made myself sick from thinking about it too much."

"She knows?"

I can see him trying to bite down an embarrassed smile. "They both do. I had to tell *someone.*"

"I can't believe Julia would do that."

He clenches his jaw. "Can't you?"

I pause. I feel dangerously close to tears. "I was so happy when I called her."

"Hey." Dillan turns to me. "We got past it. It's okay."

I must look stricken, though, because after a second, he pulls me into a hug.

I manage to gasp into his shoulder, "It's *not* okay."

But it's a little better now that we're so close. I wrap my arms around him like it's instinct. The way he smells instantly takes me back to kissing him in his living room. "Everything with Julia aside, we could have had a whole *year*. And now you're leaving in January, and I . . ."

His arms tighten around me. "No. Don't think about that. We got here eventually, didn't we?"

I let my head rest against his shoulder. "Eventually."

He sighs, and the kiss he drops on the top of my head is feather-light, almost like it's a secret.

It makes my chest hurt. "I can't believe you're going away tomorrow. That's not fair. I won't survive a whole week."

When he laughs, I can feel it in my body too, and I think it's probably my favorite part about hugging him, but then he strokes my shoulder, and I decide *that's* my favorite part.

Even though I wish we could, I know we can't just stand there forever, so I pull away. The way he smiles at me when he steps back makes me feel chaotic and strange, as though my internal wiring is running twice as fast as it should.

"I know. I keep telling myself it's just a week, but that is a *lot* of hours."

With careful steps, I walk past him down the aisle. I feel sick, poisoned with the knowledge that Julia intentionally lied to Dillan. Why would she have gone that far? What was the *point*? I've never thought about what it would feel like to experience relief and betrayal at the same time, but it's happening right now.

A whole year, lost. At least there's now.

I decide I can't think about Julia anymore, because right now thinking about her makes my chest burn. "Promise me you'll still have fun."

He laughs, falling into step beside me. "I promise."

Our knuckles brush together. I feel something electric hum in my chest.

I see him glance at me out of the corner of his eye, and I can't stop myself from smiling. It occurs to me that I could hold his hand, and so just like with the kiss last year, I do it before I can stop myself, slipping my fingers through his.

I can't look at him, though, so I just smile at the ground. For some reason this feels more intimate than it did to hug him. The pressure of his hand in mind feels perfectly right.

For a long time, we don't say anything. It's enough to just walk around the market hand in hand, admiring the stalls.

I watch him like I'm learning his face. I have an urge to sink my fingers into his curls. I want to drag him by the hand somewhere away from all these people.

Then Dillan looks over at me, head tilted, and he smiles. Like he's reading my mind, he pulls his keys out of his pocket and asks, "Do you want to get out of here?"

I look at him warily. "Not home, right?"

He tosses the keys in the air, and they jingle when they hit his palm. "Nah. I was thinking we could get some juice."

FIFTY-ONE

Before

The week after everything dissolved was one of the worst of my life.

Rejected. I'd been rejected.

I hadn't realized how much I'd been hoping for different news until my chance was gone.

Neither Eve nor I was speaking to Julia, but we weren't really speaking to each other, either, though that was less out of animosity than a mutual sense that we were both hurting too much to be anything but bitter.

It was sort of just me and Dillan, but even he seemed distracted by something beyond my understanding. When I tried to bring up Julia, he got strangely quiet.

It made sense after I'd thought about it. Dillan had flirted with Julia. The look on his face had been *so* strange and charged, almost urgent, that night at the Christmas market, and now he couldn't look me in the eye when I said her name.

They had a secret.

At least, to my relief, he didn't ask questions. That was our rhythm. Asking questions felt like mutually assured destruction, so we didn't.

The days crawled by with agonizing apathy.

Life without Julia felt strange, because she was still right there, and we were still in all the same classes. But I couldn't look at her without thinking about my journal and Eve's secret, and feeling acid burn the back of my throat.

I hadn't realized how much space Julia took up in my life until she went quiet. The space between our desks hadn't felt like a canyon before. Up until that point, I'd never have known to describe silence as cold.

I just wished that were the worst of it. Maybe we could have come back from it if we'd left it there, if that had been all.

But we were never going to come back from it.

And all of us knew it, even then.

When I was walking to my locker at the end of the day on Friday, I saw Julia and Dillan already there and deeply involved in some kind of discussion.

At something he said, she rolled her eyes, and when she spoke, she jabbed him in the chest.

He recoiled, looking annoyed—no. Hurt. Let down.

When I joined them, they looked up at the same time and fell silent.

I cleared my throat.

They glanced at each other, then away, both looking equally guilty.

"Nora," Julia said, then swallowed. "I was wondering . . . did you want to meet up tonight? To talk?"

It was a desperate, last-ditch effort, and we both knew it.

I shook my head, frantically racking my brain for an excuse. "Not today. I—I have a headache, and—"

"And she agreed to help me with an essay." Dillan stepped in smoothly.

Something indeterminate passed between them. Julia's eyes flashed, but Dillan's gaze was steady.

I looked at them, not sure precisely what I was watching for but feeling decidedly unsettled by the exchange.

Julia's tone was clipped. "Fine. Have it your way."

It looked like she was going to turn and leave, but then at the last second, she darted forward and whispered something to Dillan. His eyebrows shot straight up, but he did an impressive job of schooling his features. Maybe if I didn't know him, I wouldn't have recognized the electric shock of hurt on his face, there one instant and gone the next.

Then she pulled back, looked at him very pointedly, spun around, and stalked down the hallway.

"What was that about?"

He shook his head. "Nothing important."

"It *looked* important," I said, then regretted poking, because Dillan's shoulders hunched defensively.

"It's nothing," he snapped, then clenched his jaw.

I pressed my hand against my forehead and heaved a sigh. "Whatever. I don't want to fight with you, too."

"Sorry," Dillan said, then fell silent.

I allowed myself to stand there feeling bereft and hollowed out, and then I straightened my shoulders and set my jaw.

When I looked up, he was watching me carefully.

I tilted my head. "What?"

"I changed my mind," Dillan said. "I need to tell you something."

I *hated* the way he was looking at me. Like he thought I was going to hate whatever he had to say. I pushed past the ache and nodded. "Okay. What is it?"

He looked at me for a second, uncertain, but then he nodded, knocking lightly on his locker. "Will you be at home later tonight?"

"I should be, yeah. Is it important?"

Then he sighed. "I'll tell you about it tonight. I gotta go pick up Angie or I'd get into it now, but—yeah. I'll come around this evening, if that's okay with you?"

I shrugged. "Fine by me."

I wasn't sure how it made me feel that there was something so important that Dillan felt we needed to set apart time to talk about it. Probably, I realized, with a sharp and stabbing ache, he was going to tell me about Julia. The idea was so painful that I almost didn't notice him start to walk away.

"I'll see you later, then." He looked over his shoulder, a little apologetic. "I'm sorry I can't stay now."

I shrugged him off. "No problem. Yeah, I'll see you later."

But I wouldn't.

At least, not the way I'd thought.

FIFTY-TWO

After

feel alive and awake, full of this restlessness, this *purpose*. I
can't quite define it or describe it, but when I look over at
Dillan, I feel it thrumming beneath my sternum.

Neither of us says anything on the way to the grocery store.
It's just that kind of night. I roll down the window, stick my
head out. The wind on my face is cool but not cold, unseasonably lovely for a November evening. I'm so relieved it burns.

When we get there, Dillan parks the car and looks at me.

"Okay. What kind of juice?" I ask.

He pauses, and grins. "Whatever is on sale."

My heart skips a beat. He remembers.

He bites his lip, grinning at me with that specific Dillan
smile, the one that says: *I know you.* I want to blurt out, *And I
know you, too,* but I don't.

The store is dead as I push the door open. The bell jingles,
and the lone cashier shoots us an annoyed look.

"Okay," Dillan says. "Juice."

Everything in the store is the same as the last time we were here, yet everything between us is different. I watch him as he scans the aisle lists, wondering what he's thinking.

He smiles, sidles up next to me, and just like that—like it's just that easy, like it's natural—he grabs my hand, lacing our fingers together, and I die a little on the inside as he pulls me toward the juice aisle.

We bicker for a moment about juice flavors before falling silent. He lets go of my hand to reach a bottle high on the shelf.

I pretend to be heavily invested in comparing prices.

"Hey. Nor?"

"Hmm?"

"Can I ask you something?"

My fingers still against the glass of the fridge. "Shoot."

"When did you know?" Dillan's voice is casual in the practiced way that tells me he's been dying to ask.

"Know what?"

"About me. That I was more than a friend. This time. Because when we talked about it a few weeks ago, I thought for sure that was my last chance."

I smile wistfully. "Studio Bell. Well, just before. On the train."

His eyebrows arch. "So *that's* why you were being weird that day."

"I wasn't!" I object. "I just . . . it felt so strange. It wasn't like a realization or anything like that."

He's looking at me intently.

"It felt more like I was remembering something I already knew. No, that doesn't make any sense. It feels like . . . it feels like it's been true for a long time. Probably, it has been. Just after last year, you know . . ."

He's looking at me with soft eyes again. I suddenly feel so overwhelmed, so full of emotion, that I have to look away.

"What about you?" I ask.

"Honestly?"

"Yeah. Be honest."

He shrugs, glances at me over his shoulder. "I don't want to freak you out."

"You won't." I feel my heart flutter a little bit.

He laughs, sounding uncertain, tugging a hand through his hair so that it stands up on end. "I don't remember ever not loving you."

As soon as he says it, he looks into the freezer, face lit by the fluorescent glow. His eyelashes are nearly transparent.

Even if it's a lie, I don't care.

Even if it's impossible, I don't care.

"Dillan." I'm whispering now.

"You don't have to say that back to me," he says, still looking at the freezer.

I don't—can't—say anything at all.

"It's . . . a lot. I know that, and it's way, *way* too early on for that to be appropriate, but—"

"Did you just tell me you love me in the freezer aisle of a Safeway?"

He winces, but then I laugh, and he's looking at me, and the corners of his mouth pull up and he's smiling too, despite himself. "Maybe."

"You mean it?"

He looks right at me when he nods, serious again. "Always have."

All I can do is stare at him. It feels, for a moment, impossible that this is happening, impossible that it's real, that he's *here,* but he is.

It feels like this is the moment. He feels magnetic. I'm not sure if it's me or if it's him that moves first, but it's like there's a gravitational pull that I can't escape.

Achingly slow, we step toward each other. I can see every freckle on his face, every individual eyelash. I've never been so nervous in my life, but it's electrifying, the best kind of nervous to be.

He rests his forehead against mine, and he's too close to look at anymore, so I shut my eyes and drink in the moment. The way he smells is dizzying. His hair brushes against the side of my cheek.

I whisper, "Are you going to kiss me in the freezer aisle of this Safeway too?"

He laughs, pulling back, and I open my eyes just so I can see him again. He lingers, inches away. "Do I have permission?"

I nod.

He smiles a little bit, and whispers, "Do-over."

Then he leans in, so close, pausing in the split second before our lips meet to brush my hair behind my ear. He traces the slope of my neck with the pads of his fingers.

When he kisses me, it feels like everything all at once.

His lips are soft on mine, warm and pleasant, asking for nothing. I'm struck by everything I remember. I know Dillan at once, like I've been living in the same moment on repeat for all of the months between now and then, and now that it's happening again, my hands and mouth know what to do.

He pulls away, touches the tip of his nose to mine. "Okay?"

"Okay." I'm a little breathless, a little giddy. "Also, I'm in love with you."

It feels ridiculous to say once it's out loud, but I've said it, and it's true, so I guess it doesn't matter.

"You—what?" He tilts my chin up so I have to look at him. "Really?"

"I had to one-up you. You said you love me, so I had to say I'm *in* love—"

"Nora. I'm serious."

"So am I."

When I say it, I can actually feel the tension leave his body. He laughs, and it's a delightful sound. "You're in love with me."

"Yes." I'm laughing now too, shaking a little bit. "I am."

This time when he kisses me, he nearly knocks me over. His hand finds the small of my back and he pulls me closer, and finally, *finally,* I reach up and sink my hands into his hair, winding his soft curls between my fingers. I feel like I'm flying, and in the same moment I'm more grounded than I've been in a long time.

I've never been kissed like this. I'm dizzy and exhilarated, and all I want is for it to go on forever. The way we fit together is addicting. I slide my hand down to his neck, and I can feel his pulse fluttering just under his skin.

I don't know how long we stand there, but it feels like time isn't real. We kiss until my heart is beating too fast, and I pull away. "Okay. Okay."

He kisses my nose and my forehead. "Okay."

"We should . . ." I don't know what we should do. I want to drag him out of there by the front of his jacket. I want to find somewhere where it's just us, because now that I've kissed him once I don't ever want to stop. "We should get some juice."

"Yes."

"Not strawberry-kiwi."

"Definitely not."

I laugh, but it comes out shaky.

He taps the side of my cheek and pulls a bottle of juice off the shelf without looking to see what it is. "Let's get out of here?"

I pay for the juice. My fingers are trembling. Dillan's hands are on me the whole time—on my waist, then my hip, then his fingers skirt past my shoulder and graze my neck and I almost drop my debit card while I'm putting it back in my wallet.

It all feels extremely indecent—the way I'm *thinking* is indecent—for no real reason. It's just hands. It's just the tip of his finger on the knob of my spine at my neck, and it's just elbows knocking together on our way out of the store, but nothing about any of it is innocent at all.

I clutch the receipt. Dillan's hand fumbles to find mine in the dark of the parking lot. The cold bites at the exposed skin by my collarbone, and when he unlocks the car door, I feel sparks pirouette behind my belly button. I'm *so* awake.

I consider cutting to the chase and just getting into the backseat right off the bat, but that seems a little bit forward, so I open the passenger door with only a little reluctance.

We sit. Neither of us puts on seat belts.

Dillan unscrews the cap and takes a swig of the juice, then hands me the bottle with one eyebrow raised.

We lock eyes, and I don't look away as I tilt the bottle back to my lips. The juice is better this time, something tropical. I taste mango and orange.

I cap the bottle and place it in the cup holder between us. "It's good."

He says, "Yeah."

I look at him.

He looks back.

Then he says, "Come here."

I've never been so relieved to touch someone. It feels like I didn't know my own skin until right now. I'd never been aware of the place my neck meets my jaw until he touches it, and then everything I know about myself blooms from that one spot. His fingers wind upward through my hair, and when he kisses me, his lips barely ghost over mine.

I want it even while it's happening. When he kisses me for real, I can't help the little sigh that escapes, and he smiles, and then I smile, and we have to stop kissing before we've even really started.

I ask, "When was it really, for you? When did you know? It can't have been forever."

He laughs, and then he kisses me again, and again. "Oh. I don't know. I think I loved you right from when you turned around that first day in English."

"Really?"

"But I also think . . . I loved you before that."

I kiss him, once on the mouth, once on his cheek, a third time on his jaw. "You didn't even know me."

"When we were kids, I mean. You were my first crush."

I'm putty in his hands. "No way."

"It's true. In third grade I used to watch you read, because you'd always pick that one spot in the sun and it made your hair all shiny."

I suddenly feel like I might cry. "Really?"

"It was so pretty." He's grinning, but it slowly fades at the same time my own smile dims. His voice is quiet. "I'm really sorry about the other night."

It takes me a moment to catch up with what he's talking about. Then I remember his basement, his reluctance to talk, and it makes what I'm about to ask that much more real. "Don't worry about it."

"No," Dillan says. "I was scared, and tired, and Kayla and I had *just* called it off and I was busy feeling sorry for myself about how I was going to be alone *literally* forever, and—"

"That's where you were coming from," I whisper. I'm as still as I possibly can be. "I had no idea."

He shakes his head. "I didn't want you to know."

I'm quiet for as long as he wants to be, just thinking.

Dillan pulls back to look at me. "I'm only going to ask once, and if you don't want to talk about it, we don't have to."

"You don't have to ask." I shift in the seat so that my knees are facing him, heart sinking even as I'm saying, "You're my best friend. And you know I wanted to talk about it anyway. It's time."

"I don't want to push you."

"You're not. Besides, if we're gonna do this properly"—I gesture between us—"we probably should talk about it, right?"

Dillan's expression flickers, and he's so hard to read I'm convinced that either he knows exactly what I'm about to say, or he has no idea at all. Eventually, he just says, "Okay? What do *you* think there is to talk about?"

If it didn't make me a little bit furious, I'd be impressed with his casual diplomacy. "Nice," I say, immediately guarded and feeling immensely fragile. "Clever."

"What?" he asks, cautious. "It's a serious question."

"No," I say, crossing my arms tight. I can't help it—my head flashes back to that night, to that horrible ugly conversation. To everything Julia told me. "You're just covering your ass."

Now I'm not imagining it—Dillan looks afraid. "What do you mean?"

It's more than a little infuriating that he won't just *admit* it.

Steeling myself, I take a deep breath, and then I tell him the truth. "I know about you and Julia."

FIFTY-THREE

Before

That evening I was a nervous wreck.

Around eight-thirty, I checked Instagram, and immediately wished I hadn't, because Julia had updated her story. When I opened it, I saw a looped video of her and some of the girls on the soccer team doing shots, music loud in the background.

It didn't seem right at all that Julia was at a party and I didn't know about it.

Whatever. What she did was none of my business.

Miserable, I opened my email and stared at the message from TMU. Rejected? I'd been so hopeful. Maybe with fresh eyes on the essay, I'd be able to see what went wrong with it.

I waited for the login page to load, then clicked open the file I'd attached and scanned the opening lines.

Then I had to read through them again, more carefully.

I blinked at the screen.

My stomach plummeted.

No way.

There was no way.

This wasn't the essay I'd written. This was *nothing* like the essay I'd written. This was riddled with spelling and grammatical errors, and was so confusing I couldn't even tell what it was supposed to be about, even though I recognized some of the ideas I'd had.

I double-checked that I was on the right page. The file had the same name as the one on my computer, which was the real essay, so this couldn't be an accident. This had to have been uploaded from somewhere else.

A sick, creeping feeling coursed through me.

It *couldn't* be an accident.

Who knew how to sneak around behind my back? Who knew all my passwords? Who was a genius with computers?

Of course she was calm when she revealed she already knew about TMU. She'd known all along that I was never going to get to go. She'd known all along that she was going to sabotage me.

Julia must have snuck into my account and swapped the attachments. The thought made my chest hurt. I knew I hadn't been as excited about McGill as she'd wanted me to be, but to go this far? She'd stolen my journal, she'd outed our friend, and now this?

I couldn't breathe. I couldn't *breathe*.

Frantic, so furious my hands shook, I scrambled for my journal. Let her read it! This is what she'd find, next time she tried.

I pushed my pen so hard into the page, I was engraving my words. Underlining the sentence so I wouldn't forget: **<u>Julia Hoskins is a liar, a traitor, and a BAD FUCKING FRIEND.</u>**

I slammed it closed, hurled it onto my duvet, and sank down to the floor.

What could I do? I couldn't resubmit the essay. I wasn't going to TMU.

Then, with the kind of clarity that can only come after blinding rage, I knew what I had to do.

I had to go to that party.

It took a bit of snooping to figure out where it was. I evidently looked so distraught that when I asked my mom for a ride, she didn't even ask me why. On the drive, I went over and over in my head what I was going to say, until I'd almost convinced myself out of it, two sides of my consciousness at war.

This was a terrible idea.

It was my best idea.

This was the *only way*.

By the time we were on the highway, I felt like I was going to be sick. The dread of knowing what I was about to do threatened to choke me.

The party was in full swing when I got there. I tugged my coat around myself and waved goodbye to my mom, who gave me a worried look but let me go with the promise that I'd call her if I needed anything. As I walked up the driveway, I slid on a thin layer of ice, staying upright at the last second.

It didn't take long for me to find Julia. She was sitting on the edge of a couch, listening to one of the lacrosse players regale the others with an enthusiastic rendition of a game-winning goal; Julia looked utterly bored, swinging her lanyard in a lazy circle.

When she saw me, for a second, her face brightened. Then her expression flattened out, and she turned her head away.

"Julia." I stood in front of her. "We need to talk."

"Do we?" She sighed. "You could have fooled me."

"Get up," I hissed.

"Here? You want to do this now?"

I glowered at her until she stood.

We walked out into the hallway.

She turned, looking haughty. I was glad she wasn't wasted. This conversation was going to be a lot easier if she remembered it the next day.

"You want to talk?" she said. "Fine. Start talking."

"I just—" I clenched my fists. "I want to know *why*."

"Why *what*?" Her upper lip curled into a sneer.

"Do we really have to do this?"

"I don't—"

"Can you *stop* denying it for a second? Please?" I snatched Julia's still-swinging lanyard from her, shoving her keys deep into my pocket. I was starting to feel helpless. "I know you did it. It all makes sense. You have to admit it makes sense, right?"

She took a deep breath. "Yes, okay? All right? Yeah. I took it. I read your stupid journal."

I blinked. "I meant the submission essay. What is your problem?"

"I don't know what you're talking about," she said. But by the way she set her jaw, I knew that she knew *exactly* what I meant.

"Right. Okay, Julia. I totally believe you." I wanted to sound calm, but I was shaking. "Why would you do that? What's wrong with you? I had a real chance to follow a dream! You fucked with *my* dream. I could have had a future doing something I love, and you stole that from me!"

Julia flinched like I'd slapped her, then stared at me, eyes wide, mouth half open.

My words hung between us.

Her shock dissolved into betrayal, shoulders tensing. "You were about to break a promise!"

"I never promised to go to McGill with you!" I burst out. "It was never a promise!"

Julia gaped.

Now that I'd gotten started, I couldn't stop. "Why were you even reading my journal in the first place? What did you need to know so badly? I tell you everything!"

"You *don't*, obviously!"

"I was *going* to tell you about TMU. And you had to have been reading it anyway to know about Eve."

Julia let out a huff. "I just didn't know how to be a good enough friend anymore. I always felt like you were choosing other people—and I wanted to—I wanted to *know* you better."

"You *do* know me!" It came out explosively, and I looked around furtively, aware that people were listening in. I lowered my voice to a hiss. "Julia! We're best friends. You've known me since grade five. Come *on*."

"I just wanted to figure out how to be a better friend."

"Not like that, Julia." I shook my head, tears hot behind my eyes. "That wasn't the way. And how was you sabotaging my essay being a good friend?"

She looked away.

I'd known she wasn't telling me the whole truth, but it hadn't felt real until right then.

I'd made excuses. I'd downplayed. I'd called her bad behavior part of who she was. No apology? Fine, forgiven.

It was easier to be her friend than to even think about what it would be like to not have her in my life.

This was the first time I'd stood up to her. I felt strangely unhinged, like I was watching myself burn, my fury barely contained.

At that point, it didn't even matter if she told me what she'd done. It was written all over her face.

"I can't do this anymore," I said.

Julia looked incredulously at the way I gestured between us. "What, *us*?"

"I'm tired of you sneaking around and lying and being a—a *horrible* friend to Eve. I'm sick of defending you."

"Are you?" Her voice was frigid.

"Yeah," I said, with a surge of confidence. "Yeah, I am. I think you know you don't have anything *left* to lord over me, and you're grasping at straws to keep me from walking away."

"Oh, *really*?" Julia had gone so deadly calm that my confidence drained away in a wash of dread. "You think I'm grasping at straws?"

Coming here was a mistake.

"I have to go," I snapped, remembering that I was expecting a guest tonight. "I have somewhere else to be."

"What, got plans with Dillan?" Julia asked, mocking. Then, when I didn't deny it, she laughed, bright and loud and cutting. "Good *luck*."

"What's that supposed to mean?"

"It means," Julia said, "that he's a horrible person, and if you had two brain cells to rub together, you'd see it."

When I flinched away, she laughed. "What's that supposed to mean?" I said again.

"Has he tried to cover his ass yet?" She swayed a little.

I stared at her. She'd *looked* sober, but then I remembered the shots. "How much have you been drinking?"

"Not even that much." Julia rolled her eyes. "Why do you even care?"

"I *don't*. What's he—why would Dillan be covering his ass?"

"You wanna know why it's been so weird between us?" Julia asked, ignoring my question, and I could hear a glint of victory in her voice. "Because when he's bored, he comes to *me*."

I gaped at her.

"You really think you're the only one he goes on those cute little nighttime drives with? You think you're the only one of us he's kissed?"

My stomach dropped.

"He'll deny it if you ask him, because he's terrified of confrontation, or he'll try to tell you some bullshit story about why he ghosted you, when you wanna know the real reason?"

"I—"

"It was just because he doesn't fucking like you that much," she spat. "And he's not gonna want to look bad for it."

It would have been better if she'd just slapped me.

"I don't believe you," I whispered.

"Believe me," Julia hissed back. She whipped out her phone.

Dread rose like bile in my throat as she scrolled through photos until she found what she was looking for.

I knew what it was going to be before she turned the phone around, but that didn't make it any less painful.

The photo was a little blurry, and Julia took up most of the shot, but the person she was kissing on Dillan's front porch had his curly red hair.

"Who—" I started, but couldn't finish.

"I had to tell you," Julia said. "Because I was trying to be a good friend."

I swallowed hard, unable to look away. "How is you kissing him being a good friend to me?"

"I was trying to prove that he wasn't worth a scrap of your attention," she said, turning the screen off and shoving her phone in her pocket. "And clearly, I was right, because *hello*, if he'd kiss your best friend, what line wouldn't he cross? So you're welcome."

"I don't understand," I whispered.

"Let me summarize for you," Julia said viciously. "I'm the only one in your life who has your fucking back."

I gaped at her.

"And when you realize that, feel free to come crawling back. I'll think about forgiving you."

I wanted to scream. I wanted to hit her. I wanted—I wanted her to *go away*. I wanted Julia out of my life. I wanted her to die.

I threw the lanyard back at her.

She caught it against her chest, keys rattling, eyebrows shooting up. "What's—"

"Fuck you," I said, chest heaving. "Fuck you, Julia, go home."

Julia laughed, sharp and derisive. "Excuse me?"

"I'm not cleaning up your messes anymore," I said, out of breath. "So go *home*."

Her mouth dropped open, and then she shut it. "Fuck *you*."

When she turned and walked away, I didn't stop her.

I stood there for a *long* time, shaking and staring at the floor. I stood by myself until the sounds of the house started to register. Music drifted from an open door down the hall. People laughed somewhere far away.

And then I realized what I'd done.

Terror clawed its way up my throat and I tore back down the hallway.

Julia couldn't *drive*. Not like this.

I threw open the front door and hurtled out onto the steps, but I'd forgotten it was icy. I slipped forward and landed on my hand, so hard I felt the skin of my palm tear.

Scrambling to my feet, I swore at the sight of red beads of blood. Ignoring the ache in my elbow, I skidded down the steps to the street, where I watched her car pulling away from the curb.

"Julia, STOP!" I screamed.

But it was already happening.

She was driving away.

FIFTY-FOUR

After

"What about me and Julia?" Dillan's brow furrows.

I feel strangely disoriented; I can barely get the words out. "She told me, that night, she said that you guys were—"

"That we were what?" Dillan asks.

There's enough dread in his expression that I can't look at him, so I turn my attention back to the juice bottle. "I'm not mad at you."

"Why would—?" Dillan swallows, then exhales, slow and resigned. "She told you, didn't she?"

I'd thought I was done feeling so *gutted* about this. I just nod.

"Fuck." Dillan sucks in a shaky breath. "She said she was going to, and she must have—this whole time, you . . . ?"

I cross my arms, misery pooling tight.

"What did she say?" he whispers, voice constricted.

"She said that the two of you had been hooking up." I spit the words out before I can convince myself not to.

Dillan swears again.

He's scrambling out of the car before I can stop him, and it feels like a part of me is being wrenched out through my throat.

"Dillan—" I start, but the door snaps shut. I allow myself a single choked sob before I push my door open too.

Dillan is leaning against the car, looking up into the endless night. His expression is scraped so raw it hurts to look at, but I can't stop. I don't think I've ever seen Dillan *angry* before.

It feels like there's nothing else to look at in the world. Even if all this happiness is about to be torn away from me somehow—and it feels like it is—I'm still clinging to it, as desperate now as I've ever been.

When my door closes, he says, voice ragged, "It's not true."

I feel like I've slipped on ice, even though I'm standing perfectly still.

"It's not true. I never—*shit.*" Dillan turns, so he's looking at me over the top of the car. "I never looked twice at Julia. I never kissed her. Well—technically, but I didn't start it, or see it coming, and I pushed her away. I would never have done it on purpose. I swear we were never involved, but she threatened me. She blackmailed me with that picture!"

Dillan yanks his hands through his hair and looks down, jaw clenched so tight the cords of his neck stand out.

He takes a deep breath. "Julia said if I told you, she'd make it sound like I came on to her or something, or that I tried— that I'd done something horrible."

I stand there in stunned silence. She'd always known what would make me bleed. I'd never have believed that Dillan tried anything aggressive with her, and she must have known that, so instead—

God, she was an awful person.

My best friend was a manipulative, lying bitch.

"She made it sound like you two were sneaking around," I tell him breathlessly. "Like you were—like you kissed me and then decided you wanted her instead."

"*No.*" Dillan is so emphatic it's almost startling. "Fuck no."

Pieces start to slide together. The resulting picture is ugly.

Dillan strides around the front of the car.

"I can't believe that feels worse, somehow," Dillan says, once he's in front of me, and rubs at his face. "Jesus. No, I never wanted *Julia.* This whole time, you thought that?"

"I thought you didn't want to talk about her because you were *mourning* her," I burst out. "I thought you were grieving, just like I was."

"Grieving Julia?" A wild edge of hysterical laughter escapes into the night air. "She lied to me and ruined everything between us, then trapped me in this horrible ultimatum so I couldn't even *tell* you when I'd figured it out."

All I can do is stare.

"And I didn't even know if you'd believe me," Dillan whispers. "This is what I was trying to tell you that night, except I was terrified, because what if she convinced you I was lying? Then I'd lose you properly. She was *such* a good liar."

I close my eyes, and that whole evening suddenly makes sense. "She told me when we fought."

"That night," Dillan whispers. He's shivering.

So am I, even though I barely feel the cold. I nod.

He bows his head.

"I'm sorry," I whisper. "I'm sorry this happened, I—I swear I didn't know, I'm *sorry*."

"You have nothing to apologize for," Dillan says. *"Nothing."*

I step toward him at the same moment he steps toward me, so it's less of a hug and more two vortices colliding.

"I'm still sorry," I say, right into his shoulder as I fling my arms around him.

"So'm I," Dillan murmurs into my hair.

"It was really never her?" I ask. "It was never her you wanted?"

"No," he says, hoarse, holding on to me tighter. Something about him sounds like he's been cracked open. Wrecked. "Never. Never her."

I regret bringing this up at all, even though I'm so relieved I feel like I'm going to fly away if Dillan lets go.

But he does, and I don't fly away.

"Let's get back in the car," I say, teeth chattering. "I am *so* cold."

Dillan laughs. He still sounds a little bit ruined. When I get back into the passenger seat, he rounds the car, and when he slides into the driver's side, he looks a little more attached to his body. He starts the engine so the heater roars to life, and for some reason it's easier to talk when it's loud.

I swallow. "She said I wasn't the only one you went on drives with, and—"

"She knew about those because she can track both of us," Dillan said. "On our phones. Some app or something. She showed up at my house one night and said we needed to talk, and what was I supposed to do? She knew we'd been seeing each other without her, and I think she got worried that I was going to try to tell you how I felt, and how I never meant to hurt you. And she was right. I was going to tell you."

I feel sick.

"In the spirit of full disclosure . . . ," Dillan says, then stops. He takes a deep breath, then runs through a sentence so garbled I can barely make sense of it. "She kissed me, which was fucking confusing, and then she told me she hated my guts, which was even more confusing, and then she told me I wasn't allowed to tell you, which like, I *wasn't going to,* because *obviously,* and that's really how I started to figure it all out."

His words hang in the air.

"I can't imagine how confused you must be," Dillan says, after a moment. "Jesus. I can't believe you thought I wanted her this whole time."

This whole time I'd thought I had the truth. Now . . .

No truth. Only stories.

But I don't think Dillan would lie to me. I don't think he ever has.

"That was Julia," I say. "I always thought what she wanted me to think."

"Can we just—" Dillan swallows. "Can we reset?"

I glance over at him, unable to stop the weak smile that's trying to twist its way out of me. "You mean, to when we were making out?"

To my delight, he flushes so violently that I can see it in the dim light of the car. "No! That's not what I meant."

"What *did* you mean, then?"

"I just hate this," he says helplessly.

"It had to happen."

"That doesn't make me hate it less."

I take a deep breath, and when I let it out, it shakes. "I know."

I'll think about this later—I'll ruminate on it endlessly, probably—but I don't want to right now.

"Okay. Reset," I whisper.

Dillan nods, and turns down the heater so it's not blowing scalding air. "Reset."

I don't know what I'm going to do until I'm doing it, but then I'm sticking my hands out and shooting him finger guns.

His smile takes over his whole face, and then we're off: finger guns, fist bump, handshake, second fist bump, explosion.

This time, neither of us hesitates. We link our pinkies together, and it feels like something significant and important slots back into place. Like maybe it's okay. Or it will be.

Bittersweet, but okay.

"Reset," I whisper again. "Hi. I'm Nora."

"Dillan," he whispers. "Can it not be a *total* reset? I want to keep some things."

"Like what?" I ask, even as we're leaning toward each other.

I kiss him soft and slow, just like I've been thinking about, like I've been dying to do. Like we have all the time in the world, like this is the only thing that matters. Every square centimeter of my skin that touches his skin burns, as though he's branding me, and I want him to.

The kisses don't stay slow, though. I twine my fingers through his hair, pulling him closer, and his hand on the back of my neck pulls me deeper into the kiss. I don't want to have to breathe. I don't ever want to have to pull away.

Right now, kissing feels like rage, and defiance. It feels like yelling desperately into the dark, a vicious whisper: *mine.*

I didn't know how hungry I'd been. There's some part of me that's been starving for this for months—a *year*—and now that it's actually happening, I'm overcome by it. I don't know how to think. There's only this: Dillan's mouth, Dillan's skin, his hand on my neck. Dillan, warm, Dillan, wanting, Dillan, pliable under my fingers.

There's nothing convenient about kissing in a car. The gearshift digs into my leg, and I'm twisted in half trying to get to him, and a few weeks ago I wouldn't have had the guts to do this, but tonight it doesn't feel like bravery, just necessity.

I climb over the gearshift and into his lap.

At first, he just stares at me, half surprised and half awed, but he doesn't push me away or tell me to stop. I'm aware of how close we are, and I can tell he is too, because there's something different about the way he looks at me. I decide right then that I love the way it feels to have his arms around me as his hand drifts up my spine and plays at the baby hairs on my neck. I'm glad it's dark.

I whisper his name so quietly that I don't even hear it, just so that I feel the way my mouth moves around the word. Then, in the same way, I tell him, "I love you."

It feels even more real, somehow, on the other side of the truth.

Before he can say anything, I kiss him again, so that when he says it back, it's through breathless gasps in between.

I don't know how long we sit like that, how long we kiss. Time seems to both stretch and rush. He runs his hands through my hair senselessly, fingertips brushing past my ears, always pulling me closer.

My phone rings. I don't want to even look. I don't want to do anything that prevents this moment from going on and on.

Dillan pulls away, though. "Are you going to get that?"

I shake my head.

"What if it's important?"

"It's not you, so probably not."

He grins. "Flattering, but you should still see who it is."

"If it's a spam call," I grumble, "I'm throwing it out the window."

It's my mom.

I show him the screen, and he nods, so with some reluctance, I press the phone to my ear. "Hello?"

"Hey, hon." Mom sounds slightly concerned, and I can hear the careful footsteps that mean she's pacing. "Where are you?"

Dillan leans forward and presses a kiss to my neck, but then he doesn't pull back—instead, his lips rest there, and I have to use every piece of my willpower to drag myself back down from space to focus on the conversation. "Out. Um. With Dillan."

"Oh." Her pacing stops. "Still?"

Dillan's mouth makes patterns on the skin beneath my jaw. When he finds my pulse, my eyes flutter shut. I drag my free hand though his hair and grip his head. "Is something wrong?"

"No." Her sigh is heavy. "I was just wondering."

"I'm safe, Mom. I'll be home—soon." The last word comes out a little strangled. "Okay?"

"All right," she says. "I'll wait up."

I almost tell her not to. "Okay."

"See you in a bit." She pauses. "Be careful. Love you."

His teeth graze my skin and I officially lose the ability to track her words.

"Um." I struggle to formulate a coherent sentence. "You too. Uh. Love you."

When I hang up, I gasp, "You're the devil."

"I think you liked it." He murmurs into my neck.

I can't manage anything beyond a slight whimper.

He pulls back then, lets out the ghost of a laugh, and draws me down against his chest. I feel like I'm on fire, but I close my eyes as I rest my head on his shoulder. I can feel his heart beating against my sternum, almost as fast as my own.

I sigh. "How did we ever manage without this?"

"Patience," he says immediately. "A lot of it. And—uh. Cold showers."

I bury my laughter in the crook of his neck.

He begins to draw loose patterns on my back through my jacket.

We sit like that for a long time, until heartbeats slow. Neither of us says anything. It's not the kind of silence that needs filling.

I don't quite feel real. This moment feels too impossible to have ever happened, but he's reassuringly solid under my fingers, and so I remind myself that it's true enough times that I start to believe it.

Eventually, he sighs. "What if I just . . . didn't go tomorrow?"

"Stop it." I reach up and trace the contour of his cheek until he shivers. "I'll be here when you get back."

He kisses the top of my head. "I hope so."

"Count on it. I'm not going anywhere."

Dillan's arms tighten around me, and then he shifts a little bit and I hear his breath catch. His laughter is helpless and a little embarrassed. "We fogged up the windows."

I sit up and see that he's right. A flush prickles my cheeks and neck, and I drag my index finger through the condensation on the driver's window. Then I press it against his cheek, doing my level best to keep my voice from wavering. "Might have to make a habit of it."

"God. Nora." He sucks in a shuddering breath. "You're—"

"Incorrigible?"

He laughs, sounding a little unsteady, then reaches up to catch my hand, pressing a kiss to each knuckle. "One of many things."

"I'd like to hear them all."

"One day." He laughs, then he swallows. "I should take you home."

"Probably."

Neither of us moves.

For just a few seconds, I let myself wonder what this year would have looked like if we'd ended up together all those months ago. Would I have gone to that party? Would Julia still be alive?

I would never have gone out with Nate. I wonder if I regret that decision. This moment right here feels perfect enough that it's difficult to imagine regretting anything that brought me to it.

I reluctantly disentangle myself from Dillan and climb back over the gearshift into the passenger seat.

My whole body feels cold where I'm not touching him, and I wrap my jacket around myself.

We're quiet on the drive home. It feels like every late-night drive we've had before except not at all.

I reach over and place my hand on his knee.

He looks at me out of the corner of his eye, and his mouth quirks upward. He takes one hand off the steering wheel and rests it on top of mine.

When we get to my house, he turns to me. "I'm going to walk you up."

"What is this, the sixties?"

He flushes. "I used to do that before. When we were just friends. I don't want things to be different. Do you know what I mean?"

"Not really." I just look at him.

"I just mean like—I used to walk you up and say hi to your mom before we were . . . this, and you know, you'd call me sometimes if you were having a hard night, and I don't want to lose any of that."

"We don't have to lose any of it," I whisper. "We don't have to lose anything."

He reaches over and tucks a strand of my hair behind my ear. "I'd like that."

Then he walks me up.

FIFTY-FIVE

Before

Slipping occasionally on the ice, I tore after her. Julia's car was inching slowly down a side street crusted with ice and salt that hadn't been properly cleared. By the time she reached the stop sign at the end of the road, I caught up and slammed my hands against the passenger window.

Julia didn't have time to lock the door before I wrenched it open.

"What the fuck are you doing?" she asked.

"You can't drive," I panted. "You've been drinking."

"I'm fine."

I got into the passenger seat and slammed the door shut behind me. "Stop. Let me drive."

"I'm not drunk," Julia said. "Do you want me to prove it, or what?"

"I want you to *stop*," I said.

Julia snorted. "You're the one who told me to go home."

Behind us, somebody honked.

She turned right.

I swore under my breath and yanked my seat belt on. "Julia, seriously!"

"I said I'm fine."

"You were doing shots!"

"Ages ago. Chill out."

"I'm not going to—"

My phone buzzed. Triple tap.

Apparently Julia had heard it, because she laughed disdainfully. "That's Dillan, right? That's your stupid text alert for him. What's he got to say?"

I swallowed, but pulled my phone out.

you home? i'm coming over. be there at 10

"Shit," I mumbled.

"What?" Julia's expression was stony.

"He was going to come over."

"Weren't you guys just hanging out this afternoon?" She braked a little too suddenly. The car slid several inches on the ice.

Nervous, I gripped the grab handle. "Uh, no."

"So he was just covering for you?"

"No, that makes it sound—"

"Wasn't he, though?"

I couldn't tell her he wasn't unless I wanted to lie, and I didn't. I was sick of lies. "Sort of. Maybe. Maybe it's because he was being a *good friend*."

"And the role of a good friend is to protect you from *me*?" she snapped. "I see how it is."

We slid around a corner. She bumped over the curb.

"Jeez." I gripped the armrest. "Careful. Seriously. Can I take over? We can swap?"

"I know how to fucking drive, okay?" Julia snarled. "I'm sober. I'm fine."

I let out a trembling breath, and then I started typing a message to Dillan.

> Had to sort something out. Heading home hopefully soon, just

Before I finished the message, I looked over at Julia. The set of her mouth was grim and determined. At first, I thought she was staring intently at the road, but she wasn't. Her eyes were locked on the steering wheel in an expression that screamed *Danger.*

I swallowed. "Julia, hey. It's not a big deal. It was—we were fighting, and he'd been there, and . . . I don't know."

"You wanted nothing to do with me."

"No, I needed time to think."

"To *think*," she repeated, tone laced with derision.

I pressed my lips together.

Then Julia burst into tears.

"You're—" Her shoulders shook, and she sucked in a sharp breath before she continued. "You're all I have, Nora."

I stared at her. "What do you *mean*?"

Tears ran freely down her cheeks, shining reflectively in the headlight beams of every passing car. "You're *all* I have."

Eyes wide, I shook my head. "That's not true."

"It *is*," Julia insisted. "It is true, I don't have anybody else, and you have—"

"Hey." I touched her shoulder, and she flinched. "Hey, Julia."

"I can't lose you." Julia was sobbing hard enough that she hiccupped. "I can't."

"You won't," I said, and I knew that it was true. "You didn't have to— Why didn't you just tell me?"

"You were choosing them. And you would've—" Julia squeezed her eyes shut for a moment, and then looked over, eyes off the road. "You were going to leave me."

We might have been locked in that silence for hours.

That was a condemnation, and she was right. I'd been walking away for weeks.

"I'm not," I whispered. "I won't."

She didn't look away.

I glanced at the upcoming traffic lights and my gut twisted. My heart hammered against my ribs. "Julia, it's red. Julia, it's— JULIA!"

She slammed on the brakes, but not soon enough. We slid into the intersection.

I knew we were going to be hit before it happened. Bright lights pierced the driver's-side window, and more than one horn blared, but it didn't feel real. A small voice in my head said *This is it*—and then it was.

The impact didn't happen in one single moment. It happened, and then it happened again, and then it hadn't happened yet and it was over. A deafening crash, the pop and crunch of splintering glass, sliding on the ice, spinning, again and again and again.

Time stretched and snapped back in blurs.

There was noise, and then there was silence.

Somebody was screaming Julia's name—it must have been me.

Something was burning. There was something sticky on the side of my face.

"Julia?" My voice came out strangled. I tried again. "Julia?"

There was no response.

The lights were bright. *Too* bright. I thought I could hear shouting, but it was as though it were coming through a thick veil.

I couldn't see *anything*. My eyes wouldn't focus.

Had we really been hit? Was I—was *Julia*—

I gasped in hot air. "Julia!"

There was nothing.

FIFTY-SIX

After

While Dillan is gone, my worlds collide.

I've been worrying about what it would be like to hang out with both Eve and Kayla, but once we're all together, it's startlingly pleasant.

Kayla is the sort of person to wear affection on the outside, and Eve is the sort to starve for it, so when we're in my basement and she sprawls on the floor with her ankle touching Eve's leg, it feels natural.

And Eve looks *happy*.

"So?" Kayla is practically bursting at the seams as I hand her a wineglass. "What happened?"

"I'll second that question." Eve downs the rest of her glass. "It was almost physically painful watching the two of you. I was starting to worry it was never going to happen."

"Did you know they kissed last year?" Kayla raises her eyebrows at Eve, who smirks.

I gasp, pressing my hand against my sternum in mock offense. "He told you about that?"

Kayla tosses her hair over her shoulder. "Yes. He was *hope-
less.*"

I grin. I take a moment to think about whether I want
them to know the details, and then I realize—I want them
to know.

I want to trust them with more than just surface-level facts
about my life. I know nobody could ever replace Julia, even
Dillan—especially Dillan, now that we're more than friends—
but I'm not looking for another Julia. I'm looking for something better.

And I think I have that with Eve and Kayla. I trust them
with this.

I take a deep breath, and I tell them everything: about what
Julia had told me and Dillan separately, about how Julia and I
had fought. About figuring out the truth.

And they listen. They listen without interrupting. I don't
know what I expected, but it's such a relief to have them both
obviously *care.* They're indignant in the right places, furious
when it matters. And when it's over, neither of them is awkward about it.

Well, mostly.

"So, did you guys kiss yet?" Eve's tone is matter-of-fact.

I almost choke on my drink as my eyes dart over to Kayla.
"You sure this isn't, like, weird for you?"

"God, no. Dillan and I are ancient history. And look at how
smiley you are!"

"I'm not"—I swat in her direction—"smiley."

She gives me a suspiciously knowing look.

My phone buzzes. I know it's Dillan.

Maybe I *am* all smiley.

"Ten bucks says they'll say they love each other within like three weeks." Kayla smirks at Eve, knocking their knees together.

I can already feel my mortified grin taking over, ears warming.

"Hmm." Eve considers. "Two." Then she looks over at me and her mouth drops open. "Wait. Wait. Nora. *What?*"

"You already dropped the L bomb?" Kayla's eyes are wide and round.

I raise my hands in surrender. "What? He said it first. I wasn't going to *not* say it back. And it's true."

"First date," Kayla says. "Wow. I think that's got to break a record or something."

"That's their style, all right." Eve laughs. "Dance around each other for literal *years* and then confess their love."

Kayla grimaces. "All that tension. I bet it was cathartic, eh?"

I cover my face with my hands. "Yeah. It was."

The two of them giggle like schoolgirls.

"When's he coming back, again?"

I hold up two fingers. "Friday night."

"And then in January, do you think you'll do long-distance?" Eve tilts her head.

I frown. "I hope so. We haven't talked about it. I hope he won't think that's too much."

She just rolls her eyes. "I think you could ask him to cut off his left hand and he wouldn't think it was too much."

"Oh, as *if.*" I laugh and then gesture between them. "Okay.

Here's what I've been wondering. How on earth did *this* end up happening?"

Eve flushes darker, which looks strange on her. I don't think I've ever seen her look embarrassed before. She catches Kayla's eye. "Uh—do you want to say?"

Kayla flips her hair. "Easy. I saw her at the Halloween party and was like, *nice,* and then we hooked up and both sort of thought that was it. But it wasn't."

Eve is looking at her with undisguised fondness, which makes something in my chest squeeze. "Yeah," she says. "It wasn't. I couldn't get her out of my head, and I didn't think I was looking for anything, you know, *serious,* but then when I texted her and asked her to hang out, I *really* hoped she'd say yes."

Kayla presses a hand to her forehead. "It was super weird to be seeing both you and Dillan at the same time. I wasn't really sure what I was doing, but it was like . . . I'm really hitting hard on the Nora Inner Circle here. And then it was totally obvious that it wasn't going anywhere with Dillan, because of"—she waves a hand toward me—"you know. But I just kept wanting to see Eve. Just to hang out. I was like, *gross.* Who *am* I?"

"And here we are." Eve still looks faintly embarrassed, but pleased. "Holding the future loosely."

"Yeah." Kayla nods. "But not *too* loosely."

Eve smiles as she echoes, "Not too loosely."

That feels right. I like the idea of looking at my future through fingers splayed wide.

FIFTY-SEVEN

Before

My arm was broken.

My phone wasn't.

It seemed almost funny to me, even though nothing about it was funny. When they gave it back, there wasn't even a scratch on it. I had a cast, and my phone wasn't broken, and I still had no idea what had happened to Julia. It had been hours, I thought, or maybe just minutes. The clock on the wall said it wasn't even ten-thirty yet, but that seemed impossible.

The ambulance ride had been a hazy dream. There was nothing about tonight that felt real, just bits and pieces of something that *could* be real—flashing lights and colors, unfamiliar voices.

I had thirty-six text messages. Twelve of them were from Dillan. The rest of them were from my mom and Julia's mom, and even though there were lots of them, they all said pretty much the same thing: *Are you okay?*

There wasn't an answer to that.

I was moved to a different room, and there wasn't a clock. For a while, I used my phone to keep track of time, but then it died, and there was nothing.

Just me in a dim room, afraid.

Eventually, the door opened, and a nurse came in, and behind the nurse was my mom. I sat up just in time for her to dash across the room and envelop me in a tight hug.

I was suffocating again. The air in the room was too hot, and my mom was crying so hard I could feel it in my body.

I'd been crying at some point too, because my eyes hurt. But I didn't remember it. What was real?

There were more people. Simon was right behind my mom, crying, and my dad was there, and for some reason, so was Dillan, though I couldn't really make sense of why.

There was talking and there was silence, and I couldn't make myself speak. I only had one question, and I couldn't ask it.

They knew. And still, I couldn't ask.

Dillan wasn't looking at me. His hands were shaking, even though he had clasped them together.

"Julia?" My voice hurt, like I'd been screaming. Maybe I had been.

"She—" My mom sat down hard in one of the chairs, hand raised to her mouth.

"Mom. What?"

But I already knew.

She didn't say anything, just looked at the floor.

"What? Mom?"

The pain wasn't just in my arm anymore. It was everywhere. My chest burned with the effort of every breath.

"Julia's gone." She leaned forward in the chair. It took me a second to realize that it was because she was crying, her whole body racked with sobs.

"Gone like—to another hospital?"

Simon pressed the heels of his palms against his eye sockets. Mom didn't say anything, she just cried harder.

I looked at Dillan, but he was looking down, his face utterly blank.

Black spots dotted my vision. I shook my head frantically. "No. She's not. Julia's not—she's okay. I know she is."

But she wasn't, and that had *always* been the truth, even if I didn't want to admit it. I'd probably known it since the crash, and the horrible silence after.

That same silence was yawning inside me. That was the worst of it. My friend was gone, and it was quiet.

My best friend was dead, and nothing would ever be the same.

FIFTY-EIGHT

After

The text buzzes in and I snatch my phone, but it isn't Dillan. It's Maria, Dillan's mom. I frown at the screen, and it takes a few seconds for the words to register.

> Do you want to come to the airport with us?

I'm a little embarrassed by how quickly I reply.

> Yes please

I'm in the middle of changing my shirt when a car honks in our driveway, and I almost dash out the door without a sweater.

Sara takes one look at me and breaks out into a wide Dillan-style grin. "Are you so excited?"

I don't really know how to answer this, and she must see the indecision in my face, because she laughs. "He told us."

Maria smacks her shoulder. "We promised not to tell her we knew!"

I feel my cheeks flush as I climb into the car and settle next to Angie, whose attention is on her Switch.

"Oh, but we couldn't resist surprising him, could we?" Sara gives me a conspiratorial grin as she twists around in her seat. "You'll come over for dinner after?"

Maria backs out of the driveway. "Don't rush them!"

"What! I'm not!" Sara protests. "I'm just saying, dinner at our house?"

"Yes, please." I've hardly caught my breath. I pull my phone out and look at the last text from Dillan, two hours ago.

> taking off—text you when i land :)

I've stared at that one smiley face for a long time.

Sara asks me a dozen questions as we drive up to the airport, and I'm grateful for the distraction, because in typical Sara fashion, the questions don't touch on anything I don't want to talk about. The answers come easily, which is good, because I can hardly think straight. Most of my brain is occupied with soon, soon, *soon*.

I'm so antsy it's nearly unbearable by the time we pull into the parking lot. I hold Angie's hand on the way inside, and if she notices that my palms are sweating, she doesn't say anything. The December air bites.

My phone buzzes in my hand. I tell them, "Landed."

A second later, Sara's phone lights up. She clutches at her chest in mock hurt. "He texted you first? Oh, how the mighty have fallen."

My stomach jumps with something like nerves, but it takes me a second to realize that I'm not nervous. It's anticipation. My hands are balled into fists, and I have to make a conscious effort to unclench my fingers. I'm so excited I feel like I'm vibrating. One week has felt like a year.

We wait inside by the double doors for an excruciatingly long time. Angie pulls out her Switch again, leaning against Sara and occasionally peeking around to look for her brother. Sara's phone buzzes again.

"He's on his way down now," she says.

My stomach does a complicated flip-flop. Olympic-level.

The doors open, and a crowd of middle schoolers shuffle through. Maria cranes her neck, trying to see over the throng.

I see his hair before I see anything else, a shock of bright orange against the neutrals, closely surrounded by a group of people I don't recognize.

When his face comes into view, my heart clenches. He is deeply involved in conversation with a dark-haired girl, and when he laughs, I think he's the prettiest thing I've ever seen.

Then he looks over. He must only register the orange of his mom's hair among the people waiting, because nothing in his face changes, he just flashes a grin and waves a hand. He turns to the girl and bumps knuckles with her and another boy, waving to the rest of them, bag slung casually over one shoulder, before he looks back again.

That's when he sees me. I know he does because his eyebrows arch suddenly. Dillan always wears surprise on his whole face, and I see him glance incredulously between his parents and me as though he can't quite believe his eyes.

Then he breaks out into an elated grin. I can't decide

whether to run to him or not. My heart wants to, but my feet are solid concrete.

He jogs over to us, drops his bag on the ground, and greets his parents with a hug, dropping a kiss on the top of Angie's head, never looking away from me.

I don't quite register the moments in between, there's just this: we're not touching, and then we are.

He wraps me in a real Dillan hug, and I might be either laughing or crying, but I can't tell, he's squeezing me so hard.

I bury my face in his neck and inhale.

He doesn't let go. He whispers, "Hi."

"I wish you were that excited to see *us*." Maria's voice is dry behind us.

"You ratted me out." Dillan mumbles his reply into my shoulder, and his voice is on the edge of accusatory. "You're a pair of narcs. She wasn't supposed to know I told you."

"You don't look that upset by it," Sara remarks.

We break apart. I'm dizzy and rapturous; he grabs my elbow to steady me.

His smile is wide and delighted. "No. I'm not that upset by it."

I've never wanted to kiss anyone so badly.

Dillan bends low to scoop up his bag and throws it over one shoulder, then laces our fingers together. My cheeks flush.

I'm suddenly hyperaware of Maria's and Sara's eyes on us, and it feels supremely weird to be holding hands in front of them. But Dillan doesn't seem fazed, and I'm so, *so* relieved to be touching him again that I let out a long breath and relax.

He squeezes my hand as we file out the doors and back into the cold, and doesn't let go until we're back to the minivan. Ordinarily, one of us would crawl into the back, but tonight we sandwich into the middle seat, thighs and shoulders pressed together. It's almost, *almost* too much to bear.

I don't dare look at him until the car starts and we're pulling out of the parking lot. He's already looking back. I feel heat rising in my cheeks, and when I look away, he grabs my hand again, squeezes three times.

"Tell us about Queen's." Sara twists in the passenger seat. I flinch when her eyes land on our fingers twined together, but she doesn't miss a beat. "Did you like it?"

Dillan lets his head fall back against the headrest. "*Loved* it. I met a bunch more people who are going in January, and some of the professors, too—I can't *wait* to start classes."

Sara and Maria have a million questions, but I only listen halfway. I'm just happy. I don't remember feeling like this maybe ever. When he brushes my thumb with his it sends shock waves through me. I can't help but compare—even in our limited experience, nothing Nate ever did made me feel anything like this. All Dillan has to do is look at me while we're sitting next to each other in the half dark and I'm a ruin.

We pull up to their house—finally—and unload. It's both wonderful and unbearable to be so close and so far apart. I drink in the sight of him; it's enough and not enough to just be in the same room.

He brushes against me while we're setting the table. I keep finding excuses to touch him—tapping his arm when I pass by him, letting our hands and wrists bump together when we're setting out the silverware. We've done this a dozen times, at least, but I've never been quite so focused on straightening napkins before.

Once we're seated around the table, Maria and Sara tell us they have a work event to attend together that evening, so they'll need us to put Angie to bed. When Sara says not to expect them back until after eleven, Maria fixes us with a knowing glance, and both Dillan and I flush scarlet.

Sara runs through the usual precautions—I'm so familiar with Angie's bedtime routine that I barely register her words, distracted by the implications of Maria's raised eyebrows.

But Sara is not content to leave it there. She clears her throat. "And you both know this already, of course, but obviously, be careful, don't do anything we wouldn't do, use pro—"

"Mom!" Dillan bursts out.

"I'm just saying, I'd rather you do it *in* the house—"

"Stop! I know!" He covers his face with his hands.

"What? It's nothing to be embarrassed about—"

Maria swats her shoulder. "Enough!"

Angie looks between Maria and Sara, a frown wrinkling her brow. "Do what in the house?"

Dillan shakes his head wildly. "Nothing, Ange. Uh. Nothing."

I know full well I'm blushing to my roots, and I look down into my bowl, mortified.

Dillan groans. *"Thanks* for that, Mom."

Angie is still squinting at him with obvious suspicion. I'm thinking that I'll never be able to look any of them in the eye ever again, so when Sara and Maria bounce back to chipper conversation, I'm immensely relieved.

Then Dillan puts his hand on my knee under the table. I glance at him out of the corner of my eye, but he isn't looking at me, he's looking at Sara, nodding intently as she speaks enthusiastically about the party they're going to.

I can't breathe. His hand doesn't move, it just stays there. Slowly, cautiously, I place my hand over his.

He squeezes once, and I feel it all the way up my leg.

The animated chatter doesn't stop as we wash dishes, and this time I join in. I like when Sara laughs at my jokes. I *really* like how it feels to be in this moment, with Dillan beside me, even though the tension between us is thick enough to grab hold of.

Maria and Sara are two clucking hens as they get ready to leave. Their whole house is awake in a way mine never is, and it makes sense why Dillan is loud when he's happy, because so is everyone else. Lipstick is applied and blouses are changed, and Dillan chases Angie through the house as she screams in delight.

When Maria and Sara leave, there are forty-five minutes until Angie's bedtime.

Every one of them is excruciating.

At first, we sit with her on the floor, putting jigsaw puzzles together. She has what seems like a thousand stories about all the things Dillan missed while he was gone, and he listens to her intently, though every so often he glances over at me. His hand never leaves my shoulder.

I risk the smallest gesture—I reach over and brush my fingers through the curls by his ear, and when he looks up, there's *so much* in his gaze that I have to pull away.

It's a little better once Angie is in pajamas—I watch in amusement as the two of them sing while she brushes her teeth—and we're settled on the couch, because now I can rest my head on his shoulder.

I thought I was happy in the car; *this* is happiness.

Angie sits on his lap, and we work through a stack of picture books. She asks me to read her *The Frog and the Mouse*— I've probably read it to her a thousand times, but I'm flattered that she still wants me to—so I do, and then another, and another, until she begins to still.

Angie has never fallen asleep reading books, but I imagine the excitement of the day has gotten to her, and when I poke her arm, she doesn't react at all.

Dillan glances up at the clock. It's a few minutes early, but she's already asleep, so I close the book. He picks her up—I'm amazed this doesn't wake her—and I follow them up the stairs.

She stirs, and he raises a finger to his lips. For a second, we just stand there, looking at each other in the hallway until we're both sure she's asleep. Then he disappears into her bedroom.

I place my palm on his bedroom door—it's open a crack—and push. His bag sits on the floor, still zippered shut. The room is delightfully lived in. I've always loved Dillan's room: the posters on the wall, the papers scattered across the desk. I walk over because I see my name, and there it is, in my own handwriting, scrawled across the top of a page of sheet music: *Nora's Song*. Except now it has company; I can see at least four different versions scattered across the surface, notes scribbled in the margins. How have I not always known I love him?

I hear him murmuring something through the wall, and then the door clicks shut. I hear the sound everywhere in my body.

Idly, I run my fingers across the wood of the desk, over the stacks of loose papers.

He steps through the door.

We're less than twenty-four inches apart, but I can feel every one of them.

For a moment we just stand there, looking at each other. Then he gives the doorframe a quiet rap and comes in, sitting down on the end of his bed.

"Glad to be back?" I ask. I don't take my eyes off him as I move to sit next to him. Now we're only ten inches apart. They are cavernous inches.

He nods once, and his voice sounds far away. "You have no idea."

His gaze flits down to my mouth and back up.

I can't stop looking at him, at the way the streetlight slants through the blinds and illuminates only parts of his face. I know my desires are transparent because his eyes drop down to my lips again, and this time they stay.

He says, softly, "Ellie."

We crash together.

I'm at once sated and desperate, wild, wanting. His lips are warm, and I can feel that he's been hungry for this too, because his arms are around me and we're both pulling each other closer. We kiss like we're dying for it. I twine my fingers through his hair, and I can feel his hand against my neck, his thumb brushing against my jaw.

I gasp for breath, and in the half second we're apart I feel the absence of him so strongly I burn with relief when our lips come together again. I've thought about this every day he's been gone, and it's still better than my most vivid daydream.

I sink backward, pulling him with me until he's halfway on top of me, and it's *not enough*. He shifts on his elbow, never breaking away, and I roll onto my side so that we're lying face to face.

I kiss him hungrily, on his lips, the corner of his mouth, his jaw. His hand ghosts along my arm and finds my waist, pulling me closer so we're pressed together. My hands feel frantic, as though if I don't touch skin right now, then I never will. I drag my fingers down his back, feeling his spine through his shirt.

I kiss the place where his jaw meets his neck and his breath hitches in my ear, and when I find the hem of his shirt, I slip my fingers underneath. He makes a low involuntary sound in the back of his throat that I can feel through my lips. I decide I'm desperate to hear it again, so I let my fingers wander up to his ribs, splayed wide against his skin. I kiss down to his collarbone and for a moment I pause there, inhaling the moment. The way he smells is dizzying, I'm delirious, I can hardly believe he's real.

Then I kiss back up his neck and he gasps. When our lips meet again, he's ferocious, his hands pressed against my back. My shirt is already hitched up, and when he touches the strip of bare skin above my waistband, it burns. I feel it everywhere.

His fingers pause, hovering near the hem, as though he's unsure, and so I remove my hand from under his shirt and guide his fingers under the fabric. Then his hands are on my skin, fingers cautious, gentle, as he works his way up to my rib cage. I thought I would be embarrassed, but I'm not, I feel both senseless and hyperaware of where his hands are. He breaks away to kiss my neck and I sigh happily. He explores my skin slowly—too slowly—but then he finds my pulse point with his lips and sucks lightly, and I let out a helpless whimper.

He jerks away.

We're both breathing hard. My skin burns where he was touching it.

I feel like I might die. "What?"

"We should"—he closes his eyes—"probably talk about this."

I let my head fall back onto the duvet. I don't want to talk—I want to do anything *but* talk—but I don't want to rush this. "Probably."

I close my eyes when he lies back next to me. My fingers itch to touch him again. I feel impatient, impossibly, improbably charged, like one look from him could set me on fire.

He turns his head toward me, and I turn to him. Our noses brush. I ache to lean in again, but I know that if I start it's unlikely that I'll be able to stop. It doesn't help that I see the wanting reflected in his eyes.

"I thought about you every day," I whisper.

He smiles, looking just as delirious as I feel. "Every minute."

I reach up and do what I've been longing to do—lightly brush my fingers between the dark freckle on his temple and its twin just below his jaw.

He shivers, and his voice is a warning. "Nora."

I push one of his curls behind his ear.

"Nora. You're killing me."

I let my fingers still. "Not sorry."

He closes his eyes and lets out the tiniest breathless laugh. His hand finds mine; I bring it to my lips and kiss along his knuckles.

"*Nora.*"

I'm delighted to have such an effect on him. I want him to know I feel the same way. I want him to know how much power he has.

I kiss his wrist where his pulse flutters, and he groans. "Jesus. Nora. I don't have that much self-control."

"So talk, then. We're talking. Let's talk."

I'm glad I can see his face when he's looking at me. It's almost too much to keep eye contact, but I feel like looking away would be worse. I never thought it was possible to feel loved with just a look, but there it is. He doesn't have to say it. The idea of it is right there.

"Be my girlfriend," Dillan whispers. Then he swallows. "Will you? Please?"

I reach up and brush my thumb across his cheekbone, admiring how his lashes flutter down. "That's what you wanted to talk about?"

"I never asked you properly before I left." His voice is so, so quiet. "I didn't want to ask over the phone or something, but I want it to be real."

"It's real," I whisper. "Yes, obviously."

I ghost my fingers over his bottom lip when he smiles. It's a luxurious sort of smile. "What else did you want to talk about?"

He props himself up on one elbow. "Everything, I guess."

There's no way he could know how perfectly he's answered, and for a second I just stare up at him, smiling, and he's smiling back. I don't think I've ever adored someone before, and now that I do, I don't quite know how I lived without feeling this way. I'm weightless and giddy and my face hurts from smiling. I love him. I *love* him.

I whisper, "I have something to tell you."

For a second, he looks alarmed, but then I shake my head. "No, it's good. Don't worry."

"What is it?"

"You know how last year I didn't get in to TMU?" I rest my hand on his chest.

His expression is wary. "Yes."

I take a deep breath. "I reapplied."

He sits bolt upright. "What? *Really?*"

"There, and UOttawa, and UVic, and Concordia, but . . ." I laugh. "Yeah. So."

"Nora. Are you serious?" He reaches up to brush my hair back, examining my eyes. "You really applied again?"

I nod, wordless.

His face is the suggestion of a smile, not quite there yet, like he doesn't know whether to believe me. "Wait. So we might be in the same province next year?"

"Yeah." I just keep nodding. "Yeah, we might. If I get in."

He blinks twice. "You'll get in. You'll definitely . . . *Nora*."

It's really starting to sink in, because he smiles wide, looks down into his lap, and when he looks back up, his eyes are shining.

"I know we haven't really talked about the future," I say, "and that's okay, we don't have to, but—I think four months of *long* long-distance sounds a lot more doable than *years*. Toronto and Kingston aren't that far apart."

"Nora." He sinks back down onto the bed and covers his face with his hands. "You're going to—I don't—I would've—anyway—"

He sucks in a shuddering breath, and his voice sounds funny and a little bit strangled. "I'd've done it anyway, you know. If that's factoring into your decision at all. I would still choose you if it meant long-distance. I'd still choose you. I don't want your decision to be about me."

"That's a bit rich coming from you, isn't it?"

He laughs, wetly, but he doesn't remove his hands from his face.

"You know me," I say, a little quieter. "I'll make the decision for myself, when it's time."

I watch him as he lies there with his hands covering his eyes, his chest rising and falling.

"Dillan," I start, like I'm afraid, because I am. "Are you happy?"

He doesn't say anything, instead he just lets his hands

fall away from his face and reaches up to pull me down toward him.

My face is a half inch from his when he whispers, "Yes. I'm so, so happy."

We kiss slowly, languidly. Fire sparks below my navel. Everything about this moment is soft and warm and slow.

He runs his hands down my sides and back up the length of my spine, and when he pulls away, he laughs delightedly.

"What?"

"You're on my bed."

I can't help the smile that breaks over my face. "I am."

"You're my girlfriend."

"That too."

He sighs, and it's a lovely, pleasant sound. "Pinch me."

I smirk, and lightly pinch his side.

"Ow. Jesus. Nora."

I look at him. He's so handsome it sort of hurts. I say, "Dillan."

Then I say it again, and again, and again, because once I've started I can't seem to stop.

He touches his nose to mine. "That's me."

I let my eyes close. I say, "I love you," like it's a sigh. Like it's a truth that he would have known even if it had never escaped.

He breathes it back to me like he doesn't have to think about it.

I murmur, "I want," and then I stop, because I don't know how to say what I want.

I open my eyes.

His expression is quiet reverence.

He says, "Come here."

FIFTY-NINE

Before

After the funeral, I sat alone in a side hallway of the small Baptist church.

Her family was all out there, somewhere. *My* family was out there, somewhere.

Sitting with my back against the wall wasn't comfortable, but that was good. I let the wooden trim dig into my spine until it hurt, and then I stayed there.

It had been too quiet inside my head to be in the crowd. There were too many people having feelings. I wasn't feeling *anything*, even though I knew I was supposed to.

Julia was gone. Closed-casket gone.

My heart burned with gray static.

The carpet was rough under my calves. The nylon of my tights didn't conceal the bruises that had blossomed, stark and ugly, on my legs. My fingers played with the rough edge of my cast.

There was a sound to my right. Dillan stood in the doorway. I looked up at him. I didn't smile.

Neither did he.

He just sighed, and then he knocked lightly on the doorframe and sat on the floor next to me.

He didn't say anything.

I didn't either, not for a long time. I didn't think there was anything *to* say, like maybe it'd never be necessary to speak ever again. But then the truth was simmering at the surface and I couldn't ignore it any longer. "It was my fault."

He sighed. "No it wasn't."

"No, Dillan. It was. I started our fight that night."

"How were you supposed to know?"

We were silent for several minutes.

At last, I said, "I gave her the keys."

Then he repeated, "It wasn't your fault."

"I shouldn't have let her go. I should have tried harder to stop her."

"It *wasn't your fault,*" he said, with such ferocity that I shivered a little.

I didn't think I'd ever believe that.

Dillan didn't know what I'd been thinking at the party.

I'd never wanted to see her again. I'd wanted her gone. I'd *told* her to go. I'd handed her the murder weapon.

I gave fucking drunk, can't-drive-for-shit-even-while-sober Julia the keys. To a car.

I killed my best friend.

It was my fault.

And no one was going to tell me otherwise.

"It wasn't, okay?" His voice was a little softer.

I couldn't look at him. It didn't really matter what he

thought, because I knew the truth. If I hadn't gone to that stupid party, none of this would have happened.

"Everyone"—my voice nearly failed me—"wants to talk about her. Everyone remembers how awesome she was. And she *was*. She was awesome. It was just that, also . . ."

I couldn't find the right words. I had been good at words. Where had they all gone?

"She was a complicated person," he said.

A shot of rage stabbed through me. Of course he would think so. Of course he was ready to make excuses for her.

I wished I would cry, but I didn't have anything left in me.

"We don't ever have to talk about her if you don't want to."

It was impossible for him to know that was what I wanted to hear, but it was, and gratitude welled up behind my eyes.

If I could go the rest of my life without even *thinking* about any of this ever again, I would.

"Never, unless you want to."

I felt like something important was going to snap in my chest, pressure building slowly with no sign of escape. I looked over at him as the panic threatened to explode. "Promise?"

He looked right at me. "Yeah. I promise."

SIXTY

After

The funeral was a year ago today.

I'm trying not to think about it too hard, but how could I think about anything else?

Dillan is flat on his back reading for school, his head in my lap while I play with his hair. His curls are really soft—I always thought they would be, but now that I know it's true, I can't stop touching them.

If Julia had lived, would this ever have happened? Would we have ever been honest with each other? I like to think we would have figured it out, eventually, but I don't really know. I know who I used to be.

Who was *he*? He's told me about their secret interactions in bits and pieces, and even though I try not to, I can't stop thinking about what it must have been like.

I *kissed* him and the next thing he got was a phone call

claiming that I was angry with him. What would that have been like? I've resented him a little for a whole year about the week when he ignored me, but with the full truth now, it makes sense. It just makes guilt and sadness eat at me.

Will that ever go away?

"What?" he asks.

I glance down at him.

He's closed the book, thumb between the pages to hold his place.

I raise my eyebrows. *"What,* what?"

"Just—I don't know." He looks up at me. "It seems like you got sad."

"I'm not sad." I stroke the side of his cheek. "I'm with you."

"You can be with me and still be sad."

I sigh. "I don't know. I'm not exactly sad. I'm . . ."

"Are you thinking about Julia too?"

I nod.

There's a little hesitancy behind his voice. "Do you want to talk about it?"

Something enormous and hollow opens in my chest. "I don't know."

He's silent for long enough that I realize it's permission, either to continue or to change the subject.

I don't want to change the subject. Anger is sharp and acrid, and it's been burning me from the inside out for *so long*.

I take a deep breath. "I'm angry with her."

It's the truth.

He nods.

"I miss her."

This is the truth too.

"I feel so guilty sometimes it's overwhelming."

Dillan struggles for a second to sit up, and then turns to face me. "It wasn't your fault. You know that, right?"

"So you keep saying."

"Hey, I mean it."

I let out a long breath. "I know it wasn't my fault. Now. But that's not why I feel guilty."

He just sits and watches me.

"I feel awful for saying any of it out loud, but I can't help it, you know? I feel like I'll always be wondering what things would be like if I hadn't let her manipulate me for so long."

"It wasn't about 'letting.' Julia was . . ." He rubs the heel of his palm against his forehead and sighs. "She was really good at it. It took me *weeks* to see that she was making things up."

"Still. I feel like I should have been able to stand up to her."

"It's not fair to put that on yourself. It was never supposed to be your job to do that."

"I just didn't *know,*" I tell him. "I didn't know what friendship was supposed to be like. I didn't know ours wasn't healthy. I feel . . ."

He waits.

"I feel robbed, you know?"

"What do you mean?"

"I feel like I was supposed to be somebody, and she stole that from me. I know it's awful."

"It's not awful."

"She knew exactly what to say so that it hurt the worst. And then she could still somehow convince me that *I* was the awful friend."

He reaches over and wipes a tear from my cheek. "You weren't awful."

"Sometimes I get so angry with her that I feel wrong for missing her. And then I miss her so badly that I feel guilty for being relieved I never have to deal with her again."

I take a deep, shuddering breath, then continue. "I'm not angry all the time. I'm so happy when I'm with you, and then I feel terrible for being happy, because it's not fair. She didn't deserve that. Even though she was terrible. *Nobody* deserves what happened to her. Sometimes she was good. I can't forget that, either. Even if in the end all that good was eclipsed by all that bad. But now I'm happy, and she'll never get to experience that for herself. And that makes me angry all over again."

I have to stop, because I'm not just crying anymore—it's full-on sobs, the sort that make the back of my throat close so I can't even speak.

Dillan pulls me against his chest and holds on tightly, so that I have no choice but to breathe a little more evenly.

I choke out my last question. "Will I ever stop being angry?"

Dillan doesn't say anything for a long time.

For several long minutes it's just me and his shoulder, shirt wet from my tears.

Then he rests his cheek against the top of my head, and says, "You will."

It sounds true. I hope he's right.

"One day." Then, much quieter, he says, "Thank you for telling me."

I pull back, scrubbing at my eyes, and for some reason, I laugh a little. "Of course. I *want* to tell you about this stuff."

I'm finally discovering who I am without Julia, and I think I like that person. She's complicated and messy and not as afraid. And I can't wait to share that with Dillan—with the world, really.

"There was a time I never could have imagined life after Julia," I tell him. "I definitely couldn't have pictured losing her the way we did. She was so—so full of *life*. And maybe I thought I needed to be like she was when all I really needed to be was myself."

He pushes some of my hair behind my ear and tears threaten to spill over again.

"It's hard sometimes," I whisper. "I have bad days where I wish I could call her, and she'd pick up. Isn't that . . . backward?"

"No." He kisses my forehead. "It's not. And you don't have to deal with this alone."

I nod. "I know. I have Eve and Kayla now."

He gives me a look.

"And you," I concede with a watery smile, and he grins.

"And me. Even in January. You'll call me on the hard days?"

I nod and kiss him, even though my mouth is wet. "I'll call you on all of the days."

"Nora. I'm serious."

"Yes," I whisper. "I'll call you on the hard days."

"Promise?"

I look up, right into his eyes. "I promise."

EPILOGUE

Dear Ms. Eleanor Radford,

Thank you for your inquiry into Toronto Metropolitan University's School of Journalism. Dean Fonsatti received your letter regarding the situation you found yourself in last fall—as well as the personal essay you enclosed.

First, we'd like to offer our heartfelt condolences on the losses you suffered, as well as the indignities that resulted in the loss of your placement with our school.

Welcome to the Toronto Metropolitan University Journalism Program. Your Spring Semester acceptance and, we are pleased to share, your full-scholarship information are enclosed. That was quite the essay, Ms. Radford.

We look forward to coming alongside you as you come into your own.

Sincerely,

Ahmed Mebarek
Director of Admissions
Toronto Metropolitan University

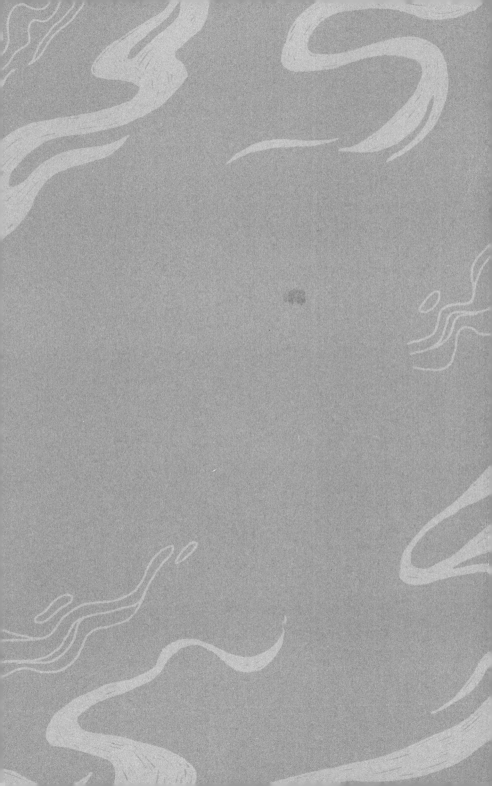

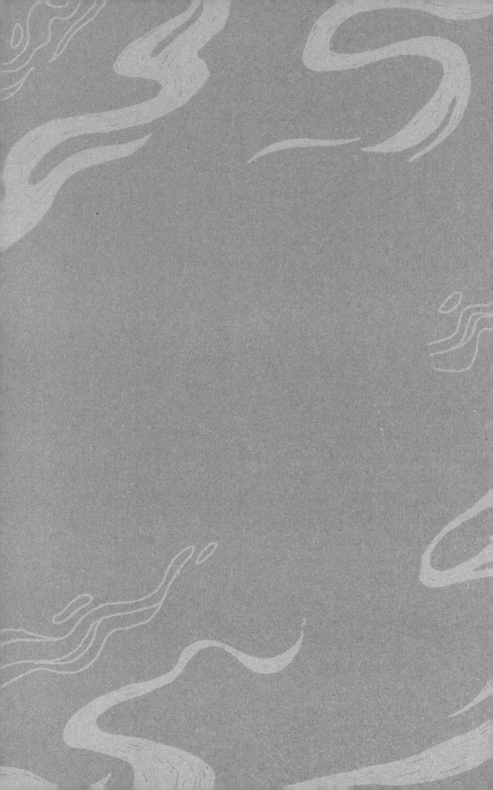

ACKNOWLEDGMENTS

It goes without saying that stories like this one are usually important to the writer, but I'll say it anyway: this book is a little piece of my life and my world in a nutshell. When I was very young, I remember wondering if I'd ever get to really explain the sort of hurt I was going through, and while this story and its contents are entirely fictional, the feelings are very much an honest reflection. I'd love to go back and tell little me we got there. And by "we," I mean a village. I owe this book to many people—most of whom I met well after draft one.

Ali, my wonderful agent and first window into the publishing world, thank you for championing Nora's story and believing in the heart of this book. Our journey together has been serendipitous from the start!

Dana, you saw such potential in the story, even as it changed and shifted so much throughout the editing process. Thank you for everything you caught that I never would have thought of.

To the brilliant minds at RHCB, thank you. This book wouldn't sparkle the way it does without Barbara Perris, Artie Bennett, Alison Kolani, and Lisa Leventer, the incredible grammar wizards. Max Reed and Alix Northrup, your cover brought this book to life. All my thanks to Ray Shappell and Ken Crossland for the incredible design work, and to our managing editor, Jake Eldred, not to mention the wonderful folks in publicity, marketing, production, and sub rights who have supported this book so well.

Kirsteen—man, oh, man. This book is in the wild because of how hard you loved it. Your belief in this story, and in Nora and (especially) Dillan, means the world to me. I envision many days together in the future, walking through European streets and talking about what's next with our stories.

Yasmi: Where would I be without you? You are every writer's *dream*. I trust you implicitly. Beyond being an incredibly stalwart reader and supporter, you have a hawklike ability to spot what everyone else misses, and with every single book I write, your advice has been invaluable. Some authors get a person like this in their career, but I don't think very many get such a solid and enduring friendship out of it. I wouldn't be half the writer I am without you.

Mikala, you were my first reader. You have, over and over, been the first to believe in me, the first to tell me to chase a dream, the first to step up and encourage this journey. You were my oasis during a very lonely time in my life, and you've been a fountain ever since. Thank you. I can't wait to live out our wildest aspirations together.

Jamie, every day it makes me laugh that we bonded so hard over made-up little guys that now you live in my house. You have sustained my belief in myself during periods of doubt and repeatedly affirmed that I'm doing the right thing. I will always be grateful to you for showing up exactly when I needed you.

To Jules, whom I met *after* giving names to the characters

of this book and who has been an incredible friend, editor, and confidant: Thanks for not taking it personally. You're a star.

To my faithful beta readers: You rock my world. Your feedback took this story from a jumbled mess to something meaningful. Sincerely, thank you to all of you.

To my parents, thank you for fostering in me a love of reading. Sophia, thank you for your long-standing belief in me and the little dudes living in my head. Braeden, you made a safe space for this story to come to life. Thank you.

To the person who inspired a lot of the feelings that went into this book: This was nothing like our story, but betrayals come in so many forms that I'm not sure it makes a difference. You taught me how to advocate for myself. You taught me how to be proud of myself and the things that bring me joy, despite scorn. You taught me how to think critically. A lot of the way I operate in the world comes down to you and me in a sandbox. I hope you're doing well.

And finally, last but not least in the slightest, Jack. I didn't know that the kind of love I write about was real until you. I'll be the first to admit that the romances that live in my books always felt like a fantasy, or some kind of escape, just realistic enough to be believable. You are *magic*. You are an ever-present source of sunlight. You are my best friend. Since you walked into my life, I get what artists through the ages talk about when they say the word *muse*. My favorite story is ours, hands down, no question. No line.

ABOUT THE AUTHOR

Alex Ritany is a lifelong reader and writer. When they're not at the keyboard, you can find them hosting tabletop game night, working on illustrations, or at their other keyboard, composing music. Alex's love of art, music, and the western Canadian landscape regularly spills into their writing, which tends to feature complex friendships, twisty romances, and explorations of queerness. They live in Calgary with their roommate, cat, and dice collection. *Dead Girls Don't Say Sorry* is their debut novel.

aritany.com
🐦 @a_ritany